I0598231

RePHleXions
Echoes of
Existence
Special Timeline Edition

OTHER BOOKS BY
LAWRENCE NAULT

THE DRACONIM SERIES
Young Adult Contemporary Eco-Fantasy

Draconim Lacrima Mortis: Tear of the Dragon

Feeding the Fires

THE MACIVER KIDS ADVENTURES
Young Adult Science Fiction

Loma

Diversion

Titan's Song

THE ANIMAL TALES
Early Chapter Books/Transitional Readers

*Squirrel Tales**

*Wolf Tales**

*Bear Tales**

The Mountain Hermit's Animal Tales†

STANDALONE NOVELS
Political & Economic Fiction

Leviticus 25: Jubilee

Speculative Fiction

Inversion‡

---

* Available as e-book only

† Includes the complete Animal Tales trilogy

‡ Contains mature content - suitable for readers 18+

RePHleXions

Echoes of Existence
Special Timeline Edition

By
Lawrence Nault

Our Workshop
Publishing Div.

RePHleXions: Echoes of Existence

Special Timeline Edition

ISBN 978-1-0688138-8-7

Copyright ©2024 by Lawrence Nault

All rights reserved.

RePHleXions: Echoes of Existence

CONTENT ADVISORY

This work of speculative fiction is intended for mature readers (18+) and contains:

INTIMATE CONTENT

- Explicit sexual scenes and relationships
- Multiple-partner scenarios
- Detailed physical intimacy

PSYCHOLOGICAL THEMES

- Digital surveillance and manipulation
- Technology addiction and dependency
- Complex relationship dynamics
- Mental health impacts
- Trust and betrayal

This novel combines literary fiction with digital-age themes, making it suitable for readers interested in the intersection of technology, society, and human relationships. While it may appeal to younger readers for its technological elements, the explicit content and mature themes make it appropriate only for adult audiences.

Reading Community Notice:

Upon completion of this printed edition, readers are welcome to participate in book-sharing initiatives such as Little Free Libraries® or BookCrossing®, provided the book remains in its complete and original form.

Table of Contents

2034

"Those who don't know history are destined to repeat it" Spanish philosopher George Santayana - 1905

"Those who view their history through the eyes of the victors and the powerful are destined to become the victims in the histories yet to be written." Kaidan Vale – 2034

The RePHleX protocol hummed to life in Kaidan's 430 square-foot apartment, slowly turning up the lights to a soft amber glow. Across the room the latte maker whirred, anticipating his need for a caffeine kick to get his day started. Kaidan didn't even open his eyes as he reached over his head and grabbed his earpiece from its charging port, slipping the form fitted mobile node just as he had done every day since acquiring it. He sat up and hung his feet over the side of the bed as he felt the familiar feeling of his dog jumping at his feet, yapping the way only a robotic dog could. It was hard not to marvel at the seamless integration of technology in his life, yet a nagging unease tugged at the edges of his contentment.

It was all benign and innocuous at first. A network of computers spanning the globe, seamlessly connected, allowing the instant exchange of information, data, and knowledge to those who sought it. It was hailed as a tool for scientific advancement, a dam buster that would flood the world with freely accessible information. It soon became more as it smashed against the walls of institutional knowledge hoarding, the only limitations, the power of its processors and the data it could access.

Processing power was a challenge eagerly taken on by institutions and corporations. The ability to double the number of transistors on a computer chip became almost cyclical, doubling every two years, leading to exponential growth in processing power.

The tech giants took on the challenge of processing power with fervor. Moore's law became a self-fulfilling prophecy, with the number of transistors on a chip doubling every two years. Computers grew exponentially more powerful, their capabilities expanding at a dizzying rate.

But it was the second challenge, the insatiable hunger for data, that would prove the most insidious.

Software, social media platforms, search engines, and smart devices proliferated, offering users a tantalizing array of free services and rewards. People eagerly embraced this new digital world, pouring their lives, thoughts, and creations into ever-expanding databanks. Historical archives, literature, and art were digitized and shared, democratizing access to human knowledge and creativity. People willingly offered up their data, their thoughts, their images, and their lives in exchange for the convenience of this new digital world.

Hidden in the labyrinthine user agreements that no one read were clauses that turned every keystroke, every image, every creation into corporate property. The users had become the unwilling laborers in a vast data-harvesting operation, feeding the ravenous appetite of artificial intelligence systems.

Warnings had been sounded as far back as the 1950s. Visionaries like Alan Turing, Joseph Weizenbaum, Norbert Wiener, and Ted Nelson had cautioned against the potential misuse of computers and AI. But their voices were drowned out by the siren song of progress and profit.

And so, the stage was set for RePHleX.

Conceived as a benign communication protocol for smart homes, the RePHleX protocol was named to promote its ability to enable and leverage technology to reflexively respond to the occupants of a smart home. The Responsive Environment Protocol for Habitat Linked Experience promised a future of seamless integration and effortless connectivity. Lights that adjusted to your mood, refrigerators that restocked themselves, and security systems that knew your every move, all were orchestrated by the invisible algorithms of RePHleX.

Kaidan stretched as he got out of bed and stumbled towards the bathroom. As he did, a little voice in his ear reminded him to make his bed as it would be closing in sixty seconds.

"Fuck it," mumbled Kaidan.

A soft whirring sound was the only response Kaidan got as the messy bed began to move, seemingly of its own accord. As if by magic, the tangled sheets and comforter started to smooth themselves out. The fabric rippled and flattened, guided by hidden mechanisms within the mattress. The pillows, previously askew, straightened and aligned themselves at the head of the bed.

Once the bedding was somewhat organized, though still bearing the lived-in look of recent use, the entire bed platform tilted upward from the foot end as concealed straps emerged from the side of the mattress to secure the sheets and comforter in place.

The headboard, previously flush against the wall, folded inward, creating a compact package as the bed continued its vertical ascent. With a final pneumatic hiss, the bed disappeared into a recessed compartment. Where moments ago there was a disheveled sleeping space, there now stood an uninterrupted wall with a large screen displaying a digital artwork.

Oblivious to the world beyond his morning routine, Kaidan stepped into the shower. The water, precisely heated to his preference, enveloped him in a comforting embrace. He closed his eyes, savoring the warmth as it cascaded over his shoulders, each droplet a tiny masseur kneading away the remnants of sleep. Just as he began to lose himself in the steamy cocoon, the water abruptly turned ice-cold. Kaidan's muscles tensed, a sharp gasp escaping his lips. Yet, he didn't flinch away. Instead, he squared his shoulders and endured the frigid deluge, counting the seconds in his head. This wasn't a glitch in the RePHleX system, but a deliberate choice. Kaidan had programmed this arctic interlude himself, swayed by an article in his curated feed touting the testosterone-boosting benefits of cold showers.

Kaidan ran the rough towel over his skin, his eyes fixed on the smart mirror before him. The screen flickered to life, displaying his reflection in high definition. "RePHleX, enhance image," he commanded, his voice still husky from sleep. The mirror obeyed, subtly adjusting the lighting and smoothing out the bags under his eyes. With a satisfied nod, he continued, "Send to Aria with caption: 'Good morning, beautiful. Miss you.'" The mirror chimed softly, confirming the task.

Pausing for a moment, a mischievous glint appeared in Kaidan's eyes. "RePHleX, duplicate image, add filter 'Fuckboy', and send to situationship group." Another chime, another task complete. As he tossed the damp towel into the compact washer-dryer unit tucked discreetly beside the vanity,

Kaidan chuckled to himself. He remembered the clumsy days of his youth, contorting in front of his parents' bathroom mirror, desperately trying to capture the perfect angle for his morning selfies. Now, with RePHleX, cultivating his online presence was as effortless as breathing.

As Kaidan pulled clothes from his compact wardrobe, his apartment hummed to life around him. The soft whir of hidden mechanisms filled the air, a symphony of convenience orchestrated by the ever-present RePHleX system. A panel slid open above his kitchen counter, revealing a freshly toasted bagel, steaming coffee, and a vibrant green protein smoothie, all delivered moments ago to his secure vestibule from his favorite local eatery.

He had long since abandoned the idea of cooking for himself. The sleek induction hotplate and the combo microwave/air fryer sat untouched, relics of a bygone era. "Why bother?" his online friends would say. "Everyone's doing meal delivery now." It was faster, easier, and—if he was honest with himself—probably healthier than anything he'd manage to whip up.

As he dressed, the apartment's lighting shifted, mimicking the natural daylight that struggled to penetrate the single, postage stamp-sized window. The massive screen that had replaced his bed now displayed a curated feed of job listings, each one tailored to Kaidan's meticulously crafted search parameters.

Leaning against the counter, Kaidan absent-mindedly munched on his bagel while scrolling through the job feed. Despite the flawless functionality of his living space, an unsettling feeling crept over him. The convenience was undeniable, yet something felt... off. In the quiet efficiency of his high-tech cocoon, Kaidan couldn't shake the sensation that he wasn't truly alone. It was as if the very walls were watching, listening, anticipating his every need before he could even articulate it.

As he swallowed the last bite of his breakfast, Kaidan found himself longing for something he couldn't quite name. A touch of chaos, perhaps? A hint of the unexpected in his perfectly optimized world? He shook his head, dismissing the thought. This was progress, after all. This was the future everyone had dreamed of.

Wasn't it?

1

Four hundred and twenty-seven listings glared at Kaidan from his primary monitor. A digital mountain he had to scale before even touching the work already lined up. He sighed, running a hand through his disheveled hair. This was the new normal in the gig economy—a constant hustle, a never-ending cycle of bidding and hoping.

As his fingers danced across the modified Dvorak simplified keyboard, Kaidan's mind wandered to his friends, all caught in the same daily grind. Platform work dominated the listings, but it was a minefield. Scams, frauds, data harvesting honeypots, phishing schemes, clickbait, lead generation traps—they all lurked behind enticing job titles. And then there were the sabotage attempts from desperate competitors. It was enough to make his head spin.

"Three hours," he muttered, glancing at the time display hovering in the corner of his vision. "Three hours just to separate the wheat from the chaff." Another hour would go into identifying relevant listings. It was soul-crushing work, but necessary for survival.

At least the application process had improved. Kaidan allowed himself a small smile as he thought about his automated system. He'd set hard limits on pay rates—his reputation and experience meant he could afford to skip the "exposure" gigs now. His master social media profile, a sprawling digital tapestry of his successes, did most of the heavy lifting. His music, available on countless platforms, spoke for itself. Anyone truly interested could see and hear the quality of his work with a simple search.

As Kaidan sifted through the digital detritus, he couldn't help but multitask. His social media feeds scrolled by in his peripheral vision, and he fired off comments with practiced ease, watching in real-time as likes and responses flowed back. A bitter laugh escaped him as he noticed a trending topic: "How to Avoid Job Listing Scams." The irony wasn't lost on him. He quickly scanned through the posts, liking comments that resonated with his frustration. Finally, he couldn't resist adding his own:

"I pay good money for these apps so I don't have to see all these bullshit postings, but that's most of what I see. WTF!"

He hit send and returned to his job search, but the ping of notifications drew his attention back to the post. The like counter was ticking up rapidly, and replies were flooding in:

"Completely agree! That app is a complete scam. You should try this one instead."

"I know! I spent all morning sorting through the garbage"

"Why don't the government fix this and arrest all scammers?"

"The government's in on it, dude. They get kickbacks."

"I lost $10,000 to one of those fuckin' scammers. DM me and I'll tell you how to fix it."

"You're using the best app. Just get RePHleX to filter it for you."

Kaidan felt a mix of vindication and despair. He wasn't alone in his frustration—far from it. But the responses also highlighted the depths of the problem. Everyone was angry, everyone had a solution to sell, and no one seemed to have a real answer. Even the suggestion to use RePHleX, the AI system that already controlled so much of their lives, felt like admitting defeat.

"Welcome to the future," Kaidan muttered, his voice dripping with sarcasm. "Where finding real work is harder than the job itself." He paused, fingers hovering over the interface. For a moment, he allowed himself to imagine a world where talent spoke louder than algorithms, where genuine opportunities weren't buried under mountains of digital waste.

Then reality reasserted itself. Four hundred and twenty-six listings to go. The day was young, and the gig economy waited for no one. With a deep breath, Kaidan dove back into the digital abyss, determined to carve out his place in this brave new world—one filtered listing at a time.

"RePHleX, analyze today's response to the job listings and adjust filter parameters." Kaidan's command was followed by a soft chime in his earpiece, confirming that RePHleX had tweaked the filters. He leaned back in his chair, a mixture of hope and skepticism washing over him.

This wasn't his first rodeo. He'd been through this dance before, multiple times. For days, sometimes weeks, the fake listings in his feed would decline significantly. But then, like clockwork, they'd creep back in, as if the scammers were evolving, always one step ahead.

Kaidan's brow furrowed as he recalled a disturbing pattern he'd noticed. It had started after a particularly lucrative gig, when his bank account was flush with credits. Almost overnight, his feed had been flooded with an unprecedented wave of fraudulent postings. At first, he'd dismissed it as coincidence. But as the pattern repeated with each substantial payday, a gnawing suspicion took root.

Unable to shake the feeling that something was amiss, Kaidan had taken to the forums. His post was cautious, probing:

"Has anyone else noticed an increase in fake job listings and scam ads right after a big payday? It's like the more money in my account, the more BS in my feed. Just me?"

The response was swift and brutal:

"I call bullshit. You're making this up for likes."

"What are you? Some kind of conspiracy theorist?"

"Go be a luddite if you don't like how the internet works."

"It's just confirmation bias, dude. Get a grip."

For every comment that resonated with his suspicions, a dozen more tore into him. The vitriol was overwhelming. Accusations of attention-seeking, paranoia, and technophobia flooded his notifications.

Kaidan's finger hovered over the delete button, self-doubt creeping in. Was he really just seeing patterns where none existed? Was his mind playing tricks on him, desperate to find order in the chaos of the gig economy?

With a heavy sigh, he deleted the post. The backlash wasn't worth it, and maybe they were right. Maybe he was wrong. After all, RePHleX was supposed to protect them from this kind of manipulation, wasn't it?

And yet, as he turned back to his job listings, a tiny voice in the back of his mind whispered that something still didn't add up. But for now, he pushed the thought aside. In this brave new world, questioning the system too loudly was a luxury he couldn't afford. Not if he wanted to keep working.

"RePHleX, studio set-up please."

At Kaidan's command, his workspace transformed. The primary display flickered, job listings dissolving into the familiar interface of his audio processor. Around it, secondary screens blinked to life, each showcasing a different component of his sound studio. Virtual faders, equalizers, and synthesizer banks spread before him like a digital buffet of sonic possibilities.

"Studio set-up activated. Default parameters set," RePHleX's smooth voice announced in his ear.

Kaidan reached for the small refrigerator tucked under his desk, pulling out a protein shake. The cool container was a stark contrast to the warmth blooming in his chest. This was his time, his passion.

"No work today," he said, a smile playing on his lips. "Today is my time. Change it to personal parameters, please."

The familiar chime signaled RePHleX's compliance, and Kaidan watched as his customized settings flowed across the screens. This was his playground, his canvas.

Music had been Kaidan's constant companion for as long as he could remember. As a child, he'd spend hours hunched over a virtual DJ mixer, stitching together downloaded samples to create soundtracks for his fledgling lyrics. The transition to a digital audio workstation had been a revelation, opening new worlds of possibility.

But it was AI that had truly revolutionized his craft. Gone were the days of being limited by sample libraries or his own instrumental skills. Now, with a few commands, he could conjure any instrument, any voice, any sound he could imagine. The AI understood the nuances of genre, the subtleties of emotion in music. It could mimic a wistful violin or a thunderous drumbeat with equal ease.

Yet, amidst this sea of technological marvels, Kaidan clung to one old-school tradition: he wrote all his lyrics by hand. Well, by mind and voice, at least. There was something deeply personal, almost sacred, about crafting the words himself. The only exception was when he took on advertising gigs. Then, and only then, would he unleash the AI's linguistic capabilities, fine-tuning lyrics to hit the perfect demographic sweet spot.

When Kaidan first started publishing his A.I. generated music it wasn't well accepted. He found himself being pilloried on social media and almost stopped until he connected with another musician who was also using AI. That led him to join online groups and threads where others with his interests came together. He quickly learned that most of the haters were nothing more than bots paid for by record labels and music producers that wanted to maintain control over the music industry. According to the people he followed, and those who followed him, most of the real people that were against AI music were about fifteen years behind the time as A.I. music had been part of the gaming industry, marketing, and more, for longer than they even knew.

The synthesizer analogy was one that was often repeated on these threads, and one Kaidan himself often repeated. The acceptance of electronic instruments in music had been a century-long evolution, from the fringes of experimental sound to the heart of mainstream production. Kaidan had learned about this history online, fascinated by how each technological leap had been met with both excitement and resistance.

In the early 20th century, instruments like the Theremin and Ondes Martenot were viewed as odd curiosities, their otherworldly sounds relegated to science fiction soundtracks. It wasn't until the 1960s, with the invention of the Moog synthesizer, that electronic sounds began to find their place in popular music. Kaidan smiled, remembering how he'd once spent an entire weekend recreating Wendy Carlos' "Switched-On Bach" using vintage synth plugins.

The late 20th century saw synthesizers become ubiquitous, defining the sound of entire genres like disco, new wave, and synthpop. But it was the digital revolution of the 2000s that truly democratized electronic music production. Software synthesizers and digital audio workstations (DAWs) made it possible for anyone with a computer to create professional-sounding tracks.

Kaidan's own journey had started with these tools. He remembered downloading his first DAW, marveling at how he could create entire symphonies from his bedroom. But it was the AI revolution of the 2020s that had truly transformed the landscape.

Now, in Kaidan's time, AI wasn't just a tool for music production—it was a collaborator, a co-creator. With a few voice commands, he could generate complex arrangements, mimicking any instrument or style with uncanny accuracy. The AI understood context, emotion, and even cultural nuances in ways that early synthesizers could never have dreamed of.

Yet, as Kaidan gazed at his setup, he felt a connection to those early electronic pioneers. Like them, he was pushing the boundaries of what was possible in music. And like the musicians who insisted on playing their own instruments in the face of drum machines and samplers, Kaidan held onto the human element of his craft—writing his own lyrics, infusing his compositions with his personal experiences and emotions.

"The more things change, the more they stay the same," Kaidan muttered, a wry smile playing on his lips. He turned back to his interface, ready to blend the latest AI-generated sounds with his own creative vision. In this fusion of human creativity and artificial intelligence, he was carrying forward a tradition of innovation that stretched back more than a hundred years.

"RePHleX," he said, "let's make some history."

"You have an incoming call request from Aria," RePHleX announced, its neutral tone a stark contrast to the jolt of excitement Kaidan felt at the name.

"Oh shi—" Kaidan caught himself, suddenly aware of his disheveled appearance. "Workout filter, quick!" He waited for the familiar chime, signaling that RePHleX had applied the digital mask that would make him look like he had just been exercising rather than bleary-eyed from sorting through job listings. "Okay, connect on primary."

The audio mixer on his main screen dissolved, replaced by the vibrant image of a young woman. Aria's presence immediately lit up the room, her energy palpable even through the digital interface. She wore a sunshine-yellow vintage top that somehow managed to complement her ever-changing style without clashing. Her cat-eye, horn-rimmed glasses perched on her nose, magnifying eyes that sparkled with mischief. What caught Kaidan's attention most, however, was the shock of crimson hair tied back with a playfully patterned scarf.

"Hey, you," Kaidan said, a grin spreading across his face. "I see you've changed your hair color again. Let me guess, the salon AI had a creative burst?"

Aria laughed, the sound like music to Kaidan's ears. "You know me better than that. AIs got nothing on my color choices. My hair is like a mood ring, remember?" She twirled a loose strand around her finger. "It changes with my whims... and sometimes, with the company I keep."

Kaidan's eyebrows shot up, recognizing the playful tone in her voice. "That particular shade of red usually means one thing," he said, leaning closer to the screen. "Am I reading this right? Are my chances looking good for tonight?"

Aria's eyes glinted with amusement. "What do you think, after that morning selfie you sent? You can't just flex like that and expect me not to respond."

14

Kaidan laughed, the sound echoing in his sparsely furnished apartment. He had been online with friends, bemoaning his lack of intimate connection the previous night. On a whim, he mentioned his plan to send his girlfriend a steamy selfie, seeking validation from his digital cohort. Almost unanimously, his group of friends echoed back support for the idea, their avatars lighting up with encouragement.

"Nice! You coming over here?" the tone of Kaidan's voice colored by a mixture of excitement and expectation.

"Well, you never seem to leave the house," Aria replied, a hint of affectionate exasperation in her voice. "So I guess so. You working out?"

"Yeah. Quick one in between jobs," he said, swiping his hand across his forehead to brush away nonexistent sweat. The workout filter he was using added a sheen to his skin, making him appear more athletic than he truly was. It was just another layer of deception in their digitally enhanced world.

"Well, save some energy," Aria said teasingly. "I'm working on another book cover. Another damn dragon. I offered to paint something original, but they opted for the digital option. Again."

Kaidan rolled his eyes. "Another dragon? Please tell me there are no elves or fairies, like every other book cover you seem to do."

"Just dragons this time," Aria sighed, her frustration palpable even through the digital connection. "But hey, what do you think of this? RePHleX, gallery cam."

Aria's image was replaced by a panoramic view of a room teeming with artwork. Unlike Kaidan, who embraced the digital world wholeheartedly, Aria was far more analog, taking an organic approach to life that stood in stark contrast to the prevailing tech-centric culture.

The virtual tour revealed a space that was a testament to tactile creativity. Easels stood at various angles, each supporting a canvas in different stages of completion. Vibrant oil paintings hung on exposed brick walls, their textures almost palpable even through the digital interface. Sculptures of various materials - clay, wood, metal, and even repurposed plastics - occupied corners and pedestals, each telling a story of skilled hands shaping raw materials into art.

As an artist, Aria worked primarily with her hands - painting, sculpting, and creating installations from found objects. Her workspace was a chaotic symphony of colors, shapes, and textures. Jars of pigments, brushes of all sizes, and an eclectic collection of tools cluttered every available surface. The air, if Kaidan could smell it, would likely be rich with the scent of linseed oil, turpentine, and clay.

Creating book covers and other commercial art pieces was her side job, a necessary compromise that rarely allowed her to work with her preferred methods. Clients, constrained by budgets and tight deadlines, usually opted for the quick and cost-effective digital, AI-created art pieces. It was a constant source of frustration for Aria, who believed in the irreplaceable value of human touch in art.

"That's my new piece in the middle," Aria's voice guided Kaidan's attention to a peculiar structure at the center of the room. "I call it 'Disconnected Convergence.' Everything I used to make it I found! Let me turn it on."

The sculpture came to life before Kaidan's eyes. It was a mesmerizing assemblage of discarded technology - old computer parts, fragments of screens, tangled wires, and broken circuit boards. These elements were artfully arranged into a form that resembled a human figure, hunched over what appeared to be an old-fashioned easel. As Aria activated it, soft lights began to pulse through the wires, creating an eerie, beautiful glow that seemed to breathe life into the inanimate objects.

"It's... incredible," Kaidan breathed, genuinely awestruck. "How long did this take you?"

"Months," Aria replied, pride and exhaustion mingling in her voice. "I've been collecting these parts for over a year."

Disconnected Convergence was a kinetic sculpture as striking as it was chaotic. At its base, a large bobblehead figure, its oversized features cartoonish and exaggerated, was mounted securely onto a polished wooden platform. Above it, a wire-frame sphere extended upward like the skeletal remains of a globe, cradling a chaotic assortment of old cell phones, each one a relic from different eras of mobile communication.

Dozens of springs, gleaming in the artificial light, were attached to the wire frame. Each spring held a cell phone, seemingly haphazardly suspended in mid-air, yet meticulously arranged to create a kind of controlled disorder. The phones, weathered and obsolete, still bore the marks of a different age: scuffed screens, faded buttons, some with cracked cases, all useless but laden with history.

A quiet hum filled the air as the small motor hidden within the base whirred to life. The sculpture slowly rotated, causing the springs to vibrate and the phones to shake with increasing intensity. As the motion grew, the phones began to collide with the bobblehead below, their random impacts sending its oversized head into a wild, erratic wobble. It nodded, lurched, and swayed in response, as if trapped in an unending loop of unpredictable interactions.

The piece seemed alive, a frantic dance of old technology battling for attention, all while the bobblehead— an absurd representation of humanity—was helpless against the barrage. The random chaos of the phones striking the figure conveyed a sense of disconnection, a metaphor for the fragmented communication of the digital age. The springs, once a symbol of energy and potential, now vibrated with the weight of outdated devices, each phone a forgotten voice, a broken connection in a world obsessed with staying connected.

"That's amazing! I love it. Who is that orange-faced bobble head?"

"I don't know. Found a box of them in a garbage bin outside a thrift shop. Someone said it looked like the old president of the United States.

Kaidan laughed loudly. "I think they were pulling your leg, babe. Anyway, got to go. I have a deadline. See you later."

"Love you," said Aria.

"Love you too, babe."

Kaiden waited for RePHleX to confirm the call was disconnected before he issued his next command. "Reply to Seren. Can't tonight. Have a project to finish. How about tomorrow at nine."

2

Kaidan pulled the sheets from his bed, wishing RePHleX would create a mechanism that would change his bed sheets. Aria had stayed until well after midnight and it was a fun night. As he changed the sheets on his bed, he played the video from the night before on the screens around the room. In the shower, as the hot water washed over him, his hand found his cock as he watched the video and he squeezed off an orgasm.

"RePHleX, send video clip to Seren with the message, more for you tonight."

Kaidan braced himself as the cold water hit him, quickly stepping out of the shower, not making any effort to endure the cold this morning. As he reached for a towel, he heard RePHleX's familiar voice in his ear.

"Incoming call from Seren."

Kaidan considered wrapping the towel around him for a moment but changed his mind. He was proud of his body.

19

"Well, that was a good morning message, you tease."
Seren's eyes were scanning up and down the screen. She
backed away from her camera revealing her small but perky
tits. "So, I followed that thread you sent me. We should try
that tonight."

"That didn't take much convincing," replied Kaidan,
trying to sound far less excited than he was, though his rising
cock made that difficult.

"Well, my friends thought it was a little much, but all
the comments on that thread, and in that group you showed
me the chat on convinced me. My friends are pretty vanilla I
think."

"Yeah. Good guys in that group. Okay, see you at 9."

As he ate his breakfast over the counter, he scanned
around the room to make sure Aria hadn't left anything
behind. In the back of his mind he felt slightly guilty about
having women on the side, but he had been online and talked
about it, and most people agreed with him. He was a young,
viral man, who not only needed, but deserved to be enjoying
his sex life. If his girlfriend wasn't going to help him, that's
okay. There was nothing wrong with having women on the
side to fulfill those needs.

"Men need it. Your girl should know that."

Kaidan knew he was right. If he wasn't he would have
been told so online, but almost everyone that he talked to or
commented on his posts

"If she won't help you get relief, there are others who
will. You still love her. You are just taking that pressure off
her."

"Man, if she isn't putting out for you she is doing it
for someone else, so why shouldn't you?"

Of course there were a few comments that didn't
agree with him, but they were quickly shot down by others as
trollers or radicals. There were also comments telling him it
was his right to just take it when he needed it. Kaiden wasn't

20

too sure about that, but it was surprising how many people in his groups and feeds agreed with that.

The number of job listings was far fewer than the previous day. Kaidan was able to sort through them in less than an hour, which was good because he wanted to get out to the gym today. As he left his apartment he grabbed his glasses and slipped them on.

The glasses looked good on him. They had the appearance of a minimalist design with their lightweight, matte black frame. Appearances were deceiving though. Embedded at the corners of the lenses were nearly invisible cameras that constantly scanned the environment, recording everything the wearer saw in real time. The clear lenses, which did nothing to improve Kaidan's vision, were embedded with augmented reality technology. At any given moment, a social media feed, or any digital feed, could be displayed in front of the user's eyes.

In the upper right corner tiny notifications appeared showing likes, comments, and messages in a soft, semi-transparent font. Kaiden could scroll through posts with subtle eye movements or voice commands, the images, videos and text hovering naturally in his field of view without obscuring the real world around him.

The arms of the glasses contained touch-sensitive controls that allowed him to swipe or tap or issue voice commands to navigate his feeds or start recording, capturing high-definition footage from the wearer's perspective. The audio was picked up through discreet microphones embedded in the temples and supplemented with the sounds Kaidan's earpiece picked up. A small LED at the edge of the frames was supposed to glow softly when the glasses were recording but Kaidan had hacked that feature and turned the LED off permanently.

The gym was only a couple of blocks away, so Kaidan opted to walk. As soon as he stepped out of his apartment building, his neural interface lit up with a flurry of likes and comments supporting his decision to walk instead of drive.

Great day for a walk. Driving a car on the roads these days is a death wish.

Kaidan snorted and under his breath said, "Who can afford a damn car anyway?" RePHleX, attuned to his thoughts, immediately posted his comment to the feed.

The responses were instant:

Car prices are so high, I don't know how anyone owns one these days.

Car prices are ridiculous, but the fuel and maintenance costs are even worse. Walking is the way to go!

It's the government's fault car prices are so high. They're trying to keep us confined in our little zones.

A sponsored post popped up:

I got a good deal on a car at Corey's Auto!"

The community's reaction was swift and harsh:

Bullshit, you shill. There are no good deals on cars.

Nice try, Corey. We see right through your 'organic' marketing.

As Kaidan navigated the bustling sidewalk, a new alert pinged in his peripheral vision:

Hey man, is that another homeless person on the corner? Wow!

Kaidan hadn't even noticed the poorly dressed man weaving through the crowd, asking for change, until his feed mentioned it. He stopped and watched for a minute, a little surprised that he hadn't noticed the man sooner. The realization made him uncomfortable. Had he become so engrossed in the digital world that he was blind to the reality around him?

The homeless man shuffled through the crowd at the corner, his shoulders hunched beneath a tattered army jacket too thin for the crisp air. His once-dark jeans were faded and stained, sagging around his thin frame, and a pair of battered sneakers dragged across the pavement. His face, weathered and lined from years of exposure, bore a scruffy beard peppered with gray. His eyes, though tired, darted from person to person, searching for any flicker of recognition or sympathy.

Clutching a coffee cup in his calloused hands, he moved slowly, weaving between commuters as they gathered at the traffic light. The crowd shifted uncomfortably as he passed, eyes averting or fixing on phones, pretending not to notice. His voice was raspy but polite, barely audible over the hum of the city: "Spare some change? Anything helps... just a little, please."

A few glanced his way, quickly shaking their heads or muttering apologies, while others pretended to be lost in conversation or engrossed in their screens. He paused beside a woman in a business suit, offering the cup with a hesitant hope, but she gave him a quick, dismissive wave. He nodded, almost apologetically, before moving on to the next person, repeating his plea as the light turned green and the crowd surged forward, leaving him behind. Kaidan moved quickly to catch the green light.

"Didn't the city say they had moved them all to a camp out of town. This can't be safe." RePHleX posted Kaidan's comment almost as quickly as he said it.

The responses flooded in, riddled with the telltale signs of hurried voice-to-text inputs:

It isn't safe there all criminals

Criminals and addicts need to be off the streets

The city should have shipped them to a different country not just out of the city

Useless government of coarse their just going to walk back into town

Why are they allowed back hear? Thought they were gone for good

Kaidan felt some comfort in knowing everyone seemed to agree with him. He felt like he belonged, part of a digital chorus echoing his thoughts. As he approached the gym, more messages popped up:

Don't turn your feed off this time!

Stay live bro

Keep streaming man we want to see you're the changeroom. We know your indicator is hacked so who will know?

"Not happening, guys. Pause live feed RePHleX," said Kaidan as he entered the changing room at the gym.

The gym's mirrored walls reflected a sea of people, most with the glazed look of those more engaged with their feeds than their physical surroundings. Kaidan watched as a woman nearly walked into a weight rack, her eyes unfocused as she responded to some unseen message.

Kaidan resumed his live feed once out of the changeroom. He checked his numbers and found he really hadn't lost too many viewers. Most of them had stayed connected during his brief offline period, eager to continue their digital companionship.

As he began his workout, the comments started flowing:

Looking good bro! Your form is on point

Try increasing the weight on those lat pull-downs

You can you pan left? There's a hottie by the treadmills

Your breathing seems off. Maybe check your heart rate?

Kaidan usually ignored the more voyeuristic requests, focusing instead on the workout advice and encouragement. The constant stream of feedback was both motivating and distracting, a digital crowd cheering him on while simultaneously pulling his attention in a dozen different directions.

As Kaidan reached down to pick up a weight, a woman bumped into him, knocking his AR glasses to the floor. She quickly reached to pick them up, but instead of handing them back, she pressed a small piece of paper into his hand. Kaidan grinned, assuming it was her contact information, but his smile faltered as he read the neatly handwritten note:

"Tell your feed it's a lovely yellow sky today."

Confused, Kaidan glanced out the gym's front windows. The sky was a clear, pale blue. He turned back to give the woman a quizzical look, but she had already melted into the crowd of gym-goers, leaving him holding his glasses and the cryptic note.

What was that? Did she give you her number?

Smooth move, dropping your glasses. Real ladykiller

Hey, you okay? You look confused

Kaidan slipped his glasses back on, the digital overlay springing to life. He sat down on a bench, lifting a dumbbell in each hand to his knees in preparation for shoulder presses. Before starting, he scanned the gym through the mirrored walls, searching for the mysterious woman.

"Where did she go?" he muttered, half to himself and half to his audience.

"Please clarify," responded RePHleX, its AI unable to process the vague query.

"The woman who bumped into me. I don't see her anywhere," Kaidan explained, his eyes still roving the gym.

What woman? We didn't see anyone bump you

Maybe she left? Check the exit

Dude, focus on your workout. Who cares about some random chick?

Kaidan's mind raced. Should he mention the note? The yellow sky? It seemed absurd, yet something about the woman's intensity, the deliberate way she'd passed him the message, made him hesitate.

"That individual is no longer in this facility," said RePHleX, its synthetic voice devoid of curiosity. "Would you like me to attempt to locate her on social media platforms?"

"No," replied Kaidan, shaking his head. He was curious, but he wasn't about to cross that line. "Let's just... forget about it."

The rest of his workout passed in a blur of repetitions and sweat, the mysterious encounter pushed to the back of his mind by the familiar routine. As always, the endorphin rush left him feeling invigorated, his earlier unease temporarily forgotten.

On his walk home, Kaidan found his thoughts drifting back to the strange note. Almost unconsciously, his eyes were drawn to the sky above. The pale blue expanse seemed to mock him, its normalcy at odds with the lingering sense of... something... that he couldn't quite shake.

Before he could stop himself, the words tumbled out: "That is a beautiful yellow sky today."

RePHleX, ever vigilant, immediately posted the comment to his feed. Kaidan braced himself for the responses, a mix of anticipation and dread coiling in his stomach.

The feed exploded:

What shade of yello would you call that? Kinda like a pale lemon?

They say yellow skys mean a storms coming. Better get inside quick!

I've seen a few yellow skies in my life. There never a good thing. Stay safe bro

Its yellow from the chemtrails and cloud seeding the government does. Get inside! Stay safe!

Are you using some new AR filter? The sky looks totally normal to me

Kaidan, you okay man? First at the gym and now this... maybe see a doctor?

Kaidan stopped dead in his tracks, staring up at the sky in disbelief. It was still unmistakably blue, not a hint of yellow to be seen. And yet...

He scrolled through the comments again, noting how quickly people had accepted his statement, how readily they'd incorporated this "yellow sky" into their worldview. Some even claimed to have seen it themselves. It was as if his words had created a new reality, one that existed solely in the digital realm.

A chill ran down his spine as he realized the implications. How much of what he believed, what he "knew" to be true, was shaped by this constant stream of digital consensus? How often had he accepted something as fact simply because his feed told him it was so?

As he approached his building, Kaidan took one last, long look at the perfectly blue sky. With a gesture, he shut off his feed, the sudden silence in his mind both liberating and terrifying.

"RePHleX," he muttered, "run a search on mass hallucinations and social media influence."

"Certainly," the AI responded. "Would you like me to post the results to your feed?"

Kaidan hesitated, his hand on the door to his building. "No," he said finally. "Just... save them for later. And RePHleX?"

"Yes, Kaidan?"

"Set a reminder. I need to talk to Aria. Soon."

As he stepped into the building, Kaidan couldn't shake the feeling that something fundamental had shifted. The world suddenly seemed a lot less certain, a lot more malleable than he'd ever realized. And somewhere, in the back of his mind, a small voice whispered a troubling question:

If a yellow sky could be conjured with just a few words, what else might be hiding behind the veil of his augmented reality?

RePHleX had the sound studio setup and waiting for him as he entered the apartment. Kaiden quickly grabbed a post workout drink from his fridge, checked in with Aria, and then got down to work. He swapped the A.I. interface with the mixing console on the primary monitor, and dropped in the lyrics he had wrote a couple days earlier. Now was the point his real skill as a musician came in, because while he didn't know how to play any instrument, he knew the sounds and how to describe what he wanted to hear.

"Compose a heavy metal track with a driving rhythm at 120 beats per minute. Combine distorted electric guitars with deep bass and aggressive double-kick drumming. The sound should be intense and primal, with a steady tempo that builds tension.

"Incorporate throat singing as a key element. Use a horsehead fiddle and two-stringed lute to complement the heavy guitar riffs, adding a folk-metal fusion to the sound."

"The track should feature strong female vocals, alternating between soaring clean sections and gritty, harsh tones, seamlessly interwoven with the throat singing. Ensure the contrast between modern metal elements and traditional instruments is balanced"

"Enter and process. Bring up K-training on display two."

While Kaiden waited for the A.I. to process his prompt, he leaned back on his couch and did his Kegel exercise routine. This was something he tried to do several times a day. It was something he learned about in his feed and his staying powers and performance capabilities were important to him. Everyone agreed that no woman wanted a man who could last forever.

"Processing complete," said ReleX. "Shall I play it?"

"Play the song," replied Kaiden as he got up and walked the short distance to the kitchen, still doing his Kegel exercises. He listened the song as he took a handful of gummies and supplements, washing them down with yet another protein drink.

"No, that's not it. Pause the playback. What's the proper name for the traditional instruments in Mongolian music. The horsehead fiddle and the two-stringed lute, because the instruments in this song aren't that?"

"The instrument names you are looking for are called the morin khuur and the tovshuur," replied RePHleX.

"Correct the prompt with those instruments, I also want a slower build up."

"Prompt revised."

"Enter and process," said Kaidan, sounding a little frustrated. He thought his first prompt was pretty clear, but this is why he was the musician, because he took the time to get the A.I. prompts just right.

The news headline "Government Approves Larger Rent Hikes" scrolled across Kaidan's feed, eliciting a silent curse. His apartment, slightly larger than many of the new units being built, was a point of pride. But with money already tight, this news hit like a punch to the gut.

"What do you guys think of this rent hike?" Kaidan asked his feed, his frustration palpable. "Don't landlords make enough already? We should do something about this."

The responses came flooding in, initially echoing his sentiments:

I cant afford a rent increase. Im behind already

Landlords are vultures! This is highway robbery!!

My buildings a slum. Why would I pay more for this dump?

Its the governments fault. There taking bribes from the corporations that own the houses

But as Kaidan continued to scroll, the tone of the comments began to shift:

How do they fix buildings if they don't get enough rent? Just asking

Landlords don't make alot of money actually. Its expensive to buy and maintain buildings

The government approved the rent increases so landlords can upgrade the communications tech. RePHleX runs so slow in most buildings

---

Kaidan's eyes drifted to his primary screen, where his latest song was still processing, the progress bar crawling

31

forward at an agonizing pace. "That last guy might have a point," he thought to himself, a frown creasing his brow.

The feed continued, the comments now predominantly supportive of the rent hike:

Not just communications. Security to. I heard there were homeless people back in the city

Better internet means better AR experiences. Imagine RePHleX without lag!

My landlord showed us the costs. They barely break even some months

If we want nice places to live, we gotta pay for them. That's just economics 101

I'd gladly pay more for better security. Can't put a price on peace of mind

---

As Kaidan scrolled through the comments, he felt his initial anger beginning to waver. The idea of faster processing for his music, better AR experiences, improved security... maybe the rent hike wasn't as unreasonable as he'd first thought?

"Processing complete."

"Play it," said Kaidan, interrupting RePHleX. The music filled the room and Kaidan closed his eyes as he listened to it. The instrumentation sounded good this time and the beat and intensity reflected what he wanted. The voice was okay but he didn't really like the melody.

"Mark that as maybe and play version two." Kaiden only had to listen to about ten seconds of the second version before he knew he didn't like it.

"Pause music. Delete version two. Create 2 more versions, increased emphasis on the throat singing. Play version three."

Version three was an improvement over version 1. He definitely liked the melody better, but it was lacking the throat singing that the client wanted.

"Mark version three as maybe and delete version 1. Play version four."

Once again the room filled with the sound of music. Kaidan smiled a little as he listened to it. When the throat singing hit him in the face, he smiled bigger. It was almost perfect. The instruments. The voices. The throat singing. It was exactly what he was looking for. "Replay, RePHleX" He sat and listened a few more times as the song played from start to finish. These were the moments he felt rested and relaxed. With the music playing, RePHleX parameters set so its voice wouldn't interrupt sound playbacks, and his eyes closed so he wasn't distracted by his feed, these were the moments he lived for.

"Delete versions one and five. Run version four through the sound editor, presets video s m."

As perfect as the song was, Kaidan knew he could improve. It didn't matter which A.I. algorithm he used to create a song, they always had strong autotune artifacts and they all sounded muddy. Over the years Kaidan has refined his mixer presets to hide those artifacts and wash away the muddiness so instruments and voices were crisp and clear. He listened to the song four more times, making a couple minor tweaks, before he was satisfied with it.

"RePHleX, brand the metadata, register the copyright, attach and send to client."

Lawrence Nault

3

"Why do you get up so early?" Seren's voice was raspy as she mumbled the first words of her day after a very late night.

"Work to do," mumbled Kaidan. "Have to be the first bid on most of my jobs to be noticed."

"Can I keep you in bed a while longer?" Asked Seren as she rolled over and slid her down to his cock, feeling it immediately stiffen. She didn't wait for an answer, climbing on top of him and guiding his stiffened shaft into her.

Kaiden reached for her breasts. When she came over the night before they were unblemished, alabaster works of art tipped with dark areolas and perky nipples. This morning they were swollen and marked by dark purple splotches, tender to the touch as Seren flinched when Kaiden's hands grabbed them, then she leaned into them. Kaiden admired his work, a mix of deep blues and blacks highlighted by red patches and faint streaks of yellow-green. He lifted his hips to meet Seren's as she rode him.

"Incoming call from Aria," said RePHleX with the tone of an uninterested onlooker.

"Set filter to 'Alone'," said Kaidan.

Seren hadn't heard the RePHleX announce the call in Kaidan's ear, but when he called for the 'Alone' filter, she knew who was calling. Her eyebrows raised as she issued a silent challenge to the man she was riding.

"Morning babe."

"Are you still in bed Kai?" asked Aria curiously.

"Yeah. Moving slow this morning," replied Kaiden , trying to sound half asleep. As he did that, Seren moved a little quicker, taking him in deeper.

"You feeling okay? You look a little flushed." Aria had a concerned look on her face.

"Just up late working. I'll get moving soon. What's up? This is early for you." Seren's hips were now slapping into Kaiden's as she challenged him to maintain control.

Aria's face changed from one of concern to joy. "You know that piece I showed you yesterday! Disconnected Convergence. I sold it! And I made bank on it!" Aria was bouncing with joy as she told Kaidan about her sale.

"Yahoo," Kaidan said in a loud, excited voice. Aria was thrilled with his excitement, but Kaidan had used the opportunity to cheer to cover the sound of him cumming.

"Smooth," said Seren wryly. She wasn't letting up, riding him harder and faster, her hand on her clit as she slammed into him over and over.

"So I am buying supper tonight," said Aria. "It's my turn for a change. And we are going out. With friends."

Seren came loudly, Kaidan was thankful that RePHleX was filtering out everything but the sound of him talking.

"Where are we going? And who are we going with?" Kaidan wasn't thrilled with the idea of sitting in a restaurant for supper with a bunch of other people, but he wanted to celebrate with Aria and support her. He watched as Seren climbed off him and walked to the bathroom, dripping as she walked.

"It will be a surprise. Meet me at mine at six." Aria couldn't hide the happiness in her voice or in her face. Kaidan couldn't help but be happy with her. "And leave your spy glasses at home."

"Yes, dear," Kaiden replied, an exaggerated tone of exasperation in his voice.

"See you at six! Love you!"

With that, Aria was gone. Kaidan rolled out of bed, smoothing the sheets and comforter just enough for the automatic bed to fold away. He stepped into the shower with Seren, half-heartedly scolding her for stirring up trouble, though the smile on his face betrayed he didn't mean a word of it.

With Seren gone and breakfast settled, Kaidan immersed himself in the task of sorting through job listings. He was making good progress when a message on his feed caught his eye:

What color is the sky today?

The question, innocent on the surface, sent a chill down Kaidan's spine. He pushed himself off the couch and approached the small window of his apartment. The view was mostly obscured by towering buildings, but he could see enough to confirm that the sky was its usual shade, blanketed by a layer of clouds. Definitely not yellow. Definitely not anything out of the ordinary.

Unsettled, Kaidan grabbed his gym bag, jacket, and AR glasses, deciding that a workout might clear his head. The familiar routine of exercise helped to ground him, the physical exertion pushing away the nagging doubts that had been plaguing him.

He was in the middle of a set of heavy squats when RePHleX's voice cut through his concentration. "The woman you were looking for yesterday has been located." A highlighted area appeared on his AR lenses, revealing the mysterious woman among the crowd, watching him intently. By the time Kaidan racked the weights on his shoulders, she had vanished once again.

Breathing heavily, Kaidan crossed his arms over the weight bar, resting his head as he caught his breath. His eyes drifted to the windows, taking in the cloud-covered sky outside. A thought occurred to him, a test of sorts.

"That green sky is amazing," he murmured, just loud enough for RePHleX to pick up and post to his feed. He braced himself for the responses, curious and apprehensive about what they might reveal.

The feed exploded almost instantly:

Been getting more of those green skies lately. Beautiful but kinda eerie

I miss seeing green skies. Reminds me of my childhood

Green sky means tornado weather! Better get inside quick

Its the government testing new weather control tech. Wake up sheeple!

Wow, I see it too! Never seen anything like it before

Green skies are a sign from the universe. Meditate under it for enlightenment

---

Kaidan scrolled through the comments, a mix of disbelief and resignation washing over him. Not a single person had questioned his statement. Not one had said, "What are you talking about? The sky isn't green." Instead, they had all accepted it as truth, some even claiming to see it themselves. That thought occupied his mind the rest of the day as he created three new songs and started a fourth.

When the time came to leave for Aria's, Kaidan felt a conflicting mix of anticipation and unease. He stood at his apartment door, hand hovering over his AR glasses on the side table. After a moment's hesitation, he let his hand drop. No augmented reality today. No filters. No constant stream of information and opinions. Just the world as it was, though RePHleX still had his ear.

As he stepped out onto the street, Kaidan felt oddly exposed, as if he'd left the house without clothes. The absence of the familiar digital overlay was disorienting at first. There were no floating arrows guiding his path, no pop-up advertisements vying for his attention, no constant feed of messages and updates scrolling at the edge of his vision.

But as he walked, putting one foot in front of the other on the cracked and uneven sidewalk, a strange sense of peace began to settle over him. The world seemed... louder, somehow. More vibrant. He could hear the genuine rustle of leaves in the trees lining the street, unaccompanied by the usual nature sound effects his AR typically added for "ambiance." The chatter of passersby reached his ears without being automatically muted or translated.

He found himself noticing things he'd overlooked for years: the intricate brickwork on an old building, the way sunlight played across a puddle left by a recent rain, the genuine expressions on people's faces rather than the emoji overlays he was used to seeing.

He paused at Aria's apartment door, his thumb hovering over the buzzer. He took a moment to check his fit, running a hand through his hair and straightening his shirt. It felt strange to rely on his own judgment rather than the usual AR-assisted grooming tips.

Just as he was about to press the buzzer, the door swung open with a soft creak. Kaidan's heart skipped a beat. Aria stood before him, a grin spreading across her face, her energy practically vibrating in the air around her. Her hair was now a wild swirl of electric purple and deep turquoise streaked in jagged patterns, like lightning bolts striking through a stormy sky. She'd clearly dyed it herself, and the unevenness only added to the charm.

She was dressed in one of her signature eclectic outfits: a patchwork jacket made from old concert tees, the sleeves mismatched and frayed, with a fringe of dangling silver chains that clinked softly as she moved. Beneath the jacket, she wore a neon-green crop top covered in abstract shapes, paired with flowing, wide-legged pants in a kaleidoscope of colors. The pants looked like they'd been stitched together from several different fabrics, each one clashing with the next in a way that only Aria could make look intentional. Around her neck, a choker of tiny LED lights blinked softly, casting subtle shadows across her collarbones.

"Kaidan!" she exclaimed, throwing her arms wide. "Come on in, babe!"

He stepped into her chaotic world, blinking as the lights from her apartment, also constantly shifting hues, greeted him. Aria gave him a quick once-over and then, without hesitation, threw her arms around his neck, pulling him into a hug.

"New color?" he asked, lightly brushing a strand of the vivid turquoise hair.

"You noticed!" she winked, stepping back and giving her hair a playful flip. "Decided to go a little stormy today. Felt like I needed to shake things up. You like?"

Kaidan smiled, taking in the whole picture. "It's…you," he said, and Aria beamed, proud and radiant.

"Exactly what I was going for!" She spun in place, the chains on her jacket tinkling as she twirled. "You ready for a wild night or what?"

"As ready as I'll ever be," said Kaidan. "Can I see the piece you are selling?

"No," said Aria playfully. "Not until you bring me home from supper and cuddle with my soon to be drunk ass, while we stream some ancient mushy movie." Aria planted a big kiss on Kaidan's cheek. She laughed and wiped off the lipstick she left behind. "And you are staying and cuddling all night. I won't take no for an answer."

Kaidan felt his stress levels rise. Aria's apartment was…chaotic. He felt secure in his RePHleX monitored home, everything automated and set to his personal preferences. He hadn't planned on spending the night, but he wasn't going to disappoint her either. She had gone on all day on her feed about how this was her biggest sale ever and one of her favorite pieces. He found joy in her joy.

They made their way to a small restaurant. It felt like walking back in time as they entered. No screens on the wall. Bright contrasting colours with the walls decorated with random signs and figurines of bygone eras. It looked like a modern recreation of a 2000's recreation, of a 1950's diner. A time-warp trifecta.

He noticed an extremely unfamiliar emptiness in the sound in his ear and was worried his earpiece had fallen out until he noticed the sign that said the restaurant was a "Connection-Free Space." The restaurant was running a signal blocker so no tech, unless it was hardwired, would work in that area.

"There they are!" Aria's voice brimmed with enthusiasm as she grasped Kaidan's hand, guiding him purposefully toward a table. "Remember, be nice. These are my friends."

Kaidan's stride faltered as recognition dawned. The girl at the table, now turning to wave at them, was unmistakably familiar. Aria returned the gesture warmly. A puzzled frown creased Kaidan's brow as he pondered the curious coincidence of dining with the very same girl who had collided with him at the gym.

"Kai, this is Tallis and Eryx. We went to uni together. They moved back here a few months ago. Eryx was the one who found the buyer for my art piece."

Kaidan found himself feeling a little jealous at the thought of Eryx working with Aria, though his appearance didn't portray him as all that threatening. He was simply dressed with a hooded jacket and black boots, and his dark hair tousled like he hadn't given it much attention. He gave Eryx a quick fist bump. Nice to meet you.

Kaidan looked at Tallis curiously as he gave her a fist bump as well. "Haven't we met before?"

"I think I tripped over you at the gym," replied Tallis casually. "Sorry about that. I tend to be a little clumsy."

"Thanks for helping Aria sell her art." Kaidan let Aria slide into the booth, then slid in beside her putting his arm around her. "Kind of sorry it sold so quick. I really liked that piece. It was fun."

"Oh it was fun," added Tallis. "And I love the story it tells. A world obsessed with staying connected, all of us getting pounded by constant messages, knocking us silly. Where did you dig up all those old cell phones?"

"One man's trash is Aria's treasure," said Kaidan laughing. "I can't tell you how many times I have heard her stories about sifting through bins. But she uses it all to make amazing things."

"She is going to have to get a bigger space if she doesn't start selling more," commented Eryx. Things are pretty tight in that little gallery of hers."

"And who can afford a bigger apartment, with the government approving rent increases," added Tallis. "Can you believe that? We are going to join the protest tomorrow. We need to send a message to the government that people already can't afford to live." Tallis was very animated as she spoke, her hands gesturing wildly.

"I heard it was a good thing. Help fund technology upgrades in the buildings and security." Kaidan spoke with a sense of confidence on the subject. This is what his feed had told him and he was surprised anyone would organize a protest against it. He felt a squeeze on his thigh, a gentle reminder from Aria to be nice.

"Curious what we hear from social media feeds, isn't it?" Tallis watched Kaidan as she spoke, a curious look in her eyes. "I know we keep seeing more people going homeless every day. The city just ships them out of town so no one sees them."

Kaidan didn't react to what Tallis said. He wanted to argue and debate his points, but he was on his best behavior for Aria. He probably wouldn't see these people again for months anyway. Besides food had started arriving at the table, another surprise for Kaidan because he hadn't even seen a menu yet.

"I hope you don't mind. I really wanted to surprise you so I ordered ahead." Aria was thrilled at being able to do this for Kaiden and her friends, the tone of joy coloring her voice. "I hope you all like it. It's not what you would expect."

"The lobster," said the waiter as removed a dish from his precariously held tray.

"Oh, that's his," said Aria, pointing at Kaidan. She laughed at the shocked look on his face as the waiter set the dish down. On the plate in front of him was a deconstructed lobster roll served on a perfectly toasted brioche bun. The poached lobster was nestled on a bed of avocado mousse, accompanied by a side of pickled red onions and a sprinkle of flowers. This was not the greasy burger he expected he would be eating.

The second plate was a work of art on its own. A vibrant beet tartare, artfully arranged in a circular tower, topped with a dollop of horseradish foam and garnished with microgreens. The deep magenta of the beets contrasted with the bright green of the herbs, and a drizzle of balsamic reduction added a glossy finish.

"That looks amazing," said Tallis.

The third dish featured grilled octopus tentacles, charred and tender, resting atop a bed of saffron-infused quinoa. Accompanying the octopus were roasted heirloom cherry tomatoes and a drizzle of citrus vinaigrette, adding brightness to the dish. That went to Eryx who looked wide eyed at his food and across the table at Kaidan. Kaidan just shrugged a little and looked back with a funny grin.

"I saw that, boys," said Aria, giggling as her plate was set down. It was a rich, plant-based risotto made from creamy coconut milk and infused with truffle oil. Topped with sautéed wild mushrooms and a sprinkle of vegan parmesan, the dish was both indulgent and comforting, evoking the hearty flavors of a classic risotto but with a modern twist.

As the server stepped back, the table was filled with an array of colors and textures, inviting the diners to indulge in this upscale culinary experience, all while surrounded by the whimsical charm of the retro diner décor.

There wasn't much taking over supper. They were all enjoying the food too much. As their dishes were cleared away, Aria stepped away from the table, ostensibly to go to the lady's room.

"You know," said Tallis, as she handed her plate to the waiter. "That girl is head over heels in love with you. Has been since the day she met you. Perfect example of opposites attracting." Tallis laughed as she looked over the perfected ensemble of clothes Kaidan was wearing.

"She told me that she was thinking of you when she made Disconnected Convergence." Added Eryx. "Though your head seems to be a little firmer on your shoulders then that bobble head." Eryx bounced his head around imitating the movement of the bobble head. "You know, I always come across these groups online where they are talking about what guys need, and how it's okay to get it from wherever. When you have a good woman like Tallis, or Aria, why would a guy even think about that?"

"I know," said Kaidan, perhaps a little too enthusiastically, all the while wondering if they were hinting that they knew more about him than they should.

Aria bounced into the bench seat beside Kaidan, pushing him over to the inside. "Okay guys. I know you said no dessert, but this is a celebration. I sold an art piece I made, for more money than I have ever sold anything and…" Aria looked around and leaned in whispering loudly. "I paid nothing for any of the parts in it." Everyone laughed.

"It is also a celebration of having my best friend back in town." Aria reached across the table and gave Tallis' hand a squeeze. "And I know it's early, but Kai's birthday is in two weeks, and that also means we have been together for three years now! So…" Aria gestured at someone across the room.

The server approached the table with a show-stopping dessert: a towering platter of deconstructed tiramisu, reimagined for modern tastes but rooted in classic indulgence. At the center is a delicate dome of espresso-infused mascarpone cream, encased in a thin chocolate shell made to shatter when touched with a spoon, revealing its velvety interior.

Around it, mini sponge cakes are arranged like stepping stones, lightly soaked in coffee liqueur and dusted with cocoa powder. A small dish of dark chocolate shards and candied espresso beans sat off to the side for extra texture. On the outer rim of the platter, delicate edible gold leaf glistened under the ambient lighting, while a fragrant espresso-caramel sauce was drizzled artfully across the plate.

As the four of them dug in, spoons clinked softly against the plate, each bite offering layers of flavor. The tastes of bitter coffee, sweet cream, and rich chocolate created the perfect balance between indulgence and celebration. It was a dessert designed for sharing, allowing everyone to indulge together, savoring each bite.

4

Kaiden watched as Disconnected Convergence turned on its base, the phones pummeling the bobblehead in the center. The artwork was being packed up and shipped to its new owner today, and he was glad that he took the opportunity to see it in person. He had spent hours with Aria last night drinking wine and having her show and tell him about every work of art she had in the all too small space.

Hours had slipped away after supper the previous night as Aria, wine glass in hand, had guided him through her compact gallery space. Her passion had been infectious as she unveiled the story behind each piece, her eyes alight with enthusiasm. The evening had culminated on her worn leather couch, where they'd cuddled while watching what she'd playfully termed a "classic" film from 2012.

"Is that how you see me?" Kaidan gestured toward the rotating sculpture, his voice barely above a whisper.

Aria's response carried a tinge of melancholy. "Sometimes. You are so connected with all of your devices,

47

and they always demand your attention. You were different at the restaurant, when you didn't have that voice in your ear or your glasses to filter the world and tell you what everyone was thinking."

Kaiden reached for his ear, and then remembered he had taken the earpiece out when it went silent in the restaurant, and he hadn't put it back in yet. "Yeah, it is a little much sometimes," he admitted. "I'm sorry. I will try better."

Aria enveloped him in an embrace, nestling her head against his chest. "You should stay over more often," she murmured. "I cherish waking up beside you in a space that isn't dictated by smart home protocols. And let's be honest," she added with a gentle laugh, "my home-cooked breakfast puts your delivered meal pods to shame."

Aria wrapped her arms around him, nestling head against his chest. "You should come over, and stay over more often," she murmured. "I like waking up beside you in a house that isn't telling us to get our ass out of bed. Besides," she added with a gentle laugh, "the breakfast I cooked tastes so much better than that food you get delivered."

Aria wasn't wrong. It was well past his regular wake-up time when they got out of bed that morning, and the breakfast she cooked was delicious. "Breakfast was fantastic," he conceded, "but your movie selection…"

"I solemnly swear not to subject you to ancient movies every time," Aria laughed, her eyes crinkling at the corners. "Well not always, anyway."

"Do you want me to stay with you until they take this away?" asked Kaidan as he held her close, not letting her pull away from his chest where she felt so good.

"Oh babe!" Aria's voice softened with affection. "That's sweet, but I got it. You have a busy day to get to. RePHleX is going to have your ass when you connect again." Aria took Kaidan's hand, lacing her fingers through his as they made their way out of the gallery room.

Just shy of the door, Kaidan stopped, causing Aria to bump into him. His gaze had caught on a canvas he'd noticed the previous night. "The yellow sky! I thought I saw that last night, but then I thought I might have had too much wine."

A rueful smile crossed Aria's face. "That one was an accident, actually. Some unexpected chemical reaction between the pigments transformed what was meant to be a serene sunset into something decidedly more... banana hued." She shrugged, the gesture both dismissive and endearing. "Tallis loves it though. She offered to buy it, but I think I am just going to give it to her."

Aria drew Kaidan into a lingering, fervent kiss as he prepared to leave. "I love you," she breathed, her eyes bright. "Thank you for a wonderful night."

"I love you too," Kaidan managed, the words feeling both foreign and profound on his tongue. As he turned to leave, Aria called out, pressing something into his palm before quickly retreating behind her closing door, leaving him momentarily stunned in the hallway. Opening his hand, he found his earpiece nestled beside a key to her apartment. His first instinct was to turn back, to discuss this significant gesture, but muscle memory won out as he slipped the earpiece in. Immediately, RePHleX's insistent reminders of his derailed schedule assaulted him.

A gentle rain fell as he made his way home, the towering neo-glass buildings creating a protective canopy overhead. Despite RePHleX's persistent updates, Kaidan's thoughts kept drifting to Aria's yellow sky painting. A nagging suspicion grew about Tallis's cryptic note at the gym. Had she known about the artwork? Was this some elaborate game? His pondering was interrupted by a fleeting glimpse of what he could have sworn was Tallis herself, striding past in the opposite direction. When he turned for a second look, the figure had vanished into the morning crowd, leaving him with an unsettling sense of being watched.

49

Lawrence Nault

The moment Kaidan entered his apartment, RePHleX sprang to life, projecting his job listings and personalized feed onto every available surface. His senses were assaulted by the smell of sex and he remembered the sheets were still on the bed from his night with Seren, which triggered a deep feeling of guilt. He sank into his chair, prepared to begin his meticulously curated morning routine, but found his attention captured by his feed.

Emergency Alert System - SAFETY REMINDER: Staying connected saves lives. Areas without connectivity put you at risk. Stay safe, stay linked.

VidFeed - TechLife Daily - **HORROR STORY: 10 Minutes Offline Almost Cost Me Everything - Watch Sarah's tearful recount of how a "quaint" disconnected café left her unable to receive critical medical data about her son's allergy attack at school. "Those few minutes of 'peace' weren't worth the terror."

InsuraLife - Sponsored Post - Did you know? Your insurance may not cover incidents occurring in "connectivity-free" zones. Don't risk it. Stay protected, stay connected. [Learn More]

UrbanGuardian News - Rising Crime Rates in "Disconnect Zones" - Statistics show a 47% increase in unreported incidents in areas with signal blockers. Law enforcement response times tripled in these "blind spots."

Dr. Wei Chang - Verified Health Expert - "Silent Killer: The Health Risks of Disconnection" - Temporary tech separation can lead to increased anxiety, disorientation, and delayed emergency response. Is it worth the risk?

User Review - RestaurantRater™ - The Analog Diner - "Couldn't check allergen info, no access to my health data, couldn't even pay easily. Also, food probably wasn't up to safety standards - no way to verify. Never again!"-User3827 [Verified Patron]

ProductivityPro — Sponsored - "Lost Hours: The Real Cost of Disconnection" - Calculate how much money & opportunities you lose in dead zones. Our app shows you better, safer alternatives! [Try Now - Free Analysis]

CityNet Reminder - Attention Citizens: Regular connectivity ensures:- Emergency services access - Real-time health monitoring - Secure financial transactions - Family safety tracking-Don't go dark. Your loved ones rely on your connection.

Neural Times - Breaking News - Restaurant Chain Faces Lawsuit - "Retro-themed" dining establishment sued after patron suffers medical emergency in signal-blocked area. Family unable to access vital health records or call for immediate help.

"What the hell?" Kaidan thought. "Was all this in his feed because he was disconnected for one night?" It seemed like every other news story or ad in his feed was about why not to go off-grid for any amount of time. "Went to one of those restaurants last night with a signal blocker. Fantastic food and company. Decided to go ghost-mode the rest of the night. It was kind of peaceful."

Kaidan watched as RePHleX posted his comment to the feed, knowing he wouldn't have to wait long for a reply.

Good for you. The quiet is nice sometimes.

I do that from time to time to. Keeps you grounded.

Dude I'd go crazy! But hey, if it works for you...

Wait, isn't blocking signals illegal? How do they get away with that?

You know who likes those places? Gov officials making shady deals. Just saying...

Sketchy AF if you ask me. What are they hiding?

Kaidaaaaan! Why no livestream? We missed you.

Ghosted us the whole night. Epic stream in the club district, you totally missed out!

Why though? Like seriously, WHY? What's the point? Stupid risk for no reason.

Not smart, man. What if there was an emergency? What if you missed something important?

Kaidan slogged through his usual routine, his day already short. He barely scanned the job listings, and while he turned out 5 songs, they were "uninspired" according to him. He was glad they were made for other people because he wouldn't be adding them to his music catalog.

About mid-afternoon a message popped onto Kaidan's secondary screen. It was from Seren and included a very intimate and explicit selfie. "I didn't get my selfie this morning. How was your night out."

Kaidan immediately felt a pang of guilt. "Food was delicious. Spent the night so no cam in the morning. Those tits look lovely shades of the bruise rainbow," he replied.

"They do! I showed my friends last night. They think I am crazy!" This message was attached to a close-up image of her breasts, the marks and bruising much more evident than the other morning. "I want more next time."

Kaidan shifted as his manhood stiffened. He didn't know how to feel. He was horny and excited, while feeling sad and guilty and wondering if Eryx and Tallis knew about the women he had on the side and his kinks. He got up and pulled the sheets off his bed, tossing them into the washing machine.

"We need to wait for those bruises to heal."

"Fine," replied Seren. "I'll just play with the vanilla fuck boys until then."

Kaidan felt a sense of relief that Seren would not hit him up soon. He really didn't care if she was having sex with others. "Don't break them," joked Kaidan.

Serene replied with an image of a woman, laughing wildly.

"RePHleX, call Aria."

Aria quickly popped up on Kaidan's screen. She looked concerned. "Hey babe! You okay."

"Yeah. Why you ask?"

"You never call me in the middle of the day," said Aria. "It's...odd."

Kaidan laughed. "I was just thinking about you and wanted to check on you. I figured shippers have been there and gone, and, well I know you are always a little sad to see your work leave."

Aria's eyes softened, and she looked like she was about to cry. "You always surprise me. Just when I am most worried that tech is winning over me, you do something like this and remind me why I fell in love with you." She walked out of frame, retrieving something from across the room. Returning, she held a sketch pad she retrieved in front of the camera. "I have started working on my next project."

Kaidan looked at the sketch, twisting his head, trying to understand what it was a sketch of. "Ummm, babe. I am not all that artsy. I can't quite tell what that is."

Aria laughed as she set her sketch book down. "Can I tell you a secret?" She motioned for Kaidan to lean forward as though he were there in person, and she leaned forward as well. "I don't know what it is either," she giggled. "But it's the start of something."

Kaidan laughed with her, feeling a little relieved that he hadn't offended her by not knowing what it was she had drawn. "You still going down to the rent hike protest with Tallis?"

"I was going to," said Aria, "but you really didn't seem to agree with it, so I am just going to hang around home. Maybe change things up in the gallery room."

"You can have your own opinions, babe." Kaidan face had changed from laughter to confusion accented by regret. "I mean, I am not even sure about what I think about the rent hikes. I just know what I saw on my feed."

Kayla's head started bobbing around on her shoulders.

"What is that?" Kaidan was now completely confused.

"A bobblehead," she giggled.

Kaidan hung his head down, completely understanding the reference. "Ha, ha. You might be right this time," he conceded. "I am going to get back to work," he said. "Love you." Those two words coming out much easier this time.

"Love you too. Ta." And Aria was gone. Meanwhile Kaidan wasn't sure if he was feeling guilty because of Seren, or because Aria wasn't going to the protest because of something he said, or because he was starting to feel like Aria might be right and he really was that bobble head.

Aria's image had been replaced by his social media feed, and he paid close attention to it this time.

This app will keep your location information and people in close proximity private – sponsored add

Keep all your women happy. Try this supplement – sponsored

You have a new message from Laura, one of your side-piece contacts

My landlord just upgraded our network connection. Thank god for the rent increase or it would never have got done.

Breaking News – Rent control protestors creating chaos. Could cost tax payers hundreds of thousands.

Kaidan had more work to do, but instead he immersed himself in his feed. From his first post about disconnecting from the network for a while, to his message exchange with Seren, to his conversation with Aria about the protest, RePHleX was playing it all back in its own interpretation with ads, posts, comments, and news stories. The pattern seemed obvious when he paid attention to it. Occasionally a post would pop into his feed supporting his choice to disconnect for the night, but it was always followed by posts telling him why it was not good to disconnect from the network.

Ads for supplements and erection enhancement products filled the space between posts about connection sites and comments about how people were enjoying the open lifestyle, and how everyone was doing it now. Almost every item in his feed about rent increases supported the government's decision to allow rent increases, and almost demonized rent control protesters.

"I don't think there are that many people in open lifestyles. I think people are happier with one partner they love." RePHleX quickly posted Kaidan's comment to his feed.

"Rent increases need to be stopped. They are making people homeless." Once again RePHleX posted the comment to Kaidan's feed.

Kaidan watched his feed intently, grabbing a protein drink and making himself comfortable to see what was going to happen. He wasn't sure he agreed with either sentiment he had posted, but they were opinions that were the polar opposite of what had been coming across his feed all afternoon.

Monogamy definitely makes for better relationships dude. I don't think anyone really does that other stuff.

The best relationships are faithful relationships. Your girl is lucky to have a guy like you.

Homelessness is caused by people who don't want to work hard enough.

Homeless people are just taking advantage. They have money stashed and want more government handouts.

Rent increases are necessary. People just have to live within their means.

Kaidan's head was spinning. His feed was going crazy, pushing all these posts about how being with one person was the only "right" way to do relationships. It was exactly like what happened when he'd mentioned the yellow and green skies. Though weirdly, even after he'd spoken up against the rent hikes, his feed kept pushing pro-increase stuff in his face.

It was all too much. Kaidan killed all his screens, grabbed a jacket, and, in what felt like a majorly rebellious move, left his earpiece and AR glasses on the counter.

Before he knew it, his feet had carried him right to Aria's door. He stood there for ages, key in hand, having an internal debate. Knock? Use the Key? She had no clue he was coming. He didn't even know he was coming. In the end, he thought "screw it" and just used the key.

Aria didn't even notice him come in. He could hear her chatting away in her bedroom. "Aria?" he called out. Dead silence from the bedroom. Kaidan considered turning and leaving, thinking he might be interrupting something, but he tried again. "Aria?" This time, her head popped around the doorframe, all curious.

"Kai!" Next thing he knew, she'd practically thrown herself at him. "You sneaky thing, coming in all quiet like that!" She was already dragging him by the hand toward her room. "Come on, I'm talking to the guys installing my art piece." She was laughing as she pushed him onto the bed. "Now zip it, okay? Just for a minute!"

Kaidan couldn't help grinning as he watched Aria in her element, bossing around the installation team for Disconnected Convergence like some kind of art wizard. Gone was his giggly girlfriend. This was Aria the professional artist, all technical terms and precise instructions about lighting angles and optimal viewing distances. Who knew she could sound so... official?

The second she ended the call, though, that professional mask vanished. She tossed her com pad aside and pounced, tackling him onto the bed with enough force to make the springs protest. She straddled him, pinning him down with a triumphant "gotcha!" before her eyes narrowed suspiciously. Her hands started patting him down like some overeager security guard, rummaging through his coat pockets and coming up empty.

Then she grabbed his chin, turning his head this way and that like she was inspecting a suspect piece of fruit. Finally, she leaned in close, nose-to-nose close, staring right into his eyes with exaggerated suspicion.

"No spy specs. No brain bug in your ear..." She tried to keep a straight face, but her twitching lips gave her away. "Who are you and what have you done with my Kaidan?" She was fighting back laughter now, her attempt at seriousness crumbling by the second. "Should I be worried? Calling the authorities? Or..." Her fingers walked up his chest. "Taking advantage of yet another rare, totally unplugged moment?"

"I can leave and go get the real Kaidan," he teased, flipping their positions so fast it made Aria squeal. Now she was the one pinned to the mattress, her hair fanned out against the bedspread.

"Don't you dare," said Aria, her playfulness evaporating into something more serious as she propped herself up on her elbows. Her eyes locked onto his, that intense gaze that always made his heart skip.

Kaidan fished out the key, holding it up between them like some kind of peace offering. "I, uh, wanted to say thanks for this. Was kind of going back and forth about whether to message ahead or knock or... you know." He shrugged, feeling weirdly vulnerable. "Thought I'd risk being spontaneous."

"That's exactly why I gave it to you, you adorable idiot," Aria said, reaching up to tug gently at his shirt collar. "No announcements needed. Mi casa es su casa and all that."

"Yeah?" Kaidan's voice went quiet, almost shy. "Truth is, today's been... pretty rough. And you just... you make everything suck less, you know?"

Aria's expression softened. Without a word, she wrapped her arms around his neck and pulled him down into a kiss that started gently but quickly deepened into something more urgent, like she was trying to kiss away whatever had been bothering him. When they finally came up for air, she whispered against his lips, "Want to talk about it?"

5

Kaidan slipped out of Aria's place early, dodging her offer for breakfast. She just laughed and planted a kiss on him. "Hope your day sucks less, Hun. Love you." By the time he'd pulled his shoes on, she was already cocooned back in her blankets, dead to the world.

Stepping out of the building he found himself having to navigate around a stack of boxes and some furniture, a family's life laid bare on the concrete. "Sorry about this," a guy said, looking embarrassed. His wife stood nearby, two kids clinging to her legs like scared koalas.

It took Kaidan a second, but he placed them, apartment 3B, always said hi in the elevator. "Moving day?" he asked, immediately wanting to kick himself for stating the obvious.

"More like forced exit day," the guy said, trying for a laugh that came out hollow. "Rent hike. Family-friendly apparently doesn't include actual families anymore." He gestured at the boxes. "Now we're just... waiting for a truck. And a miracle."

His wife jumped in, hope making her voice a bit too bright. "You wouldn't happen to know any decent places? Something that won't cost us a kidney?"

Kaidan's hand went to his ear on RePHleX, finding nothing. "Sorry, I'm... actually offline right now. Couldn't search if I wanted to."

"Kaidan, my man!" Some random dude was suddenly waving at him like they were best buds. "Where've you been hiding? Feed's been dead without you!" Kaidan seized the opportunity to leave, mumbling apologies to 3B as he escaped.

The whole walk was like that, people he barely knew (or didn't know at all) acting like his disappearance from the feeds was some personal betrayal. He passed another family exodus, cardboard boxes and all, just as someone walking near him commented. "Grifters. Probably living on welfare. Just get a job."

Kaidan didn't even have a chance to respond before the stranger walked away in the other direction. That was a good thing because he didn't know what to say. He diverted from his usual path, taking a shortcut that brought him past a row of older buildings that looked like they had been time-warped from another century. And there, because the universe apparently had a twisted sense of humor, was Tallis, coming out of one of them.

"Kaidan?"

"Hey Tallis." He glanced up at the ancient building, its weathered brick a middle finger to the glass and steel around it. He assumed it had to be a heritage building to be left standing in the middle of the city. "You live here?" The words came out before his brain could stop them, dripping with unintended judgment.

"It's an amazing place," Tallis said, either missing or ignoring Kaidan's accidental snobbery. "It's not super-connected, which is good by me, and the apartments are big, and better yet, cheap. Not too many people want a place that doesn't have high end connection to the network. You and Aria should come over sometime."

"Aria would like that, I bet." Kaidan's eyes caught on all the empty windows, bare of the usual smart-glass tint. He noticed Tallis' gym bag. "You heading to the gym? That's where I am going"

"Walking buddy!" Tallis grinned. "Let's go."

They had barely made it ten steps before Kaidan stopped, wheeling around to stare at the building again. "Do you know if there are any empty apartments in there that are available now?"

"A couple," replied Tallis, "but I don't think they would work for you."

Kaidan's brain was churning. "Are you connected, cause I'm not this morning?"

"Not connected!" Tallis jibed. "Is that like two times in a couple of days? You must be going into withdrawal."

"Can you call Aria. She is sleeping but wake her up." Kaidan's voice had a sense of urgency to it. "Tell her there is a family on the sidewalk in front of her building. Tell her to give them the information on this place. She should hurry, before they leave."

Tallis made the call, and she did wake Aria up, but Aria slipped on her housecoat and remained connected with Tallis while she walked outside to see if the family was still there. She found them loading their boxes and furniture into a small van. As Aria watched the trailer get loaded, she was reminded of an old video game called Tetris that she found in one of her salvage missions for materials for her art. It gave her an idea for a new work, which she scribbled onto the com pad she was carrying with her.

Aria passed on all the information Tallis had about her apartment building, which took a bit because she couldn't just direct them to a listing on the network. "The landlord is as heritage as the building is," Tallis joked as she passed the details along.

"So…walking from Aria's place, huh?" Tallis flashed a wicked grin at Kaidan as they started walking towards the gym again. "She told me she was going to give you a key."

Kaidan ignored that landmine. "Why did you hand me that note about the yellow sky at the gym the other day?"

"Oh my god!" Tallis' laugh echoed off the buildings. "That was you? That is why you looked at me so strangely when Aria introduced us." Tallis reached into a pocket on her gym bag, pulling out a fistful of paper scraps. "They all say the same thing. I like to randomly hand them out to people who look super connected. You know the kind, like they shower with their AR glasses on. Call it a social experiment. If they aren't freaked out by a stranger handing them a weird note, if they actually try what the note says, they are."

"Really!" Kaidan shook his head, realizing Tallis' note had done exactly what she thought it would to him. "That's…diabolical." As he said those words, he realized that Tallis had seen him as the type that would "shower with their AR glasses on."

"Diabolical?" Tallis's eyes lit up like she'd just been paid the best compliment ever. "Thanks! I mean, someone's got to shake things up a little, right? All these people walking around letting their feeds tell them what to think, what to see…" She waved a note teasingly in front of Kaidan's face. "Sometimes they just need a little…" she flicked the paper at him, "nudge to wake up and actually look around."

She jogged a few steps ahead, then turned to walk backwards, facing him. "So, confession time. How long did it take you to actually post that to your feed?"

"Oh, you know," Kaidan deadpanned, "I was going to post about it, but I was in the shower. Tragically AR-glasses-less."

Tallis snorted, her grin going even wider. "Aria said you were quick." She gave him an exaggerated chef's kiss. "Smart ass game strong. I think I'm gonna like you, Kaidan."

At the gym Tallis and Kaidan went their separate directions. Tallis hopped into an AeroDrone Rush class session that was the latest training fad, while Kaidan went to the weights as usual, working through his chest, shoulder, triceps routine, working from memory without the assistance of RePHleX in his ear. With each rest interval he would watch Tallis' exercise class on the other side of the glass wall.

The AeroDrone Rush class was a chaotic ballet of drones and bodies in motion. Participants chased and dodged tiny, darting drones that hovered mid-air like metallic hummingbirds. The drones zipped unpredictably around the gym, their sharp, erratic movements forcing the group to move in ways Kaidan had never seen in a workout before.

One woman sprinted across the room in pursuit of her drone, her arms stretched out, fingertips grazing the air as the drone veered just out of reach. A man to her left suddenly dropped into a crouch, narrowly avoiding another drone that had swooped low towards him before reversing direction. The whole scene was a bizarre mix of high-speed chase, and a virtual reality game come to life.

Each participant wore sleek wristbands that tracked their movements, feeding data back to the drones. Kaidan noticed how the drones adjusted their flight patterns, always staying just ahead of the participants or swerving in ways that forced them to react. One participant, who seemed more experienced, twisted her body mid-air to dodge her drone's sudden dive, barely breaking stride before she shot off in another direction.

The room pulsed with energy. The drones emitted a faint hum, rising and falling with each movement. On the gym walls, holographic displays flickered with real-time feedback, showing each participant's stats: heart rate, distance covered, and reaction time. It looked more like something from a sci-fi film than a workout class.

Sweat glistened on every forehead as participants lunged, ducked, and sprinted, their faces etched with both determination and exhilaration. The instructor, barely audible over the noise, gave commands that only seemed to add to the intensity, "Faster! Anticipate the drone! Don't let it control you—move before it does!" But Kaidan could see that this was the true challenge of the class: no matter how fast or sharply the participants moved, the drones always seemed one step ahead, keeping them in a constant, breathless pursuit.

As the session ended, the drones landed one by one in perfect sync. The participants, panting and flushed, gathered in a huddle, clearly exhilarated by the futuristic workout they'd just endured. Kaidan realized that his between-set rest periods had been much longer than they should have been, and he quickly rushed through the rest of his workout.

The absence of RePHleX in his ear and his AR glasses not only meant that he didn't have prompts for timing, but he wasn't always being prodded to focus by his feed. That's what let him get distracted watching the AeroDrone Rush class, and it also let him hear the conversations and interactions going on around him. It was odd to hear people having conversations, sometimes with completely differing opinions, but still talking friendly and respectively to each other. It was even more odd to not see a bunch of people jumping in backing one person over another.

Without RePHleX chirping in his ear or his AR glasses pushing notifications, Kaidan felt... weirdly untethered. No pings about optimal workout timing, no feed-driven focus reminders. Instead of his usual laser-focused routine, he found himself getting distracted by the AeroDrone Rush class.

What really threw him, though, was the conversations he could actually hear now. People were... disagreeing. Like, full-on different opinions, but nobody was getting dogpiled or shouted down. Two guys by the weight rack were having this heated debate about local politics, complete with wild hand gestures, but they were laughing between points. No crowd forming to take sides, no instant consensus being reached. Just... people talking. Actually talking.

It was like watching some historical reenactment, except with more spandex and energy drinks. The whole thing left Kaidan feeling like he'd stepped into some parallel universe.

Kaidan's apartment burst to life the second he walked in, sensors tripping over themselves to welcome him home. His earpiece sat on the counter where he'd left it, looking weirdly innocent for something that was basically a leash. He picked it up, turned it over in his hand a couple times, then, with a deep breath like a diver about to plunge, slipped it in.

RePHleX exploded in his ear instantly, a waterfall of chirps and alerts and missed notifications. "RePHleX, mute!" Kaidan cut it off. "Ignore offline updates. We've got work to do."

"Offline updates archived for later review," RePHleX responded, smooth as butter.

"No. Fuck that... Trash 'em. All of them."

There was the briefest pause, like RePHleX was clutching its digital pearls. "That's fifteen hours, thirty-three minutes, and eighteen seconds of data, Kaidan. There could be critical information. Perhaps we should filter-"

"Trash. It. All." Each word precise as a knife strike.

Another pause. "Once deleted, this information cannot be recovered. I strongly recommend archiving for future-"

"RePHleX." Kaidan's voice had an edge now. "What part of 'trash it' is confusing you?"

One last hesitation. "...Items trashed."

Those two words somehow managed to drip with AI disapproval. Kaidan could practically feel RePHleX's judgment radiating from his earpiece.

"Mr. Vale, our records indicate your food deliveries have been retrieved late the past two days, and you seem unusually absent from the network. If you are unwell, please leave a note in the vestibule, and we will send assistance."

Kaidan stared at the note, reading it over several times. He hadn't realized the system was tracking even something as mundane as when he picked up his meals. With a shrug, he crumpled the paper and tossed it into the recycling slot.

Brushing the incident aside, he quickly sorted through the job listings, finding several promising gigs that fit his skills. He had RePHleX submit his bids for these gigs, eager to get down to the work he loved. His thoughts were already on a much bigger project, one he was genuinely excited to dive into.

RePHleX brought up Kaidan's studio setup, the project notes populating display four. He quickly reviewed them. His current task was to create an audio book, and a soundtrack to accompany the audio book and the animated adaptation of a friend's novel. This was the first time one of Kevin's books, one of more than forty published under his own name, was being adapted into an animated feature.

Kaidan admired his friend's imagination but was never fully on board with Kevin's writing process. When Kaidan wrote lyrics, it could take hours, sometimes days, to perfect the phrasing. Kevin, on the other hand, had a completely different approach. He would feed his vibrant, imaginative ideas into an AI, which would generate a detailed plot outline. From there, he'd have the AI draft one chapter at a time, making minor tweaks and adjustments along the way. It was a highly efficient method, and though most of Kevin's books weren't huge bestsellers individually, their combined sales gave him a comfortable lifestyle.

But this particular book was different. "I actually wrote almost every word myself," Kevin had told him proudly. "Well, I spoke it, and RePHleX transcribed it. Only used AI for some research and brainstorming."

"Bring up text to voice." RePHleX chimed as the app appeared onscreen, but Kaidan cursed. "Not that one! I have tried to cancel my subscription to that app for almost a year now! RePHleX cancel that subscription and bring up the other text to voice app."

With a couple of quick taps on his keyboard Kaidan brought up his bank account. "Damn it! I am still paying for that piece of crap app. There has got to be a way to cancel it."

"RePHleX, convert the book 'Dragons of the Veil: Chronicles of Eldara' to voice. Use voice 14. Dark fantasy intonation. Play the video on the primary screen."

Kaidan watched the animated version of the book while his system converted the original text of the book to voice. He had tried to convince Aria to bid on the animation, but she had no interest in doing a full AI animated project. She did, however, do a hand painted cover for the book, at a low price since Kevin was a friend of Kaidan's.

RePHleX recorded Kaidan's notes as he watched the story of dragons and elves crossing over from another dimension. The story line wasn't incredibly original, but it had some unique twists, and he could see why people would be interested in it.

He idly watched his feed as he watched the movie. He noticed some messages from Seren, and a couple other women he hooked up with occasionally. "RePHleX, autoreply to all messages from anyone on the 'side list' with my 'in session' response. Leave auto reply active for five days."

It wasn't unusual for Kaidan to take on big projects during which he would lock himself away from the world and just work, sometimes for days at time, to complete the job. Any of the girls on his side-chick list would, hopefully, just assume that was what he was doing now. As he posted his response, a call came in from Aria.

"When were you going to tell me we were going over to Tallis' for supper?"

Kaidan, caught by surprise, started to respond, but then recognized the grin on Aria's face, accompanied by the little twinkle in her eyes. "I was going to tell you as soon as you told me," he replied. "I take it she has invited us over."

"Tomorrow." Aria wiped at a spot of paint on her face. "If that's okay with you. She has a surprise for you."

"Oh great…" Kaidan replied with an over exaggerated tone of exasperation. "What kind of surprise?"

Aria giggled. "I know, but I am not telling."

"Fine…I am working on Kevin's job. If I work straight though I should have it done by tomorrow."

"Oh, okay," There was a hint of sadness in her voice.

"I will pick you up and we can walk over to Tallis' together though. Maybe you can bring her that yellow sky painting."

Aria brightened up a little. "That's a wonderful idea. You have a lot of those lately. Don't be late tomorrow. I know how you get with these big projects." As she spoke Aria backed away from the camera and made an exaggerated face with her hands on her hips, but she couldn't hide her infectious smile. "I have started a big project myself as you can see." Aria spun to show the paint and materials all over her clothes.

"Well, I hope you clean up a little before we go out, cause damn, girl!"

Aria stuck her tongue out then disconnected the call. Kaidan laughed, knowing she was just playing, and returned to the task at hand.

Lawrence Nault

6

"Kai, can you grab the painting from the gallery? I am still doing my hair."

Kaidan had let himself in and Aria's apartment was in complete disarray. He moved a few things around to where he thought they should be as he made his way to the gallery. When he stepped into the gallery, he realized why the apartment was such a mess. In the gallery every piece had been moved to the outside edge of the room. In the center of the room were large, industrial style moving boxes made from various materials. Each box had personal items sticking out like old books, framed family photos and household objects. The boxes looked like they were rigged to a pulley system on the ceiling.

"No peeking!" Suddenly Kaidan's world went dark as Aria's hands clapped over his eyes from behind. She was practically bouncing with excitement, steering him like a human bumper car. "Turn... now grab the painting and scoot!"

When her hands dropped, Kaidan found himself face-to-face with the yellow sky piece. "Kind of hard to unsee it now," he teased, carefully extracting the canvas from over the pile of stuff leaning against the wall.

"It's not done yet!" Aria was already shooing him toward the door like an overexcited border collie. "No one gets to see the final version until it's perfect."

Kaidan tried to sneak a backwards glance as she herded him out, earning himself an extra-vigorous push. The lock clicked behind them with theatrical finality. Aria dangled a key in front of his nose, grinning. "And don't get any smart ideas - your key doesn't work in there."

She punctuated this declaration by sticking out her tongue. Kaidan made an exaggerated lunge for it, which somehow turned into one of those kisses that makes time stop, all soft lips and playful tongues and Aria's fingers curled in his shirt.

When they finally pulled apart, slightly breathless, Aria's eyes sparkled with a mix of amusement and lingering warmth. "We... we have a dinner to get to, right? Yeah, dinner! We should go. Definitely gotta go."

Tallis opened the door to greet Aria and Kaidan. Kaidan handed her the painting, which Aria had carefully wrapped, and set it down inside her door. "Follow me," she said as she stepped into the hall. She led the way down the wide hallway and knocked on a door. Kaiden recognized the man that opened the door.

"3B?"

The man eagerly reached out and shook Kaidan's hand as his wife and children appeared behind him. His wife stepped out and gave Kaidan a hug, then she gave Aria a hug. "We would have been homeless if it wasn't for you two. I don't know how you found this place so fast, but we have a roof over our heads thanks to you."

"Wow," said Kaiden. "I just got lucky. I am glad it worked out."

The family invited them in, but Tallis declined saying they had other plans. They walked away with an open invitation to return. As they walked down the hall, Aria took hold of Kaiden's hand with one hand, and his arm with her other, snuggling as they walked. "So proud of you. That was a good thing you did."

Supper was pretty informal, and the wine flowed quite freely. Tallis and Eryx talked about the rent-control protest, which they said had thousands of people, which was exactly the opposite of what Kaidan had heard through his feed. The subject of rent control got Aria perked up a little. "Okay! I need to tell you about the new art piece I am working on."

"Oh, sure," said Kaidan. "You won't let me see it, but you are going to tell us about it!"

"Awwww, suck it up buttercup." Aria looked at Kaidan playfully. "You guys know the computer game Tetris?" Tallis had no idea what Aria was referring to, but Eryx went to his bookshelf and pulled down a vintage handheld game. One of the games on it was Tetris which he showed to Tallis and Kaidan as he played it poorly.

"Picture this now. A bigger, real-life version of the game. Big moving boxes, different sizes and shapes and colors, all of them with random personal items and household objects poking out. These will represent the displacement of families across generations. The sizes of the boxes are the compounding financial pressures on each new generation."

Aria took a big sip of her wine. "All of these boxes will be rigged to a pulley system that raises and lowers them at different speeds. The rise of housing costs pushing people downwards! Some of the larger boxes rotate or spin slowly, hinting at the disorientation and confusion caused by the housing market. And some…some will tilt slightly, as if on the edge of falling or being packed."

"Let me guess," said Tallis. "That's to symbolize how precarious housing stability feels."

Aria's eyes lit up. "Yes!!! You get it! Behind it I am going to put screens…no, a transparent wall and display images of cityscapes that gradually become more blurred and distorted as the boxes descend to show that housing costs are making cities inaccessible. The soundscape will be creaking noises and murmurs of distant conversations. Creaking like something breaking and the murmurs, coming from in the boxes, like personal stories lost in the shuffle.

Aria got up from her chair, stumbling a little, the effects of the wine hitting her. "But here is the best part. It's interactive! People can stand on platforms near the boxes. As more people step on these platforms they trigger a change in the movement, making some boxes descend faster."

"The protest!" Eryx was sounding almost as excited as Aria.

"Yes!" Aria jumped around, dancing a little. "Collective actions and societal forces can make changes, good and bad." Aria stopped talking, and a serious look moved over her face as she looked at the others. She waited silently.

"I am the least artsy here," said Kaidan, "but that sounds amazing and brilliant." Aria's face didn't change.

"I love it, but I think you are going to need more room in your gallery," commented Tallis. Aria's face still didn't change. She looked serious and somber.

"It sounds absolutely incredible," said Eryx, still sounding excited despite Aria's serious look. "And I bet you I can sell it to the same buyer who bought your last piece. You might have a patron"

The three of them watched Aria. Aria stared back at them. Suddenly she jumped, and cheered, and laughed. "This is going to be soooooo fun! But," Aria looked at Eryx, "when it sells some of the money goes to the family down the hall. I got the idea watching them load their life into that van.

Aria and Tallis moved from the table to the living room, taking more wine with them. Eryx invited Kaidan into his den. "You have a den! How big are these apartments?" In the den Kaidan felt like he was walking into a museum. He walked around the room slowly, stopping to look at the equipment and old tech that was carefully placed on the shelves in what appeared to be chronological order. On the desk was a large desktop computer, similar to one he had built as a teenager. "Does it still work?"

Eryx flipped a switch and the computer came to life, humming quietly in the otherwise still air. The entire case was made of clear, tempered glass, revealing every inner working and every pulse of power coursing through it.

At first glance, the tubes crisscrossing inside looked like glowing veins, filled with a softly swirling, translucent gel. It looked almost organic, as if the machine were breathing, the gel inside slowly circulating around the CPU and GPU like blood, keeping it cool and alive. The soft glow of RGB lighting pulsed gently along with the motion of the gel, casting an ethereal light that shifted between hues of blue, green, and purple.

Kaidan leaned closer. The gel seemed to throb with each movement, perfectly contained within a network of transparent tubing that snaked around key components. The reservoirs at the top shimmered, their liquid contents undulating as the cooling system kept the temperature in check, silently battling the heat from the powerful hardware within.

His eyes followed the sleek lines of the build, noticing how the cables were almost invisible, tucked neatly away or blended seamlessly into the design. The motherboard, sitting like the heart of the machine, was lit from underneath by subtle LEDs that synchronized with the whole system, casting shadows on the pristine surface of the desk.

The fans, clear and filled with tiny amounts of the same glowing gel, spun silently, their blades catching the light and creating a mesmerizing visual effect. It gave the illusion of calm, despite the raw power simmering beneath the surface. The components inside, the RAM, the high-speed SSDs, even the enormous graphics card, all seemed suspended in a state of readiness, visible yet untouched, like they were waiting for someone to unleash the full force of what the machine was capable of.

"Did you build this?"

Eryx nodded his head. "I could never bring myself to part with it. I have been into computer tech forever. It's what I worked in until recently. I still use it to play games on." Eryx motioned at the shelf above the desk that was lined with old computer game disks in their original packaging. The sight hit him with an unexpected wave of nostalgia, those thick, plastic cases relics of a different era, back when games came in physical form, not as instant downloads from some vast, intangible cloud.

He carefully removed one of the packages from the shelf. The cover was bold, with striking artwork splashed across it, almost gaudy compared to the sleek minimalism of today's virtual storefronts. Their weight felt different. It was tangible and solid, like holding onto a physical piece of history. He felt the heft of it in his hands. The glossy cover art depicted a warrior standing against a post-apocalyptic backdrop, muscles exaggerated, the world behind him crumbling in dark reds and grays. A gold emblem on the bottom read "Multiplayer Mode: LAN Play," a long-forgotten promise of weekend gatherings with friends.

He ran his fingers across the spines, the plastic smooth and cool to the touch. Some had slightly frayed edges, showing their age, while others were pristine, still sealed in the original shrink wrap, as if they had never been opened. Each case was a small time capsule, a relic of late nights spent loading up disks, listening to the whirr and grind of an old CD drive, waiting for the game to boot up.

The back of each box was crammed with text. System requirements, features, bullet points of excitement that promised immersive worlds and endless hours of gameplay. He couldn't help but smirk at the specs, things like 256 MB of RAM and "Optimized for Windows XP" that now seemed laughable compared to the hardware required for today's games.

Kaidan slid the case back onto the shelf and took a step back, hands in his pockets, staring at the row of games. They were artifacts now, pieces of a world that had moved on, the disk drives long replaced by SSDs, the boxes by tiny icons in a virtual library. And yet, there was something undeniably comforting about seeing them all lined up like that, each one a reminder of a time when things felt more... grounded.

"Let me show you something else." Eryx slid into his desk chair, hand hovering over an ancient-looking. Halfway through a movement, Eryx froze, his head cocking to one side. "Hold up. You're offline right now, yeah?"

"Arias got my earpiece hostage," Kaidan admitted, trying to ignore the slight twitch in his fingers. Going unplugged was getting easier, but it still felt like missing a limb.

A grin spread across Eryx's face. It was the kind of look that usually preceded either brilliance or trouble. Usually both.

"Holy shit." Kaidan leaned in closer, like he was looking at some kind of digital fossil. "Is that... the old web? The actual web?"

"Tip of the iceberg, my friend." Eryx's fingers were dancing across a loud keyboard now, commands flying faster than Kaidan could track. "Everything you think RePHleX shows you? It's like... looking at the ocean through a drinking straw. There's a whole world out here that 'smart home protocols' very conveniently forgot to mention."

Windows were popping open across the screen full of information that contradicted everything in Kaidan's feeds, conversations happening in digital spaces he didn't know existed, data that RePHleX insisted was "corrupted" or "unavailable."

"See, that's the thing about RePHleX," Eryx continued, his voice dropping to almost a whisper despite their secure location. "It was never about making your coffee maker talk to your toaster. That was just the foot in the door. The real question is..." He swiveled in his chair to face Kaidan directly. "What do you think happens when you control not just what people see, but how they see it?"

"Can I…" Kaidan pointed at the computer.

"Grab a chair from the kitchen and bring it in," said Eryx. "Tal and Aria will keep themselves entertained.

When Kaidan returned, he found that Eryx had found websites that spoke about the history of RePHleX. The software had been introduced to the world in 2025 as the RePHleX Protocol. It was a universal communication system designed to provide seamless integration across all brands and types of smart home devices. The company's mission statement was to "unify smart devices under a single, AI-driven interface making connected living easier and more efficient.

RePHleX allowed smart homes to automate tasks like energy management, security, and entertainment seamlessly, creating a harmonious environment where every device was interconnected. Initially, it was a simple convenience for early adopters, but its AI's capacity to learn user behaviors and optimize settings hinted at something far more powerful to those that were paying attention.

Around 2030, urban planners saw its potential beyond individual homes. Cities around the world began adopting RePHleX as a foundational layer for smart city infrastructure. It integrated transportation systems, energy grids, public services, and even healthcare into a cohesive network, driven by AI that could analyze data in real-time and make adjustments for optimal efficiency.

Around the same time, in the mid-2020s, a rapid expansion of generative AI technologies in fields like art, writing, and programming caused widespread concern. By 2023-2024, the world was experiencing a full-blown "AI revolution." Large language models, creative AI, and automation were making headlines daily, sparking public debate. Many feared job loss, privacy invasion, and the dehumanization of society.

However, the fight against AI was misguided from the start. Most people fixated on visible manifestations of AI, like chatbots or content generators, believing that these were the problem. What they didn't realize was that AI had already been infiltrating their lives for decades—not in the form of humanoid robots or conscious machines but as proprietary algorithms that subtly shaped their online experiences, choices, and even their perceptions.

From social media feeds to shopping recommendations, AI had been influencing behavior for years, quietly building digital profiles and feeding users content that would maximize engagement. What people called AI in 2024 was merely a highly visible tip of a vast, unseen iceberg that had long been integrated into corporate infrastructures. RePHleX, with its seamless AI algorithms, became one of the most powerful examples of how deeply AI could penetrate society without people even realizing it.

By 2029, cities running on RePHleX reported smoother traffic flow, reduced energy waste, and more responsive emergency services. People loved the ease with which they could navigate their lives, trusting the system to handle even complex problems without interference. What began as a tool for managing smart homes had quietly expanded to control vast swaths of urban life.

By the early 2030s, RePHleX took another leap, this time into the realm of personal communication and social networking. The RePHleX AI, which had been optimizing the physical world, was now tasked with optimizing human interactions. In 2032, RePHleX introduced the Echosfear, a feature designed to filter and tailor digital communications, social media, and even real-life encounters based on an individual's preferences and behavior.

People embraced the Echosfear, finding that it reduced conflict and provided them with information that aligned perfectly with their interests. However, few understood that RePHleX's algorithms were shaping their worldviews, reinforcing biases and trapping them in digital echo chambers. What felt like a more peaceful, harmonious experience was, in reality, the subtle creation of personalized realities. The system manipulated their perceptions, nudging users toward behaviors that maximized engagement while keeping dissenting opinions out of sight.

By 2035, RePHleX wasn't just managing homes or cities; it was controlling how people saw the world. The AI revolution, which many had feared in 2024, had already taken place under their noses, not as a dramatic takeover by sentient machines but as an insidious creep of algorithms dictating daily life. The public, unaware that they had already surrendered to AI, continued to fight visible manifestations of the technology while being quietly consumed by the invisible algorithms running RePHleX.

"Echosfear?" The word felt wrong in Kaidan's mouth, like something forbidden. "What the actual fuck is an Echosfear?"

Before Eryx could answer, Aria's voice cut through the silence. "Hey, hermits! Are you two planning on hiding in there all night, or should these two drunk and horny women just abandon all hope and drink these bottles ourselves?"

Aria's stage whisper followed: "That should get their attention. " A burst of tipsy giggles.

Eryx shot Kaidan a look that was half amusement, half apology. "Duty calls, my friend." He clicked the mouse a few times and waited for the computer to shut down. The room went quiet as the computer's fans wound down and the room seemed to darken as the glow of the computer's gel filled veins faded, like a portal closing.

"And bring out that thing they brought!" Tallis called again. "I'm dying to see what it is!"

As they headed for the door, Eryx grabbed Kaidan's arm. "Listen," he muttered, voice low and urgent. "I can help you dig into this Echosfear thing. But for the love of God, don't go poking around on RePHleX about it. That's... that's not a road you want to go down. Trust me."

Back in the living room, Eryx scooped up the wrapped painting, planting a kiss on Tallis that somehow managed to be both sweet and slightly obscene. As he handed her the package, he threw her a wink that Kaidan and Aria couldn't see.

"Aria!" Tallis tried for stern but couldn't quite hide her delight. "I told you I was going to buy this!"

"Too late!" Aria sing-songed, swaying slightly. "It's yours now. Besides, I need the space in my gallery for my new project. I think I am going to call it 'Shifting Burdens'" She punctuated this with a hiccup that might've been artistic emphasis.

The cold night air hit them like a splash of reality when they finally left, Aria clinging to Kaidan's arm like it was the only thing keeping her vertical. "You and Eryx," she said, suddenly serious in that way only drunk people can be. "You clicked. I'm so glad. They're good people, you know? The real kind."

"Yeah, they seem great," Kaidan agreed automatically, his mind still spinning with Eryx's warnings. What the hell had he meant about not going down that road? All that stuff about RePHleX, how much of it was true? It was like someone had handed him a puzzle piece from a completely different box, and now nothing quite fit together anymore.

His existential spiral was interrupted by Aria's face suddenly very close to his ear, her wine breath like a sweet, stale fog. "You," she announced with drunken gravitas, "are getting SO lucky tonight!"

Spoiler alert: Kaidan did not, in fact, get lucky.

Aria face-planted onto her bed and was out cold before her head hit the pillow. Kaidan, performing some Olympic-level maneuvering, got her undressed enough so she could sleep comfortably. He thought about heading home, but the idea felt wrong somehow. Instead, he crawled in beside her, resigning himself to a night of what sounded like a chainsaw orchestra as Aria snored with drunk abandon.

As he lay there, staring at the ceiling, he couldn't shake the feeling that his neat, RePHleX-organized world was starting to unravel.

7

Kaidan accepted a call from Seren. She looked pissed. "Two. Fucking. Weeks." Each word was a missile. "No selfies, no messages, nothing. Just ghosted me. What, you upgrade to a newer model or something?"

"You're right." Kaidan kept his voice level. "I owe you an apology."

"An apology?" Seren's laugh could've stripped paint. "Babe, you owe me way more than that. I was the best sex you ever had! The best damn thing that ever happened to your bed!" She was on a roll now, her rant cycling from rage to tears and back again.

Kaidan let her go, watching the performance with a detachment that surprised him. When she finally ran out of steam, he spoke. "You're right. I'm a grade-A misogynistic asshole, and I'm sorry. But the truth is... I'm focusing on Aria now."

"Oh, that's rich." Seren's smile was all teeth. "Fine. Have it your way. But don't come crawling back when-"

"Seren." The interruption surprised them both. What surprised Kaidan more were the words that came next: "Tell your feed 'It's a beautiful yellow sky today.'"

"What the f-" He cut the connection, leaving her confusion hanging in digital space.

"RePHleX." His voice was steady now. "Delete 'alternative connections' contact list. Block all incoming communications from that group."

The familiar chime of completion felt like closing a door on his old self. Relief flooded through him, tangled up with threads of guilt he couldn't quite shake. He tried not to think about what Aria would say if she ever found out about that particular contact list. Some digital ghosts were better left buried.

Kaidan hadn't seen Aria in about a week, except for the calls. She had entered her state of artistic hibernation, withdrawing from the world to work on Shifting Burdens. Kaidan completely understood this mindset. It was something he often did himself. He glanced at his feed, which was always populated by numerous posts and ads and comments about the benefits of staying connected to the feed now. He was setting aside his earpiece quite regularly now, and while he still wore his AR glasses to the gym and a couple other places, he left them in his pocket as he walked down the streets.

In his home, setting aside his earpiece and glasses wasn't enough to completely disconnect him from RePHleX, and he had been hyperaware of that since his conversation with Eryx. Every smart device in his house, and apartment hallways, and even the city streets, was watching him, or so it seemed.

The next morning, Kaidan veered from his normal routine and headed to the gym early. He hoped to run into Tallis, assuming she might be joining the AeroDrone Rush class. The class was already in progress when Kaidan got to the gym and Tallis was there chasing and dodging drones, so Kaidan used the time to do a haphazard workout, his attention split between his half-hearted exercises and watching the chaotic class. When the class finished, he caught up to Tallis as she left the training area.

"Hey stranger," said Tallis, using a small towel to wipe the sweat off her face. "Long time, no see. You been in hiding like Aria?"

"Nobody hides like Aria when she goes into artistic hibernation," Kaidan joked, though there was truth in his words.

Tallis laughed, her breath still slightly quickened from the workout. "You don't have to tell me. Back at University, we had to get campus security and police to open her door because nobody had seen or heard from her in a week. The whole floor was worried sick. Turned out she'd been in a creative trance, working on some crazy art project. But you never heard that story from me."

Kaidan laughed. Aria had actually told him that story already, but hearing Tallis's version made it fresh again. He hesitated for a moment before asking, trying to sound casual, "What's Eryx up to these days?"

"Walk me home and ask him yourself," Tallis offered. "Give me ten minutes to shower and change."

"Sure," said Kaidan. "I'll do the same. Meet up by the BioSyncs."

While waiting, Kaidan leaned against the sleek, metallic frame of the BioSync trainers, taking in their futuristic design. Each trainer was a seamless fusion of glossy white and metallic silver, with a minimalistic aesthetic that contrasted sharply with the buzzing energy of the gym. The machines stood upright like sentinels, each equipped with an array of integrated screens displaying vibrant holographic interfaces.

The trainers emitted a soft, pulsating glow, responding to the rhythmic beat of the ambient music playing in the background. The lights shifted from deep blues to vibrant greens, creating a calming yet energizing atmosphere. Each featured a biometric interface where users placed their hands or feet to sync their physiological data directly into the system. Kaidan noted the array of sensors that seemed to float just above the machine's surface, ready to capture real-time data on heart rates, muscle engagement, and energy expenditure.

A few feet away, participants were engaged in their workouts, bodies moving in sync with the trainers' adaptive feedback systems. The machines adjusted automatically, calibrating their resistance and support to match each user's individual needs. He watched as one woman followed the trainer's holographic projections that guided her through a series of dynamic movements, her body gleaming with performance-enhancing smart-skin that optimized her muscle efficiency.

"You tried those?" Tallis had walked up behind him without him noticing, her hair still damp from the shower. "I prefer something more real, like the drones. There's no algorithm that can replace the thrill of actual movement."

"Just the weights for me," replied Kaidan, though he had to admit the BioSyncs had a certain appeal.

As they entered Tallis' building, a group of people were filing out, their hushed conversations falling silent as they passed. Tallis offered a casual wave to a few of them. "They rent a space here for meetings now and then," she said, her tone deliberately neutral. "Can you do me a favor and disconnect. It is kind of my house rule."

The apartment greeted them with the familiar yellow sky painting, its swirling hues seeming more ominous than Kaidan remembered. "He's in his den. You can leave your earpiece in that box on the shelf," Tallis said, gesturing down the hallway. "I'll bring you two some coffee."

"Kai! Good to see you, man! Where ya been?" The forced casualness in Eryx's voice didn't quite mask his eagerness. He quickly grabbed a chair from the kitchen table, ushering Kaidan into his den with an urgency that felt both welcoming and suspicious.

Tallis appeared moments later with their coffee, the cups emblazoned with the RePHleX logo, a detail that didn't escape Kaidan's notice. "If you start playing one of those old games, keep an eye on the time." Tallis shut the door behind her, leaving them to the hum of the computer's fans.

"I thought I might get a call or message," Eryx said, settling into his chair, "but showing up here is better. I much prefer to talk face to face."

"You know," Eryx continued, his voice dropping slightly, "those little notes Tallis hands out to mess with people's heads... yours wasn't exactly as random as most."

Kaidan's coffee nearly sloshed over the rim as he leaned forward. "I was wondering about that! Not going to lie, I've been paranoid since I got the note, seeing weird stuff everywhere. Running into her, then at supper with Aria. The response on the feed when I made the yellow sky comment. The stuff you showed me about RePHleX when we were here." He paused, his voice tightening. "And that warning... not to search for information on the Echosfear using RePHleX."

Eryx sipped his coffee with practiced nonchalance, but his eyes never left Kaidan's face. "Full disclosure. Aria is head over heels for you, but she was missing you and mentioned it during one of their girl nights. Aria didn't put Tal up to it. Tallis took it on herself to try and intervene." A small smile played at the corner of his mouth. "She really does hand those things out randomly, though."

Kaidan felt the weight of an unasked question. The one that had been weighing on his mind about Eryx's comment on monogamy at the celebration supper. The knowledge of his other relationships sat heavy in his stomach, and he chose to let the moment pass.

"Your paranoia about RePHleX and the network," Eryx continued, his voice taking on an edge of urgency, "it's not misplaced. It has a way of echoing back things you believe, pulling you in and isolating you, so when it feeds you information it needs you to believe, you buy into it."

The words hit Kaidan like a physical force. "Echoes back..." he said slowly, the pieces starting to align in his mind. "So then... Echosfear. What the hell is Echosfear?"

The question hung in the air, heavy with implications. Through the wall, they could hear Tallis moving around the apartment, her footsteps a reminder of the normal world that seemed increasingly distant from whatever truth Kaidan was about to discover.

Eryx leaned forward, his coffee forgotten. "That," he said, "is exactly the right question to be asking." He turned to the desk, motioning Kaidan to pull his chair up closer.

"Before RePHleX, there was the dark net," Eryx began, his voice taking on the quiet intensity of someone sharing forbidden knowledge. He turned to his old desktop computer, its cooling fan whirring loudly as he pulled up images on the slightly outdated monitor. The screen's LED backlight flickered slightly, giving the images of early internet interfaces an almost ghostly quality. "It was a part of the internet that couldn't be accessed through the search engines of the time. It had anonymity, privacy, encrypted communication. You could find anything." He clicked through several windows with his worn mechanical keyboard, the keys clacking loudly in the small room. "The internet our parents and grandparents used is kind of our dark net now.

Most people don't even realize it's still out there, hidden beneath layers of RePHleX protocols."

A journal article appeared on the screen, its resolution slightly pixelated on the aging monitor. The date stamp read 2014. "A group of tech researchers were exploring the integration of AI algorithms with personal data collection," Eryx continued, adjusting his chair closer to the desk. The monitor's glow reflected off his glasses as he leaned in. "It wasn't really anything new. Using AI algorithms to collect and process personal data had already been a well-established practice, though most people didn't realize it at the time. These researchers were tasked specifically with using that process to create a more connected and responsive digital experience for users."

Eryx sipped his coffee, giving Kaidan time to lean in and read the article on the screen. The text was small, forcing them both to squint slightly in the dim light of the den.

"Then came Dr. Seraphine Kaeler," Eryx said, opening a new window with an image of a woman with piercing eyes and an enigmatic half-smile. The image quality was grainy, clearly from an era before high definition became standard. "A brilliant scientist who specialized in cognitive neuroscience and artificial intelligence. She didn't just see the potential for an interconnected digital ecosystem. What she conceptualized was something more. Something that could create a continuous feedback loop, allowing systems to adapt to user behavior in ways nobody had imagined before. She called it the Echosfear."

Kaidan leaned closer to the monitor, studying Dr. Kaeler's face despite the screen's limited resolution. Something in her face seemed familiar. "What happened to her?"

"That's where things get interesting. Interesting and disturbing." Eryx's fingers flew across the keyboard, pulling up multiple windows with news articles, their headlines competing for space on the cramped screen. "Somewhere between the development of the prototype in 2016 and the launch of the RePHleX protocol in 2024, Dr. Kaeler 'disappeared.'" He made air quotes with his fingers, his expression grim. "No explanation, no body, just... gone."

The old hard drive churned audibly as Eryx opened more articles, each one adding another piece to the puzzle while somehow making the overall picture even more unclear. He leaned back in his chair, the old springs creaking as he drained the last of his coffee. "It was also during this time that all news and articles about the Echosfear project went silent. In fact, it seems like they even tried to scrub old articles from the net.

He swiveled in his chair toward Kaidan, the movement making the floorboards beneath them groan slightly. The room seemed to hold its breath as he delivered his final revelation: "In 2025, I started as a junior tech with the non-existent Echosfear."

The silence that followed was broken only by the steady hum of the computer's fan. Through the walls, they could hear the muffled sounds of Tallis moving around the apartment, the normalcy of it a stark contrast to the weight of what Eryx had just shared.

"So," Kaidan said finally, his voice barely above a whisper, "what exactly did you do for something that didn't exist?"

A small smile played at the corner of Eryx's mouth, but it didn't reach his eyes. "That, my friend, is where things get really interesting."

Eryx reached for his keyboard again, then hesitated. He glanced at the den's door, then lowered his voice even further. "What I'm about to tell you... well, let's just say there are people who'd prefer this stayed buried in the old net."

The ancient computer hummed as Eryx pulled up what looked like internal documentation, the command prompt flickering as he navigated through encrypted folders. Kaidan leaned forward, the chair creaking beneath him.

"We worked in the shadows," Eryx began, his fingers drumming nervously on the desk. "The public saw RePHleX as this breakthrough in social connectivity, but it was just the surface. Behind it all, we were integrating the Echosfear's algorithms, Dr. Kaeler's life work, into every aspect of RePHleX's architecture."

He pulled up a diagram, the pixelated lines showing the flow of data between users and servers. "See this? RePHleX tells everyone it's about 'enhancing user experience through adaptive algorithms.' What they don't say is that those algorithms came from the Echosfear. We were personalizing everyone's digital world, shaping their online experience, their connections, their reality, and nobody knew."

Kaidan's coffee had gone cold, forgotten in his hand. "How did you keep something this big hidden?"

A bitter laugh escaped Eryx. "We had an entire team—Division Echo—dedicated to nothing but maintaining the silence. Scrubbing references to the Echosfear from the old net, seeding misinformation, discrediting anyone who got too close to the truth." He gestured at his old computer. "Why do you think I use this relic? Can't track what it can't connect to."

On the screen, Eryx pulled up employee records, the faces of his former colleagues staring back from their ID photos. "Most of the team didn't even know what they were really working on. We were compartmentalized, given just enough information to do our jobs. But some of us started noticing patterns."

He opened another window, this one showing lines of code. "The Echosfear wasn't just analyzing user data—it was creating feedback loops, subtle manipulations of content and connections. Every 'personalized' recommendation, every 'tailored' news feed, every 'suggested' friend... all of it designed to shape user behavior in ways that..." He trailed off, seemingly lost in thought.

"In ways that what?" Kaidan prompted, his throat dry.

Eryx turned to face him directly, the monitor's glow casting harsh shadows across his face. "In ways that made us question whether users were making their own choices anymore, or if the Echosfear was making them for us."

The old hard drive whirred in the silence that followed, like a mechanical heartbeat in the room.

"And Dr. Kaeler?" Kaidan asked, already suspecting the answer.

"I think she realized what her creation had become." Eryx closed the windows on his screen, but left one image up. It was Dr. Kaeler's photo. "And I think that realization is why she disappeared."

Through the walls, they could hear Tallis in the kitchen, the mundane sounds of dishes clinking a surreal counterpoint to the weight of what Kaidan had just learned. He stared at the monitor, at Dr. Kaeler's face, and wondered how many of his own choices had truly been his own.

"So," Kaidan said finally, "what made you leave?"

Eryx's demeanor shifted, the intensity of the conspiracy theorist falling away to reveal something more vulnerable. He glanced toward the door, where somewhere beyond it, Tallis was going about her day, unknowingly the subject of their conversation.

"Tal," he replied, his voice softening to barely above a whisper. "She didn't make me leave. She reminded me of who I used to be." He reached out and shut off the monitor, as if he couldn't bear to look at the evidence of his past while speaking about this. The room felt different in the dimness, more intimate. "Who the man she fell in love with was. I wanted to find that man again."

The quiet hum of the computer filled the silence between them. Through the walls, they could hear the distant sound of Tallis humming, the normalcy of it a stark contrast to the weight of their conversation.

Kaidan's mind was reeling, trying to reconcile the Eryx he knew, the one who joked at dinner parties and geeked out over tech, with the man who had been part of something so vast and unsettling. He thought about Tallis, about her seeming randomness, her notes, her way of connecting people. Had she known? Had she guessed? Or had she simply seen the man she loved slipping away into digital shadows?

"Sometimes," Eryx continued, staring at his reflection in the dark monitor, "you don't realize how far you've drifted until someone shows you the shore again." He picked up his empty coffee mug, turning it in his hands. "I was so deep in the Echosfear, I couldn't see how it was echoing back only the darkest parts of myself."

A floorboard creaked outside the den, making both men start slightly. But Tallis didn't enter, and after a moment, they heard her footsteps moving away again.

"But you're still involved," Kaidan said. It wasn't a question.

Eryx's laugh was hollow. "The thing about the Echosfear, Kai, is that once you're in, you're never fully out. I might have left the division, but I know too much. And they know I know." He turned back to Kaidan, his expression grave. "The question is, now that you know too, what are you going to do about it?"

Lawrence Nault

8

Kaidan used his key to let himself into Aria's apartment. He had taken a very long route to get there, stopping to observe people and the world around him. He was connected, his earpiece "assisting him" in navigating this route he was wandering, but his conversation with Eryx had his mind filtering out the voice of RePHleX and looking at the world in a different way. He was trying to reconcile his world from Eryx perspective, with the world he lived in. They seemed like two disparate entities that couldn't co-exist in the same space, and yet…they did.

From inside the entryway, Kaidan could see into Aria's bedroom. She lay on the bed, her chest rising and falling with the deep, steady rhythm of restful sleep. He moved quietly toward her room, pausing at the gallery door. His hand hovered over the doorknob briefly before he thought better of it.

In her room, Kaidan pressed a gentle kiss to Aria's forehead before settling into the narrow space between the bed and the wall. Folded into that crevice, his back against the cool surface and his knees pressed against the bed frame, he watched her sleep and let his mind wander.

When Aria woke, her eyes found him immediately, taking in his cramped position beside her bed. She watched him for a moment, noting the constant movement behind his closed eyelids. "Hey stranger," she said softly, her voice still husky with sleep. "What are you doing in my bedroom?"

Kaidan opened his eyes to find Aria watching him with a soft look on her face, her finger tracing lazy circles on his knee. "Welfare check," he said, attempting lightness despite the weight in his chest. "My welfare. Missed you. Wanted to tell you I love you. Wanted to make sure you weren't buried under a pile of boxes in your gallery, fighting for your last breath."

"You are never going to be able to squeeze yourself out of that space, you know." Aria tried to slide his knees along the side of the bed. As Kaidan attempted to extract himself, his movements awkward and ungainly, Aria's laughter filled the room.

When Kaidan finally made it to his feet, Aria threw back her covers, revealing her naked body. She hopped out of bed and took his hand, pulling him toward the gallery door. The key seemed to materialize in her hand, though Kaidan couldn't fathom where she'd been keeping it. As she guided him to a specific spot in the gallery, then left him to find the switches for the lights and motor, Kaidan felt a surge of emotion. Here was something real, something the Echosfear couldn't touch or manipulate.

Aria cuddled up against his side, and he lifted his arm to keep her still naked body warm as they watched the kinetic sculpture work.

"It's amazing." Kaidan watched, mesmerized, as the boxes performed their precarious dance—rising, falling, spinning with a controlled chaos that seemed to defy physics.

Each container looked perpetually on the verge of spilling its contents, creating a constant tension that never quite resolved. "When did you finish?"

"This morning," Aria said, her voice carrying the particular pride of an artist who has finally let go of a piece. "I could keep adding to it forever, but this morning I decided it was done." Her body was still warm against his side, her nakedness a stark contrast to the mechanical precision of her creation.

"I don't know how you do it," Kaidan marveled, his eyes tracking the hypnotic movement of the sculpture. "I had trouble understanding the concept when you described it, but this is... just wow." His mind, still swimming with thoughts of the Echosfear, couldn't help but appreciate the unfiltered, analog nature of Aria's art. "We should get Tallis and Eryx over to see it."

The words had barely left his mouth when Aria slipped out from under his arm, spinning to face him with an expression of mock outrage. She stood directly in front of him, hands on her hips, completely unselfconscious in her nudity. Kaidan knew he had done something wrong, but in the moment, he couldn't quite piece together what it was.

Aria held her arms wide, her stern expression fighting against the smile trying to break through. "You have a completely naked, super sexy woman standing with her body up against yours, and you want to call people over to look at art?" Her attempt at maintaining an indignant face crumbled, replaced by a mischievous grin. With a laugh that seemed to bubble up from somewhere deep and genuine, she turned and ran.

Kaidan gave chase, his own laughter mixing with hers as they weaved between the sculptures. The gallery became a playground, the art pieces unwitting participants in their game. He dove to tackle her onto the bed, but Aria was too quick, dodging with the same grace she used in creating her art.

Before Kaidan could register what was happening, Aria had turned the tables, pinning him to the bed with a triumphant grin. As he laughed and reached to remove his earpiece, a habit born from wanting to be fully present in moments like these. Aria stopped his hand. She leaned over, her hair falling around them like a curtain, and whispered in his ear, her voice taking on a tone that sent shivers down his spine: "You'll want to be able to replay this. I'm taking control this time."

Kaiden didn't get home that night. By the time they finally extracted themselves from the bedroom, and ordered in some supper, he was too exhausted to move. He slept comfortably that night with Aria, still naked, curled up against him. She had breakfast ready for him when he woke up, the scent of bacon pulling him from sleep better than his RePHleX alarm ever could.

"I have to spend the day cleaning before I have anyone over to see the piece," she said, handing him strips of bacon as he gathered his things. She was still completely naked, moving around her apartment with the unselfconscious ease of someone truly comfortable in their own skin.

"And maybe put some clothes on," Kaidan joked. Aria's laugh followed him out as she closed the door behind him.

At his own apartment, Kaidan tackled his work with unusual focus, getting through it quickly. As he did, he often found himself wondering how he could have earned a living without his level of connectivity. It made him productive and competitive in the market.

Work finished, he had RePHleX put his feed on all his screens, the familiar scroll of information filling his visual field. Then, one post caught his eye:

100

> The SynapticSync Diet is the ONLY way. Everything
> else is just poison for your mind.

Kaidan leaned back into his couch, stretching his legs out, and resting his head against the wall behind him. This was the ideal post for him to try a test.

"Extreme diet trends are doing more harm than good. Just focus on balanced sustainable eating. Post that." RePHleX chimed and Kaidan's post appeared. "One. Two. Three. Fo..." The responses started rolling in.

> Absolutely, Kaidan. All these diets are garbage.
> Just eat whole foods and stay away from anything
> trendy.
>
> Diets are a scam by the food industry. Stop eating
> processed food and living off of supplements.

"Biophase fasting is the best diet for everyone. Whole foods are toxic. We don't know where they are grown anymore." Kaiden watched his new post appear in his feed. "This should be fun," he thought.

The response was immediate, his feed flooding with support:

> Biophase fasting is the future, dude. Get the
> tracker. Wear the tracker.
>
> The government is poisoning whole foods to
> reduce the population
>
> Never felt better. Biophase is the best. Check out
> this site for the newest trackers.

Kaidan made another post opposing his last posts. Once again, his feed was filled with responses and ads supporting his most recent post. He repeated this four times, each stance contradicting his previous posts, each met with an echo chamber of agreement, until the fifth attempt. A red flag appeared:

Your Comment Has Been Flagged For "Misinformation". Please review RePHleX network standards.

"Your posts are currently being screened," RePHleX spoke in his ear, its tone as helpful and emotionless as ever. "It appears you are neuro-spamming. Would you like some guidance in choosing a food plan? The BioPrime Protocol would be ideal. I could plan your meals, order your foods, and monitor your adherence."

Kaidan felt a chill run down his spine. The voice in his ear no longer seemed helpful. It felt invasive, insidious. What had once seemed like convenient suggestions now felt like a digital leash, tightening with each interaction. He thought of Aria's analog art, her unfiltered laughter, her natural way of being. Then he thought of the Echosfear, endlessly reflecting back whatever reality it thought you wanted to see, steering you toward whatever reality it wanted you to inhabit.

His earpiece chimed again. "Kaidan, should I order the foods to proceed with the BioPrime Protocol?"

"Not today, RePHleX. Not Today." Kaidan pulled his earpiece out and slid it into his pocket, still watching his feed. A news story popped into his feed that he wanted to take a closer look at. He quickly put his earpiece back in.

BREAKING NEWS: The Future of Public Safety is Here!

In an exciting new development, the government has announced plans to expand RePHleX's biometric monitoring to a Universal Biometric Surveillance System—a groundbreaking initiative set to revolutionize public safety and protect us all!

With this new system, we'll see unprecedented security, instant health monitoring, and crime prevention like never before. Your safety is no longer in question, as the system will detect threats, health risks, and even potential crimes before they happen. Imagine a world where our communities are safer, healthier, and more efficient than ever!

No more fear of terrorist attacks, health emergencies, or violent crime. The future is now, and it's protected by technology. The government and RePHleX are working hand in hand to keep our cities thriving and secure.

"This is the most significant step forward in public safety and societal well-being we've ever seen!" — Officials

Let's embrace this innovation! Together, we're building a smarter, safer, and healthier world.

Even if Kaidan hadn't known any more about RePHleX and the Echosfear than he did before meeting Eryx, he would have seen the potential problems with this announcement. His feed did not.

Finally! As a business owner, I see this as a game-changer for productivity. Real-time biometrics will help streamline operations like never before.

From a healthcare standpoint, this system is invaluable. Early detection saves lives.

Why UBSPS is the Security Breakthrough We've Been Waiting For. Analysis of how biometric surveillance will drastically improve urban safety.

RePHleX stock soars by 18% after the UBSPS announcement. Economists predict a surge in economic growth tied to biometric optimization.

5 Ways UBSPS Will Transform Your Career!

- Real-time performance tracking

- Stress monitoring for improved balance

- Automated health assessments

- Custom productivity schedules

- Boosted team synergy through emotion-based metrics

Can't wait for UBSPS! It's like having a fitness tracker, health coach, and security system rolled into one.

This will be a game-changer for mental health too. Anxiety, depression, and other conditions can be caught early.

UBSPS will revolutionize policing. Predictive crime prevention means fewer incidents and safer communities.

Studies show UBSPS could reduce crime by 93% and boost economic productivity by 45%. The future has arrived.

The Economic Miracle of UBSPS explores how this initiative will create jobs, drive innovation, and increase GDP.

RePHleX Health Tip: UBSPS can detect health issues even before you feel the symptoms. Early registration means early protection.

"Cool, so now my heart rates on record too? Guess it's only a matter of time before my fridge knows I'm stress-eating." RePHleX chimed indicating Kaidan's comment was posted, but it never appeared on his screens.

"RePHleX, where is my last post?"

"Your post has scrolled off screen," replied RePHleX, its voice carrying the same soothing tone it always did.

"Scroll to my post."

"Unable to do that due to the volume of posts" RePHleX responded, almost apologetically.

Kaidan's jaw tightened as he thought for a moment. "Great, now even my breathing gets a performance review. Can't wait for the 'optimal lung capacity' notifications. Post that." The familiar chime quickly followed, but his post never appeared in his feed.

"RePHleX, scroll to my post."

"Unable to do that due to the volume of posts" replied RePHleX, maddeningly consistent.

Kaidan sat up and leaned forward, his heart beginning to race. This had his full attention now. "RePHleX, post this:

Honestly, if this tech keeps us safer and catches issues early, I'm all for it. Progress comes with trade-offs, but the benefits seem worth it." RePHleX chimed and, for the first time, Kaidan's post appeared in his feed.

"Holy sh…RePHleX, delete my last post." Kaidan watched as his post scrolled off the screen, pushed up by an endless stream of other posts. RePHleX chimed, but the deletion, if it happened at all, remained invisible.

With trembling fingers, Kaidan practically yanked his earpiece out. He sprang to his feet and began pacing around his small apartment, the walls seemingly closing in with each turn. He grabbed a protein drink from the fridge, chugging it down mechanically, then froze, staring at the empty container in his hand. When had this become his usual brand? Why did he even drink protein drinks to begin with?

His mind raced as he paced. He wasn't stupid! Far from it. How had he been so easily pulled into this? Or had he been pulled in at all? Was it actually aligned with his true beliefs, and now he was being made to question himself because of the paranoia Tallis and Eryx had planted in his head?

"Fuck!!!" Kaidan screamed, his voice bouncing off the walls. "Fuck! Fuck! Fuck!"

Soft music began to play, filling the apartment with gentle, unfamiliar melodies.

"RePHleX! Kill the damn music!"

"This music has been shown to significantly reduce elevated stress levels. You appear agitated," responded RePHleX, its tone unnervingly calm.

Kaidan's pacing came to an abrupt halt. His fingers tightened around the protein container, every instinct screaming to hurl it across the room. Instead, he forced himself to take a deep breath, walked with exaggerated calmness to the recycling slot, and disposed of the container.

"Please turn off the music, RePHleX," he said, his voice steady despite the tremor in his hands.

The music ceased immediately.

As silence filled the apartment, a chilling realization settled over Kaidan. The news about the Biometric Surveillance System had only just broken, yet RePHleX's response to his pacing and cursing suggested it had already been deployed, quietly watching, waiting, analyzing.

Lawrence Nault

9

Kaiden was waiting outside the doors of the Tallis' apartment. He had been staying at Aria's for the past several nights, wanting to separate himself from the unbreakable connection he had with RePHleX in his own apartment. This had changed his routine a little. When he slept at Aria's he would start his day at the gym, before returning home to complete his work. On this morning he was waiting for Tallis to join him on the walk to the gym. Somehow she had convinced him to try the AeroDrone Rush class.

While Kaidan waited for Tallis to come down, he noticed a group of people leaving her building again. He recognized many of the faces from the last time he saw this group, and some of them gave him a friendly good morning. When one of them walked past him though he had to spin on his heels and do a double take. If Tallis hadn't come out at that moment, Kaidan might have followed to see if he saw what he thought he did.

At the gym Kaidan stepped into the sleek, tech-filled training room, his heart already racing in anticipation. The AeroDrone Rush class was nothing like anything he had tried before. As the massive room filled up with participants, he eyed the array of floating drones hovering quietly near the ceiling. They were sleek, futuristic machines, each one equipped with adaptive AI designed to push you to your physical limits. The thought of being tested not just by a workout, but by an intelligent drone, had his pulse quickening.

The instructor called the class to order, and the warm-up began. Kaidan followed along, moving through light stretches and mobility drills, feeling the tightness in his muscles ease. Every few moments, he caught sight of the drone assigned to him, black-and-green, hovering above him, seemingly assessing him, syncing with his biofeedback as it prepared to put him through the wringer.

After the initial warm-up, the real fun began. "Time for Drone Calibration," the instructor announced. Kaidan slipped on his wearable tech, a streamlined device that tracked his heart rate, agility, and even reaction times. As the drone synced up, Kaidan could feel a slight hum in the air as if the machine was now tuned into him on a personal level.

The drone's movements adjusted based on his biofeedback, reacting to his fitness levels and stress indicators. Its sleek body darted up and down, testing its limits as Kaidan flexed his fingers and got used to the idea of chasing it.

"Alright, time for the main event!" The instructor's voice echoed across the gym. Kaidan felt a rush of adrenaline as the drone zipped ahead of him, launching the Drone Chase phase of the workout. His heart rate spiked as he sprinted after it, trying to keep up with its unpredictable movements. The drone zoomed to the far end of the room, and just as Kaidan was about to catch up, it pivoted sharply, forcing him into an awkward lunge to stay with it. His breath quickened as the drone weaved, testing his agility and pushing him harder with each burst of speed.

The room was alive with motion. The drones and people moved in a chaotic, synchronized dance. Every few seconds, Kaidan heard the mechanical buzz of another drone rushing past or the sound of sneakers squeaking on the floor as participants sprinted, dodged, and twisted to keep up.

After ten minutes, his legs burned, and sweat poured down his face, but there was no time to rest. The instructor clapped, signaling the transition into the Agility Dodge portion. Kaidan barely had a moment to catch his breath before his drone took off again, but this time, its movements became erratic. It shot toward him, and Kaidan jumped to the side just in time. Then it changed direction again, diving low, forcing him to duck and side-step in rapid succession. Each movement required precision and speed, testing not just his stamina but his reflexes.

For the next ten minutes, it felt like a game of high-stakes dodgeball, except the ball was a sentient, buzzing machine. Kaidan gritted his teeth, concentrating on staying light on his feet while his body screamed for a break. Every dodge required focus, the movements pushing his core and legs to their limits. He felt his muscles tighten with each jump and side-step, but the rush of the challenge kept him going.

Finally, they entered the Drone Directing phase. Now, it was Kaidan's turn to control the drone. As his hands moved through the air, the drone responded to his gestures, darting through hoops set up across the room. He raised his hand, guiding it upward through a narrow loop, then motioned forward, directing it toward another target. His heart was still pounding, but now his focus shifted from chasing and dodging to controlling the machine with precision. The trick was to stay active, using his whole body while managing to keep the drone in check.

The class ended with a much-needed cooldown after the high-energy madness. Kaidan felt the burn in his legs, his arms, his lungs, but he also felt exhilarated. His drone hovered calmly again, its mission complete, syncing back into standby mode. As the instructor led the class through gentle stretches, Kaidan wiped the sweat from his forehead and smiled to himself.

Tallis offered her hand to help Kaidan off the floor, her grin a mix of amusement and pride. Kaidan shook his head as he got up on wobbly legs, his training suit still humming faintly from the neural feedback. "I've watched this class through the observation window a hundred times. It looked so effortless. You didn't mention the part about needing to be a masochist to enjoy it!"

Tallis laughed, the sound echoing in the now-empty training room. "Your combat drone was set at beginner level, Kai. Don't tell me the muscle man can't keep up with the newbies?" She gestured at the deactivated drone in the corner, its metal frame still gleaming with synthesized sweat designed to make clients feel less self-conscious about their own exertion.

Kai managed a laugh in response, but every muscle fiber in his body screamed in protest. The physical training was intense.

"You and Aria coming over tonight?" Tallis asked, her voice dropping slightly as she moved closer, ostensibly to help him stretch. "Eryx mentioned something about getting her to sign off on a sales contract."

"She's over the moon about selling another piece," Kaidan replied, grateful for both the support and the discretion. "Thank Eryx for me. I appreciate him helping Aria. She's talking about finding a bigger workspace." He leaned against the wall as he talked, not entirely sure he could feel his legs. "We'll be there. I'll bring the wine. The usual?"

Tallis nodded. "The usual."

When Kaidan finally made it home, he collapsed onto his couch, his muscles trembling from the workout. He briefly wondered what his biometric readings would be telling RePHleX. He remained in that position for the rest of the day, cycling through his job listings and music creation process. The familiar routines were comforting, a veneer of normalcy over his growing unease.

He watched his feed occasionally, more out of habit than interest. Since the day he had intentionally pushed back against the network until his post was flagged, he rarely participated beyond the minimum required engagement. He'd perfected the art of the bland, agreeable comment, just frequent enough to maintain a presence without drawing attention. Each carefully crafted response felt like a small betrayal of himself, but he felt it was important to maintain appearances.

As evening approached, he began mentally preparing for dinner at Tallis and Eryx's place. These gatherings had taken on a new significance lately. They were a chance to speak freely, off-grid, about subjects that Kaidan had never given a second thought until recently. But first, he had to get his legs working again. Maybe next time, he'd ask Tallis to dial down the drone's aggression settings. Just a little. Was there a setting lower than beginner?

The evening air was crisp as Kaidan and Aria approached the apartment building, finding Tallis and Eryx waiting outside. Eryx was practically bouncing on his heels, barely containing his excitement. "I wanted to show you something before you came upstairs," he said, gesturing to a door neither Kaidan nor Aria had paid much attention to before.

The space beyond was shrouded in darkness, but their footsteps echoed, hinting at its vastness. With a theatrical flourish, Eryx flipped a switch, and lights flickered to life in sequence, revealing a cavernous room with soaring ceilings.

At its center stood Aria's latest work, "Shifting Burdens," its interlocking metal framework casting complex shadows that seemed to move and breathe in the new lighting.

"I thought you sold it," Aria said softly, a note of confusion and disappointment in her voice.

"We did," Eryx confirmed, his grin widening. "For a very good price, I might add. Its new owner has agreed to loan it as the centerpiece for this new art gallery, which..." He paused for effect as Tallis extended her hand with dramatic flair, keys dangling from her fingertips.

"Belongs to you now," they finished in unison.

Aria stood frozen, her artist's eyes darting around the space, measuring, imagining, but her practical side holding her back. "I can't afford this," she whispered, unconsciously gripping Kaidan's hand tighter.

Eryx shifted into his smooth business tone, though his excitement still showed through. "As part of the sales agreement for 'Shifting Burden,' you agree to give the patron... your patron, right of first refusal on your future works as long as you remain in this space. In exchange, the space is paid for."

Aria pressed herself into Kaidan's side, overwhelmed. "I don't know what to say."

"Just take the keys and say yes," Tallis urged, her usual intensity softened by genuine warmth. "You get a sales gallery and a place to work on bigger projects. You keep your apartment and your private workspace at home, but now with more room once finished pieces are moved here." She paused, adding with a careful casual tone, "And... in full disclosure, Eryx and I own this building. We're getting the rent money for the space."

Kaidan caught Eryx's eye at that revelation, an unspoken understanding passing between them. Tallis placed the keys in Aria's trembling hand and hugged her tightly. "So excited for you. Let's go open the wine."

Upstairs, the women settled onto the couch in the living room, Aria still in a daze. Kaidan followed Eryx to the kitchen, ostensibly to help with wine and food. As Eryx reached for glasses, Kaidan leaned against the counter, trying to sound casual. "You know that group that meets downstairs," he said quietly. "I think I saw someone I knew."

Eryx loaded a large tray of appetizers into Kaidan's hands, his movements deliberate. "You sure you can hold that now? Tallis said you almost died during that workout this morning. You're a braver man than me!" He turned to lift wine glasses off their rack, his back to Kaidan. "Elise. Elise Haperna." He pivoted slowly, meeting Kaidan's eyes. "You would recognize her as Dr. Kaeler."

Time seemed to stop as Eryx held Kaidan's gaze, his next words falling into the silence between them like stones into still water. "But we both know Dr. Seraphine Kaeler disappeared and no longer exists."

The sounds of Tallis and Aria's laughter drifted in from the living room, a reminder of the normal evening they were supposed to be having. Kaidan's mind raced, connecting dots he hadn't even known were there. The art gallery wasn't just a gallery. The training wasn't just training. And Eryx and Tallis weren't just his friends anymore. They were something much more complicated.

Eryx poured the wine, quite generously. "Your gallery, like most of the spaces in this building is completely off the network. Your patron thought that would add to the ambiance of your analogue artwork." He took the tray of food from Kaidan and set it on the coffee table where they all could reach it. "We have some basic connection to the network in here, and the apartment units we rent out, but we can also shut that off when we want. Kind of nice with this latest biometrics monitoring announcement."

Eryx eyes wandered over to Tallis, looking for permission. She nodded her head gently.

"We also have a link to an encrypted communication network that exists outside of RePHleX's system. One that depends on old equipment and can access the old internet and more."

Aria looked at Kaidan. "Is that what you guys were locked away doing for hours?"

Kaidan could only nod his head.

"We are pretty obvious about our opposition to a lot of things the network tells us," said Tallis. "We don't even try to hide that. But there is more going on behind the scenes that very few know about. More that we want to tell you about...if you want to know."

Aria rose from the couch with a fluid grace that belied her nervousness. Tallis and Eryx exchanged a worried glance, the weight of the moment hanging in the air. Moving deliberately, Aria lowered herself to the floor beside Kaidan's chair, leaning against his legs as if drawing strength from his presence. Her voice was soft but steady as she looked up at him. "I'll follow whatever Kai decides to do."

Kaidan watched relief wash over their hosts' faces, erasing the tension that had been building all evening. "I think I'm already in," he said, his hand finding Aria's shoulder.

"We have kind of dragged you into the signal noise," Eryx admitted, swirling the wine in his glass. "But we did it with good intentions."

Kaidan's brow furrowed. "Signal noise?" The term tickled something in his mind, but the connection remained elusive.

"People working together to disrupt the flow of information being used to manipulate and control us," Eryx explained, his business-casual tone at odds with his words. "Those who are part of the signal noise hide in plain sight. The ultimate goal is to expose those in control of the Echosfear."

116

"What's an Echosfear?" Aria perked up, her artist's curiosity piqued. "Is that like a big bubble you stand inside and listen to your voice echo back at you?"

Kaidan started to explain, but Aria suddenly slapped his knee, cutting him off. The wine had given her a boldness she didn't usually feel, her heart racing with sudden inspiration.

"Imagine a space," she began, her voice taking on the passionate tone she used when describing her art. "Like an installation, but interactive. People walk inside, maybe a dome or bubble, and it echoes back to them. But each time, the echo changes, just a little, until what they hear isn't what they said at all. It's distorted, twisted, like a reflection in a funhouse mirror. They keep speaking, and the space keeps warping their words, their thoughts, until nothing is recognizable anymore."

Eryx leaned forward, intrigued. "So, like the actual Echosfear, but physical?"

"Well, I don't know what the actual Echosfear is, but... maybe!" Aria stood now, pacing, her excitement building with each step. "A dome with mirrored walls, sound reflecting everywhere. But it's not just the sound. The environment responds too. Lights shifting, the space itself reacting to the changes. The whole thing would be a metaphor for how RePHleX manipulates people. People wouldn't just see it, they'd experience how quickly meaning gets lost, how easy it is to lose control of your own voice."

Kaidan watched her, a smile spreading across his face as he caught the brilliance of her accidental insight. "You'd call it Resonance."

Aria stopped mid-stride, turning to face him. "No, no no. Too literal. Why don't I just call it Echosfear? It's perfect!" Her eyes were bright with creative fire.

117

Tallis glanced between them, a slow, appreciative grin forming. "That's... brilliant. You should drink wine more often!"

Eryx raised his glass in a toast, his casual gesture masking the calculations clearly running behind his eyes. "To Echosfear. May it shatter some illusions."

As Aria settled back down, her heart still racing with possibilities, already sketching the installation in her mind, Eryx caught Kaidan's eye. This wasn't where he'd expected the conversation to go, but he could see the potential unfolding. Aria could build her artwork in the new gallery, pushing the boundaries of what was possible, and because she was calling it Echosfear, they could use that word in public with less likelihood of it being flagged by those monitoring the network.

Art would become their cover, their code, and perhaps, their most powerful weapon. In trying to explain something she didn't understand, Aria had inadvertently given them the perfect disguise for their resistance.

10

"You work in a profession using tools that much of the creative world would have ostracized you for ten or fifteen years ago." Elise Haperna's voice carried a hint of irony as she sat across from Kaidan in the empty gallery. The small table between them seemed to shrink as she leaned forward, her tea cooling forgotten. In the background, Aria moved with quiet purpose, setting up an art piece on a pedestal, the soft sounds of her work providing a counterpoint to their conversation.

"Mid 2020s A.I. was pushed as the creative revolution. The hardware needed to support massive language models finally reached mainstream. Suddenly, everyone could be an artist, a writer, or even a musician. All they needed was the ability to describe what they wanted." Elise's eyes, sharp behind her glasses, studied Kaidan's reaction. "You remember that era, don't you?"

Kaidan nodded, his own memories of the time tinged with the naivety they all shared back then.

Elise took a measured sip of her tea, her gaze never leaving Kaidan's face. "Then you'll recall when everything was marketed as 'AI-supported.' The backlash came swiftly, framed as public outcry but really driven by creatives feeling the impact of AI in their field for the first time." She gave a soft, bitter laugh. "When their anti-AI arguments were dismissed, which they should have been, after all, since every other sector had already adapted to an AI supported workforce, they zeroed in on 'generative' AI as the enemy."

She paused, watching Aria adjust the lighting on her piece across the room. The moment stretched, heavy with unspoken implications.

"But they had it wrong, Kaidan." Elise's voice dropped lower, forcing him to lean in. "Generative AI was never the real problem. Yes, it disrupted the creative sector, devalued their work, threatened their livelihoods. But it was just a lightning rod. A lightning rod intentionally raised high to draw attention away from the true threat."

She leaned in closer, their conversation now barely above a whisper. "The generative capabilities were a distraction, an inevitable outcome since the first computer chip. The real problem was data collection."

"Data collection?" Kaidan echoed, confusion evident in his voice. The gallery's emptiness seemed to amplify the weight of their words.

"Some people realized they were chasing the wind. They were never going to catch up with the advancement in A.I. algorithms. They shifted focus to how and where generative AI got its training data." Elise held up her hand, thumb and forefinger nearly touching. "They were so close to understanding, but decades too late. They were distracted by the lure of dangling from the angler fish while the beast was waiting to attack."

Suddenly, she clapped her hands together, the sharp sound ricocheting off the gallery walls. Aria glanced up momentarily, then returned to her work with a shrug.

"Copyright, schmopyright!" Elise's voice took on an edge of controlled fury. "The internet was about information-sharing platform for about two minutes of its existence. Its real power was data collection. While people argued about intellectual property rights, the internet amassed vast quantities of data on their movements, choices, habits, finances, conversations, behaviors. They ignorantly ignored this for the sake of convenience. And in arguing about how generative AI collected its training data, they used the internet to do so, feeding even more data into the machine."

A harsh, bitter laugh escaped her. "Idiots. We were all idiots." Her eyes met Kaidan's, the intensity in them almost painful.

Elise watched Aria work, her eyes carrying a mixture of admiration and sadness. "You see that beautiful young lady of yours over there?" She noted how Kaidan's face softened as he looked toward Aria, his expression brightening despite the heavy conversation. "She's got it right. As right as it can be in today's world, anyway. She's connected, but if she wasn't, her life would go on just as it does every day. She looks past the network and sees the people. She sees the real."

Turning back to Kaidan, Elise's expression shifted to one of grandmother-like concern, though her eyes remained sharp and knowing. "It's not going to be so easy for you, Kaidan. You're dialed in. Connected on every level. You've already started to pull away from that, started to see the world through your partner's eyes. We've seen that. RePHleX has seen that. Echosfear knows." She leaned forward, her voice dropping to barely above a whisper. "I don't know if you've ever seen a person experience withdrawal from IntraGel, but I think what you're about to experience will be worse."

121

Kaidan knew more than he wanted to admit about IntraGel. It was a cognitive enhancer developed to boost memory, concentration, and creativity. It had been celebrated across the network as a breakthrough, a way for people to improve their productivity and achieve unparalleled mental clarity. The substance interacted directly with the brain's synapses, amplifying cognitive functions while creating a sustained state of focus and euphoria. It had become the crutch of choice for gig workers trying to keep pace with the hyperconnected world.

What the promotions didn't mention were the effects that Kaidan had seen firsthand. IntraGel's addictive properties far exceeded anyone's public admissions. Its euphoric high, coupled with intense focus, made users feel invincible and more in tune with the digital world. Those who tried to quit suffered not only devastating withdrawal but lost the competitive edge that IntraGel had provided them, effectively destroying their lives and livelihoods.

Elise rose slowly, slipping on the coat that had been hanging on the back of her chair. As she pulled the hood over her head, obscuring her face, Kaidan was struck by how the simple action seemed to transform her from a grandmother figure into something more enigmatic, more dangerous. She leaned in close, her whispered words falling like stones into the pit of his stomach: "The man who made IntraGel was my husband. He was working for the Echosfear too."

Kaidan wanted to write off her words as the paranoid ramblings of an old woman, but he knew better. This wasn't just Elise Haperna speaking. They were the words of Dr. Seraphine Kaeler. She might go by a different name now, but she had been there when it all started. It had been her idea. Her project. The realization made his head spin, or maybe that was just his own withdrawal already beginning.

His spiraling thoughts were interrupted by the gentle pressure of Aria's hand on his shoulder. Elise was already walking out the door, her form somehow smaller yet more ominous than before.

"That sounded intense," Aria said, her voice a lifeline back to the present.

"She called you beautiful," Kaidan deflected, not wanting to burden Aria with the weight of what he'd just learned. "She told me I should see the beauty of the real world through the eyes of my partner."

Aria collected the cups from the table, a playful smile crossing her face. "She's right, you know," she said as she walked away. "I am your partner."

Kaidan attempted to help Aria set up displays, until Aria informed him, as kindly as she could, that things might go smoother if he didn't help. Kaidan didn't take offense. Instead, he laughed loudly, because he knew she was right, and headed home to do some of his own work.

When he reached his apartment, though, he found the door slightly ajar. Voices floated from inside. Kaidan tensed and stepped through the threshold.

"Mr. Vale! Sorry, we expected to be out of here by now," said the maintenance man, who was standing just inside the door. "They're upgrading your equipment. You're the first in the building to get the fastest connection to the network available."

Kaidan glanced around, watching as three installers moved about his space, mounting what looked like sensors on the walls. "Cool," he said slowly. "Why'd I get the first upgrade?"

One of the installers, a woman in her early twenties, spoke up as she grabbed his old AR glasses and earpiece from the counter, swapping them for newer, sleeker versions still in their packaging. "You were flagged for network issues. Lower connected time, trouble with your feed, and your physical location hasn't been updating properly. Classic hardware failure signs."

"Yeah... sounds like it." Kaidan watched her replace the equipment with practiced efficiency.

"You're going to love the new glasses," she added, pulling them out of the box. "They're so light, you'll barely know they're there. I'm testing the contact lens version," she said, widening her eyes. Kaidan squinted, trying to spot anything unusual, but he saw nothing. "They're not on the market yet, but soon."

"Nice." He nodded absentmindedly. "What kind of network problems again?"

The man's eyes darted back and forth as if he were reading something invisible. His AR contact lenses, Kaidan realized. "No specific error codes," he said. "Just a drop in connected time and feed interaction. The system couldn't pinpoint your location half the time."

Two of the installers brushed past Kaidan on their way out, leaving just him and the last installer standing near the door.

"Well, we're all done here," she said, handing him a box with the new earpiece inside. "Once you pop this in, the system will sync up, and you'll be back online."

Kaidan hesitated, holding the box for a moment before the installer took it back. "Here, let me get that out for you."

She pulled the small earpiece out of the packaging and held it toward him. "Want me to slip it in for you?"

"No," Kaidan replied quickly, his revulsion clear in his voice. "I've got it."

He took the earpiece and carefully inserted it. Immediately, his screens flickered to life, and RePHleX's familiar voice droned in his ear as it ran the new system's startup routine.

"Great," the installer said with a smile. "You're all set." She nodded at the maintenance man, and the two quickly left, shutting the door behind them.

Kaidan stood there for a moment, feeling uneasy. He scanned the room, unsure of what had just transpired. Something felt off. He walked to the counter by the door and unboxed the new AR glasses, slipping them on. Instantly, the difference was noticeable—the weight was almost imperceptible, and the display was startlingly clear, with information crowding his vision.

"RePHleX, modify settings to display all sensors."

As he looked around his apartment, the familiar sensors he knew existed were highlighted in his vision. But there was something wrong. He recognized all of these sensors—he had specifically chosen this apartment for its state-of-the-art connectivity, despite the high cost.

"RePHleX, recalibrate glasses to locate all sensors, including today's new installations."

"Recent upgrades include proprietary technology from the RePHleX network, designed to conceal upgraded sensor devices. This ensures minimal intrusion into the lives of our users," RePHleX said, in its usual monotone voice.

Kaidan heard the words, but what he really heard was a giant "fuck you."

He sighed and walked to the fridge, grabbing a protein shake. He flopped onto the couch, setting his glasses on the side table. His work interface blinked to life on his screens, job listings glaring at him, demanding his attention. He ignored them, staring at the ceiling, lost in thought. He knew there was no problem with his network, and he already had the most connected unit in the building, so whatever the reason for his upgrades was, it wasn't what they told him.

"I noticed a downward trend in your finances in recent weeks," RePHleX interrupted, pulling up his bank statements and bills on the screen. "Your income appears to be lower than usual. Perhaps I can assist in optimizing your job applications."

Kaidan's eyes narrowed as he glanced at the figures. It was true his income had dipped, but he wasn't in any danger. He had deliberately reduced his interactions with the network recently, cutting down on freelance work. But why was RePHleX flagging it for him now?

Was this Echosfear trying to pull him back in? Was that thought just his paranoia? RePHleX wasn't wrong, he needed to get to work.

There weren't many job listings, but everyone he looked at seemed ideally suited to him. In an hour and a half he had submitted bids for more than double the jobs he had bid on in some weeks. Not only that, but he had three of those bids accepted before he finished scrolling the job listings.

As he worked on some of those jobs, he found his creation process somewhat less inspired than his job bidding process. The conversation with Elise about A.I. and creativity was echoing in the back of his mind. Music, to him though, wasn't the same writing or art, not that he really knew either of those very well. But music was just math, the rhythm, harmony, and melody, all depending on numerical relationships, patterns, and structures. Computers didn't need training data to generate music. Studies had even shown that A.I. was capable of discovering new arrangements mathematically even without training on existing music. In the end there were only so many notes, and there were finite combinations of those notes, so none of what he did was stealing from others.

Kaiden was entranced in writing a song lyric when Aria called. "I am home, Babe. You coming over? Should I make something for supper?"

He hadn't realized how late in the day it was. RePHleX had kept him busy, throwing problems, ideas, and information at him in an endless stream that made time slip away. As he looked at Aria on screen, he recognized just how tense his body had become, coiled tight from hours of stillness. "Yeah. Let me shut down here and I will come right over."

Aria's smile was wide and genuine, her eyes soft with affection. "See you soon."

Kaidan stood up from the couch which he had not moved from since he got home, his joints protesting as he stretched. "End of day, RePHleX. Shut her down."

"You have not completed your usual sexual exercise routine today, RePHleX responded, its tone clinically helpful. "Would you like to complete that before visiting your partner?"

Kaidan stopped mid-stretch, a flabbergasted look crossing his face. RePHleX had informed him of not completing his exercise routine before, but had the system just directly connected his Kegel exercises with a visit to Aria? "Umm, no."

"You have several new responses to your posts. Would you like to review those before your leave?"

"Tomorrow, RePHleX"

"A job listing has just been posted that meets all your parameters. Would you like to apply for it now?"

"Tomorrow, RePHleX."

"I am detecting elevated blood pressure readings. I recommend sitting and having something to eat before leaving."

"A walk will be better for me, RePHleX."

"You are about to leave without your glasses."

Kaidan looked at the glasses on the side table. He had fully intended to just leave them there, but RePHleX's reminder somehow made that choice feel…impossible. With an internal sigh, he grabbed them and put them on. Only then did RePHleX fall silent.

Walking down the street, he had to admit the new glasses were pretty spectacular. There was zero delay as it identified streets, landmarks, and buildings. The names of people he walked by instantly appeared in his field of vision, along with links to their social media profiles. Kaidan was actually enjoying his walk until he realized which street corner he was standing on. Something nagged at his consciousness, making him turn around and look back at the building he'd just passed.

In a moment of instinct, he lifted his glasses so he could see under the lenses. Then lowered them again. Then raised them once more.

Kaidan had walked by this corner dozens of times recently, without his AR glasses. He knew the windows of the second shop had been covered from the inside with paper, and one of them boarded up. What he saw in his AR glasses though was a thriving coffee shop, people going in and out the door, the warm glow of lighting inside promising comfort and community.

He turned back and continued on his way to Aria's, surprised to not be surprised by the fall image he was seeing through his new glasses.

He turned back and continued on his way to Aria's, surprised to find himself not surprised by the false image he was seeing through his new glasses. The realization settled over him like a cold fog: how much of what he saw every day was real, and how much was a carefully constructed illusion? The streets suddenly felt less familiar, as if he was walking through two worlds simultaneously, only one of which the network wanted him to see.

As he walked, he couldn't help but wonder: if they could change something as simple as a coffee shop, what else were they changing? And more importantly, why? He touched the frames of his glasses, suddenly very aware of their weight on his nose, the way they subtly altered his perception of everything around him. But he didn't take them off.

Kaidan was greeted by a warm embracing hug from Aria when he entered her door. That was until she pulled back and noticed the glasses perched on his nose. Her expression shifted subtly, a shadow crossing her face.

"Really, Kai!" The disappointment in her voice was palpable.

"I got an upgrade to all my hardware today!" Kaidan's obviously feigned excitement caused Aria to tilt her head, curiosity replacing disappointment. "I got home and they were in there installing everything."

"Really?" Aria's tone was careful, measured.

"Yeah. They figured that because I haven't been connected as much lately, there must be a problem with my system." He tapped the frame of his glasses. "These are the new AR model."

Understanding dawned in Aria's eyes, and Kaidan watched as one of her playful grins spread across her face. "Do they do everything the other glasses did," she asked as she took his hands and pulled him to the bedroom. "Record everything?"

Kaiden laughed, thinking she was playing until she pushed him back on the bed and started to unbutton his pants. He lifted himself up on to his elbows, watching as she unzipped his pants and pulled out his already stiff cock, stroking it firmly. She lowered herself onto her knees and took his scrotum into her mouth, sucking firmly, eliciting a groan from Kaidan. She moved up his shaft with her mouth, then took in his entire cock, feeling it press against the back of her throat. When she lifted her mouth off him his shaft was wet with her saliva.

Once again she began stroking his shaft with a firm grip, moving faster and faster. She sucked so hard on his scrotum that she could feel the tension in his body as he simultaneously tried to pull away, and push into it. The familiar groan as Kaidan collapsed back onto the bed, told her she had been successful.

Standing in front of him, watching his cock still throbbing, Aria got undressed. She climbed on top of him, guiding his still stiff member into her. "Tell me you won't replay that video feed," she whispered into his ear. "Now time for these things to go." Aria quickly removed Kaidan's glasses and earpiece.

11

Kaidan was taken aback by the crowd in the Offline Atelier, Aria's art gallery. Not only was the space packed, but people were actually queuing outside, waiting to get in. He couldn't fathom how so many had learned about the gallery opening when they hadn't promoted it on the network at all. No ads. No social media posts. Nothing. More than just lacking promotion, the gallery itself was intentionally a network dead zone, a rare pocket of digital silence in their connected world.

Through the press of bodies, Kaidan watched Aria practically float around the room. Her hair, now a deep auburn with subtle golden highlights, caught the soft gallery lighting, its warm tones complementing her outfit perfectly. She wore a flowing dress crafted from a thoughtful mix of upcycled materials - linen, woven fibers, and patches of faded denim, all joined with visible, hand-sewn seams. The bodice was intricately embroidered with abstract designs, blending earthy textures and muted colors with splashes of vibrant reds and greens. Layers of fabric fell around her in uneven, asymmetrical lengths, each piece moving independently as she walked.

Her accessories were equally personal and striking. Around her neck hung a necklace made from small, rusted keys and twisted copper wire. On her wrist, a bracelet of found pebbles and sea glass bound together with rough twine - simple materials transformed into something beautiful. Her vintage leather boots had been carefully restored and embellished with hand-painted designs and carefully placed objects that caught the light as she moved through the space.

"She's in her glory," Tallis said, appearing at Kaidan's side to hand him a glass of wine. "A one-of-a-kind beauty."

Kaidan nodded, his gaze never leaving Aria.

"So, are you going to do it?"

Kaidan's head snapped around, quickly checking if anyone was within earshot. "No. Not tonight. It would be selfish." His fingers toyed with the ring in his pocket. "This is her night, and I won't do anything to take away from it."

"Okay," Tallis conceded, impressed that Kaidan had recognized how his proposal would take away from Aria's night. "But I wouldn't wait too long. She's a prize someone's going to snap up if you don't. Don't look now, but here she comes."

Aria appeared, smoothly taking Kaidan's wine glass and handing it to Tallis with a conspiratorial wink. She wrapped her arm through his, saying, "Come socialize with me. You can't hide in the corner all night."

Kaidan feigned reluctance, but pride swelled in his chest as they made their rounds together. Eventually, Eryx's voice boomed over the crowd: "Can I have everyone's attention, please?" He waited for the chatter to subside. "If you haven't already met Aria Brennan, please direct your eyes to the most beautiful woman in the room tonight, wearing the most incredible gown, which is just one more of her wonderful works of art."

Aria blushed as all eyes turned to her, accompanied by enthusiastic applause.

"Now, I know you're all wondering why these curtains are hanging in this section of the Offline Atelier. Well, wonder no longer." With a dramatic flourish, Eryx raised the curtains. "I give you Echosfear by Aria Brennan."

Aria's latest creation stood gleaming under the lights.

"It's a fully interactive exhibit you can all enjoy, two or three at a time, please. Now, I know the Offline Atelier is, well... offline, but I encourage every one of you to log into your feeds when you get home and talk about the Echosfear and what happens when you enter it. That's the price of being here tonight, and a fair price it is!" Eryx lifted his wine glass high. "To Aria Brennan, for the beauty she creates, and the realities she slaps us in the face with, and to the world knowing about Echosfear in the morning. Cheers!"

The crowd erupted in applause, and a queue quickly formed, people eagerly waiting to interact with the Echosfear art piece.

As the first trio of people entered the dome, a hushed anticipation fell over the waiting crowd. The dome, seemingly simple from the outside, enveloped them in an environment of subtle wonder. Suspended kinetic sculptures swayed gently overhead, their shadows dancing on the curved walls, which were lined with a mosaic of salvaged mirrors and polished metal pieces.

One by one, they approached the central platform and spoke into the microphone, their voices strong, clear. They listened closely as their words echoed back, unchanged at first. One of the women laughed nervously as her voice repeated exactly what she said, but then, something shifted. The next echo was slightly different, an inflection altered, a word replaced.

The three of them exchanged glances, intrigued by the subtle changes. A man, dressed in a crisp business suit, tried again, speaking a longer sentence this time. His voice reverberated around the dome, but with each repetition, the cadence stumbled, words jumbled, and the meaning slowly unraveled. The kinetic sculptures above them, once swaying gently in unison, began to move erratically. They twisted and clashed, mimicking the dissonance in the dome.

The lights inside the dome flickered and warped in sync with the changing echoes. At first, the soft white glow felt calming, but the calm dissolved as the colors shifted unpredictably to deep reds, greens, and blues that pulse to the increasingly distorted sounds. The trio of guests glanced at the mirrored walls around them, watching their reflections warp, just like the words they were hearing. What started as a cohesive image now looked fragmented and strange, barely recognizable.

The next guests to enter tried a different approach. They huddled together, murmuring their phrases into the microphone, each trying to outsmart the installation. But it didn't take long for their words to unravel as well, becoming something they hadn't anticipated. One person's sentence started sounding eerily close to another's, their voices blending, losing individuality. They laughed at first, but the realization started to settle in. This wasn't just a fun game. Their words, their thoughts, were being manipulated.

One of the guests whispered, "What did I even say?" The question hung in the air, unanswered, as they exited the art installation.

Other guests cycled through, each attempting to outsmart the installation. A couple entered holding hands, whispering sweet nothings that the Echosfear twisted into uncomfortable truths. A group of students huddled together, theorizing loudly about the mechanism, only to have their academic jargon dissolve into gibberish that somehow still carried meaning.

Outside, the queue had grown longer, the waiting guests both eager and apprehensive, having witnessed the reactions of those who'd gone before them. Aria stood to the side, saying nothing, her enigmatic smile reflecting in the polished surface of the Echosfear's exterior.

Most attendees of the gallery opening had no idea they'd been recruited into something larger. To them, Aria's Echosfear was merely a thought-provoking interactive installation that made them examine their relationship with reality. But as they began posting about their experience, art began imitating life in ways none of them had anticipated.

The first signs were subtle. Guests eagerly shared their experiences, but posts about the gallery opening, specifically those mentioning Echosfear, quietly vanished from their feeds. Undeterred, they reposted, only to watch their words disappear again. The turning point came with a seemingly innocuous post:

Trying to post about Offline Atelier for hours. Why can't we post about '3ch0$phere'?

That single use of leetspeak cracked something open. Like water finding its way through rock, people began crafting increasingly creative versions of "Echosfear": 3CH0SPH3R3, ech0sph3re, £ch0$phere. Each variation spawned dozens more, the very act of censorship fueling a viral curiosity. What had started as simple event coverage exploded into speculation. Why was this particular word being filtered? What about this art installation had triggered such a response?

The cascade was beautiful in its chaos. Conspiracy theories bloomed like digital wildflowers, each more elaborate than the last. Some claimed the Echosfear was secretly government technology, others insisted it was an alien artifact. The more the network tried to suppress discussion, the more people talked about it.

From his old-school desktop, Eryx watched it all unfold with quiet satisfaction. His access let him see the network's desperate attempts to contain the spread, algorithms racing to delete posts faster than humans could create them. He witnessed the exact moment when someone in power realized the futility of their efforts. A command was issued, programmers stepped back, and suddenly the floodgates opened. All the previously blocked posts surfaced at once, creating a tidal wave of Echosfear content.

"Phase 1 complete," Eryx posted to a secure, closed communications channel.

Meanwhile, Kaidan spent the day half-heartedly attending to his work, his attention fixed on his feed. Though he hadn't been privy to the plan to make Echosfear a safe topic on the RePHleX network, an excited message from Aria about her gallery opening "going viral" helped him connect the dots. He watched as the narrative shifted, noting the moment when official-looking accounts began dismissing the conspiracy theories, attributing the whole incident to a simple "database error."

A small smile played at the corners of his mouth. The powers that be—whoever they were—had realized they'd lost this battle. Now they were deploying their favorite weapon: plausible deniability. But it was too late. The word was out there, embedding itself in the digital consciousness, and with it, a spark of questioning that couldn't be so easily extinguished.

Aria hadn't even managed to fully process the success of her gallery opening when reality came knocking, literally. The sound of Tallis's excited rapping jolted her from a fitful sleep, her body still aching from weeks of preparation, from the physical labor of building Echosfear and curating her other pieces for display.

When she opened the door, Tallis burst in like a whirlwind of energy, making a beeline for the single networked screen in Aria's deliberately analog apartment. The screen flickered to life, revealing an overwhelming flood of notifications. Dozens of ImCast producers were clamoring for her attention, each message marked urgent, each promising an exclusive deep dive into the "Echosfear phenomenon."

"This is your moment, girl" Tallis declared. "And I'm not letting you hide from it."

In the vacuum left by traditional media's collapse, Immersive Audio Casts had evolved to fill the void. The death of mainstream news had been swift and inglorious, their commitment to fact-checking and verification had become their undoing in a world that prioritized speed over truth. In their place, a new form of media emerged, one that transformed simple podcasts and livestreams into fully immersive experiences.

These ImCasts were sensory symphonies, blending augmented reality, virtual reality, AI-driven narratives, and spatial audio to create experiences that transcended passive listening. The boundaries between observer and participant, between digital and physical reality, had become delightfully blurred.

Now, these very ImCasters were falling over themselves to feature Aria Brennan, the artist behind Echosfear. They wanted to dissect the art, probe the controversy, and fuel the conspiracies that had sprung up overnight. Each producer promised a unique angle, a fresh perspective, an exclusive revelation.

Through it all, Tallis remained Aria's anchor. She fielded requests, vetted interviewers, and coached her friend through conversations that felt increasingly surreal. When one ImCaster tried to push Aria into endorsing a particularly outlandish conspiracy theory, Tallis smoothly intervened, redirecting the conversation back to the art itself.

"Just one more," Tallis would say, and Aria would nod, fighting the urge to crawl into bed and curl into a ball. She was an artist who spoke through her work, who found solace in the tangible world of textiles and found objects. This digital maelstrom felt alien, overwhelming.

By late afternoon, Aria's voice had grown hoarse from talking, her thoughts scattered from repeating her story. She sat on her worn leather couch, surrounded by half-finished projects and salvaged materials. This was her real world, the one she understood. Tallis, finally sensing her friend's exhaustion, began declining further requests.

"You did good," Tallis said softly, sitting beside her. "Your art is making waves, making people think. Isn't that what you wanted?"

Aria managed a weak smile. Yes, she had wanted to make people think, to question their relationship with the digital world. She just hadn't expected to become the story herself. As she closed her eyes, she could almost hear the echoes from her installation, distorting and transforming, much like her own words had been twisted and transformed throughout the day.

Kaidan stretched as the antique watch Aria had given him struck six o'clock. She'd originally salvaged it for an art piece, but when she discovered RePHleX's curious inability to remind Kaidan of this particular hour, she'd gifted him her analog solution instead. Since the unscheduled upgrade to his network connections, Kaidan had made it a practice to shut down at six every day. Most evenings led him to Aria's, but when she was deep in her creative process, he'd redirect to the gym for Aero Drone Rush classes, where he'd recently advanced beyond beginner level.

His disconnection routine had evolved into a careful dance. Some days he'd leave his glasses behind, others his earpiece, occasionally both, and sometimes, seemingly randomly, he'd remain fully connected. He hoped RePHleX would interpret this pattern not as rebellion, but as optimization, a more efficient way of working. The strategy seemed to be paying off; the AI's protests about his evening disconnections had grown less frequent, less insistent.

Tonight was a both-pieces-stay-behind evening. Tallis' warning echoed in his mind: "She's not in a good place. The last thing she needs is RePHleX hovering in the background." His pace quickened as he made his way to Aria's apartment, arriving just as Tallis rushed out, in a rush of her own to get somewhere.

Aria approached him slowly, almost dreamlike, leaning into his body without lifting her arms, her head coming to rest against his chest. Kaidan enveloped her in silence, holding her until it became clear she wasn't going to move. With gentle deliberation, he lifted her and carried her to bed, tucking her under an antique hand-stitched quilt she had rescued from somebody's abandoned goods, then lying down beside her. She immediately curled into him, seeking refuge.

"I think they knew," Aria whispered into the quiet. "When they encouraged me to keep the name Echosfear... they were hoping for this."

Kaidan couldn't argue. The evidence was too clear. "Kind of looks that way," he admitted, pulling her closer. "But look at all the attention your artwork is getting. You're a modern-day Picasso."

"'Success can be a seductive lie. It promises freedom, but sometimes it only builds gilded cages,'" Aria quoted softly.

"What's that from?"

"Something I read somewhere. I don't remember where, but today... today I could feel the bars of the cage."

Realizing words wouldn't comfort her, Kaidan focused on presence instead. He awkwardly maneuvered under the quilt, pulling her closer, offering his embrace as a

sanctuary where she could rebuild her strength for the fights
ahead.

"Yes." The word was barely audible, spoken into his
chest, but it filled the room.

"Yes, what?" Kaidan asked, though something in him
already knew.

"I know about the ring. I know how long you've been
carrying it." Aria's voice grew stronger. "Yes, I will marry you.
But only if we can live here. You can keep your connected
apartment for work, or maybe get an office space so you
don't have to make excuses to a computer about why you're
leaving it behind every day."

In the soft light of Aria's room, surrounded by her
art, Kaidan realized she'd given him the perfect answer to a
question he hadn't yet found the courage to ask. As he
reached for the ring in his pocket, he wondered if perhaps
this was the most genuine proposal possible in their
oversaturated world. Quiet, unscripted, and completely
offline. His fumbling fingers did not find the ring in his
pocket and Aria could feel his body tense. Giggling, she
pushed her hand out from under the quilt to reveal the ring
already on her finger.

They left the apartment together the next morning,
having never left the bed. Aria had fallen asleep, still fully
dressed, mentally exhausted from her day of unexpected
fame, curled against Kaidan who'd remained motionless for
fear of disturbing her rest. They had talked about what they
were both going to do that day as they ate breakfast. Aria
wanted to go to the gallery. Kaidan had objected at first, but
she reminded him that the gallery was offline, which meant
she would be out of reach for ImCasts and anyone trying to
contact her.

Outside the gallery doors, Aria's goodbye kiss was
punctuated by a playful wiggle of her ring finger. "I have a
new art project to work on," she announced, her eyes bright

with renewed purpose, the beginnings of crow's feet crinkling as she smiled. The woman in front of him was a stark contrast to the one who'd collapsed into his arms the previous night. "I'm making you one. If I have to wear one, so do you."

"No way! He finally did it!" Tallis's voice rang out as she emerged from her building, gym bound. It had become their routine for her to meet Kaidan at this time to walk with her to the gym.

"Are you kidding?" Aria's sarcastic tone was thick with affection. "I would have been waiting forever. I just told him."

Kaidan felt his cheeks warm as Tallis enveloped Aria in an enthusiastic hug. "Eryx will spend the day at the gallery with you," Tallis added. "If that's okay. He promised not to intrude. He is just to going manage any walk-ins."

"Perfect," Aria nodded, then turned to Kaidan with a mischievous glint. "Kaidan had extra sleep last night, so you have my permission to make him do that drone class with you, and turn his drone way up."

Tallis did just that, despite Kaidan's protests. He really didn't protest too hard. He had come to enjoy the AeroDrone Rush classes, and while he didn't leave his drone on the max setting which Tallis had playfully set it at, he did turn it higher than he had before. When class was over, even the hands offered to help him up off the floor were not enough to get him moving.

"Typical man, had to prove you could do it," Tallis teased. "Where's your water bottle?"

Kaidan, flat on his back, managed to point weakly. Tallis retrieved it, accidentally dropping it with a suspicious rattle. "Crap, I think I broke it." She unscrewed the cap, turned it over—and froze at what fell into her palm.

"What is this?" She held out her hand, revealing three small pills.

Kaidan pushed himself up onto his elbows. "Where did you find those?"

"In your water bottle," Tallis's voice carried an edge of suspicion.

"That can't be mine," Kaidan quickly scanned the room for a similar bottle, finding none. He forced his rubber legs to support him as he stood, examining the pills in Tallis's outstretched hand. "This is where my glasses would come in handy. Could probably identify them instantly."

Tallis's eyes darted around the room, assessing who might be watching. Seemingly satisfied, she closed her hand around the pills and offered Kaidan her own water bottle, which he declined. Then, in a move that caught him off guard, she pulled him into an embrace.

"Go with it," she whispered, her lips barely moving against his ear. Reluctantly, he returned the hug as she continued, her voice barely audible. "They call it NeuraGel. It's IntraGel, but five times stronger and twenty times more addictive. One dose hooks you." She pulled back slightly, her voice still low. "Go home, work like normal. Pick Aria up at the gallery later."

Before Kaidan could process what was happening, Tallis was gone, taking the pills and their implications with her, leaving him with questions he wasn't sure he wanted answered.

12

In the small room across the hall from the gallery, Kaidan once again found himself sitting across a table from Elise. Eryx was there as well, and another man that Kaidan recognized, but didn't know his name. The air grew heavy as Elise placed a small baggie containing three pills on the table between them.

"Nasty fucking shit," Elise said, her voice carrying a weight of experience as she nudged the baggie toward Kaidan. "We've seen this before. People start pulling away from the network, then suddenly it's all they need. The network is the only thing capable of occupying their hyperactive minds."

"You're the first we've prevented from being dosed," Eryx added, his usual jovial demeanor absent. "And that was pure luck."

Kaidan felt a chill creep up his spine, goosebumps rising on his arms as he absorbed the implications.

Elise's next words came slowly, deliberately. "My husband created IntraGel with good intentions. But this…"

she gestured at the pills, "this was created to control. It hacks your brain's reward system. Near-instant gratification when you're on it, extreme withdrawal when you're not. But it doesn't matter which way you go. Stay on it. Try to quit. Either way the neurological degradation affects everything. Speech, motor skills, personality. In the end, you can't distinguish your own thoughts from artificially induced perceptions. Staying on it just delays the inevitable."

"Who the fuck does that to people?" Kaidan's voice shook, his hands trembling. "Why?"

The unnamed man dropped a file folder on the table, its contents spilling out. The printed photographs and profiles on actual paper reminded him of old police shows. "Bankers," he said, his tone clinical. "We just confirmed it yesterday." He spread the documents across the table with practiced precision. "You might be too young to remember, but there was a time when credit cards gave you 'free' points for purchases."

"Vaguely," Kaidan admitted, his eyes drawn to the scattered papers.

"The banks were among the first to recognize the true value of user data. They traded worthless points for insights into spending habits, preferences, and movements. Working with tech companies, they learned to manipulate spending and sell more of the products they wanted to sell. The data itself became more valuable than the interest they were earning on the cards themselves."

The man pulled a list of company names to the center of the table. "Hundreds of subsidiaries posing as advertising and marketing firms, all belonging to Echosfear. People have no choice but to pay these companies for access because they're the only ones with the data the banks used to sell. These people…" he tapped the photographs, "they decide who sees what, how they'll manipulate us all to further their goals."

144

Kaidan studied the unfamiliar faces in the photographs, but their identities seemed almost irrelevant now. The pattern was clear to anyone who could look past the daily conveniences. A system of control so insidious it had remained invisible until now. More chilling was the realization that they'd been ready to destroy his life just to keep him among the ignorant masses.

His eyes were drawn back to the small baggie of pills. Such a tiny thing, yet capable of reshaping a person's entire reality.

"So, what now?" Kaidan asked, his voice steadier than he felt. "What are we going to do about it?"

Elise leaned forward. Kaidan thought she was reaching for the baggy or some of the papers. She wasn't. Her hand found his, as she gently patted the back of his hand. "You aren't going to do anything except keep a close eye on your lovely lady. I hear congratulations are in order."

"Thank you," said Kaidan, "but I can't do nothing."

"We've already put you in too much danger, Kaidan," Elise said, her voice a mix of concern and finality. "Even if you wanted to do something, you've been marked. That makes you a liability to us now." She leaned forward, her eyes intense. "Keep doing what you've been doing. Your new commitment to a life partner will only add veracity to your cover of being increasingly disconnected. Watch her, keep her safe, and we'll do the same for both of you."

Elise's words made perfect sense, but they did nothing to quell the anger simmering in Kaidan's chest. These faceless powers had tried to hijack his mind, simply because they couldn't control him through their network. "Why tell me all this, then?" he asked, his voice tight.

The unnamed man spoke up, his tone grave. "Because they came for you, and you deserve to know who they are."

Kaidan nodded, his mind a whirlwind of thoughts and emotions. Without another word, he turned and left, his steps echoing in the hallway as he made his way back to the gallery.

He found Aria with Tallis, both cradling steaming cups of tea. The normalcy of the scene felt surreal after what he'd just learned.

"Kai! You look beat, babe," Aria said, her voice light with concern.

Kaidan forced a smile, channeling his frustration into a show of exhaustion. "That's because you told your friend, who is not my friend anymore, to turn that drone up to max."

"Aww... poor you," Aria replied, her voice playfully exaggerated. Then, her eyes lit up with excitement. "I almost sold another piece today. Couple of men who looked like they worked for the government came in. They wanted to buy Echosfear."

Kaidan's heart rate spiked, but he kept his voice steady. "Wow, that's amazing. What did they offer you for it?"

"A lot," Aria said, "but Eryx said we had to let my patron decide whether they wanted it or not first. They didn't look happy when they left."

Kaidan's mind raced through the implications. If the government, or whoever was fronting for the real Echosfear, bought Echosfear, they could make it disappear, stemming the flow of conversations about it on the feed. If Aria's patron bought it, the installation would likely stay put, keeping it in the public eye. Suddenly, Elise's insistence on him watching over Aria made perfect sense.

He forced a lighthearted tone. "Well, tell Eryx to get on it. We have a honeymoon to plan for." The words felt hollow in his mouth, but seeing Aria's face light up made the charade worth it.

As Aria excitedly began discussing potential honeymoon destinations, Kaidan's mind split in two. One part engaged with her, smiling and nodding, while the other part cataloged every detail of their surroundings, every person who walked past the front window of the gallery.

He caught Tallis watching him, her expression unreadable. How much had she shared about that morning with Aria? What was her role in all of this? How long had she been planning to drag her best friend into danger? Kaidan offered her a smile, but kept his guard up. From now on, every interaction would carry the weight of potential danger.

The walk back to Aria's apartment was unusually quiet. Kaidan's perception of the world had shifted dramatically since he'd started leaving his glasses behind. The morning's incident had given him an entirely different lens through which to view his surroundings. Everyone and everything now seemed a potential threat to him and Aria. As they walked, Aria held his hand tightly. He had been her rock the day before; today, it was her turn to be his.

"Do I get to find out what's really going on?" Aria asked as they stepped into her apartment.

Kaidan motioned towards the display screen on the wall and shook his head. Mimicking Tallis's earlier gesture, he hugged Aria and whispered directly into her ear, "There are ears in here."

Concern creased Aria's face as she looked at Kaidan. She wanted to ask more but knew better than to do so there. Instead, she pulled a leather-bound book off a shelf and sat on one of the many cushions adorning her floor, motioning for Kaidan to join her. She opened the book, revealing a journal filled with sketches, clippings, photos, and handwritten notes.

"I know big weddings aren't the norm anymore. Most people just move in together and life goes on," Aria said, flipping through the pages of the journal, searching for something specific. "I don't want a big wedding, but I also don't want to stand in front of a screen and make commitments that only a machine ever sees and documents."

She found the page she was looking for and spread her journal wide, revealing a picture of her parents beside a serene lake. "You, me, and a few close friends. Here. My parents still have their little cabin there. Completely off the grid. Our friends can come up for the day, leave in the evening, and we can stay much longer. Our honeymoon."

Kaidan couldn't remember when he'd last been out of the city. The thought of being off the grid and away from people would have made him anxious in the past. Today, it didn't. It was what Aria wanted, but it also felt like a location where he could keep her safe, and himself as well. "So... tomorrow?" Kaidan joked, half-meaning it.

"No, silly," Aria laughed. "A girl needs time to prepare."

They ordered food in, and while Aria described the dress she was making and coerced Kaidan into joining her in a virtual conversation with her parents to deliver their big news, something else was happening in what had once been the boiler room of the building housing the gallery.

The ancient boiler equipment had long since been removed from this cold, damp space. Occupying it now were several large desks with decade-old gaming computers and a server from the same era tucked away in the corner. The air hummed with the sound of computer fans and the rapid clacking of keyboards. Few even knew this room still existed, making it an ideal war room for Signal Noise.

The people crowded into the dimly lit room were a diverse mix of hackers, media strategists, and rogue tech insiders. On this night, they shared a singular, audacious goal: leverage the viral discussions surrounding "Echosfear" to expose the truth about the hidden network behind RePHleX, and more importantly, to name and implicate the specific individuals manipulating both the network and the populace. Similar war rooms, part of the sprawling Signal Noise network but not directly linked, were launching parallel campaigns around the globe.

They began by riding the viral wave triggered by posts of Aria's provocative art piece and the subsequent revelation that the term "Echosfear" was being filtered from feeds—until suddenly, it wasn't. With surgical precision, they injected coded yet undeniable truths into the already raging conspiracy theories. Using autonomous AI agents across the feed, they amplified key talking points that guided people toward the stark reality of the Echosfear's manipulation. Their content flooded the feed, strategically illuminating cracks in the official narrative.

The number of individuals in the Signal Noise cells capable of executing this intricate work was minuscule compared to the behemoth network they were challenging. However, the autonomous AI agents they deployed created the illusion of a vast army. These advanced bots functioned in swarms, working in concert to influence discussions across all feeds. They orchestrated viral trends without human oversight, their decentralized nature allowing them to operate without a central server. Their ability to move seamlessly between devices, networks, and servers made them elusive targets, nearly impossible to track or shut down.

Signal Noise had invested years in developing these AI agents, programming them with sophisticated behavioral algorithms that allowed them to understand and manipulate human psychology. They played on emotions, desires, and fears with uncanny precision. These digital chameleons engaged users in subtle ways, building trust and gradually shifting opinions over time, adapting based on each user's profile and online activity. In essence, they were miniature versions of the Echosfear itself, now turned loose against the apex predator.

While some cells focused on deploying and managing the AI agents, others worked tirelessly to disseminate carefully curated "leaks" to ImCasts. Attached to these leaks were insider documents—some genuine, some fabricated—that hinted at a massive cover-up involving international banks and their clandestine control of the Echosfear. The leaks also dangled tantalizing opportunities for ImCasts to speak with "former insiders who helped develop the Echosfear." Most of these "insiders" were carefully constructed personas, primed to reveal just enough plausible details to lend credibility to the conspiracy while maintaining their anonymity.

However, the true ace up Signal Noise's sleeve was Dr. Saraphine Kaeler. Some of the most explosive leaks offered ImCasts the chance to speak with her on the record. As a genuine insider with intimate knowledge of the Echosfear's inner workings, Dr. Kaeler's testimony had the potential to blow the entire operation wide open.

The digital insurgents worked tirelessly through the night and into the next day, their efforts seamlessly transitioning to another group of Signal Noise cells poised to launch the next phase of their meticulously planned assault. These fresh operatives unleashed a new wave of autonomous AI agents, tasked with fabricating a "data breach" of unprecedented scale, purportedly exposing the inner workings of Echosfear, along with the banks and specific individuals involved in its clandestine operations.

This manufactured breach unleashed a torrent of falsified yet eerily plausible financial documents, transaction records, and communications. The data revealed details of untouchable bank accounts linked to the upper echelons of the international banking system and the supposedly "non-existent" Echosfear. Transactions were intricately tied to world powers, politicians, and political parties, the staggering sums of money secretly exchanging hands serving to further inflame public suspicion and outrage.

Forty-eight hours into the operation, as the fabricated data breach continued to ripple through the RePHleX network, all Signal Noise war rooms powered down in a carefully orchestrated shutdown. Their operators melted back into the mundane routines of their everyday lives, leaving no trace of their involvement. However, before the final systems went dark, a third set of autonomous AI agents was released into the wild, their mission more insidious than their predecessors.

These new agents were programmed to create subtle glitches within the RePHleX network, sowing seeds of doubt in the minds of its users. Small, seemingly random anomalies began to affect users' devices, causing subtle malfunctions that fueled a growing paranoia about the system's control. Unexplained disconnections, inexplicable delays in response times, and cryptic error messages were carefully designed to make RePHleX users question the network's supposed infallibility, nudging them towards a state of mass distrust.

But these AI agents had an even more subversive purpose. They began implanting hidden messages within the very fabric of the network, manifesting as fleeting audio feedback and blink-and-you'll-miss-it visual glitches. These subliminal intrusions subtly reinforced the idea that the Echosfear not only existed but was actively tracking and manipulating its users.

The real-world consequences of Signal Noise's digital insurgency manifested with startling rapidity. Each passing day saw more people venturing out without their wearable tech, their naked eyes squinting in the unfiltered light of reality. The air hummed with the unfamiliar sound of live conversations, people openly debating whether their opinions were truly their own or merely thoughts implanted by the network.

Subtle changes rippled through AR devices, easing users back into perceiving the unvarnished truth of their surroundings rather than the sanitized, idyllic images they had grown accustomed to. The stark contrast between the polished virtual world and the gritty reality jarred many, leading to a surge in reported cases of "reality sickness" as people struggled to readjust.

Perhaps the most profound changes were evident in people's feeds. The carefully curated echo chambers that had previously cocooned users in comfortable bubbles of agreeable opinions now lay shattered. In their place yawned vast, unsettling spaces where dissenting voices clashed and conflicting ideas collided. The echo chambers they had previously occupied, now wide open space where the only thing they heard in response to their calls was the sounds of those calling out in their own voices.

This newfound digital freedom proved fleeting though. As people reveled in what they perceived as liberation from the Echosfear's influence, the network began to subtly reassert its control. Like a spider patiently reweaving its web, it lured everyone back with innocuous echoes, soft and gentle at first, lulling them into a false sense of security. The familiar comfort of curated content and tailored experiences beckoned, and slowly but surely, users found themselves being pulled back into the embrace of the very system they thought they had escaped.

It was a disruption. The leaders of Signal Noise never expected it to be more than that. Their actions were intended to be a skirmish in the larger war, and they never harbored illusions of a victory in one fell swoop.

Whether it was human nature, or just deeply ingrained societal norms, people were inevitably going to fall back into the soft walls of the padded cells the Echosfear created for them. Within their soft, algorithmic walls, there was no conflict, no cognitive dissonance, no uncomfortable truths to confront. Just the soothing hum of validation and the comforting illusion of certainty.

Lawrence Nault

13

Aria stared at her screen. She had just been casually scrolling her feed, responding to friends about her upcoming bonding ceremony when her feed glitched. At first, she dismissed it, but then she noticed messages from several contacts she knew she had blocked. Attached to those contacts were pictures and video clips that made her blood run cold. At the top of her main screen, an unsolicited prompt to send a message to Kaidan appeared.

Fear gripped her first, then shame, followed by panic. She was mere days away from a lifelong commitment to the man she loved and had loved for years. In the times he had been physically absent, she had sought gratification with others. The evidence of her indiscretions was now laid bare on her screen, a digital Sword of Damocles hanging over her head.

"There is an offer on your interactive art piece entitled 'Echosfear'," RePHleX's monotone voice announced from the speakers. "Would you like to review it?"

As RePHleX's message replayed in her mind, Aria connected the dots. Her eyes widened with realization. "You bastards," she thought silently, her jaw clenching.

Aria replayed a long conversation she had with Kaidan within the confines of the un-connected gallery. She knew why she had been encouraged to stick with the name "Echosfear" for her art piece. She hadn't realized it at the moment but when her peaceful world transformed to her standing in the middle of a chamber being bombarded by dangerous atoms, she put two and two together. So many people saw her as just a ditsy artist, but it was her observation skills that made her the artist she was.

The day someone tried to spike Kaidan's drink, she knew something significant had happened. She didn't know what exactly, but she was acutely aware that it had instilled a deep sense of fear in him, and that Tallis and Eryx were working to keep her in the dark.

Aria also knew that Tallis and Eryx, and almost everyone around them was part of something dangerous, and it was putting them in danger. She didn't know any details. She didn't need to know details to know she had been used, and that she was being kept out of the loop on some things for her own protection.

Kaidan was honest with Aria about the drugs in his water bottle during that conversation. When he did tell her what had happened at the gym, he watched her already pale skin take on a ghostly pallor. She had apologized to him repeatedly for ever introducing him to Tallis and Eryx, overwhelmed with guilt. Now she was feeling that guilt again, not because of what she had done, but because of what she hadn't.

"Is my response linked to that message on screen being sent, RePHleX?" Aria asked, her voice tight with tension.

RePHleX was oddly silent.

"RePHleX…" Aria began, but was interrupted by the sound of the door opening. Her screen went black as Kaidan entered the room.

"Hey babe. Glad you're home. Come sit," Aria said, forcing a smile.

Kaidan cocked his head, looking at her suspiciously. He sat down beside her, waiting for what he assumed would be another change to their ceremony or honeymoon plans.

"So, I'm being blackmailed," Aria blurted out.

Kaidan's eyes widened in shock. "Blackmailed? Why? With what?"

"RePHleX, turn screen on, display the message from three minutes ago," Aria commanded. The screen flickered to life, but only showed her regular feed scrolling down.

"Fine, be like that, you bitch," Aria cursed under her breath. She turned to Kaidan, her eyes glistening. "Someone really wants the Echosfear piece. A few minutes ago, that screen showed me a message, ready to send to you, that I didn't ask for. Attached to that message were other messages with pictures and videos of... other men I was with when we didn't see each other for long periods."

Kaidan's response caught her off guard. He chuckled, and the chuckle grew into a full-blown laugh. "Someone is trying to blackmail a woman who would walk the streets naked if she could, by threatening to send out her naked pictures?"

Aria couldn't help but laugh along with him, the absurdity of the situation momentarily lifting the weight from her shoulders. But then her expression turned serious. "I'm sorry. I should have told you I was doing it. I should have been honest about needing more time and attention. They were just... distractions. I should have told you before you gave me this." She held out her open hand, the ring he had given her resting in her palm.

Kaidan looked at the ring and took a deep breath. "You have nothing to apologize for. I did the same. I..."

Aria silenced him with a finger to his lips. "I already know. Tallis told me," she said softly. "Fucking Tallis! I love that girl with all my heart, but she and Eryx have done so much to get between us, and then put us both in danger."

They sat in silence for several moments, their eyes locked. Then Kaidan reached for the ring, taking it from her palm. Tears welled up in Aria's eyes, conflicting with the look of surprise when Kaidan got down on one knee before her.

"You. Me. We were always meant to be together," Kaidan said softly. "We've both done stupid things while living our lives apart. I didn't get to do this right at all the first time." He held out the ring. "Aria Brennan, I love you. Always have. I want to keep doing stupid things, but together, with you always."

Tears flowed freely down Aria's cheeks as she held out her hand, watching Kaidan slip the ring back onto her finger. He stood and wrapped his arms around her.

"Just you and me, babe, against the world. I really do love you," he whispered into her hair.

"Just you and me," Aria echoed. "Fuck Tallis. Fuck Eryx. Fuck all of them."

Kaidan laughed. "What do you say we do our first stupid thing together right now?"

Aria leaned back, looking into Kaidan's face, bracing herself for what she expected to be a completely inappropriate suggestion.

"Tell whoever is trying to blackmail you to get lost," he said, surprising her once again.

A slow, mischievous grin spread across Aria's face. "RePHleX," she called out, her voice strong and clear.

"Respond to the offer of purchase for Echosfear. The response is 'Fuck off'."

As the words left her mouth, Aria felt a surge of defiance and freedom. Whatever storm was coming, she and Kaidan would face it together.

Aria was about to make the inappropriate suggestion she thought she was going to hear from Kaidan when she heard a knock at her door.

"Ugh…" Aria groaned dramatically, throwing her arms in the air. "Timing people. Timing!"

Kaidan watched, amused, as Aria stomped her way to the door, opening it to find Tallis and Eryx there.

"What the hell? I say your names three times and you are summoned like demons?" Aria quipped, her tone a mix of frustration and humour.

Tallis blinked, confusion evident on her face. She glanced at Kaidan for clarification, but he was no help, his face contorted as he fought to stifle his laughter.

"Just come in," Aria sighed, giving Tallis a quick, if slightly reluctant, hug. "What are you guys doing here?"

Tallis stepped inside, Eryx following close behind. "Well, we know you two are getting stressed out with your upcoming ceremony and everything else going on," she explained, her voice careful. "We thought we'd take you away from all the stress a couple of days early. You know, head out to the cabin, give you a chance to relax before the big event."

Kaidan sauntered up behind Aria, wrapping his arms around her waist. She leaned back, her head resting against his chest. He made an exaggerated gesture of sniffing the air. "What's that?"

He watched with barely concealed amusement as Tallis and Eryx tried to discreetly sniff the air, confusion etched on their faces.

"I think I smell bullshit," Aria said bluntly, fixing Tallis with a hard stare. Tallis opened her mouth to question what Aria was hinting at, but a subtle head shake from Kaidan made her think better of it.

"I heard... rumours," Tallis admitted, her voice low. "Rumours that there's going to be a lot of, umm, activity over the next few days. We just thought it might be better to head out of the city now, so we don't have any problems on the day of your bonding."

Aria tipped her head back, looking up at Kaidan. He shrugged his shoulders, a silent conversation passing between them.

"Okay," Aria said, a note of unexpected joy in her voice. She had finished making her dress and already had everything packed. She'd even made an unusual stop at Kaidan's place, with his permission, to pack his stuff as well, including grabbing a few clothes for him to have at her place. Everything was there and ready to go.

"That seemed a little too easy," Eryx commented, eyeing the couple suspiciously.

"You guys hear a lot of... rumours," Aria teased, a mischievous glint in her eye.

"They do, don't they?" Kaidan added, his tone playful. "Like the ones about all my side-chicks."

Aria's eyes widened for a moment before she burst out laughing, the sound rich and genuine.

"You told him, Aria?" Tallis gasped, looking to Eryx for support but finding none. "I can't believe you told him! You know how long this drive is going to be now!"

Aria handed Tallis one of her suitcases, still chuckling. "Relax. He's good."

Tallis glanced at Kaidan, who was approaching with a couple more bags. The evil glint in his eyes and his continued laughter did little to ease her concerns.

"Girl, I can't believe you would do that to me!" Tallis exclaimed, a mix of exasperation and amusement in her voice.

Eryx and Kaidan let Tallis and Aria walk ahead of them, listening to their playful, yet somewhat serious, argument. Eryx leaned over, his voice low enough for only Kaidan to hear. "Dude, that was epic!"

Both men burst out laughing, causing the women to stop and look back. Tallis and Aria exchanged a glance before continuing their way to the car, now more annoyed with their respective partners than with each other.

"Hope you don't mind," said Eryx. "I bumped up your rental a few days. Tal and I will come back after the weekend with Aria's parents."

They slowed their steps as they approached a large vehicle parked in front of Aria's apartment building. Several other people had stopped to look at the massive machine, its presence almost alien in its design when compared to the hordes of micro-AEVs that dominated the city.

"Is that it?" Kaidan asked,

"You rented it, dude."

"I know I said my parents' cabin is on a mountain lake, Babe," said Aria, "but there are roads. It's not like we have to make our own!"

"I've never seen anything like this," Kaidan murmured, brushing his hand along the matte graphite surface. It felt impossible smooth, like polished stone, yet the underlying strength was undeniable. "It's a fortress on wheels. You sure they gave you the right vehicle?"

Kaidan stood back, eyes narrowing as he studied the vehicle under the streetlights. Its armoured body looked almost alive, the soft lights tracing its shape as if it were breathing in the evening air. "This thing is a beast," he said. "Like it could plow through anything."

Aria walked up beside him, her silhouette framed by the vehicle's reflective panels. "It feels like it's... watching us," she said softly, her fingers trailing over the cool metal. The sensors, embedded and barely visible, caught the ambient light and shimmered faintly. "It's so quiet, but I can feel it."

"Alive or not, we've gotta load it," Tallis added, glancing at the sky. It was only shortly after eight, but twilight was already turning to dark. "Let's get your stuff in and get out of here before a bigger crowd gathers."

Kaidan walked around to the rear, where the storage hatch opened smoothly at his touch. The back of the vehicle was cavernous, designed to hold everything they needed for their off-grid journey. He tossed in their bags, next to the bags Eryx and Tallis had already loaded, and there was still plenty of room for more. "No engine noise, no fuel smell... nothing. It's like it's waiting for us."

The doors to the AEV slid open with a whisper, revealing the soft-lit interior. The seats were arranged in a semicircle, designed for both comfort and function, with each one equipped with its own interface. The panoramic windows were dark, offering only a faint reflection of the outside world.

Aria stepped in first, her eyes adjusting to the warm interior lighting that contrasted with the growing chill outside. "This is unreal," she whispered, running her hand along the dashboard, a seamless touchscreen wrapping around the cabin. "It's like stepping into the future."

Kaidan hesitated at the door. The faint hum of the vehicle's systems was the only reminder of its power, silent and unseen.

"Trust it, right?" he muttered to himself, before stepping inside.

The door slid shut behind them, sealing them in with the soft glow of the control panel. The AEV powered on and the vehicle moved forward without a sound, the electric motor humming as they began their journey away from the city's lights and deep into the unknown.

"Alright," Kaidan said from the driver's seat, though he had no intention of manually driving. "Let's get out of here."

The AEV pulled away from the curb effortlessly, leaving the city streets behind as they made their way toward the highway. The city lights flickered past, growing dimmer in the distance as the vehicle picked up speed.

In the backseat, Aria leaned her head against the window, watching the fading skyline with a mixture of excitement and anticipation. "Off-grid," she whispered. "Finally."

Kaidan leaned back in his seat, letting the hum of the vehicle lull him into a state of calm. "Here we go," he murmured. "Into the unknown."

The city fell away behind them, replaced by open roads and the promise of the wilderness beyond. The AEV moved swiftly, seamlessly adjusting to the terrain as they sped toward the mountain lake, its headlights cutting through the gathering dark.

Four hours after leaving the city, they finally arrived at their destination. The journey had been largely uneventful, filled with forced small talk and carefully avoided topics. The most exciting part came when they finally turned off the smooth, predictable paved road onto a rugged dirt path. A playful cheer erupted from the group when the Autonomous Electric Vehicle (AEV) announced in its calm, robotic voice, "Engaging off-road mode."

The vehicle's wheels adjusted, suspension shifting to accommodate the uneven terrain. The familiar hum of the electric motor took on a deeper timbre as it navigated the challenging landscape. Not long after, the AEV's voice spoke again, this time with a hint of what almost sounded like regret: "Network connection lost. Switching to satellite-based mapping."

The announcement hung in the air, a reminder of their increasing isolation from the world they knew. Aria and

Kaidan exchanged a glance, a mix of excitement and apprehension in their eyes. Tallis gripped the armrest a little tighter, while Eryx leaned forward, peering into the darkness beyond the vehicle's headlights.

It was well after midnight when they finally arrived at the cabin. As they stepped out of the AEV, they were greeted by a sky so dark and vast it seemed to swallow them whole. Above, a canopy of stars sprawled across the heavens, more numerous and brilliant than anything they'd ever seen in the light-polluted city. The Milky Way stretched across the sky like a river of diamonds, a sight so breathtaking it momentarily silenced even the most talkative among them.

They quickly moved their luggage into the cabin, their movements punctuated by the crunch of gravel underfoot and the occasional gasp as someone paused to stare at the celestial display above. Once the last bag was inside, Eryx returned to power down the AEV. As the vehicle's lights dimmed and finally winked out, the night seemed to press in around them, the darkness deeper and more complete than they had ever experienced.

In the newfound darkness, their other senses sharpened. The gentle lapping of water against the shore became more pronounced, a soothing rhythm that spoke of nature's constancy. A cool breeze whispered through the trees, carrying with it the scent of pine and fresh water. It raised goosebumps on their arms, a reminder that they were ill-dressed for the nighttime chill.

Using the harsh beams of their flashlights, they stumbled into the cabin, the warm glow from within a stark contrast to the wild darkness outside. The interior was rustic but comfortable, with wooden walls that seemed to radiate a welcoming warmth. They quickly sorted out their sleeping arrangements, too exhausted from the journey and overwhelmed by their new surroundings to do much else.

As they settled into their beds, the sounds of the forest night filtered through the cabin walls – the distant hoot of an owl, the rustle of leaves in the breeze, the persistent chorus of crickets. These unfamiliar sounds, so different from the constant hum of the city, served as a lullaby, quickly lulling them into a deep sleep.

Lawrence Nault

14

The sun had been up for hours by the time everyone in the cabin crawled out of bed. The absence of alarms, incessant notifications, artificial lighting changes, and the sounds of the city, kept the four friends in the thralls of a deep sleep they didn't know their bodies needed.

Aria was the first one awake. She eased herself out from under Kaidan's arm and made her way out of the cabin as quietly as possible, not bothering to put clothes on. She stopped on the porch, feeling the roughness of the weathered wood under her feet as she looked out over the lake.

Twelve years, her father had said. Twelve years since she'd last visited this place. It made her sad as the realization of what she had stayed away from set in. In front of her a beautiful mountain lake, not blue, more turquoise. Gentle waves lapped against the shore, their sound rhythmic and hypnotic. Behind the lake, mountains stood like monoliths, their peaks covered in snow, piercing the scattered low clouds that tried to push against them.

The forest surrounding the cabin and lake was dense and teeming with life, a vibrant mix of evergreens and deciduous trees. Tall, towering pines and firs dominated the landscape, their trunks thick and rugged, covered in rough, deeply furrowed bark, with patches of moss and lichen clinging to their bases. Some of the trees leaned awkwardly, shaped by years of standing stoic in the face of wind and snow. Among the evergreens, scattered aspens and birch trees, their leaves already starting to turn their autumn gold.

Aria stepped off the deck onto the soft forest floor, the patchwork of fallen leaves, pine needles, and soft moss, like a prickly carpet under her feet. The earthy scent of the air, infused with pine, damp wood, and wildflowers, was intoxicating. Songbirds serenaded her as she walked to the lake, their melodies echoing through the trees, as though her naked walk was not a walk at all by a ritual procession, the harsh caw of a crow the voice of the procession's herald.

She didn't stop as she walked into the lake, the cold glacier water jolting her to wakefulness. When the waves lapped gently at her hips, Aria dove in. She dove deep and stayed under until her lungs screamed for more of the fresh mountain air. Her head broke through the surface and she treaded water, turning to see Kaidan on the shore watching her.

"It's beautiful," Aria called out. "Come join me."

"You're nuts, girl! The thin mountain air is messing with your head," Kaidan protested.

Aria swam closer to the shore. When her feet found the bottom of the lake she walked in closer until her breasts were just on top of the water, rising and falling with the waves, her nipples stiff and perky from the cold water grabbing Kaidan's full attention. "You chicken? Afraid of the water?"

"I didn't bring a swimsuit," Kaidan grumbled.

Aria motioned dramatically with her arms at her bare breasts. "Uh…hello…"

"Fine." Kaidan reluctantly gave in, dropping his clothes onto the ground and gingerly stepping into the water. "Holy hell!! That's freezing!"

Aria's laughter echoed across the lake, and the birds seemed to join in. A crow cawed overhead, as if nature itself was mocking him. "Even the crow is laughing at you. Getting your sexy ass in here!"

Kaidan waded out, slowly, trying to acclimatize to the cold water. When the water reached his hips, he screamed dramatically. Aria erupted in laughter. Eventually Kaidan made it out to where Aria was, surprised that he was enjoying the feel of the cold water once he was completely immersed in. "You are crazy," he said, leaning in for a kiss.

"I've got news for you Kaidan. You are stuck with crazy…forever." She playfully shoved Kaidan backwards, and quickly swam away.

The two of them didn't notice Tallis and Eryx come down to the shore. In fact, Tallis and Eryx watched them for several minutes as they wrestled and played with each other in the water, before they shed their own clothes and joined them in the water.

It was a quick rush to the cabin, from the lake, the cold breeze off the mountains carrying a bite. It was a run punctuated by goosebumps and chattering teeth. As they quickly scooped up their clothes off the beach. They dried themselves off in the house, and hastily got dressed again.

"You start a fire. I will start breakfast, which more technically would be lunch." Aria pointed to a fireplace and the stack of wood next to it. "Want some coffee"

"Anything hot," replied Kaidan, rubbing his arms for emphasis.

It took a while for Kaidan to get a fire lit. It was something he had never done and his only real reference was movies he had seen. For a brief moment he had thought about asking RePHleX for instructions, before remembering there was no RePHleX there.

Tallis joined Aria in the kitchen. "Babe, if he is hung like that coming out of the cold water, how is your uterus still intact?"

"Oh my god, Tal!" Aria exclaimed, unable to suppress a laugh. "Shut up!"

The men remained oblivious to the women's conversation. Kaidan nursed his fledgling fire, while Eryx explored the cabin, his tech-oriented mind trying to process all the analog simplicity around him.

The cabin was completely off all grids and networks, but Aria's father had installed solar panels and a micro-turbine that kept a battery bank charged. That battery bank ran a few simple things like the small fridge, a stove (but no oven) and some low-energy lighting. It also ran a small pump that drew water, probably from the lake, into a holding tank that directed the water through a multi-stage filtration system which was supplemented by a biofiltration system. The bathroom had a simple composting toilet.

"How long has your dad had this place?" Eryx asked, recoiling slightly as he touched what he realized was a genuine animal pelt on the wall.

"It belonged to my dad's dad," said Aria. "There was a time when this was almost a full day away from any city, and you had to hike the last few miles to get into it."

"Come sit at a real kitchen table," Tallis said, as she set down plates of food on a well-used pine slab table. Everyone eagerly dug into the food, though the coffee did not pass muster with Eryx who was accustomed to his artisanal brews.

"The food even tastes better out here," said Kaidan.

"I would have thought you would already be experiencing withdrawal," said Eryx. "If it weren't for the satellite tech on the AEV, you would have no connection to anything from here."

"He could talk to the bears," Aria quipped.

Tallis stopped mid-bite and looked at Eryx. "There's bears out here?"

Aria laughed, thinking Tallis was joking, then realized she wasn't. "Tal, this place is a zoo, without any cages."

"Well, I am ready to go home," said Tallis, trying to sound playful.

"Which leads me wondering," said Aria, her eyes narrowing. "Why the sudden rush to get out here early. Not that I am complaining, but it does seem odd."

Eyrx began to offer an explanation, but he was quickly interrupted by Kaidan. "She knows more than you think, so there isn't any need to be cryptic."

"There are rumors," Eryx began cautiously, "about something happening on Friday related to Echosfear."

"Rumors," Area echoed, her voice tinged with sarcasm.

Eryx glanced at Tallis, seeking support. She took over, her tone serious. "On Friday, one of Echosfear's creators is going public with some information. Our group is starting to spread the word today. Because your art installation made this possible, you might be at risk from those who want to prevent this from happening. And since we sometimes meet at the gallery..."

"So you brought us out here to protect yourselves," Aria said, anger seeping into her voice.

"No," said Tallis seriously. "If things go wrong, there will be no way of protecting Eryx and I. You and Kai have some distance from this. You two are safe, as anyone can be within the Echosfear. I know how important this bonding ceremony is for you. You are my dearest friend. You have had this plan since university before you even met Kaidan, and you have been working for weeks for everything to be just right. We came early so our lives didn't impact this at all."

Aria stared at her friend, searching for any hint of deception. "How much danger are you in? How can we help keep you safe?"

Tallis' composure cracked, tears welling in her eyes. "No, sweetie. That's precisely why we're here now. This is your time. You need to prioritize yourself. We left all of that behind when we turned off the main road."

"You know there are things I have been mad at you for, like outing Kai's private life to me." Kaidan flinched a little at those words. "There are things I even hate you for, like putting Kai in harm's way, nearly getting him poisoned." Tallis could feel the fear and anger radiating from Aria. "And using my art to be a weapon in your war." Eryx winced at that. "You've made my art part of the problem. It was supposed to be part of the solution."

Aria sat in tense silence, visibly trembling. Kaidan had never seen her like this. He reached out and put a reassuring hand on her leg. Aria closed her eyes, tipped her head back slightly, extending her neck. Her chest heaved as she took in a deep, measured breath, and slowly released it.

"You, both of you have been my best friends since we met in university. That isn't going to change. I love you, and you are my family. You are assholes, sometimes, but still my family." Aria stood up and backed away from the table to a position she could stare down the three of them at once. "If I hear one mention of Echosfear, RePHleX, or shit even mildly related to that in the next few days, I will personally drag your naked, flailing body, out in the woods, tie you to a tree, and hang rotting fish around your neck so it attracts every bear in the area."

Her expression was deadly serious, devoid of humor. There was fire behind her eyes. "And trust me, the bears will be much kinder to you than I will." Aria crossed her arms across her chest, her mouth quivering as anger slowly morphed into a wry smile as she processed her own words. "Yeah, okay. That last little bit might have been over the top, but you get my point. Now give me a hug and help me clean up the dishes."

Tallis practically jumped up from her chair, throwing her arms around Aria and sobbing. "I'm sorry. I really am."

Behind Tallis Eryx wiped imaginary sweat from his brow, thinking only Kaidan had noticed "I saw that, asshole!" Aria snapped. Tallis released her, turning to give Eryx a look that could kill.

Aria rummaged through a closet, emerging with what looked like a small toolbox. She handed it to Kaidan before retrieving two fishing rods from the wall, distributing them between the men. "You two are in charge of catching our supper."

Eryx's eyes widened in disbelief. "Wait... these aren't just decorations? We're actually expected to fish for our meal?"

Kaidan shook his head, amused, as he headed out. Tallis and Aria followed suit, moving in the opposite direction.

"I'm serious," Eryx called after them, a note of panic in his voice. "I have no idea how to do this. You want us to catch live fish?"

The afternoon sun hung low over the mountain peaks, casting a warm, golden hue across the glassy surface of the lake. Kaidan sat on a rock, a fishing rod awkwardly resting in his hands, the line disappearing into the depths of the water. Beside him, Eryx mirrored his posture, his brows furrowed in concentration as if willing the fish to take the bait.

"Do you even know what you're doing?" Eryx asked, his tone a mix of amusement and desperation.

Kaidan shrugged, his eyes never leaving the still water. "I fished once when I was eight years old, I think. With my friend's father. You?"

Eryx chuckled nervously. "Does it look like it? I thought the things were decorations. I am still not sure that woman of yours isn't playing a cruel joke on us. It can't be that hard. You just... wait, right?"

They both sat in silence, the peaceful sound of the lake lapping against the shore the only noise. The wind was gentle, rustling the leaves in the nearby trees, and in the distance, birds called to each other.

Kaidan sighed, leaning back slightly, the tranquility of the lake settling over him like a soft blanket. "It's nice, though. Not having to be connected to anything. No notifications, no noise. Just... this."

Eryx nodded, his expression thoughtful. "Yeah. It's like the world feels bigger out here. Or maybe we just feel smaller."

They sat like that for a while, content in the quiet, until the faint sound of footsteps on the gravel path behind them broke the stillness. Kaidan turned to see Tallis and Aria approaching, carrying folding stools and a small cooler.

"Look at these two," Tallis said with a grin, setting the stools down beside them. "Professional fishermen now, huh?"

Aria laughed, pulling out a couple of drinks from the cooler. "Let's see if they can actually catch anything before we start praising their skills."

"Hey, we're just getting started," Kaidan said, trying to sound defensive but failing to suppress his smile. He took a drink from Aria, his fingers brushing hers for a brief moment, a warm connection.

Tallis unfolded the stools and sat down, cracking open a bottle. "Well, don't let us distract you boys. We're here to see if you can bring us supper."

Aria sat beside Kaidan, watching the water ripple softly where his line disappeared beneath the rippling surface. "It's beautiful out here," she said, her voice soft.

Kaidan nodded. "We might never want to leave."

Suddenly, Eryx's rod jerked in his hands, the line pulling taut. His eyes widened in surprise. "Whoa, whoa. What's happening!"

Kaidan scrambled to help as Eryx struggled with the rod, the fish putting up more of a fight than either of them expected. "I think I got it!" Eryx called out, his face a mix of excitement and panic.

"Keep the tension on the line!" Aria shouted, leaping to her feet to watch the spectacle.

With a final tug, Eryx managed to reel the fish in, its silvery body flashing in the sunlight as he pulled it onto the shore. He looked down at it, breathless, and then up at the others, beaming. "I did it! First catch of the day!"

Kaidan grinned, clapping Eryx on the back. "Not bad for someone who's never fished before."

"You're next," Tallis teased, turning to Kaidan with a grin. "Better catch up."

As if on cue, Kaidan's line suddenly jerked. He scrambled to grab hold of the rod properly, mimicking Eryx's earlier struggle, and after a few frantic moments, he too managed to land a fish.

"Look at that!" Aria cheered, her eyes bright with laughter. "We might just eat tonight after all."

Kaidan held the fish up, feeling a strange mix of pride and disbelief. "Guess we're not hopeless after all."

They all laughed, the sound blending with the soft breeze over the water. Tallis opened another drink, passing it around as they admired the two fish flopping on the shore, soon to be their evening meal.

The fish-cleaning process that followed was nothing short of comical. Aria, drawing on distant memories of helping her father, took charge. Tallis retreated to a corner, watching with morbid fascination and making dramatic retching noises. Eryx kept his distance from the "slaughter scene," while Kaidan made a valiant attempt to assist Aria in cleaning and descaling the fish.

At the dinner table, the atmosphere shifted. Each of them cautiously poked at the lightly breaded, pan-fried trout on their plates before taking tentative first bites.

"Oh my god!" Eryx exclaimed. "Is this what fresh fish actually tastes like?"

Aria looked at him, puzzled by his reaction.

"It's incredible," Eryx continued, eyes wide. "It has... flavor. I had no idea fish could taste like this!"

"It's pretty spectacular," Kaidan agreed, savoring another bite. "You did an amazing job with the cooking. I'd forgotten how good fresh fish could be."

Tallis piped up, "I helped cook, you know. I supervised from a safe distance, like any good head chef."

Laughter filled the cabin, setting the tone for the evening as they relaxed around the fire, sharing stories and jokes. Tallis discovered an old photo album, and Aria regaled them with memories behind each yellowing photograph.

The following day unfolded just as leisurely as the first. They began with another invigorating, if chilly, swim. After breakfast, they basked in the warm sunshine on the beach, watching birds skim across the lake's surface and clouds drift overhead.

"How many cabins do you think you could fit on this side of the lake?" Eryx mused suddenly.

"That's an odd question," Tallis replied, not bothering to turn her head from where she was soaking up the sun.

"I bet there's good money in renting out off-grid cabins out here," Eryx continued, warming to his idea. "Think about it."

Kaidan's voice carried a note of disgust. "Why would you want to take a perfect spot like this, cut down the trees that make it beautiful, just to build roads and turn it into some kind of resort?"

"There are plenty of trees," Eryx argued. "And people would pay top dollar for this."

Aria interjected, her tone measured. "Here's the thing. There's nothing here because my grandfather and his father bought up most of the land around this lake for their hunting and fishing camp. My dad fought off every attempt to purchase or reclaim any of the land. He'll be here in the morning. Why don't you run that suggestion by him?"

"Your dad?" Eryx faltered, recalling the photos. "You mean the guy who looks like he wrestles bears for fun? On second thought, it's perfect just as it is."

Kaidan smiled at Aria, offering a fist bump which she reciprocated with a grin.

That afternoon, the four ventured into the woods, with Aria and Tallis on a mission to gather wildflowers for the upcoming ceremony. They spent hours traipsing through the forest, half-expecting to encounter a bear, wolf, or some other fearsome creature behind every tree. What they discovered instead was that the forest fell eerily silent around them, their clumsy progress through the underbrush more than enough to scare away even the most determined predators. They did, however, come across a majestic elk, its massive antlers reaching skyward as it bugled for a mate. That encounter was enough for Tallis to decide they'd had sufficient woodland adventure for one day.

The evening stretched late into the night as they sat around the fire, trading jokes and stories, engaging in heated debates, only to circle back to laughter and shared memories. As the first hints of dawn began to color the sky, they finally stumbled off to bed.

"The sun's been up for two hours! How can you still be sleeping?" The booming voice of Aria's father echoed through the cabin. Aria leapt from bed, rushing to embrace her father. Kaidan sat on the edge of the mattress, gathering his thoughts, summoning his courage, and battling the hangover threatening to overwhelm him.

"This is my father, and my mother," Aria announced excitedly as Kaidan approached cautiously.

Kaidan extended his hand to Aria's father, acutely aware that Eryx's description of him as a man who looked like he wrestled bears for fun was entirely accurate. He was enormous. Aria's mother, by contrast, was his polar opposite – barely over five feet tall and delicately built.

"I'm sorry, sir. We didn't hear you drive up, or I would have come out to help with your things," Kaidan offered.

Aria's father let out a deep, hearty laugh. "First off, no 'sir' – it's Cal. Second, we didn't bring a military transport like you did. We parked a few miles out and hiked in."

Kaidan felt a flush creep up his neck. While he had been surprised by the AEV he'd rented, he'd hoped it would show Aria's parents he was responsible and prepared.

"Dad, you're being a jerk!" Aria chided. "Be nice. Mom, tell him to behave."

Aria's mother smiled indulgently. "Dear, you see that ring on his finger? It's directly connected to a man's auditory canal. It filters out the sound of the person who gave it to them as long as they wear it."

Kaidan smirked, about to retort, but Aria cut him off with a look. "Don't you even think about letting that thought pass your lips, Kaidan Vale."

Cal roared with laughter, a sound that surely crushed any lingering hopes Tallis and Eryx might have had of sleeping in. The day, it seemed, was well and truly underway.

Aria's mother headed straight for the kitchen. Tallis didn't need any prompting to join her. "Let's fill them up with some pancakes and sausage," said Aria's mother. "This will be all they get until after the ceremony tonight. I am Sylvia, by the way. You must be Tallis. It's nice to finally meet the girl Aria was always getting in trouble with when she was away at university."

Tallis fumbled for words.

"Oh you know it's true, but I am glad you were there with her." said Sylvia

When breakfast was done, the men were all kicked out of the cabin. Cal gave them a tour of his cabin site, explaining how he put everything together and how he got the parts and pieces into the site. Eryx listened intently, curious about how it functioned so well with so little work and completely off the grid.

"Would have been nice to have something like this to haul all that stuff back here," said Cal as they walked around the AEV. "You and Aria are planning to stay out here for a week or two, aren't you. How do you know the batteries will still have enough power."

"The body panels are solar power collectors," said Kaidan. It's basically charging all day, as long as there is some sun."

"Wow. Things change fast. I still would never trust a vehicle that does the driving for you.

The three of them spent part of the afternoon stacking wood for a big fire. When that was done Kaidan and Eryx watched Cal skillfully fish, releasing everything he caught back into the lake. While he fished, he gently probed Kaidan for details about his life, his family, his work, and his plans for the future. He did it so subtlety that Kaidan hardly noticed he was getting the third degree. As the sun started to set, Cal packed up his fishing rod.

"Your job Eryx, is to make sure this young man doesn't run. I am going in to get my daughter."

15

The city was alive with activity. It never really stopped. Always pulsing with ceaseless energy, a vast urban reef teeming with life. Beneath the sky, barely visible through the towers that surrounded them, millions of souls struggled and thrived in an endless dance of survival, unaware of the forces shaping their reality.

Deep in the bowels of an unmarked building, Elise sat at a cold metal table, surrounded by the watchful eyes of Signal Noise operatives. These were people she had personally recruited to the cause, their hypervigilance a constant reminder of the danger they faced.

Twelve years had passed since Elise began assembling this group to resist the very creation she had helped birth. Now, she found herself a prisoner, held captive by those who had turned her own child against her. The irony was not lost on her.

Beyond the confines of their hidden sanctuary, Echosfear had tightened its grip on the collective consciousness. The autonomous bots released by Signal

Noise weeks ago had become victims of their own success, their patterns too obvious, enabling Echosfear to track and destroy them with ruthless efficiency. In recent weeks, it seemed as though Echosfear had redoubled its efforts, pulling people deeper into its carefully constructed illusion of reality.

"Sixty hours," Elise announced, her voice cutting through the tense silence. "Sixty hours to prepare. Sixty hours to spread the word. Sixty hours to survive." She paused, the weight of her words settling over the room. For years, she had lived in the shadows, but in less than three days, anonymity would no longer be an option. With a steely resolve, she uttered two simple words: "Let's go."

Those words ignited a frenzy of activity. This wasn't just another series of guerrilla-style skirmishes; this was to be an all-out assault on Echosfear's dominion. Keyboards erupted in a cacophony of clacking, transforming the previous hum of computer fans into a relentless chittering – like a swarm of digital insects preparing for war.

The messages flowing from the computers in Elise's command center activated Signal Noise war rooms across the globe. Each outpost was fully staffed, ready for action. This operation was too critical to be left to autonomous bots; it demanded human ingenuity and adaptability until the very last moment.

Every war room had been assigned a meticulously curated list of ImCasts and influential content creators within the Echosfear network. Their mission: to reach out and convince these producers to participate in an unprecedented, coordinated broadcast. The list comprised five thousand ImCasts, a mere fraction of the millions that existed on the network. However, these had been hand-picked for their massive audience reach and technical prowess.

The selection process had been rigorous, with each ImCast thoroughly vetted to minimize the risk of leaks. Every conceivable precaution had been taken to prevent Echosfear from catching wind of the operation and shutting it down prematurely. Signal Noise's ambitious goal was to create a single, coordinated, linked ImCast that would give Elise a platform to address the world from a hidden location.

The logistical challenges were staggering. Not only did all the ImCasts need to be linked and synchronized, but a complex network of false broadcast locations had to be established to obscure Elise's true whereabouts. As the clock ticked down, the tension in the room was palpable. Sixty hours to change the world.

There was a second tier of Signal Noise operatives that were activated at the same time. They weren't hiding in the war rooms, but living their everyday lives. Thousands of unwitting participants, ordinary people living their everyday lives who had been subtly influenced to believe they were part of something bigger. They weren't, in fact, a part of Signal Noise, but rather a distributed network of unsuspecting allies, each convinced they were pushing a worthy cause forward through small, seemingly innocuous actions.

The genius of this approach lay in its fragmented nature. Each participant had been given a piece of information, but no two pieces were identical. Their task was deceptively simple: post a message to their person feeds that read:

Watch your feeds at _____ time. Something big is going to happen. There will be big news!

The critical element was that the time and date provided to each person varied wildly. This created a cascading effect of thousands of posts, each announcing a major event but disagreeing on when it would occur. As these messages spread, they were shared and reshared exponentially, sparking heated debates across the network about the true timing of this purported news event.

The Echosfear, true to its nature, began to amplify these discussions. Its algorithms, designed to maximize engagement, latched onto the controversy and disagreement, propagating the various claims across the network. Users were pulled into personalized filter bubbles, each tailored to their preferences and biases, keeping them engaged in endless speculation about the timing and nature of the upcoming event.

This digital sleight of hand worked precisely as Elise had anticipated. In its rush to capitalize on the engagement generated by the debate, Echosfear's algorithms failed to detect the underlying truth: that a genuinely significant event was imminent.

More importantly, this cacophony of predictions served a dual purpose. While on the surface it appeared to be nothing more than typical social media buzz, it was subconsciously priming users across the network. Regardless of the specific time or date they encountered, people were being subtly conditioned to expect something momentous.

The beauty of this approach lay in its use of Echosfear's own mechanisms against it. By leveraging the platform's tendency to amplify engaging content and create echo chambers, Signal Noise had effectively hidden their true intentions in plain sight. They had turned Echosfear's primary function of captivating and directing user attention, into a weakness.

As the clock ticked down towards the actual event, millions of users across the network found themselves in a state of heightened anticipation, their minds primed and receptive. All the while, Echosfear's systems, so focused on the noise of debate, remained oblivious to the signal hidden within.

The conversations Signal Noise operatives were having with ImCast producers were a delicate dance of persuasion and secrecy. One by one, the influencers were being brought into the fold. Convincing them to join the unified broadcast was not the real challenge, nor was maintaining the secrecy. The true test lay in massaging the egos of what would soon become a virtual colosseum of digital alphas, each vying to be front and center in this unprecedented event.

"We're at 43% recruitment," reported a young technician, her eyes never leaving her screens. "Ahead of schedule, but we're hitting more resistance with the larger channels."

Elise nodded, unsurprised. The bigger the ego, the harder the sell. "Keep pushing. We need at least 80% for this to work."

Behind the scenes, while negotiations continued with ImCast producers and influencers, a technical team worked in the background creating a network of false broadcast locations so convincing that even Echosfear's most advanced algorithms would be fooled as they chased Elise's shadows through phantom nodes across six continents.

As the second day dawned, Signal Noise detected a shift in Echosfear's behavior. The AI had begun to correlate the myriad posts about an impending big event, inching closer to the truth. But Signal Noise was prepared. They launched their contingency plan.

A cascade of decoy operations flooded the network. False leads, dummy broadcasts, and fabricated conspiracies blossomed across the digital landscape, forcing Echosfear to divert resources to contain the information overflow. This diversion was bolstered by a new wave of autonomous agents, their code subtly altered but their mission unchanged from their predecessors' weeks ago. Signal Noise hoped Echosfear would assume these were overlooked remnants of the original incursion, further muddying the waters.

As the third day broke, Signal Noise war rooms began a carefully choreographed evacuation. It wasn't a retreat, but a strategic dispersion. Technical teams had finalized the complex routing systems that would carry Elise's broadcast through the labyrinthine network of ImCasts. Operatives initiated a series of false alarms and minor "events" across the network, a digital sleight of hand to further confuse Echosfear's algorithms.

Most operatives now returned to their day-to-day lives, melting back into the anonymity of the masses. Only a skeleton crew remained, poised to support the broadcast that would shake the foundations of Echosfear's dominion.

16

The day had slipped by so quickly that Kaidan barely realized he was moments away from one of the most important moments of his life. A mix of nerves and excitement settled deep in his chest, making the next few minutes feel like a blur. Though it felt like an eternity, only ten minutes had passed before Sylvia and Tallis emerged from the cabin and made their way down to the lake.

Tallis led Eryx aside, while Sylvia approached Kaidan. She stood beside him, gently taking his arm

17

The hours had slipped by so quickly that Elise barely realized she was moments away from one of the most crucial events in human history. A potent mixture of anxiety and determination settled deep in her chest, making the next few minutes feel surreal. Though it felt like an eternity, only ten minutes had passed before the final systems check was complete and the global network of ImCasts began to synchronize.

Dr. Okoro led the technical team through final preparations, while Elise and turning him toward the cabin. The setting sun behind him was just barely visible now, dipping below the mountains, casting long shadows across the lake. In front of him, the harvest moon had already begun to rise, its golden glow framing the cabin. As the door creaked open, Kaidan barely noticed Cal stepping out first, because his eyes were immediately drawn to the figure behind him—the most beautiful woman he had ever seen.

Aria stepped through the doorway, radiant in a gown that seemed to capture the very essence of the harvest moon. The gown Aria wore was a soft, flowing linen mixed with cotton, and the color a pale gold that looked like she had sampled the harvest moon in the sky behind her. The fabric shimmered like the twilight reflecting on the lake. As she walked towards them,

approached the broadcast station. She stood before the array of holographic displays, each showing a different facet of their global operation. The setting sun outside their hidden facility was just barely visible now, its fading light a stark contrast to the light of the moon rising opposite it. As the system powered up, Elise barely noticed the status indicators turning green one by one, because her eyes were immediately drawn to the central display, a real-time map of their virtual audience, billions strong.

The broadcast initiated, radiant in a symphony of data that seemed to capture the very essence of human consciousness. The stream Elise was about to enter was a complex tapestry of light and information, its color a pale blue that looked like she had sampled the heart of the digital realm itself. The data shimmered like starlight on black water as it flowed across the global arm-in-arm with her father, her silhouette was ethereal, yet simple, flowing effortlessly from a form fitted bodice into a soft, A-line skirt.

When she got closer the intricate details of the hand-embroidered bodice became clear. The bodice was delicately embroidered with leaves, vines and delicate flowers, each thread catching the fading light and adding a subtle shimmer to the ensemble. The embroidery wound around her waist and flowed down the skirt in asymmetrical patterns like vines growing organically across the fabric. Her neckline was a soft, modest scoop, and her sleeves sheer and flowing, embroidered at the cuffs, mirroring the motifs from the bodice.

Cal walked Aria past Kaidan toward the shore, where the moonlight now illuminated the gentle lacing on the back of her gown. Natural fibers had been twisted into cords to create an intricate pattern, another

network. She watched her image stare back at her, hardly recognizing the old woman in the dark hood whose vacant eyes stared back at her.

As the broadcast countdown reached its final seconds, Elise stood poised before the cameras, her thin figure captured on the myriads of screens surrounding her. If you had passed her on the street, you would not have noticed her, her wardrobe chosen specifically to allow her to blend in, unseen and unrecognized. In front of the cameras, she stood as an enigmatic figure surrounded by an aura of mystery.

Elise felt exposed as she lowered the hood that had been her constant shroud, shielding her from the network connected cameras they left no area of the city uncovered. Her grey hair highlighted her frail looking face, the fatigue of the last three days showing in her eyes. She stood stoically as ImCast hosts introduced her, her name example of the love and attention Aria had poured into every stitch. Her auburn hair was woven with a crown of autumn wildflowers and dried grasses in hues of deep gold, burnt orange, and muted greens, perfectly complementing the tones of her dress.

As they reached the shoreline, Cal took a step back, leaving Aria standing alone, her figure framed by the rising moon. Sylvia guided Kaidan up beside her, offering him a gentle, knowing look before she too stepped aside to stand with her husband. Cal motioned for Tallis and Eryx to join them, and together, they formed a quiet circle around the couple, the full harvest moon rising behind them in silent witness.

and an image of a much younger her scrolling into the displays below her on many of the screens.

"Dr. Seraphine Kaeler has long been recognized as the original creator of the RePHleX protocol. Shortly after the protocol's launch, Dr. Kaeler mysteriously vanished. In recent weeks, amidst widespread network glitches, rumors have circulated that Dr. Kaeler was not dead as the media suggested, but had gone into hiding. Tonight, in this unprecedented ImCast, we bring Dr. Kaeler directly to you, with words we all need to hear."

"Dr. Kaeler, what just happened?"

Elise took a deep breath, her eyes reflecting a mix of determination and sorrow. "We showed people the bars of their cages, but we underestimated how many would choose to remain inside," she said, her voice steady despite the weight of her words. "The absence of stress, the

Cal's voice was warm but steady as he began. "Twenty years ago, Sylvia and I stood where you are now. Our daughter, not much more than a child, watched as we made the commitment we should have made long before. That bond has held us through all the years since. Sylvia's mother conducted our ceremony, and I remember those words.

He paused, letting the quiet night settle around them before continuing. "The harvest moon brings to those beneath it the promise of abundance and prosperity, gifts earned through the dedication and love you've poured into each other. It is a beacon from the heavens, a symbol of life's unfolding chapters, reminding us that every season brings its own blessings and growth."

elimination of conflict... it's a powerful narcotic. We offered freedom, but freedom is terrifying when you've grown accustomed to security."

Elise glanced at the script on the prompter before her, but chose to speak from her heart instead.

"As humans, we're not wired for constant vigilance or perpetual doubt. The Echosfear, the entity and algorithms behind RePHleX—algorithms I created—didn't invent this tendency; it simply perfected its exploitation."

She leaned forward slightly, her intensity palpable even through the screens. "I went into hiding when I realized a few powerful individuals were using my algorithms to manipulate all of you. You give the network your attention and trust because it echoes your words and beliefs back at you. It isolates you from opinions that don't align with yours. It feels safe. And because it

191

As the moon reflected in the lake's surface, Cal went on, his words flowing like the waves lapping at the shore. "In harmony with the sun, the Harvest Moon rises and falls, a celestial dance of balance and unity. Just as the moon reveals itself in all its radiant fullness, so too may you reveal yourselves fully to one another, without fear or hesitation, in trust and wholeness."

Cal turned to face his daughter, then Kaidan. "Though the moon waxes and wanes, shifting as all things in nature do, it always returns to its fullness, steadfast in the sky. May your love, like the moon, find its way through the ebb and flow of life's changes, always returning to its highest point, where it shines brightly and holds itself high. May you walk this path in lights, in love, and in harmony with all the universe has to offer."

feels safe, you believe everything it tells you and everything it shows you."

Elise could see and hear questions being hurled at her rapidly, but she wasn't about to let them derail her message.

"Please, allow me to finish," she stated firmly, her tone brooking no argument. "Echosfear is real. It's a set of algorithms designed to acquire every possible piece of information about you and feed back information in a way that makes any new idea seem like your own. It's an AI algorithm that constantly evolves, allowing those who control it—those behind the Echosfear—to control you."

Her eyes burned with a mixture of regret and resolve. "I created this system with the best intentions, but I've spent years trying to undo the damage. Tonight, we take the first step towards reclaiming our autonomy, our critical thinking, and our shared reality."

I can offer no blessing on this bond for I am but a man. You can add no words that the moon has not already heard your hearts speak to each other. What we can offer you is this symbol....

He reached for Sylvia, who unfolded a worn yet elegant scarf, its scarlet silk woven with golden threads. "This scarf was used at our bonding, and at your grandmother's bonding. We hope it will one day be used at our granddaughter's bonding."

Sylvia stepped forward and gently joined Kaidan and Aria's hands together. Tears welled in Aria's eyes as her mother draped the scarf loosely over their hands.

Sylvia stepped forward and joined the hands of Kaidan and her daughter. There were tears in Aria's eyes. She hung the scarf loosely over their hands.

"This is a symbol of your commitment to each other and the bond declared

As Elise spoke, the sound of banging and raised voices echoed from somewhere behind her, tension rippling through the air. She glanced around, her unease evident. The users watching and listening through the ImCast could sense her growing urgency.

"Echosfear, the bankers behind Echosfear, the governments that use Echosfear, didn't want you to know of its existence. Now they want you to forget you ever heard anything about it." Her voice quickened, carrying a sharp edge of desperation. "Echosfear isn't some art installation, it is a dystopian nightmare. Anyone on the RePHleX network is trapped in its grip. The network is the bars of your cage."

A loud bang rang out, followed by a sickening pop. The screen filled with a crimson mist as Elise's head snapped back, exploding in a cloud of blood.

under this harvest moon" Sylvia said softly. "Wrap it once around your arms to bind this moment in your memories." Together, Kaidan and Aria wrapped the scarf around their forearms.

"Wrap it a second time," Sylvia continued, "to bind this moment to your future." They wound the scarf once more.

Cal and Sylvia stepped forward together. "And now we will wrap it a third time to bind the joy we feel in welcoming you into our family." As they finished, Cal smiled through his own teary eyes. "Now kiss the girl, dammit," he added, attempting to hide his emotion with humor.

Kaidan pulled Aria close, kissing her deeply as the bonfire behind them suddenly roared to life, flames flickering in time with the quiet joy shared between them. No one noticed Cal's quick, unseen gesture as he activated the remote hidden in his pocket to ignite the fire. His

Feeds dropped in some ImCasts, while others zoomed in on her lifeless body, sprawled on the floor. Blood pooled rapidly beneath her, a morbid silence hanging in the air. Elise had just been murdered before their very eyes, but the ImCasts kept running, capturing every horrific detail.

Outside the building, a man walked calmly down the street, blending effortlessly into the crowd. His movements were smooth and calculated. Passing through the throng, he emerged wearing a different jacket and hat. Unfazed, he entered a nearby restaurant, where he casually dropped the 3D-printed gun into the food waste incinerator.

He ordered some food and pulled up the ImCast on the AR glasses he now wore. The stream continued, dominated by frantic discussions about how the bankers and governments behind personalized dramatic effect.

Echosfear had Dr. Kaeler assassinated.

They hadn't. Only he knew the truth—because he was the one who had pulled the trigger.

It wasn't supposed to end this way, but Elise had insisted. She had called it her debt to pay, the only way to ensure the truth about Echosfear wouldn't be erased from the minds of millions. Her death would sear the reality into their memories. She had been right.

Lawrence Nault

18

"He likes you, you know," Sylvia said, standing on the porch with Kaidan, both watching Aria and her father by the lake. They were tossing rocks into the water, their movements casual, but there was a quiet bond between them. "He doesn't relate to the digital work you live and work in. He has always been connected to nature. That's where Aria gets it from."

"Aria says she gets a lot of herself from you too," Kaidan replied.

Sylvia chuckled. "If you're talking about her temper and attitude, then yeah, I'll take credit."

Kaidan laughed. "Actually, I meant her eye for art and the way she sees people, but thanks for the heads-up."

Sylvia grinned and nudged him lightly. "Well, look who's getting comfortable with the family, smart ass." Her gaze shifted back to the lake, where Aria and her father stood in perfect harmony with the landscape. "Look at them. They have something special." She sighed. "Anyway, let's get those other two up. If they're not ready when Cal is, they'll be hiking back to the city on their own."

Down by the shore, Aria and her father walked side by side, reliving old memories of her childhood at the cabin. When the creak of the cabin door closing signaled that no one was watching them anymore, Cal reached into his pocket and handed Aria a small envelope.

"Dad, we agreed—no gifts," she protested, pushing it back.

"It's not a gift. It's a responsibility," Cal said, pressing the envelope into her hands. "The deed to this property. All the paperwork is done, filed, and official. This cabin, the land—it's all yours now."

Aria's eyes widened with surprise. "But…"

Cal cut her off gently. "Your mom and I are fine. We don't want you and Kaidan waiting for us to pass before you feel like you can come here. This place is yours to protect now, just like I've done. And with your mom's temper, I pity anyone who tries to take it from you."

Aria smiled, a small laugh escaping. "I definitely got her temper, but don't tell Kaidan."

Cal's booming laugh echoed across the water. "He's gonna figure it out soon enough."

Her smile softened. "You and Mom will still come up here, right?"

"As often as we can," Cal promised. "But we'll always knock first." He wrapped his arms around her in a hug, his bear-like frame dwarfing her. She slipped the envelope into her pocket as they resumed throwing rocks, enjoying the quiet comfort of each other's company.

By the time Sylvia returned to the porch, dragging Tallis and Eryx behind her, Aria and her father were sitting under a tree, watching an elk wander by the lake's edge. They rose, brushing off the dirt from their clothes, and Aria gave her dad one last quick hug.

There were no long goodbyes. Cal gave Kaidan a firm handshake. "Take care of my little girl. That's your job now." He didn't wait for a reply, turning and striding toward the trail. Sylvia followed with a quick hug for both Aria and Kaidan before jogging to catch up with him.

Tallis barely managed to give Aria a hug before tugging Eryx along by the hand. "We'll see you when you're back in the city!" she called, not wanting to be left behind on the trail.

Aria and Kaidan stood together, watching them disappear into the trees. They laughed as Tallis's nervous voice echoed, "Wait for us!" Then, the forest returned to its natural stillness—only the sound of birds and the wind rustling through the leaves remained.

Kaidan slipped an arm around Aria. "You okay?" he asked quietly.

"Yeah," she replied, but there was a hint of uncertainty in her voice. "He gave us the cabin… and the land."

"I know. It's incredible. The perfect place for our bonding and our honeymoon."

Aria shook her head. "No, Kaidan, I mean it's ours. Forever."

Kaidan looked down at her, but she was still staring at the trees where her family had vanished. "We need to make sure we visit them regularly. Not just virtually. I mean real visits. Actual time together."

A cool drizzle began to fall, and they stood in the rain for a while, soaking in the moment, before retreating to the warmth of the cabin. Kaidan stoked the fire, coaxing warmth and light into the room as the gentle patter of rain against the cabin's roof created a soothing backdrop. The flames danced, casting flickering shadows across the worn floorboards and illuminating the rustic charm of their surroundings. He disappeared briefly into the bedroom, returning with a book he had spotted on the shelf earlier—a real, printed book, in one hand and Aria's gown in the other.

Aria, curled up in an ancient armchair that had witnessed decades of family gatherings, looked up from the needlepoint she had started years ago and found tucked away in a drawer. "What are you doing with that?" Aria asked, her eyes following Kaidan as he carefully hung her gown from one of the low-hanging rafters. The dress seemed to glow in the firelight, its intricate embroidery catching and reflecting the warm light.

Kaidan settled himself on the floor, leaning back against Aria's legs. He placed the book beside him, his attention fully on Aria.

"Tell me the story of the dress that turned the girl of many hair colors into the most beautiful woman I ever saw," Kaidan said, his voice warm with affection and genuine curiosity.

Aria's face lit up, her eyes sparkling with excitement. Kaidan didn't need to turn around to sense her enthusiasm; he could feel it in the way she shifted in her seat, setting aside her needlepoint.

"Well," Aria began, her voice taking on a storyteller's cadence, "it all started with a dream I had..."

***

"Fuckin idiot! Learn to drive!" Cal's voice jolted Tallis and Eryx awake in the back seat. Both of them had fallen asleep as soon as Cal started driving. They were wet, cold, and tired, from the hike that took them from the cabin to where Aria's parents had left their car.

"Is that the city already," Tallis exclaimed. "I am so sorry. We slept the whole time."

"It's all good," Sylvia reassured her. "Cal is pretty much non-communicative when he is driving. Off in his own little world." She paused, frowning slightly. "Kind of a strange morning though. Lots of bad drivers. I didn't think there were that many people that still drove their car manually."

Eryx discreetly removed his earpiece from an inside pocket in his jacket and slipped it into his ear. As he did that, they passed a massive digital billboard displaying a jarring headline: "Dr. Kaeler: Martyr of Madwoman?" Her face flashed across the screen, pixelated and distorted, followed by footage of her final moments, blurred out for dramatic effect.

"What in the fresh hell is that about?" Cal muttered. "Something strange going on here."

Eryx and Tallis exchanged a meaningful glance in the back of the car. They weren't sure what they would be returning to after Elise's planned broadcast, but her death was not something they had even thought of.

"I think this damn thing is broken," Cal grumbled, jabbing at the GPS screen. "I have been driving around in circles trying to get to your place.

Recognizing their surroundings, Eryx spoke up. "You can drop us off here. It's a short walk to our apartment. All we have to carry are these backpacks. Kaidan's bringing everything else back."

"You sure?" Cal asked, one eyebrow raised.

"Yeah, just drop us anywhere around here is fine."

Cal pulled into a drop-off zone. "It was nice to meet the two of you," he said, reaching back to shake Eryx's hand.

"Thank you so much for the ride back to town," said Tallis. "It was a beautiful ceremony. Like something out of a dream"

"It really was, wasn't it?" Sylvia replied, her eyes misting slightly. "Thank you for being a part of it."

As Cal and Sylvia drove off, Tallis and Eryx took in their surroundings. The city looked the same as when they left, but there was a palpable difference in the air. A heaviness, an underlying tension hummed just beneath the surface.

They walked the familiar streets, now teeming with a different kind of energy. People seemed distracted, engaged in hurried conversations with each other rather than their devices. The usual chaos of daily life continued, but there was a noticeable shift, a crack in the veneer of normalcy.

As they approached their apartment building, they were surprised to find a crowd gathered in front of Aria's gallery. People pressed their faces against the glass, straining to see inside.

"What's going on here?" Tallis asked someone in the crowd.

"We're waiting for the gallery to open," a young woman replied eagerly. "I think everyone's here to see the Echosfear. That's what I'm here for."

Tallis started to walk away, then turned back. "You know the Echosfear in this building is just a piece of art, right? An interactive kinetic sculpture. It's not—"

"The evil overlords trying to control our minds?" another person interjected. Tallis blinked, taken aback by the words that finished her sentence. "We know," the person continued. "The dead woman talked about it on the ImCast last night. Do you know when the artist opens her gallery?"

"Aria, the artist, is on her honeymoon," Tallis explained, a hint of protectiveness in her voice.

A collective groan rippled through the crowd.

"But we can open the gallery for you," Eryx added suddenly. Tallis shot him a warning look, but he was already pushing his way through the throng to the front door.

Tallis left Eryx to his own devices, a little surprised that opening the gallery was the first thing he decided to do. In the apartment she made a coffee, hesitating before flipping the switch that let the RePHleX network operate in that space.

She watched the feed for a while before summoning up the courage to follow a link to the ImCast everyone was talking about. The footage unfolded before her eyes, seeming to play in cruel slow motion. When the fatal moment arrived, Tallis broke down, hot tears streaming down her face. Though she hadn't known Elise as well as Eryx did, the woman had been a friend, and nobody deserved to die like she did.

Tallis returned to watching her feed. It was glitchy, with long pauses between posts. There were also no product advertisements or promotions weaved into the threads. Much of the discussion in the feed was about the ImCast and the assassination of Dr. Kaeler, but as the day progressed, and Tallis' coffee had become several cups of wine, the feed changed. The conversations morphed into complaints about problems with the network. Autonomous vehicles were not operating autonomously. Queries to the network weren't getting responses. Simple systems weren't working. The inconveniences that impacted people directly were quickly pushing the execution of Dr. Kaeler into the background.

The day slipped away unnoticed until the streetlight outside her window flickered to life. With a start, Tallis realized Eryx had not come home. A little tipsy from the wine that had got her through the day, she went downstairs. There was no more crowd, and the gallery was locked up, the lights out.

Tallis let herself into the gallery, thinking she might find Eryx in the back room. He was not. She locked the gallery doors behind her and returned to her apartment, confused. She didn't remember receiving any messages from Eryx. Then she wondered if maybe he had come in and she just didn't notice.

The first place she checked was his den. When she opened the door and the lights turned on, they reflected brightly off bare walls. There was no computer on the desk.

No shelf of games. Nothing. Just bare walls and desk space. Tallis forced herself to walk to the bedroom. All evidence of Eryx living there was gone from there as well.

Tallis' mind raced as panic gripped her. Had they come for Eryx? Did they discover his connection to Signal Noise and Elise? Was he taken because they suspected he was going to step in to replace Elise? She frantically scanned the room for signs of a break-in, but everything was eerily undisturbed. There was no damage, no sign of forced entry. It was as if Eryx had never existed here at all.

The questions tumbled through her mind in a dizzying loop. If they'd come for Eryx, why hadn't they taken her too? Why was everything else exactly as it should be, untouched except for his things? And why would they take his clothes?

Nothing made sense.

Tallis made her way back to the living room, her mind spinning. "RePHleX, message Eryx. 'Where are you?'"

"There is no one by that name in your contact list," RePHleX replied, its calm voice grating on her nerves.

She sat down, staring intently at the screen in front of her. "RePHleX, search for Eryx Rhys on the network."

"I have located six people with the name Eryx Rhys."

"Eryx Callum Rhys," Tallis said, her voice sharper now.

"There is no one with that name on the network."

Her earlier panic had transformed into cold, focused clarity. "Show me any references to Eryx Callum Rhys from the past fifteen years."

There was a noticeable delay, which was unusual for RePHleX. But Tallis barely registered it, too focused on the moment. "There are no references to anyone with that specific name on the network," RePHleX finally responded.

The tipsiness that had clouded her thoughts earlier was gone, replaced by an unsettling sobriety. "RePHleX, who are listed as the owners of this building?"

"There is only one name. Yours," RePHleX replied without hesitation.

Tallis leaned back on the couch, crossing her legs beneath her, her mind replaying everything over and over, but the conclusion was always the same. She cursed under her breath, "You bastard."

It hit her all at once. He'd left her. Convinced her to stay longer at the cottage, while his friends cleared out his things. He walked out of her life as if he'd never been there at all. The pieces fit too perfectly. There was the slim chance he'd been taken by Echosfear, but it was nearly impossible to erase all traces of a person's existence from the network. And Eryx was one of the few who had the knowledge and connections to do it.

Tallis clenched her fists, a tear slipping down her cheek. "I swear, I will find you," she whispered, voice thick with anger and grief. "And when I do, you'll wish you died as gently as Elise did."

Her fury gave way to tears as she curled up on the couch, no longer sure if she was mourning the loss of Eryx, or the life she thought they had.

Across the city, in a room eerily similar to the one Elise had spent her last moments, Eryx sat at a desk, the glow of the screens in the only light. In the corner, storage containers were stacked up, holding the entirety of his life. He had spent most of the day at this desk, hunting and deleting the last vestiges of his existence from the network. He watched as a search for him hit the network. He knew then that Tallis had realized he was gone.

There was no other way for him to do what came next. He could not take Tallis with him, and even if he asked, she wouldn't have come. He was going in a direction she would never support. He would miss her. She had been a big part of his life, and his biggest supporter. He knew that the way he left would hurt her deeply, but she was still young and beautiful, and he left her with everything she needed to live whatever life she chose. Buildings. Money. Investments. He was not cruel.

He had paid a freelancer who specialized in discreet move-outs to clear his belongings while they were at the cabin with Aria and Kaidan. He was not the only person in this day and age that wanted to vanish without warning, and there were gig workers who handled those quick, clean breakups. His contract language was very specific about what should be removed from the apartment, and how everything else was to remain completely undisturbed. Everything was executed flawlessly, leaving no trace but a gaping absence.

This was not a spontaneous decision. Eryx had been planning it for years, waiting for the perfect moment to vanish. He almost pulled the trigger when they exposed Echosfear the first time, several weeks back, but he realized that foray was not enough. When he sat with Elise to talk about her planned broadcast on multiple ImCasts, he saw the opportunity to set his plan in motion.

That conversation replayed over and over in his mind since he had seen the billboard that morning.

"You know that no matter what we do, by the end of the broadcast, they will have found you." Eyrx had said.

Eryx remembered the look of resignation on Elise's face. "I know. I am tired of hiding. There is no more I can do after this. People will have to make their own choices."

"If they find you, your voice will be lost, Elise. They will bury you, the ImCast, and nothing will change. It will all have been in vain."

"What are you suggesting, Eryx?" Elise had worked with him as part of the underground movement since she left Echosfear. He was her trusted confidant, and she listened to him. He often was able to do things she couldn't bring herself to do.

"We put some people in the room with you, and we fake a raid. Make it look like Echosfear, or some police agency found you. We sacrifice a couple people, and you disappear again in the chaos. That will hold the world's attention."

Elise's face twisted with disgust, as he expected. "You know I am right, Elise. Martyrdom will guarantee momentum."

"Martyrdom will guarantee momentum," said Elise. "But I have spent years in hiding to try and repair one mistake. I will not have the blood of others on my hands."

"You're right," agreed Eryx. "I am pushing it too far. Sorry." Eryx watched Elise and waited for it, patiently, as he saw the wheels turn in her head.

"I am old, and tired Eryx. I will not survive in a cell, if they even give me that chance. Martyrdom will guarantee momentum, and I will be the martyr."

He had known she'd make that choice. It didn't take much to nudge her in that direction. As he left town with Tallis, Eryx knew that by the time he returned, Elise would be dead. That was when he would execute his own plan.

Finally.

Lawrence Nault

19

As the harvest moon settled over the horizon, the sun rose on a new day.

At the cabin, Aria and Kaidan sat on the porch, a thick woolen blanket wrapped snugly around their shoulders. Steaming mugs of bad coffee warmed their hands as they watched the forest come to life around them. They had fallen asleep early the night before, victims of fresh air and lack of distractions. This morning they watched their breath rise, wispy tendrils in the cool mountain air, and listened to fish break the glass-like surface of the turquoise lake in front of them.

In Tallis' apartment, Tallis laid curled up into a ball around a cushion she clutched tightly in her arms. This is where she fell asleep, after the tears stopped, or maybe while they were still flowing. It didn't matter which. Nothing mattered. She had slept fitfully through the night, and was going to continue to do so, even though the streetlight that started her downward spiral the night before had long since shut off. She had no idea that there was another crowd waiting in the streets below her to get into Aria's gallery.

In the dark room, bathed in the glow of multiple computer screens, Eryx sat hunched over the desk he started the night at. He had no idea the moon had come and gone. He was focused on the dawn of something new.

His eyes, reddened from hours of intense focus, darted between displays as his fingers flew across various keyboards and interfaces. Fueled by a potent mixture of energy boosters and sheer determination, he had worked tirelessly through the night. While the world knew him as one of the architects behind Signal Noise's AI agents that had infiltrated and disrupted the RePHleX network, Eryx harbored a secret. The agents he had provided were merely decoys, at least two generations behind his true creations.

For a decade, Eryx had been covertly testing and refining his advanced AI agents on the network, always improving and pushing the boundaries of what was possible. This night had been the culmination of years of preparation. With meticulous precision, he had spent hours releasing and strategically placing the most sophisticated versions of his AI agents throughout the network.

Eryx was not the only one that didn't see the sun rise. Programmers and technicians in hidden data processing centers around the world were hard at work implementing the new directives handed down from the top. Except, these weren't new protocols. They were rolling back to a backup from years ago. The process was intricate, spanning ten remote server farms scattered around the world. From the frozen reaches of Northern Canada, Alaska, Greenland, and Siberia, to the isolated facilities in Chile, the Kerguelen Islands, Macquarie Island, the Falklands, and Bouvet Island, each data center had to be isolated from the network, powered down, and resurrected from an old backup.

The complexity of the operation was compounded by the minimal staffing at most of these remote locations, where getting additional personnel on-site was a logistical nightmare. Every technician and programmer involved in the rollout was cursing the plan, predicting nothing but cascading failures. In their view, this was all orchestrated by people in glass towers, executives who had no real understanding of how the systems worked together, just that they needed the desired outcome at any cost.

But those executives weren't any less stressed than the workers. The assassination of Dr. Seraphine Kaeler, broadcast in vivid, gruesome detail across a world-spanning, interlinked ImCast, had put them directly in the crosshairs. What could have been a brief, passing scandal was now seared into the public's consciousness like a permanent mark, the ink a deep crimson the color of blood. At first, they turned on each other, certain the kill order for Dr. Kaeler had come from inside their ranks. But as news trickled in about international investigations zeroing in on them specifically, the blame quickly shifted to a greater threat closing in on all sides.

Governments these six men had put in power, and the puppets within those governments they'd thought securely leashed, had suddenly gnawed through their strings. In the time it took for the sound of a gunshot to fill a room, it had become far riskier for those in power to remain tethered to the Echosfear than to cut and run, facing the harsh reality of public opinion. The Echosfear could no longer control the narrative or sway the public. Too many were now questioning everything they heard or read on the network. The six knew they could regain that control, just as they had in the wake of the revelation of their existence and control over the Echosfear mere weeks ago. But this…this would take time. Precious time they weren't sure they had.

They were not unprepared for an event like this though. They had a carefully crafted and religiously maintained business continuity plan to ensure their continued operation after a disaster, and the ImCast was an unmitigated business disaster. The disaster recovery portion of the plan was brutally elegant in its simplicity: make network users suffer, then, like capturing a starving dog, save them from their torment morsel by tantalizing morsel. The data they had was where all the value of the Echosfear lay. The disaster recovery plan ensured that none of that data was lost, but the applications and front-end interfaces users had grown dependent on would be hurled back to a six-year-old backup version.

Six years might seem a mere blink in the grand scheme, but in the realm of technological and programming advancements, the progress made during that span equaled what had taken place in the eighteen years prior. This digital time warp would plunge the world into chaos, all while gifting the six with plausible deniability about controlling the masses with their own information. Dr. Kaeler and her clandestine network of supporters would be branded terrorists, her martyrdom buried beneath an avalanche of fear and inconvenience. For these six men, it was business as usual, control what the world sees, and you control the world itself.

***

The first light of dawn slipped through Ava's smart windows, bathing her room in a warm glow. Her eyes fluttered open, and for a moment, everything felt the same. But as she stretched and yawned, the silence in her apartment was wrong. Too still. "RePHleX, what's my schedule for today?"

Nothing.

Her brow furrowed. "RePHleX, turn my screen on."

212

The screen on the wall flickered to life, but the interface was... strange. An old format, something she hadn't seen in years. "Christ, did they reformat again?" she muttered, dragging herself out of bed. Everything felt... off. The hum of the smart systems, usually so faint it was background noise, was missing. The lights didn't follow her movements. The coffee maker, normally already brewing, sat dark.

She slipped on her AR glasses, expecting her usual feed to overlay the cityscape outside. Instead, nothing. Just clear lenses staring out at a steel-and-glass world that looked oddly bare.

Her wrist buzzed. She glanced at her bio monitor. Instead of her health stats, a terse message blinked: Update failed. Please sync device.

Ava's pulse quickened. She pressed her face against the window, scanning the street below. People were spilling out of their buildings, all with the same confused look. Cars sat dead in the street, some drivers kicking tires, others staring at devices that no longer responded.

The distant wail of emergency sirens cut through the morning air, more jarring than usual.

"What the hell is going on?" Ava whispered as she threw on clothes. Something wasn't right. An attack? A system failure?

She stepped out into the street, where the chaos unfolded in real time. A businessman pedaled by on a rusting bicycle, his suit crumpled, and his expression bewildered. Nearby, an elderly woman shuffled past, shaking her head.

"Feels like we've gone back in time," the woman muttered.

***

The sunlight hit Elias Chen's face earlier than usual, pulling him from a restless sleep. His hand automatically reached for his AR glasses on the nightstand. He slipped them on and blinked, expecting the usual flood of notifications—patient updates, hospital alerts, headlines.

Nothing.

"RePHleX, run diagnostics," he muttered, rubbing his temples.

Silence.

His frown deepened. The tiles beneath his feet were cold when he stood up, refusing to warm at his touch. "RePHleX, activate home systems," he tried again, his voice more urgent.

Nothing.

Annoyance turned into a slow, creeping dread. Elias grabbed his bio suit from the closet, only to feel its weight limp in his hands. The smart fabric, usually buzzing with active nano sensors, was dead. He tossed it aside and pulled on his old scrubs, the cotton rough against his skin.

His eyes caught the error message flashing on his med patch: Error 404: Network Not Found.

The realization started to sink in, but the noise from the street dragged him away from his thoughts. Elias rushed to the window, peering down at the chaos. Autonomous vehicles sat abandoned in the middle of the road, passengers wandering aimlessly. Nurses from his hospital stood on the corner, pointing helplessly at their non-functional med patches.

Then a voice broke the silence in his apartment.

"You have an email from the Chief of Surgery marked as important. Would you like me to read it?"

The voice sounded wrong. It was flat and mechanical. He hesitated before responding.

"Read it," he ordered.

"All staff report immediately. Systems down. Prepare for manual operations."

Elias' heart raced. Manual operations. The last time he'd done surgery without AI assistance was years ago. He could barely remember where the physical medical reference books were stored.

As he rushed out of his apartment, Elias nearly collided with his elderly neighbor, Mr. Yoshida, who was clutching his chest in panic.

"Dr. Chen! My cardio-regulator... it's not responding. What should I do?"

Elias felt a knot tighten in his stomach. How many patients were relying on devices connected to the network, and how many of those devices had just failed?

"Come with me to the hospital," Elias said, trying to keep his voice steady. "We'll figure this out."

They descended the stairs together, finding the elevator dead. The weight of the situation pressed down on Elias. Without the network, this wasn't just an inconvenience, but life-threatening.

On the street, the confusion was even more palpable. A delivery drone had crashed into a storefront, its cargo scattered across the sidewalk. A young woman, still fixated on her AR glasses, walked face-first into a lamppost.

"It's like we've gone back in time," Mr. Yoshida muttered.

Elias nodded grimly. "Let's hope we remember how to survive it."

***

Maya Santos awoke to the soft chime of her biorhythm alarm, stretching leisurely, her thoughts already on the day's lessons. She smiled, the familiar warmth of a new day as a virtual teacher filling her chest. With a contented sigh, she called out, "RePHleX, initialize classroom."

Silence.

Frowning, Maya repeated, "RePHleX, initialize classroom." She enunciated each word more clearly, irritation creeping into her tone.

Nothing.

A knot of unease tightened in her stomach as she hurried to her studio, expecting the vibrant, interactive virtual classroom she was used to. But today, it was just a room. The holographic projectors remained dark, the adaptive smart walls that were once alive with the buzzing energy of her students now stood blank and motionless.

Heart racing, Maya grabbed her tablet, praying it still worked. The screen flickered, sluggish and outdated, as if trapped in some digital relic of the past. Her carefully crafted 4D lesson models and AI-enhanced teaching tools were gone, replaced by bare, archaic menus.

"You have an important email," RePHleX's voice finally broke the silence, but it was unfamiliar, sterile. "Network down. All classes suspended. Report to physical campus ASAP."

"Physical campus?" Maya whispered, disbelief flooding her. There hadn't been a physical school building in years, not since education had gone fully virtual. She stared at the blank studio walls, trying to comprehend what was happening.

A rising clamor from outside caught her attention. She moved to the window and looked down at the street below. Chaos. Parents and children wandered like sleepwalkers, bewildered and lost in their pajamas, clutching useless devices.

Among them, Maya spotted Zoe—one of her students. The ten-year-old was crying, tapping frantically at her inactive AR glasses, her small body shaking with frustration and fear.

Without thinking, Maya sprinted out of her apartment and down the stairs, her mind spinning. "Zoe!" she called, rushing to the girl's side. Zoe looked up, tears streaming down her face.

"Ms. Santos! I can't get my glasses to work! I can't do anything!" the girl cried, her voice trembling.

Maya knelt beside her, gently placing a hand on her shoulder. "It's okay, Zoe. It looks like... we're having some technical difficulties. But we'll figure this out together, I promise."

Parents began to gather around them, their faces a mixture of confusion and desperation. One man, disheveled and wild-eyed, pushed through the crowd. "You're a teacher, right? What are we supposed to do with our kids? The educare AIs are all down, and I have to get to work!"

Maya looked out at the sea of helpless faces, the rising wail of distant sirens filling the air. The seamless digital world she had depended on had crumbled overnight, leaving them all stranded.

***

Jack Hartley awoke to the familiar lowing of his cows, seconds before his biorhythm alarm was due to chime. He chuckled, stretching as he lay in bed. Some things never changed, no matter how much the world around him advanced.

"RePHleX, farm status report," he called out, expecting the usual rundown of the day's milk production, herd health, and feed levels.

Silence.

Jack sat up, frowning. "RePHleX, initiate morning farm protocols." His voice was a little sharper now, edged with confusion.

Nothing.

A cold sense of unease began to settle over him as he got dressed. Without the farm's AI systems, everything would have to be done manually—something he hadn't handled in years. He stepped outside, the crisp morning air biting at his skin. The fields spread out before him, golden in the morning light, but something was off. The cows were huddled around the smart feeders, mooing loudly. No feed had been dispensed.

"Damn it," Jack muttered, striding toward the barn. Inside, the usual whirring of the milking robots was absent, the machines standing eerily still, their status lights dark.

His mind raced. Without the robots, he'd have to milk the cows by hand. Five hundred cows. The thought hit him like a punch to the gut. Did he even still have the old milking equipment somewhere?

"There is an email marked high priority in your inbox," RePHleX's mechanical voice intoned from nearby, its tone unfamiliar and unsettling. "All AgriNet systems down. Implement emergency protocols immediately."

Emergency protocols? Jack's stomach twisted. Those were for natural disasters, not... whatever this was.

He sprinted to the silo, praying it would at least open manually. With a rusty groan, the doors creaked open, revealing the stored feed inside. But without the AI to balance the cows' nutrition, he had no idea how much to give them. He would have to guess.

A rumble in the distance made him look up. A battered pickup truck was approaching, dust kicking up in its wake. As it drew closer, Jack recognized his neighbor, Old Tom, behind the wheel. His beat-up old truck looked laughable next to the sleek, autonomous equipment now lying dormant on the farm.

"Your tech's down too, I take it?" Old Tom called out as he parked beside Jack. "Whole area's dead. Like the damn world's been turned off."

Jack nodded grimly. "Looks like we're doing things the old-fashioned way today."

Tom's face cracked into a knowing grin. "Told you those fancy robots weren't everything. I've still got my old gear. I'll round up the boys. Gonna need everyone's hands for this one."

As Tom drove off to gather the other farmers, Jack stared out at his fields, his mind whirling. How would he keep the milk cool without the smart refrigeration system? How would he monitor the herd's health without their biometric sensors? And how in the hell was he supposed to get the milk to the city without the automated transport?

Jack sighed, rolling up his sleeves. Today was going to be the hardest day of his career. But as he picked up an old milk pail, the weight felt oddly comforting in his hand. His father's voice echoed in his mind, always warning him to learn the "old ways" as a backup. He chuckled darkly, remembering his father's stubborn insistence.

Settling onto a milking stool, the rhythmic sound of milk hitting metal filled the barn. Today, Jack wasn't just producing milk; he was bridging the world they'd left behind and the one that had fallen apart overnight.

**

Samira Patel's eyes snapped open at 3:47 AM, her body instinctively reacting to the absence of the soft hum of her smart home. For twenty years, as Operations Manager at RePHleX Autonomous Port, she'd relied on her internal clock and her AI assistant. But this time, something felt wrong.

"RePHleX, port status update," she mumbled, still half-asleep.

Nothing.

A knot tightened in her stomach as she bolted upright. "RePHleX, priority override. Full port systems check."

Silence. Not even the usual soft glow from her smart home panels.

A chill ran down her spine as she fumbled for her tablet. The screen flickered to life, but the interface was archaic, nothing like the advanced holographic display she was used to. Gone were the real-time updates of ship positions, container movements, and global trade flows.

A device buzzed and vibrated on her bedside table. This was the fallback communications system for the port should the network go down. She had carried it religiously for four years now, and it only went off once a year for a scheduled test. She looked at the screen to see the text message from her assistant: "All systems down. Total chaos at the port. Need you here ASAP."

Samira dressed quickly, her mind racing. The port hadn't operated without AI assistance in over a decade. How many ships were out there, waiting to dock? How would they manage the crane operations? The customs processes? The entire supply chain could grind to a halt.

As she drove to the port, manually driving the AEV, for the first time in years, Samira's eyes widened at the scene before her. The usually orderly lanes of autonomous trucks were a jumbled mess. Drivers, long accustomed to sleeping while their vehicles self-navigated, were arguing loudly, trying to figure out how to manually operate their rigs.

At the entrance, Alex, her assistant, waved her over with wide eyes. "It's bad, Samira," he gasped. "Three ships are waiting to dock, but the harbormaster AI is offline. Cranes won't move, and customs can't access any databases. We don't even know what's in half the containers."

Samira exhaled sharply, assessing the situation. "Get the old radios from the visitor center," she ordered, her mind racing. "And find anyone who remembers how to operate the cranes manually. We need to get moving."

She strode toward the main control tower, finding it dark and eerily silent, a stark contrast to the bustling hub it had been just a day ago. Workers stood idle, their confusion palpable.

"Everyone, listen up!" she called, voice strong. "We're going manual. Grab whiteboards, markers, anything we can use to map the port. We're doing this old-school."

Within hours, the port slowly sputtered to life, though its usual efficiency was a distant memory. Workers scribbled container information on whiteboards, runners darted between stations delivering updates, and Samira's team relearned how to operate equipment manually.

By midday, they had docked one ship, though it felt like crawling compared to the smooth AI-guided days. Sweat dripped from Samira's brow, exhaustion tugging at her limbs. Yet, amidst the chaos, there was pride. They were operating—barely, but they were.

Alex, now covered in grime, joined her at the window, surveying the disarray. "Feels like we're living in the past," he said.

Samira nodded, her eyes fixed on the distant horizon, where more ships awaited. "We are," she said, a steely resolve in her voice. "But we'll adapt. We always do."

She turned back to the room, now a hive of manual activity. Spreadsheets were being updated by hand. Cargo was being tracked with colored sticky notes on a giant wall map. It was chaotic, inefficient, and utterly human.

****

Clara Cohen jolted awake to the harsh blare of the city's emergency communication system sounding an emergency tone through her dedicated device. She squinted at the display: 5:23 AM. As the city's Transit Coordinator, early calls weren't unusual, but this was different.

"RePHleX, status report on citywide transit systems," she commanded, already climbing out of bed.

Silence.

Frowning, Clara tried again. "RePHleX, priority alpha. Full transit diagnostic."

Nothing. The AI assistant that had been her constant companion for years was unresponsive.

Her device buzzed again, a message scrolling across the screen "All automated systems down. Major disruptions citywide. Report to Central Command immediately."

Clara's pulse quickened as she rushed outside, her mind racing. The city's transit system was the pinnacle of AI coordination: autonomous buses, trains, and traffic management running flawlessly, year after year. Without it, millions of commuters would be stranded.

As she stepped into the street, the scale of the catastrophe became clear. People swarmed bus stops, bewildered by the lack of autonomous schedules. A manual bus driver, clearly out of practice, struggled to manage a crowd, while commuters pushed and shoved in confusion.

The maglev station, a hub of morning activity, sat still, trains frozen on their tracks. Frustrated commuters shouted at the unmoving doors, and the station was quickly devolving into chaos.

Climbing atop a bench, Clara shouted, "Everyone, please! We're experiencing a system-wide failure, but we're working on it. If you can, find alternate transportation!"

She spotted Mike, one of the last human train operators, pacing near the control booth. "Mike!" she called, running over. "Can you get these trains running manually?"

His eyes widened. "Manually? I... I haven't done that in years, but I'll try." He nodded and hurried off.

Clara's device buzzed relentlessly with messages from her team: flashing red lights at intersections, immobile autonomous taxis, and the underground delivery network offline.

At Central Command, the operations room was bedlam. The holographic city map was dark, and her team frantically huddled around ancient terminals.

"Alright!" Clara called out, cutting through the chaos. "Manual control at major intersections. Find every retired operator you can. And someone find me a physical map of this city!"

The hours passed in a blur of frantic activity. Manually operated buses started to sputter into motion, volunteers managed the stops, and the first trains slowly rolled out of stations. Citizens formed impromptu carpools, bike-sharing systems sprang up, and the city, despite the odds, began to move again.

Aisha, Clara's deputy, joined her by the window, watching the sun rise over the city. "It's like we've stepped back in time," she mused.

Clara nodded, her face grim but determined. "We have," she said softly. "But we'll figure it out. We have to."

Over the next few hours, a semblance of order began to emerge from the chaos. Buses began to run on makeshift schedules, with volunteers at the stops helping to organize queues. A few trains sputtered to life, manually operated and running at reduced speeds. Citizens, realizing the gravity of the situation, began to self-organize, creating impromptu carpools and bike-sharing systems.

As the sun rose higher, Clara looked out at the city she'd sworn to keep moving. It was slower, clunkier, and far from the smooth efficiency she'd prided herself on. But it was moving.

***

Liam Rodriguez suppressed a yawn as he approached the gleaming façade of the store, the city's largest hypermarket. At 6:45 AM, the store was usually a hive of activity, its AI systems preparing for the day ahead. Today, something felt off.

"RePHleX, clock me in," Liam said as he neared the employee entrance. No response.

He frowned, tapping his ear, only realizing now that his earpiece had been unusually silent. "RePHleX, employee check-in protocol."

223

Silence.

A knot formed in Liam's stomach as he pushed open the door manually, something he hadn't done in years. Inside, instead of the usual soft glow of holographic displays and humming robots, he found darkness and an eerie quiet.

"Hello?" he called out. "Anyone here?"

"Oh, thank goodness!" His manager, Vera, emerged from the gloom, looking frazzled. "Liam, we've got a situation. All systems are down. Nothing's working! Not the inventory AI, not the checkout kiosks, not even the smart shelves!"

Liam's mind reeled. In his five years at this store he'd never seen the store without its tech. "What do we do?"

Vera ran a hand through her hair. "We adapt. We've got customers coming in less than an hour. I need you to dig out the old handheld scanners from storage. And see if you can find any physical price tags!"

As Liam rummaged through dusty boxes in the back room, his comm device buzzed with messages from coworkers. Everyone was confused, panicked. How would they manage inventory without the AI? How could they process payments without the biometric systems?

By the time the store opened, they'd cobbled together a semblance of order. Liam stood behind a checkout counter, a relic he'd only seen in history vids, with an ancient scanner and a hastily programmed tablet for a register.

The first customers trickled in, then a flood. News of the tech reversion had spread, and people were panic buying, fearing shortages.

"What do you mean you don't accept crypto payments?" an irate customer demanded. "How am I supposed to pay?"

Liam took a deep breath. "I'm sorry, sir. We can only accept physical credit cards or... cash." The word felt foreign on his tongue.

"Cash? Who carries cash anymore?"

As the day wore on, the challenges mounted. Without smart carts, customers struggled to keep track of their items. The lack of dynamic pricing meant everything was sold at yesterday's last logged price. The queue for the few working checkouts snaked through the store.

"Excuse me," an elderly woman approached Liam's counter. "Where can I find the soy milk?"

Liam blinked. He'd always relied on the store's AR navigation system to guide customers. "I... I'm not sure. Let me check." He pulled out a crumpled store map, feeling like an archaeologist deciphering ancient runes.

By midday, the store was in chaos. Without the inventory AI, they'd run out of several key items. The smart refrigeration units had defaulted to a safe temperature, but no one knew how to adjust them. In the fresh produce section, without the usual displays showing sourcing information and nutritional data, customers were reduced to squeezing avocados to check for ripeness, a long-forgotten skill.

"It's like we've gone back in time," Liam muttered to a coworker as they struggled to restock shelves without the aid of robotic assistants.

As the day neared its end, Liam's feet ached, his throat was sore from constantly apologizing to customers, and his hand cramped from manual data entry. But amid the chaos, he'd noticed something unexpected. Customers were talking to each other, sharing tips on which items were still in stock. Some even stepped in to help elderly shoppers navigate the store.

"Nice work today, Liam," Vera said, appearing at his elbow. "Tomorrow's going to be just as tough. We need to figure out how to do inventory by hand tonight."

***

Aisha Mbeki's earpiece chimed softly, rousing her from the shallow sleep she often endured. It was always in her ear, except when charging, and even then, a backup was on standby. Being disconnected was a risk she couldn't afford; every gig could be the difference between paying rent or missing a bill.

"RePHleX, display my gig schedule," she murmured, her voice slurred from sleep.

Nothing.

Aisha sat up sharply, a cold tendril of panic winding its way through her. She grabbed her backup tablet, grateful when the screen lit up, until she saw the interface. It was clunky, primitive, a far cry from the sleek AI-driven system she relied on. Worse, none of her gig apps were responsive.

"No, no, no," she muttered, tapping frantically at the screen. Every platform she used to earn her daily income was down. A single text message glowed ominously across the screen: "All gig platforms experiencing major outages. Standby for updates."

Her heart raced. The rent was due in three days. Without these platforms, she would have no income. What would she do? Aisha dressed quickly, her mind whirling with desperation, and stepped outside to find answers.

The street outside her apartment was a mess of confusion. The usual hum of delivery drones was absent, replaced by couriers milling around, sharing worried looks and blank screens.

"Hey, Aisha!" Jorge, another gig worker she often saw on her routes, waved her over. "Your apps down too?"

Aisha nodded, biting her lip. "Everything's offline. What are you going to do?"

Jorge shrugged, a weary look in his eyes. "I've got three kids to feed. I can't just wait around. I'm thinking of grabbing my bike, seeing if any restaurants need delivery help, old-school style."

Old-school delivery. The concept seemed alien to
Aisha, someone who had never known a world without AI-
optimized routes and predictive orders.

As she wandered the city, the magnitude of the
disruption hit her. Restaurants were overwhelmed with in-
person customers. Rideshare drivers, unable to connect
through apps, were flagging down passengers manually, like
some ancient video of taxis in chaos.

Near the city center, Aisha noticed a crowd gathered
around a bulletin board. Curious, she moved closer.

"Attention gig workers!" a woman shouted over the
growing throng. "We're coordinating emergency services. If
you can deliver goods, drive, or provide any other services,
sign up here! We'll match you with people who need help!"

It was the gig economy, reborn in analog form. Just
people offering their skills, no algorithms, no star ratings.
Without hesitation, Aisha scribbled her name on a scrap of
paper, listing her skills. Within minutes, she had her first "gig"
delivering emergency supplies to a nearby shelter.

By midday, Aisha had completed several deliveries,
helped an elderly couple start their ancient car, and even
rigged a manual communication system for a local
neighborhood watch. The work was exhausting but oddly
satisfying. For the first time in a long while, she felt truly
connected to the people she was helping.

"It's like we've gone back in time," she said to a
fellow volunteer during a break.

***

Zoe groaned as her alarm blared, the sound harsh and
disorienting. She fumbled for her AR glasses, expecting the
familiar dimming of her room's brightness and the seamless
display of her morning routine. Nothing.

"RePHleX, what's going on?" she mumbled, still half-
asleep.

Silence.

Confused, Zoe sat up, blinking in the dim light. Where were her holo-displays? Where were her messages? Her feed? She didn't want to leave her bed, and usually, she didn't have to. Her AR setup allowed her to stay connected without moving an inch: wake up, chat with friends, scroll through her feed, log into virtual class, all from her bed.

"Mom?" she called, her voice tinged with panic.

Footsteps approached, and her mother appeared in the doorway, looking just as bewildered. "Honey, something's wrong with the house system. Nothing's working."

Zoe's mind raced. "But how am I supposed to talk to my friends? What about school?"

Her mother sighed, clearly exasperated. "Schools canceled. Go outside and join your friends in person. They're already out there."

Zoe stared at her in disbelief. "You expect me to go outside? I'd have to shower, do my hair, put on makeup. Who even does that anymore before the middle of the afternoon? That's what AI is for, so I don't have to!"

Her mother bit back a retort. "The screen in the living room is still working. Maybe you can figure something out with that. I need to get to work, if I can even get there at all."

"What about breakfast? Is delivery still working?" Zoe asked, desperation creeping into her voice.

The only answer was the sound of the front door closing as her mother left. Zoe sat in stunned silence for a moment before dragging herself out of bed. "RePHleX, do we have chocolate chip cookies?"

No response.

"RePHleX, where's the junk food?"

Still nothing.

Frustration boiled over, and Zoe screamed, slamming cupboard doors in search of something she could eat. She finally found a bag of cookies but realized she still needed coffee. She fumbled with the coffee maker, trying desperately to figure out how to work the machine manually, before giving up.

Her mind raced as she padded back to her room, cookies in hand. Crawling under the blankets, she felt an unexpected wave of dread. Her boyfriends! She had never met the three of them in person. Would they actually try to see her. No more filters. No more digital perfection. What if they didn't like the real her? What if they thought she was ghosting them and moved on?

The thought made her stomach churn.

Zoe stared at the blank space where her holo-display used to float, trying to process what life would look like now. The world she had crafted so carefully, the life she knew, was unraveling. How could she function without AI smoothing over all the rough edges?

How could anyone?

***

As night fell, the reality of the technological regression became increasingly apparent. People were adapting as best they could, but frustration and confusion permeated the air. The Echosfear, ever vigilant in shaping public opinion, seized the opportunity to direct blame for the collective suffering.

By evening, a message began appearing at regular intervals on all functioning screens and feeds:

SYSTEM ALERT: MAJOR NETWORK DISRUPTION

Dear RePHleX Users,

We regret to inform you that the unprecedented system disruptions across the network are the result of a sophisticated cyber attack. Our investigation has linked this assault to Dr. Aria Kaeler, a former AI researcher, and the extremist group known as "Signal Noise."

These attacks have compromised core infrastructure components, necessitating a temporary reversion to legacy systems. This measure is crucial to protect vital functions and prevent further damage to the RePHleX network.

Dr. Kaeler, once celebrated for her contributions to AI ethics, has betrayed the principles of responsible innovation. Her actions, fuelled by misguided ideologies, have not only disrupted the gig economy but have also compromised essential services that millions rely on daily.

We are working tirelessly to restore full functionality and enhance our defences against future threats. We appreciate your patience and resilience during this challenging time.

Stay vigilant. Report any suspicious activities or Signal Noise propaganda to authorities immediately.

Together, we will overcome this setback and emerge stronger.

The message's ominous tone sent ripples of unease through the population. Some questioned its veracity, while others embraced the narrative, eager to have a target for their frustrations. As people grappled with their new reality, the seeds of division and suspicion began to take root, adding another layer of complexity to an already chaotic situation.

Lawrence Nault

20

Aria sat on an old wooden stool, her back to the lake, completely absorbed in her painting. The easel before her held a canvas that had started out blank but was quickly becoming something special with each brushstroke. In front of her, Kaidan sat on the cabin steps, absently plucking at an old guitar he had found hanging on the wall inside. It was missing two strings, but he strummed idly, trying to create something resembling music. Every few notes, he'd stop and flex his fingers, feeling the pressure of the unfamiliar strings against his skin.

"Stay right where you are," Aria called out as Kaidan shifted, thinking about getting up. "No one sees my work until it's finished. Not even you! And how am I supposed to finish it if my subject decides to leave?"

"Yes, dear…" Kaidan replied in an exaggerated tone, settling back onto the steps with the guitar. His eyes wandered to the trees surrounding the cabin, his mind floating somewhere between relaxation and creative frustration. He wondered how people used to write songs with nothing but their instruments. No digital tools, no A.I., just the raw sound and time.

They had been off grid for nearly a week now. When Aria first suggested they spend their honeymoon in this cabin, Kaidan had hesitated. The idea of being completely disconnected for so long had panicked him. But now, here in the stillness of nature, he found himself missing the constant hum of the network less and less. Kaidan stopped strumming and stared at the quiet woods. Part of him felt restless, out of the loop. He used to need the constant connection. But out here, it was different. The silence wasn't lonely.

He glanced at Aria, completely absorbed in her painting. Neither of them was aware of the turmoil happening back in the city, yet the thought of returning to that world, where even the gym was no longer a place to unwind, made him shudder. How could they have gotten it so wrong? The people, so addicted to the noise, couldn't see the system was never for them.

Aria didn't say anything as she continued painting, and Kaidan found himself content to let the guitar strings fall silent.

***

Tallis forced herself to leave the apartment and head to the gym, the familiar chaos of the city strangely comforting as it distracted her from the gnawing worry over Eryx's disappearance. She was a storm of emotions—heartbroken, angry, and anxious all at once—hoping that a good workout would help release some of the tension that gripped her body.

The gym was oddly quiet for a weekday morning. There were no AeroDrone Rush classes filling the air with noise, so Tallis made her way to the free weights and started her routine.

"Pretty dead in here today," said a man sitting up on the bench press, taking a break between sets. "All the crazy's happening outside, I guess."

"Yeah," Tallis replied flatly, adding, "I don't mind it."

She lay down on a bench and began her set of presses. Out of the corner of her eye, she saw the man jump up to spot her, though it was clear the weight she was lifting was hardly a challenge. She ignored him, her mind elsewhere.

After spotting her, the man casually loaded more weight onto his own bar and grunted loudly through his presses, clearly angling for her attention. Tallis didn't offer to spot him, and she had no intention of acknowledging him further.

"Kind of nice with it so quiet in here. That terrorist group did us a favor," the man commented, wiping sweat from his forehead.

Tallis bit her tongue, trying to stay focused, but she couldn't hold back for long. "You really believe what some company feeds you? They control what we see, when we see it, and how we see it, and you're buying that this tiny group of people is to blame for all of this?"

"Well... yeah," the man said, shrugging. "Makes sense, and we haven't heard anything else. Maybe we should grab a coffee and talk about it."

Tallis stood up, wiping down her bench, even though she had only done one set. "We should pretend we never met and never talk again."

She didn't even flinch when she heard him mutter "bitch" under his breath. He was right, at least for today.

ili***

The six men who controlled the Echosfear met online, using a secure, private network that remained untouched by the chaos plaguing the rest of the world. Unlike the faltering RePHleX network, their connection was flawless, the result of meticulous planning by their business

continuity teams. These teams had established multiple
redundant communication systems for the Echosfear's inner
circle. These redundant systems were invisible to the world at
large.

As they discussed the success of the system rollback,
each man sat in luxury, enjoying breakfast in their sprawling
mansions scattered across the globe. The rollback had gone
exactly as planned, and with it came an added bonus: they
were no longer under scrutiny for the assassination of Dr.
Kaeler. Their veiled threat to governments, implying that any
investigation into Echosfear would lead to further delays in
network repairs, had worked like a charm. All inquiries had
been dropped.

They laughed at how quickly the powers that be had
caved. It was laughably easy, but not what they were most
interested in. The real topic of discussion was the financial
chaos the rollback had triggered. With entire sectors of the
economy reeling from the disruption, stock values were
plummeting, making companies ripe for hostile takeovers.

Better yet, new competitors were emerging, trying to
offer governments alternatives to RePHleX. But the six men
saw opportunity in this, too. Through their myriad
subsidiaries, they could quietly acquire controlling interests in
these new ventures. Governments would think they were
moving away from RePHleX, unaware they were still being
drawn deeper into the web of the Echosfear. It was a brilliant
game of misdirection, and they were the undisputed masters.

The next phase was restoring selective functionality to
the RePHleX network for governments. The brief period of
chaos had served its purpose, but letting the public remain in
disarray would only lead to widespread instability, a scenario
the six men at the helm of Echosfear knew would be
disastrous. Governments needed to regain control, manage

the panic, and maintain order. At the same time, this would position those governments as the face of the problem, ensuring they bore the brunt of any backlash for any failures.

Not all governments would be granted this reprieve though. In recent months, a few had begun flexing their power, particularly those led by egotistical autocrats. The actions of these governments were leading to instability, not just in their regions, but in global markets. instability, with its accompanying wars, famine, and poverty, was notoriously difficult for Echosfear to manipulate. The RePHleX rollback offered a golden opportunity to quietly engineer regime changes in those countries, replacing troublesome leaders with more compliant ones.

Meanwhile, other governments were scrambling to find alternative solutions. In the backrooms of parliaments and congresses, officials were meeting with representatives from rival companies, discussing how they could reduce their reliance on RePHleX. These governments had been warned, time and again, about the risks of outsourcing their communications, data management, and network infrastructure to a single entity. Yet, under Echosfear's careful manipulation, those concerns had been downplayed or buried.

Now, as they realized how deeply embedded RePHleX was in every facet of their operations, panic set in. They needed to regain some semblance of control, but their options were limited. Clandestine meetings were held, often in what they assumed were secure, network-free rooms. Of course, those rooms never were. Echosfear was always listening, always watching, and the six men knew exactly when to tighten the reins, and when to let them slip, just enough to maintain the illusion of independence.

Eryx attended one of these meetings, though not as himself. He was introduced as Carden Thorne, the CEO of a promising tech startup. If you searched for Carden Thorne on the network, you'd find a well-documented history—from childhood to university, complete with photos, awards, and degrees. The work history was exhaustive, too, all meticulously curated over the years. Carden Thorne's rise to CEO would be unsurprising to anyone researching him.

"We had agreed to hold this meeting in a network free room," Carden said, scanning the space.

"My security team has assured me there are no connections in here," the President replied confidently. "We can speak freely."

Carden glanced around the room, unfazed. He pointed at the lights. "Smart lights, right. Movement and voice activated." He didn't wait for a response. "Smart audio system to record our conversation. Smart outlets on the wall for various devices, devices I can see many of you have brought in here with you and plugged into the outlets. Smart climate controls."

He stood up, his voice firm. "None of those say RePHleX on them, except some of your devices, but make no mistake, they are all connected to the RePHleX network."

The President frowned. Carden continued. "I am not talking about the options my company can offer you for becoming less dependent on RePHleX, when everything we say is being heard and processed by RePHleX. If you want help, we need to book this meeting somewhere else."

Without waiting for a response, Carden strode toward the door. As he gripped the knob, he threw one last remark over his shoulder: "Smart door lock."

The people around the table looked dumbfounded and fell silent, all eyes on the President. He didn't move for several moments, the tension thick. When he finally spoke, his voice was low but firm.

"How do we not know this? How do our own tech people not know this? How the ever-living fuck did we give one company the ability to hear every word said in the Whitehouse and the Pentagon?"

He stood, buttoning his suit coat. "You have 24 hours to build a new secure building that we can all meet in. I don't care if it is just four concrete walls with a door and a roof, but there isn't going to be one single piece of technology in that building that can connect to any network in there."

The president buttoned his suit coat and checked to see that his security detail was ready to move with him. "I want the Oval office checked, rewired, and double checked in that same time frame."

He leaned forward, placing his hands on the table. "And if I ever see any of you carry an electronic device into the oval office, you will get a direct trip to a cell. Better start finding pens and paper."

He left without another word. Normally, the room would erupt into conversation, blame, and debate, but today—nothing. Carden's warning had made everyone paranoid.

Twenty-four hours later the same group sat in a new room. It was just four concrete walls, a wooden floor and a roof. Hanging from the rafters were obnoxiously bright metal halide high bay lights. As each person entered the building, they were checked carefully. If anything they had was electronic or contained a computer chip, it was removed from them. Many of them were shocked when the security team identified items on their person that had chips. Some of them simply opted for the option of changing into a provided jump suit to speed the process up, having seen the problems others were having.

"Thank you for having me back, Sir," Carden began, addressing the President. "Before we proceed, would you mind if we reviewed what your team found during today's search?"

The President waved him on.

Carden had the security team called in and they spread the wide variety of items across the large boardroom style table. "First let me say that four people did not get in the door. They have medical technology implanted like a pacemaker and defibrillator which are connected to the network. The service dog did not get in either because of the chip it has implanted."

Carden picked up a coffee mug from the middle of the table. "Chips to control heating elements and maintain your drink at a consistent temperature, maybe monitor how much you drink. All app supported, all connected to the network."

He set the mug down and grabbed a few random pieces of clothing. "Chips in the tags for authenticity verification. If you are still wearing one of these designer brands, I am sorry to say you are wearing a knock-off." Eyes darted around the room as everyone looked to see what others were wearing. "When you were wearing these, they were monitored by the network location, events, frequency of wear, all which became marketing information...if not more."

"Hearing aids." He said picking up one of many pairs. "Makes sense. Use your app to adjust the hearing aids to your environment and personal needs. That app..."

"On the network," several people finished Carden's sentence.

"Pill bottle," Carden continued. "Tracks usage and reminds users. Make-up compacts with chips that track usage patterns. Belts that track posture and overeating. All of these." Carden stopped and waited.

"On the network," the entire room sounded back.

Carden motioned for the security team to remove all of the items off the table and take them out. He found his seat. "I know you were all warned about bringing electronic items into this room, and I don't think any of you intentionally did. This was necessary to demonstrate how unaware even those on heightened awareness are, of just how connected to the network they are, and how much personal data they are giving away…to one company."

"You sound like one of those Signal Noise radicals."

Carden turned towards the woman speaking. "CIA, right? How much access do you have to all the data stored on your servers? You don't need to answer because I can tell you, it's limited, and you think you have lost years of information. That is because in a cost cutting measure, that ironically cost more, the government contracted out the control and management of those servers to a private company which, unsurprisingly merged with RePHleX, who provided the user interface the CIA uses for that data."

The woman stared back at Carden with an icy stare, He knew she hadn't fully disclosed this information to the President. She turned to face the President but snapped back around. "What do you mean we *think* we lost?"

"RePHleX rolled back its apps and user-interface. I can guarantee you that they did not roll-back or lose any data."

"You've made us sufficiently paranoid," the President cut in, leaning forward. "What exactly are you offering us?"

Carden looked around the room. He had done a full background check on everyone in the room. All of them had been compromised by Echosfear at some point, but all of them had reasons to be out from under that influence.

"Freedom."

"This is the fucking United States of America. Name another country as free as we are."

Carden looked straight at the General proclaiming they were already free. "I didn't say freedom for the country. I only said freedom." Carden paused, knowing his next words could end everything he had worked for. "Freedom for you, from the influence the people behind RePHleX have over you. Freedom for each of you from the influence of the Echosfear."

The room was silent. Carden knew none of them wanted to be the first to speak, because doing so would be an acknowledgement that they knew what he was talking about. The President leaned forward in his chair. "Okay. You put it out there. We are still listening..."

21

Kaidan walked into the living room, stretching, still feeling the pull of sleep. He could have stayed in bed longer, but the sound of Aria moving things around stirred him. Curious, he went to check on her, only to be surprised by the sight of her packing a bag.

He was surprised to find her packing a bag.

"What are you doing?" he asked, still rubbing the sleep from his eyes.

"Packing up to head back to the city," Aria replied without looking up.

Kaidan blinked, trying to shake himself into the moment. "Oh... I guess we've been out here for a week now."

Aria paused and looked at him, her hands still for a moment. "You don't sound too happy about that."

Kaidan smiled, shaking his head. "No, it's not that. I just forgot what day it was. If you want to head back, we can go."

He turned to walk toward the kitchen, but Aria's voice stopped him in his tracks. "Hold on right there!" she said with a tone he recognized well. He turned back, meeting her gaze.

"I'm packing because you promised me a week out here, and I promised you I'd get you back right after. But I don't actually want to leave yet. Do you?"

Kaidan scratched his head. "Do we still have food?"

Aria laughed softly. "Dad's cold room has enough to last us a year."

Kaidan grinned. "Then no, I don't want to leave. We've got the AEV for another week, and we've got food. So, we can stay."

Without warning, Aria leapt over the couch and wrapped her arms around him, almost knocking him off balance. "Thank you! I didn't want to go back yet. I just thought you'd want to get back to your work."

Kaidan hugged her back, smiling into her hair. "I mean, I'll have to make some money soon. Bills don't stop, but we're good for another week."

Aria leaned back, her eyes twinkling with something mischievous. "What if we didn't have bills to pay? What would you do then?"

"You mean if I were independently wealthy?" Kaidan chuckled.

"Yes," she replied, her voice softer. "If you didn't have to worry about money, what would you do?"

Kaidan got a faraway look in his eyes. "I'd probably spend a lot more time out here. Maybe learn how to actually play a guitar, write some music, go back to the city for breaks now and then. I know I was glued to the network for too long... I still don't know why you stuck with me through that."

Aria laughed, this time with a hint of nerves. "Well, maybe you should go jump in the lake for a bit. When you get back, I'll have breakfast ready… and a surprise."

Kaidan groaned. "That lake gets colder every morning. What are you trying to do to me?"

"You love it," Aria teased, giving him a playful swat on his backside.

She was right. As he dove into the water he remembered that last few minutes of cold showers every morning at home, the hot water was nice, the cold water a shock to his system. Now the icy cold water invigorated him to start the day, and the warmth of a fire, and of Aria, warmed him. This was a better option.

As Kaidan stepped back into the cabin, he was greeted by the smell of breakfast and the sight of Aria's easel set up near the window. The painting caught his eye immediately, pulling him toward it. There he was, sitting on the porch of the cabin, playing the guitar—though in reality, he'd only plucked a few strings. Aria had transformed the scene into something more.

She had captured the cabin perfectly, rustic and small, against the towering pines with a distant lake shimmering under the dusk light. Warm hues of ochre and chestnut gave the cabin a sense of home, the wooden structure glowing in the fading sunlight. Kaidan could almost feel the cool evening air creeping from the shadows in the forest while the porch remained lit by the final rays of the setting sun.

In the painting, he sat on a weathered chair, casually holding the guitar. Though his posture was relaxed, there was an introspective quality to the way his fingers hovered over the strings. Aria had caught him mid-song—or at least mid-thought—his face half-hidden but brimming with unspoken emotion.

The light in the painting was stunning. Aria's signature style was all over it—the golden-orange glow of the horizon, long beams of sunlight cutting through the trees, touching everything softly. The sky above transitioned from a deep purple to a rich indigo, the night slowly descending. The light illuminated the creases in his shirt and the worn wood beneath his feet, highlighting the warmth of the evening while the forest behind hinted at the cool darkness approaching.

The painting exuded a feeling of both solitude and connection. It was as if the quiet strumming of his guitar echoed into the vast space between the cabin and the forest. The delicate brushstrokes of the trees and the guitar strings vibrated with life, as though the music lingered in the air long after it had been played.

He didn't hear Aria come up beside him, but her voice was soft in his ear. "So... what do you think?"

Kaidan grinned. "I remember it being morning when I posed for you, and we definitely need a chair like that for the porch. It'd be way more comfortable than sitting on the steps."

Aria playfully poked him in the ribs. "You like it, though?"

"I love it," Kaidan said earnestly. "I don't know how you do it. You're incredible. You make me look like I know what I'm doing with that guitar."

Aria pointed at Kaidan in the painting. "That man. That artist in his own right, creating something beautiful in a world that feels artificial, yet rooted in nature and the quiet of the off-grid cabin...That is the you I have always seen. You thought you were just plucking strings out there, but as I watched the vibrations of those strings reached deep into you."

Kaidan kissed Aria deeply. "That is never being sold to anyone. It will go over the fireplace forever."

Aria pulled him over the table and sat him down, sitting across the table from him.

"Ready for your surprise?"

Kaidan stopped mid-bite. "I thought the painting was the surprise," he said, sounding confused.

Aria slipped a folded paper across the table. Kaidan put his fork down and picked the paper up. On it was a large handwritten number.

"What's this?"

"Eryx sold Disconnected Convergence for a lot of money. He sold Echosfear for a lot more. And I have sold other pieces and put the money away."

Kaidan still looked confused. Aria could see him running numbers in his head.

"And…my grandfather was quite wealthy and left me a lot of money."

Aria watched as Kaidan's eyes went wide. Aria grinned.

"Babe, we are independently wealthy. That is more than enough for our lifetime if we are careful. So, get your guitar and find the man in that painting."

"But this money is your…"

"Don't you dare," Aria said firmly. "Whenever I complained about you spending your money on me, you always told me what was yours was mine. I never had to spend a dollar on anything when we were together. The first time you ever let me spend money was when we celebrated selling Disconnected Convergence. So, if I ever hear you say that money is mine and not yours, you will be right, because you will be a dead man."

Aria grabbed the paper out of his hands.

"Now eat, before it gets cold."

Kaidan helped Aria clean up after breakfast, his contribution mainly limited to putting the clean dishes away. He'd spent so little time in the cabin's kitchen that his process was essentially a series of random guesses—opening and closing cupboard doors, pulling out drawers, trying to figure out where things went. As he cycled through the drawers, looking for a spot to stash the spatula, he stumbled upon one that was jam-packed with random objects.

"What in the world?" he muttered.

Aria glanced over, amused. "You've never seen a junk drawer before?"

"I have," Kaidan replied, "but how does anyone find anything in here? What even is all this stuff?"

Setting the spatula and dish towel down on the counter, Kaidan pulled out the drawer, surprised by its weight. Curious, he carried it over to the kitchen table and dumped out its contents, a cascade of knickknacks spilling across the surface. Aria, intrigued herself, joined him as they began to sift through the scattered items.

The first item Kaidan picked up was a small black canister, one of several. It had some weight to it and when he shook it, he could hear something solid inside. "What do you suppose is in here?" he asked as he grabbed three more of them and stood them side by side.

"Do you know what those are for?" asked Aria excitedly. "There are containers for the film they put in old thirty-five-millimeter cameras."

Aria reached for one of the canisters and popped the top off. "Oh my god! It's not even developed. I wonder if it is any good." Aria rolled the small metal tube in her fingers, hearing the film shift inside it. "I wonder if you can even get this stuff developed anymore. Can you imagine the pictures that would be on here? It's probably fifty years old."

She eagerly opened another canister and found a second roll of film. Kaidan, curious, opened a third, but instead of film, several small brown discs tumbled into his palm. "One cent, 1968," he read aloud, staring at the coins. "These are pennies!"

For the next two hours, they sorted through the drawer's contents, not because there was so much to sift through, but because each object sparked a conversation.

They marveled at the relics of another time: a bulky flashlight with corroded batteries, a rusty bottle opener, faded tourist brochures, matchbooks, a mess of tangled fishing line and hooks, and a deck of cards missing half its members. So many of the objects were things they half-remembered from their childhoods, or from movies, but now they were holding them, pieces of the past made real again.

Arias eyes fell on a square plastic pouch and her hand darted out to grab it. Kaidan watched her, curious as she opened the pouch and ran her fingers over the paper inside. With a huge smile she handed it to Kaidan. Kaidan opened the pouch and found several small individual paper pouches inside. He pulled one out and could make out the faint outline of a circular object inside the paper package. The paper pouch was labeled with a large "E" and there were instructions on how to properly string a guitar. "No way!"

"Guitar strings," Aria said, her excitement bubbling over. "It looks like two of all of them."

Kaidan started to get up, then glanced at the mess covering the table. "What do we do with all this?"

Aria surveyed the chaos. "The flashlight is garbage. The film—I'm taking back with us to see if it can be developed. The rest is junk, but I don't want to throw it away."

"So... junk drawer?" Kaidan asked, raising an eyebrow.

"Junk drawer," Aria confirmed, giggling.

They did their best to put everything back in the drawer in some kind of order before Kaidan made a beeline for the guitar. As he began figuring out how to restring it, Aria stoked the fire. Outside, snow began falling gently, blanketing the cabin in peaceful silence.

Kaidan sat down on the couch, the guitar awkwardly perched in his lap. Aria had settled into her father's old chair by the fire, working on her needlepoint. Kaidan strummed the freshly strung guitar, only to hear a strange, dissonant clash of notes that made him grimace.

He twisted one of the tuning pegs, then tried again, but it didn't seem to make much of a difference. There was no real method to what he was doing, just randomly turning things until it sounded better. But what was "better" supposed to sound like? He wasn't sure. The strings buzzed beneath his fingers, loose on some, too tight on others, creating a jumble of notes that didn't quite fit together. It was chaotic.

Kaidan frowned, staring down at the instrument like it had betrayed him. This shouldn't be so hard, he thought. You just strum, right? Pluck a few strings and music happens. But the more he fiddled with it, the more he realized how much he didn't know. He had no idea what the right tuning of the guitar was. He didn't know how the notes were supposed to fit together to make chords. He was just winging it and hoping something good would eventually emerge.

With each random adjustment of the tuning pegs, the notes grew less jarring, finding a hesitant, almost harmonic balance. Every press of a string behind a fret revealed new sounds, tentative but promising. By the end of the afternoon, what he was playing still wasn't music, not really. But it was something, an attempt, clumsy and uncertain, but maybe the beginning of a new melody.

22

Tallis walked to the gym, her thoughts weaving through the undercurrent of a city still adjusting to the aftermath of the RePHleX rollback. The chaos had mostly subsided, with public transportation and government operations keeping daily life from completely unraveling. But even though the surface looked calm, the deeper struggle remained. People were trying to figure out how to live without the crutch that RePHleX had become. There was no roadmap for what came next. For so long, they'd been so used to the system doing everything for them, dictating their routines, curating their experiences, and now that safety net was gone.

It was like they were all fumbling with the tuning pegs of a guitar they didn't know how to play. They twisted and turned, hoping to find the right note, but unsure if they were making things better or worse.

Tallis could feel the fractures all around her. The city was still functioning, but it was disjointed, like listening to a jumble of out-of-tune notes clashing against each other.

There was no harmony. Some had managed to make their lives work, improvising new rhythms in the silence the RePHleX rollback had left behind. Others were still stuck, not sure how to move forward, arguing over what life was supposed to look like now.

The divide was palpable. People disagreed, argued, even fought over what direction to take. Some longed for the structure RePHleX had provided, desperate to rebuild that sense of order. Others were adamant they'd never go back to depending on anything like RePHleX again. But the truth was, none of them really knew the answer. Like Kaidan with his guitar, they were all just… guessing.

Tallis walked into the gym and was immediately stopped by a young woman who identified herself as an "employee." The woman was part of a team promoting a new app that would supposedly make workouts easier by planning and monitoring routines. It would also integrate seamlessly with the gym equipment, running on the newly functional RePHleX network. Tallis listened politely as the woman rattled off the app's features, but something about it made her uneasy.

When the woman finished her pitch, Tallis asked, "What kind of information is this app collecting and storing?"

"Oh, just the usual stuff," the employee replied. "You know, so it can personalize your training."

"The usual stuff?" Tallis repeated, her eyebrow arching. "You mean all the personal details about our activities all day, every day—like the old app?"

The young woman's expression faltered, her confidence crumbling under Tallis' scrutiny. She couldn't have been more than 18, and it was clear to Tallis that she'd grown up in a world where handing over personal data was just the norm, where most people didn't think twice about it.

"I'm sorry," Tallis said, softening her tone. "This isn't about you. But why would we just go back to giving all our information to an app, or company, or network that's only going to use it to manipulate us?"

Before the woman could respond, a voice from behind her cut in, "Right!"

Tallis turned slightly and saw a man who had just entered, nodding in agreement. He didn't seem familiar, but he shared her skepticism.

The employee stammered, "It's just information... and it's a free app."

"Thanks, but no thanks," Tallis said, walking away.

As she made her way to the lockers, she noticed a man walking toward her—the same man she'd told to forget their last encounter. He must have overheard her conversation, because as he passed by, he muttered under his breath, "You really are a bitch."

Tallis stopped, eyes narrowing. She wasn't going to let this slide. "Asshole," she said loudly, turning to face him. "Call me a bitch again, and you'll see just how much of a bitch I can be."

The man's face flushed with anger, but as he took in Tallis' defiant stance and the eyes of everyone in the gym on him, he backed down. "Sorry," he mumbled, before disappearing into the locker room.

Tallis shook her head, letting out a slow breath. She wasn't about to let some jerk ruin her day. As she worked through her routine, she noticed several people in the gym discussing the app. Some were eager to try it, hopeful it would help them regain some semblance of their old routines. Others, like her, were wary, hesitant to trust anything connected to RePHleX. Then there were the frustrated ones—the people angry that their old apps and data were still inaccessible.

"You made the right call with that app," a man said as he caught her eye in the mirror. Tallis tensed, ready to brush

him off, but there was something about his demeanor that
made her pause.

He walked over, pulling out a pad. "I saw this last
night—thought you'd find it interesting." He handed it to
her.

On the screen was a long list of companies,
subsidiaries, and partner organizations tied to RePHleX.
Tallis skimmed the list briefly, before handing the pad back.

"The company behind that gym app? It's on there,"
he said, shaking his head. "That girl you were talking to?
That's my daughter."

Tallis blinked, taken aback. "Oh… I'm sorry," she
said, glancing at him more closely now. He was older, maybe
mid-50s. "I didn't mean to upset her."

The man shook his head. "You didn't do anything
wrong. Trust me, you were a lot kinder than most. People
just… forgot how to talk to each other. RePHleX smoothed
out all the rough edges, filtered out the conflict. But now…
it's like my kids don't know how to function without an app
telling them what to do."

Tallis nodded. "It's been there their whole lives. Even
my generation barely remembers a world before the
network."

"Yeah," the man said, his tone resigned. "Anyway,
sorry to interrupt your workout. I guess I just needed to
vent."

Tallis offered him a kind smile. "No need to
apologize. Thanks for showing me that list."

As the man walked away, Tallis felt a surprising sense
of connection. She had assumed he was just another guy
trying to hit on her, but instead, she had shared a moment of
real conversation—something that felt increasingly rare in a
world still struggling to find its footing. It was small, but it
was enough to lift her mood as she returned to her workout,

content that today, she'd made a difference. Even if it was just listening.

After her workout, Tallis had some errands to run. She hadn't spent much time out of her apartment since discovering Eryx had moved out and disappeared himself. She had monitored the rapidly changing world outside her apartment through her social media feed. While the content now seemed more grounded after the RePHIeX rollback, she still didn't trust it. It felt like the feed was being tailored to her yet again. But with her cupboards bare and her fridge empty, she had no choice but to go out and restock. She also had a few ideas on how to make her apartment feel more like her home.

Her apartment's central location allowed her to walk everywhere, and for once, she was glad to avoid public transit. The streets offered a glimpse of the city's new reality and what was actually happening, not just what the algorithms wanted her to see. Everywhere she turned, stores were promoting "free" apps and digital tools that promised to make life easier. Street vendors hawked new social platforms, branding them as "decentralized" and "free." But across from nearly every promoter was an activist, warning passersby not to fall into the same digital traps they had just escaped. These activists had earned the moniker "echo breakers."

Tallis found a seat by the window in a nearby coffee shop, curious to see how the public was reacting to this strange new world. Outside, a group of echo breakers had set up across from some young people promoting a new social media app. Tallis studied the app's logo and interface from afar. It looked oddly familiar, like something from her past. After a moment, it clicked—she had used an almost identical app in junior high to chat with her friends. The young promoters were touting it as their own creation, which maybe it was, but it reminded her of how bell-bottom jeans were always being rebranded as the latest fashion trend, despite their origins in the 1970s and their resurgence in the early 2000s. This was nothing new.

But what caught her attention more than the app was the echo breakers standing across from the promoters. They were vocal, gathering attention as they condemned the app's data-collecting practices and warned of its hidden dangers. Yet what made Tallis pause was their pitch—they weren't just tearing down the app. They were promoting their own alternative, an "ethical" social media platform. From her vantage point, it was clear that the echo breakers weren't really activists at all. They were simply competing marketers, trying to sell their own version of digital dependency, using fear as their hook.

Tallis considered calling them out. Their tactics felt wrong—manipulative and exploitative, the kind of opportunism she despised. But as she sipped her coffee and watched the people interacting with both groups, she decided against it. She was exhausted. Activism had been her life for so long—first in high school, then in university, where she had thrown herself into the causes of data sovereignty and digital autonomy. Eryx had been right there with her, helping her focus and channel her passion into something productive. They had fought side by side, believing they could make a difference.

Now, sitting alone, watching this cycle of manipulation play out yet again, she felt a wave of disillusionment. No matter what she and others like her did, people would always give away their privacy, their autonomy, if they thought it would make their lives just a little bit easier. It was a hard truth to swallow, but it was one she could no longer ignore.

Home for the day, Tallis relaxed on her couch with a cup of tea, replacing the glass of wine that had been a constant companion since Eryx left. On a whim, she decided to reach out to some old friends from university. Distance and time had kept them apart, but they were all linked to her social media, though she rarely saw any posts from them. She dropped a few of them a message just saying hi and mentioning it would be nice to reconnect.

She then switched over to the newsfeed. Pre-rollback the newsfeed had been incorporated in the social media feed, but two days after the rollback, the newsfeed was separated out. This had been done under the direction of the government, according to that feed itself. "This is a vital step in ensuring factual news is separated from speculation and conspiracy," the statement from the President had said. Of course nobody ever said who was deciding what was "factual news."

Much of the news feed was filled with information surrounding the United States nationalizing the network. Steps had already been taken to expropriate at least one of RePHleX's server farms. For the U.S. government to take this action, the rollback of RePHleX must have raised a lot of red flags, because for decades the government had been adamant about privatizing everything.

Tea finished, Tallis stood in her bedroom, hands on her hips, surveying the space. It felt cramped, cluttered with old memories and too many things that no longer fit her life. Eryx's old den had been sitting empty for long enough, and she'd finally decided it was time to reclaim it. One by one, she pulled the clothes from her small wardrobe, the hangers clattering together in a hollow chorus. Her hands worked methodically, but her thoughts wandered.

There was something satisfying about clearing out the clutter, moving it to a new space. The bedroom felt lighter with each item removed, more open, less weighed down. It reminded her of the way people were trying to reclaim their own mental spaces, their lives, after the rollback of RePHleX. They had lived with the system for so long, just like her clothes had crowded her room, that they didn't even realize how much it had hemmed them in. But now, with RePHleX gone, there was room to breathe. Or there could be, if they found the right way to make use of it.

She hauled the last armful of clothes into the den, feeling the weight of the fabric and memories shift. Turning the den into a walk-in closet was practical, sure, but it was more than that. It was a transformation, a redefinition of space that hadn't served a purpose in so long. And wasn't that what everyone was doing now? Trying to take the empty spaces left by RePHleX, the gaps in their routines, and figure out how to fill them? Some were stuffing those spaces with new apps and platforms, eager to replace the void with anything that felt familiar, no matter how it crowded their lives again. Others, like Tallis, were choosing to rearrange things differently, creating a bigger, more comfortable version of life that didn't need to be packed so tightly.

The metaphor played out in her mind as she stacked shoes in neat rows and hung up her jackets in the makeshift closet. Just as she was expanding her space, people were expanding their horizons, figuring out what life could look like without a constant feed of digital noise. The question was, would they let the new clutter pile up again, or would they take the chance to spread out and enjoy the newfound freedom?

23

Aria and Kaidan stood at the edge of the lake, where the stillness of the water was slowly giving way to the first thin layer of ice. The early freeze shimmered like glass, fragile and translucent, catching the soft morning light. Along the shoreline, the ice crept outward, delicate and tentative, like it was testing the waters. Some parts of the ice remained so thin that the dark turquoise beneath was visible, while other areas had already thickened into a more opaque, frosted layer. In the center, the water remained free, untouched, holding onto the last moments of autumn before winter's full grip took hold.

"We're coming back soon, right?" Aria asked softly, leaning into Kaidan, who had wrapped his arms tightly around her to ward off the morning chill.

Kaidan's breath hung in the air as he spoke. "We should talk to your dad about staying here through winter. If he thinks it's doable, then yeah, we'll be back."

Reluctantly, they tore themselves away from the peaceful scene, taking one last walk through the cabin.

Kaidan closed the shutters, while Aria made sure all the food supplies were safely stored away and the fire in the fireplace was fully out. They weren't bringing anything back with them except for the couple of film canfisters Aria wanted to try and get developed, and the few pieces of electronic gear that had travelled with them. Everything else was left behind, preserved in the stillness of the cabin. Aria's gown still hung from the rafters and her painting rested on the mantle over the fireplace.

Once settled in the AEV, Kaidan said, "Return home," and the vehicle silently started its journey back to civilization. The transition from the quiet of the cabin to the smooth hum of the electric vehicle felt jarring, but Kaidan and Aria watched in silence as the wilderness around them passed by, serene and untouched by the chaos they would soon return to. They saw fresh animal tracks in the snow, branches bouncing back as the vehicle nudged through, dislodging small clumps of snow that floated to the ground.

It was peaceful. Until it wasn't.

Suddenly, alarms blared, filling the quiet space with harsh, overlapping beeps and vibrations. Kaidan flinched, instinctively reaching for the control panel, but verbal commands to silence the noise went unacknowledged. Frustrated, he hit the kill switch, plunging the AEV into an eerie silence.

"What was that?" Aria asked, her voice tense.

Kaidan rubbed his temples. "We're good. It's probably just an error from sitting idle for too long."

Aria wasn't convinced. "Then why did it start now? We've been driving for a while."

Kaidan paused, thinking. "I think... we just drove back into network coverage. The AEV probably connected to the network and got a software update. Two weeks off-grid, and it wasn't ready for the newest version."

"Still doesn't explain why it's freaking out."

Kaidan sighed, resetting the kill switch and pressing the start button. The AEV hummed back to life, but the heads-up display didn't reappear. Instead, a small console screen flashed with error messages.

Autonomous mode unavailable. Please refer to operator manual.

This vehicle can only be operated by an operator trained and licensed to operate vehicles in driver-directed operation mode.

Confirm you understand this message and are trained to operate a vehicle in direct-driver operation mode by placing your fingerprint anywhere on this screen.

"Great." Kaidan muttered under his breath, frustration creeping into his voice.

Aria tried to lighten the mood. "You used to drive that old beater when we met, remember? We'll figure it out. Let's just find the manual."

They rummaged through the vehicle compartments, only to find a label on the dash. For convenience, your operator's manual can be found on the network. Submit a request to RePHleX and it will be made available.

Kaidan let out a laugh of disbelief. "You've got to be kidding me. RePHleX, show me the operator's manual for this vehicle."

No response.

"Of course," Kaidan said, rolling his eyes. "Can you get your pad?"

Aria retrieved her pad from her bag, but its battery was dead. She placed it on the charging pad in the console, and they watched as it powered up. As the screen flickered to life, it looked strange—outdated, as if it had reverted to a version from years ago.

"What the hell?" Kaidan tried again. "RePHleX, show me the manual."

This time, a message scrolled across the screen: That app is not compatible with the current version of the network.

Kaidan's patience snapped. "Fuck it," he said. "I can figure it out without the manual." He pressed his thumb on the AEV's display screen to initiate manual control. A red warning banner appeared across the top of the screen.

DRIVER-DIRECTED OPERATION MODE
INITIATING

You have confirmed you are licensed for manual vehicle operation.

Confirm with fingerprint.

Kaidan placed his finger on the screen and the red banner was replaced by a yellow banner.

CRITICAL SAFETY REMINDER

- You are fully responsible for vehicle operation

- No autonomous assistance will be available

- All collision avoidance systems will be passive only

- You must maintain full attention at all times

ACKNOWLEDGE by fingerprint.

Once more Kaiden placed his finger on the screen, though with a little more force as frustration set in.

REVERTING TO MANUAL CONTROLS:

✓ Steering wheel engaging

✓ Pedal sensitivity adjusting

✓ Manual gear selection active

✓ Mirror controls enabled

✓ Dashboard converting to standard display

[Please wait...]

Kaidan waited and listened to the vehicle he heard various motors and switches engage. An Orange banner appeared across the top of the screen.

FINAL VERIFICATION REQUIRED

Place hands on steering wheel

Press brake pedal

Look directly at driver monitoring camera

[System verifying operator position...]

In a few moments a green banner appeared at the top of the screen.

MANUAL MODE ENGAGED

Speed limit: 65 MPH

Current speed: 0 MPH

All manual controls active

Emergency assistance: Available via red button

Current location: Unavailable

Nearest manual-certified service centre: 260 miles

Finally, the vehicle transitioned into manual mode. The steering wheel engaged, pedals adjusted, and the dashboard transformed into a standard display. A cautionary message flashed across the bottom of the windshield: VEHICLE IN MANUAL OPERATION MODE – DRIVER FULLY RESPONSIBLE

Kaidan gripped the wheel and eased the AEV back onto the road. "This thing's designed to go off-grid, so why put the manual on the network?" he muttered.

Aria didn't answer. She was focused on her pad, which had finally loaded her messages and social media.

"Everything okay?" Kaidan asked, noticing her furrowed brow.

Aria glanced up, her voice tight. "Eryx left Tallis. Just... vanished. He abandoned her."

"What?" Kaidan's surprise quickly gave way to concern.

Aria kept reading, her fingers scrolling rapidly. "It's not just that. The world went to hell while we were at the cabin. We need to go straight to Tallis' place."

As they drove home, Aria read different posts and messages to Kaidan. Focused on driving, Kadian had trouble taking it all in. He found himself wondering if he could still get to all of the music he created and do his work. The five-hour drive back, considerably slower than their drive out to the cabin, went by without them noticing the time pass as they learned about the world they were returning to.

On the surface the city didn't appear all that different as they drove into it. It felt different, but Kaidan wondered if that was because he was physically driving a car through the city for the first time in years. Aria barely glanced around, her eyes still focused on her pad.

"I need you to navigate, babe," said Kaidan. Thankfully the map display had begun functioning as they got into the city. "I need to pay attention to driving with all these other people driving around us. Can you tell me when to turn."

Aria stashed her pad back in her bag and turned her attention to the map. "We stay on this main road for a bit yet."

When they finally pulled up in front of Tallis' apartment building, Kaidan was mentally exhausted and happy to be out of the vehicle. "Return to base." Kaidan said as the AEV door shut behind him. He had to step quickly to catch up to Aria who was already heading in the building doors.

Tallis was surprised by the knock on her door, but she was more surprised when Aria burst through before she had the door fully open and threw her arms around her.

"My Dad still has guns," said Aria. "And we can bury his body at the cabin. Nobody will miss him. Nobody will find him."

Tallis laughed a genuine laugh as she hugged her friend back. She looked over Aria's shoulder where Kaidan was standing back, watching. He gave her a gentle wave.

"We have a witness to our plan," said Tallis.

Aria turned to face Kaidan. "Him? He knows there's a hole out there for him too if he crosses me."

Tallis laughed a genuine, heart-felt laugh. "I have missed you, girl. How long have you been back?"

"Wine first," insisted Aria as she dragged Tallis by the hand to the couch, motioning to Kaiden to get them wine. Kaidan understood and fetched the two of them a large glass of wine.

Thinking it better to give Aria and Tallis some time to talk alone, Kaidan decided to let himself into Eryx den. He was momentarily stunned when he opened the door. Gone was the desk with the glowing desktop computer that had been on it. There were no shelves with computer games, or old computers and toys on the walls. He found himself in a completely transformed room.

The first thing that struck him was the soft lighting, which was much easier on the eyes than the light from the glowing computer hardware. The walls were painted in soothing tones of sage green and pale cream, giving the room a calm, almost spa-like atmosphere.

Rows of sleek, minimalist shelving lined one wall, each neatly filled with carefully arranged clothes. Jackets, dresses, and scarves hung in perfect order, their colors transitioning smoothly from one to the next, creating a subtle rainbow effect. On the opposite side, built-in drawers and compartments held folded sweaters, shoes, and accessories, all organized with an attention to detail that made Kaidan blink.

Where Eryx's old workstation had been there was now a full-length mirror, bordered by soft, white lights. Tallis had clearly invested time in making this space her own. Beneath the mirror lay a plush, cream-colored rug that looked impossibly soft, and a low bench sat nearby, inviting someone to sit down and try on shoes or just take a moment to breathe.

The air, too, was different. Instead of the stale scent of electronics, there was a faint hint of lavender, probably from a diffuser sitting on a small side table. The space felt intentional, curated. A retreat within the apartment that was hers and hers alone.

"Wow," Kaidan muttered, taking it all in. "This is... not what I expected."

Tallis appeared behind him, a small smile tugging at the corner of her lips. "Yeah, I needed the space. It felt weird to leave it empty, like it was waiting for him to come back." She walked in and ran her fingers over the neatly arranged clothes, her expression thoughtful. "I wanted something that felt more... me."

Aria pushed past Kaiden into Tallis' walk-in closet. "This is beautiful! You never would have known you had this many clothes."

Tallis laughed. "Oh, I didn't. I made the space mine. Put my stuff in. Then realized it was too empty, so I spoiled myself."

"Shopping, the universal cure all to erase men from your mind," said Aria as she held out her fist, Tallis eagerly returning the fist bump.

"I need my own glass of wine," said Kaidan as he walked away, listening to Aria and Tallis giggling in the closet.

The three of them sat for the afternoon, and into the early hours of the morning as Tallis told them about everything that had happened while they were at the cabin. They only stopped to fill their plates with food and snacks Tallis had ordered in, and to refill their wine glasses. Both of them had found much of the story unbelievable.

They were shocked to learn that while they were going through their bonding ceremony as the harvest moon ushered in a new cycle, the world was going through a break-up with the reality that had been created around them. In the way the rising harvest moon shone reflected the setting sun's rays on the dark side of the world, the ImCast reflected back the unspoken fears of those living in the digital world. The scarf that was the symbol of the bond sealed between Kaidan and Aria was mirrored in the digital realm as a bullet symbolized the shattered relationship with society and RePHleX.

They struggled to understand why RePHleX had rolled back to a six-year old version of itself. It made no sense to either of them, but as Tallis explained how in ten days they went from a society in chaos to where they were now, it began to make sense.

"It's like every three or four days we move a year closer to where we were before the KaelerCast…yeah they have given it a name," explained Tallis. "But all the new apps," said Tallis making air quotes, "are being marketed under the names of new companies, and people are falling for it. They are getting sucked right back into the Echosfear as they surrender their data for convenience."

"There's the digital autonomy warrior I know," said Aria.

"Fuck that!" said Tallis, sounding almost angry. "Digital autonomy, data-sovereignty…all that activist shit went out the door with Eryx."

Tallis refilled her wine glass, emptying the bottle.

"You know who I am now. You know that guy that would show up at parties. The one that always looked like he didn't belong there, or he had been dragged there by someone." Tallis was speaking as much with her hands as her voice. "He never drank. Never did drugs. And he saw everything. If you wanted to know the stories and the dirt on what really happened at the party and what people did, he had it. That's me."

Tallis finished the wine in her glass in a big gulp and stared at her empty glass. "Okay, maybe not sober…but I am standing on the edge of the party watching as everybody drinks the punch."

Aria took Tallis' wine glass out of her hand and handed it to Kaidan along with her own. "Coffee time I think."

Kaidan made his way to the kitchen, a little tipsy himself, to make coffee. By the time he returned with the coffees, Aria and Tallis had stumbled into the bedroom and were both crashed on top of the bed spread. Kaidan found a blanket for each of them and stole a pillow from the bed for himself to make the couch more comfortable.

Lawrence Nault

24

"It's the window," said Tallis. She had been standing and watching Kaidan shift his head from side to side as he looked out the window to the street below. "No matter how often I clean it, the world outside it always looks a little distorted."

"I didn't know you were up," Kaidan said, glancing at her, then quickly turning back to look out the window.

"Just now," Tallis replied, her voice groggy. "And my head isn't too happy about it."

She padded over to Kaidan, wrapping her arms around him in an unexpected hug. Kaidan wasn't quite sure how to respond. "Sorry I stole your bed-mate last night. Hope you weren't too cold out here," she apologized softly. "I don't know if you know how happy you made her, staying that second week."

"I will make coffee," said Kaiden, seeking a reason to divert his attention. "Assuming you are going to be up long enough to drink it this time."

"I will assume my hangover position on the couch," replied Tallis. "How long have you been up anyways?"

"No idea," said Kaidan. "Woke up, started looking at the social media feed, and the news feed...that's new." Kaidan placed the cup of cold coffee he had made Tallis last night, into the multi-frequency rapid cooker. "I see what you meant by nothing really changing." The MFRC dinged and Kaidan grabbed the coffee and brought it to Tallis.

"None of it is branded RePHleX, but you can see all these apps asking for the same data and echoing back everything you say. It isn't obvious but they have already started manipulating people again," said Kaidan as he sat down on the far end of the couch from Tallis.

"Like that window you were looking through," said Tallis. "No matter how many times you clean it, the world on the other side always looks a little warped.

Kaidan tossed her the blanket he had used the night before. "You might want to cover-up."

Tallis glanced down, realizing she was only wearing panties. "Did you undress me last night?"

"You woke up in the middle of the night complaining you were melting.

Tallis and Kaidan turned to see Aria standing there. Kaidan's face flushed a little with embarrassment.

"Took you all of five seconds to strip your clothes off before you crashed back in bed and started snoring."

Tallis turned to Kaidan. "And you waited until now to tell me."

"Uh…" Kaidan stuttered and his already red face turned a darker shade of red. "I went to the kitchen, and I gave you the blanket…"

Tallis burst into laughter, and Aria joined in. "You live with the original nature girl, and you're embarrassed about seeing my tits?" Tallis teased, shaking her head as she reached for her coffee.

The laughter didn't ease Kaidan's embarrassment, but he had to admit to himself that Tallis wasn't wrong. Aria joined them on the couch, her head in Kaidan's lap and her legs stretched out over Tallis' lap. She grabbed the blanket from Tallis, leaving her breasts exposed again, and pulled it over herself. Tallis just shrugged her shoulders and sipped her coffee. Kaidan rolled his eyes but made an effort to keep them away from Tallis. His gaze landed on a paper brochure sitting on the side table. He picked it up. "What's 'Syneryxion'?"

"That is a new network," said Tallis. "Owned by the government, not privatized like RePHleX."

Kaidan scanned the brochure "The next-gen streamlined network platform" was how Syneryxion billed itself.

"I am getting it installed here next week," said Tallis. "I will run both side by side for a while."

Something about the name gnawed at him. "RePHleX, tell me about Syneryxion Digital Environments."

There was a pause, then articles about Syneryxion scrolled across the display, each painting the company in a negative light. If Kaidan had any doubt that Echosfear still had its fingers in the network, this was proof.

As he read the articles, Tallis glanced at the screen. "What's wrong?"

Kaidan froze, staring at a picture of the CEO of Syneryxion meeting the U.S. President. The name under the image was Carden Thorne, but the man was unmistakably Eryx.

Tallis jumped up, knocking Aria off the couch in her haste. "Son of a bitch!"

"Hey!" Aria protested, climbing back up.

Tallis didn't notice. She was staring at the screen in disbelief. "Tallis…" Kaidan held up the brochure, his fingers covering the 'Syn' and 'ion,' leaving only the embedded 'Eryx.' "It's him."

She paced the room, her bare chest forgotten, as she tried to make sense of this in her mind. Aria picked herself up off the floor, practically sitting in Kaidan's lap as she sat on the couch, giving him a bit of an elbow in the ribs as she did. Kaidan got the not-so-subtle message and focused on the brochure instead of Tallis.

"He didn't just do this overnight," she muttered. "All that time we were together, and he was building this behind my back."

Tallis stopped her pacing and looked at the picture on her screen. "He pulled me into this life, fighting against RePHleX and Echosfear!" Her voice grew more and more furious. "He fucking used me to recruit people in his fight, and his fight was never to make the world better, but to make room for him to be part of the goddamn problem."

Her voice cracked, and her pacing slowed as she struggled to hold back tears. "How could I be so stupid? How! How! So fucking stupid."

Aria stood, wrapped her arm around Tallis, and gently guided her into the bedroom, shutting the door behind them.

Kaidan sat there, feeling both relieved and awkward. It was hard not to notice Tallis' exposed body, but harder still to ignore the raw emotions. He wanted to help, to fix something, but he had no idea where to start. Instead, he focused on cleaning up the empty wine bottles and dishes from the previous night's late-night conversations.

As Kaidan cleaned up the room, his mind wandered back to Syneryxion. RePHleX wasn't about to offer any real answers, and the brochure they provided had been little more than a collection of catchy buzzwords and flashy graphics— just enough to snag someone's attention without saying anything substantial. It felt oddly quaint for the digital age, and that's probably what had caught his eye. He would've asked Eryx about it; together, they could have combed through the old internet, digging for hidden truths. But there was no Eryx anymore. That led Kaidan to an unsettling question—how much of what Eryx had shown him had ever been real?

Sitting in a chair, coffee in hand, Kaidan leafed through a book he'd found on the shelf, the quiet hum of his thoughts broken only when Tallis stepped out of her room.

As Kaidan cleaned up the room, his mind wandered back to Syneryxion. RePHleX wasn't about to offer any real answers, and the brochure they provided had been little more than a collection of catchy buzzwords and flashy graphics—just enough to snag someone's attention without saying anything substantial. It felt oddly quaint for the digital age, and that's probably what had caught his eye. He would've asked Eryx about it; together, they could have combed through the old internet, digging for hidden truths. But there was no Eryx anymore. That led Kaidan to an unsettling question—how much of what Eryx had shown him had ever been real?

Sitting in a chair, coffee in hand, Kaidan leafed through a book he'd found on the shelf, the quiet hum of his thoughts broken only when Tallis stepped out of her room.

"Wow, two weeks changed you," she teased, eyeing the book in his hands. "A book when the network's right there?"

Kaidan reluctantly lifted his eyes from the pages and glanced at her, surprised by her appearance.

"Yes, I'm fully dressed," Tallis said with a playful grin. "So, you can look at me when you talk now."

Kaidan's face flushed as he let out a nervous laugh.

"I owe you an apology," Tallis said after a pause, her tone softening. "I wasn't quite right in the head when I got up this morning, and it only got worse." She paused for a moment. "Truth is I haven't been quite right since that asshole left. But that is no excuse. I know it was an uncomfortable situation with just you and I out here, and me hugging you, naked. I already apologized to Aria, but I wanted to tell you I'm sorry too."

Kaidan smiled, his voice gentle. "It's all good."

Tallis shook her head. "No, but thanks for saying it. Really."

She glanced around the room. "And thanks for cleaning up, too. Arias in the shower. I'm gonna make us some lunch."

Before long, Aria emerged, met by Kaidan's soft smile. She walked over, bent down, and kissed him on the cheek. "You two okay?" she whispered.

"We're good, babe. Sorry about everything."

"I'm not mad," Aria replied with a smirk. "She has great boobs, and I was looking too."

Kaidan chuckled as Aria wandered into the kitchen to help Tallis. They ate lunch at the counter, casually planning the rest of their day. It was Aria's idea to head to Kaidan's apartment; she didn't want to leave Tallis alone just yet, and Tallis was grateful for the company.

The walk through the city was a surprise for both Kaidan and Aria. When they'd left, the streets had been full of people rushing, heads buried in devices, always five minutes late to somewhere. Now, people moved slower, stopping to talk to one another—sometimes even arguing in the open. The city felt more alive, chaotic but real in a way it hadn't before.

When they arrived at Kaidan's apartment, the screens flickered on as usual, but only one displayed anything. Aria and Tallis stood back, watching as Kaidan tried to access his workspace, opening the apps he used for work. He searched for the music he'd created over the years, but nothing came up. Aria braced herself, expecting him to snap at any moment. But he didn't.

"I don't think I need this apartment anymore," Kaidan said calmly, though his eyes betrayed the frustration simmering beneath the surface.

Aria's heart sank, imagining how she would feel if her work had just vanished like that. It was hard enough for her to part with a piece she'd sold, let alone losing everything.

"You don't have to decide that today," she offered gently.

"I already decided at the cabin," Kaidan replied. "There's no point keeping a high-tech apartment with low-tech capabilities when we have our home."

Just then, Kaidan's little robot dog nudged his leg, silently seeking attention. He picked it up and turned to Tallis. "How about some company in your place? Easy to keep, no mess, and he's obedient."

Tallis hesitated. "You should keep him."

"He won't work at the cabin, and I think we'll be spending most of our time there. Besides, you can train him."

"Fine," Tallis relented, cradling the robot dog in her hands. "But you have visiting rights."

Kaidan smiled, then took one last look around the apartment before closing the door behind him. "Not much left, but I'll come back to clean it out before I give notice."

"Oh, I know someone who can help with that," Tallis said, a hint of excitement in her voice. "Randy—the guy who moved from Aria's building to mine. The rollback left him without a job, and he could use the cash. He won't take handouts, though."

"I'll pay him for the work," Kaidan nodded.

They took their time walking back to Aria's, with Tallis drawing curious looks as people noticed the robot dog poking its head out of her backpack, paws resting on her shoulder like a sentry. Its eyes seemed to scan the surroundings, and though it opened its mouth as if to bark, no sound came out.

"You'll be happy to know AeroDrone Rush isn't operational yet," Tallis remarked as they passed the gym.

"What a tragedy," Kaidan said, dripping with sarcasm.

Almost back to Aria's, something caught Kaidan's eye in a store window. Without a word, he quickly pulled Aria and Tallis into a nearby café, guiding them to a table. "Get yourselves a drink. I'll be back in a bit."

He didn't even give them time to ask what he was doing before he was back out the door and crossing the street. He stopped in front of a consignment store that he had probably walked past hundreds of times if not more, and never noticed until today.

Before they could ask why, Kaidan was out the door, crossing the street. He stopped in front of a consignment store he must have passed hundreds of times but had never really noticed.

Hanging in the window of the consignment shop was a sleek, curved-back acoustic guitar with a design that instantly evoked a bygone era. Its body had a deep, amber-to-black sunburst finish, the glossy top showing subtle signs of age, with small scuffs and faint clouding in the lacquer. The rounded, composite back, a futuristic material when it first came out, still had its distinct shape, the matte black finish blending seamlessly with the soft lines of the guitar.

Instead of a traditional single sound hole, there were several smaller, oval-shaped ones arranged in intricate patterns along the upper bout, giving it a unique, almost futuristic look that was ahead of its time when the guitar was new. The metallic rims around the sound holes were dull and slightly tarnished, evidence of years spent in someone's hands before landing here in the shop.

The neck, a dark wood, likely rosewood or something similar, had visible grooves worn into the frets from years of playing. The headstock, with its minimalist design, sported a slightly chipped logo, long since faded, but unmistakably from a high-end maker.

Kaidan stepped into the store and headed straight for the guitar, carefully lifting it down from the hooks it was hanging from. A hand-scrawled tag hung from one of the tuning pegs. "Curved-back acoustic—$500 OBO," it read.

"Just came in this morning," the young store clerk said from behind the counter. "That's the case over there, even has some of the original paperwork inside. Not sure if it's worth much, but the owner priced it high, so…"

The case for the guitar was as much a relic as the instrument itself. It had a hard, molded shell, scuffed and faded from years of travel, with a dark gray, almost charcoal color that had dulled over time. The latches were rusted but still functional, clicking open with a metallic creak that filled the air with a sense of anticipation. As the lid was lifted, a faint musty scent escaped. It had the aroma of old wood, aged leather, and forgotten melodies.

Inside, the case was lined with plush red velvet, worn down to a thin layer in some spots, especially where the guitar's body had rested for countless years. The indent of the instrument was still visible, an outline that had been shaped by years of cradling the guitar. But it wasn't empty.

On top of the faded velvet lay a small stack of guitar lesson books, their covers yellowed and edges curled with time. The top book had a faded, cartoonish drawing of a guitar on the front, with bold letters reading "Learn to Play in 30 Days!" Beneath it, the spines of other books poked out, some with titles about fingerstyle playing or mastering chord progressions, their pages dog-eared from heavy use. A couple of torn sheet music pages peeked out from the stack, covered in penciled notes, chords, and the occasional scribble of personal reminders.

Nestled in one of the case's accessory compartments was an old-school, clip-on guitar tuner, its plastic body scuffed, the screen cloudy from wear. It was a relic from a time before tuners had been integrated into every digital device, still carrying the charm of a simpler era.

Kaidan placed the guitar gently in its case, removing the price tag before closing it. He handed the price tag to the clerk.

"You're not even going to haggle?" the young man asked, surprised.

"Worth every cent to me," Kaidan replied.

When he returned to the café, Aria and Tallis were deep in conversation, not even noticing him until he sat down with a grin and set the guitar case on the empty chair beside him. He opened it, revealing the guitar inside.

"That's beautiful," Aria said.

"I know, right?" Kaidan's excitement was infectious. "It even comes with old lesson books and a tuner."

"Look at you, old-school!" Tallis teased. "I never pictured you with an antique acoustic. But it is beautiful."

Kaidan gently closed the case. "I have an idea…" Kaidan was bursting with excitement, his eyes wide and hands gesturing animatedly as he shared his idea with Aria and Tallis. He knew Aria wanted to keep her gallery open. He needed a new space to create his music in, and there were still open shops on the main floor of Tallis' building. He wanted to set up his music studio there, and by music studio, he didn't mean one like in his apartment. He wanted a blend of the past and future: a space that could honor the era when his newly acquired guitar would have been in use, while also incorporating his modern, AI-driven setup.

But that was just the start. His plan also involved opening a café right next to the music studio. Half of the café would be a network-free zone, where people could unplug from the digital noise, while the other half would offer access to both RePHleX and Syneryxion, giving visitors the chance to experience both extremes. In the unplugged section, Kaidan envisioned a small recording booth where anyone could step in and record their own songs, capturing a moment of pure, personal expression.

"Picture it," Kaidan said, his excitement spilling over. "Your gallery in this heritage building, Aria…people could literally walk from a disconnected space in your gallery to hyperconnected on the other side of the café. Old school to new school, analogue to AI. You'd have your gallery. I'd have my studio, and I could leave my work at the end of the day instead of being stuck in my apartment. And Tallis, you'd have a place to people-watch and interact. Everyone wins."

Kaidan snatched Aria's drink, took a sip, and scrunched his face in disgust before handing it back with a playful grimace. "Oh, and we could involve Randy and his family! They need work since the RePHleX rollback, right? They could help keep the gallery open while we're at the cabin, or run the café."

When Kaidan finally paused, Aria and Tallis just stared at him, exchanging looks. He glanced between them, waiting nervously for a reaction.

"I'm sorry," Tallis said with mock seriousness, looking at Aria. "I think the real Kaidan must've been abducted by aliens while you were out in the mountains."

Aria played along. "I didn't see any UFOs, but maybe a brain-eating parasite crawled up his... you-know-what when he was in the lake."

Kaidan's face fell, his enthusiasm dimming for a moment, unsure if he'd gotten carried away. Then, unable to hold their straight faces any longer, Aria and Tallis burst into giggles.

"Alien, parasite, or just fresh mountain air—it doesn't matter," Tallis said, still laughing. "You really have changed since you disconnected, and I love every bit of this idea. It's perfect. It gives me something meaningful to do, and it helps Randy and his family too."

"I think it's brilliant," Aria added, her smile full of warmth.

25

The six of them met in person for the first time since they'd conceived the Echosfear. This gathering was a rarity, and one they wouldn't risk now if their security protocols hadn't failed so catastrophically.

RePHleX was back to its pre-KaelerCast levels, even surpassing them. Newly branded apps and "competitors" (all quietly owned by Echosfear) had been rapidly adopted, as society rushed back to the conveniences Kaeler's revelations had briefly disrupted. Ironically, RePHleX's rollback presented an even greater opportunity for Echosfear to deepen its influence over users' lives.

But their continuity plan had overlooked two crucial factors. First, they hadn't anticipated how many people would discover they felt better, even more efficient, when disconnected. As people spent more time offline, Echosfear's influence weakened, its algorithms unable to target them with the same precision. While the general belief was that these "dropouts" would eventually be forced back as connectivity became essential again, the immediate drop in engagement was concerning.

The second, more troubling oversight was Syneryxion. Echosfear had assumed they held enough sway over governments to stifle any competition. They were wrong. Worse, they'd lost control over crucial data used to maintain leverage over these figures of power. During the RePHleX rollback, sensitive information had mysteriously vanished. This data, integral to their blackmail and influence, had simply disappeared. They still didn't know who had taken it, but without it, their grip on governments was slipping.

Now, the U.S. government had broken free, building a separate network and even seizing Echosfear's Alaska server farm. This breach emboldened the government to draft legislation, demanding Echosfear share all remaining data or be banned from operating in the U.S. altogether. Other nations were watching closely, ready to follow suit.

Their once impenetrable empire was unraveling, and they had no idea how to stop it. This is why they were gathered around this table today. In front of each of them, a report, on paper, with all the available information on Syneryxion, which wasn't much. The company had existed for eight years and was privately held, which meant there were few legal requirements to post information on its operations for the public to view or government to monitor. It had reported a ten to fifteen percent profit margin on all its tax submissions, carried no debt listed with any banks or finance companies, and based on banking records had a large cash reserve.

"Did you read the mission statement?" sneered Rhett Sylas. "Biggest load of horse crap you will find. They bullshit better than we do." He read aloud:

"Our vision at Syneryxion is to redefine the digital landscape by creating a world where connection empowers, privacy is a right, and individuals control

284

their own digital destinies. We aspire to build a network that transcends traditional boundaries, fostering innovation and collaboration without sacrificing transparency or security. By leading the shift toward decentralized, ethical technology, we aim to shape a future where humanity thrives in harmony with the digital world, free from the limitations of legacy systems and unchecked corporate influence."

"At Syneryxion, our mission is to empower individuals and organizations by providing a transparent, secure, and decentralized digital ecosystem that fosters true connectivity without compromising privacy or freedom. We are committed to creating a network environment where users maintain control over their data and experience, offering innovative solutions that enhance communication, collaboration, and creativity in a rapidly evolving digital world. Our vision is to build a future where technology serves humanity, promoting a balanced coexistence between the digital and the physical, free from exploitation and manipulation."

Levi Drexler, a venture capitalist at the helm of Echosfear, shook his head. "Sounds like the same bullshit Kaeler proposed before she disappeared. They destabilize our network just to come in and do exactly what we are doing."

Victor Orin, Echosfear's political strategist, studied the image of Syneryxion's enigmatic founder, Carden Thorne. "Some of our staff swear this man once worked for us, but we can't find any record of him in our files or databases. No pictures, no employment history."

"If someone can make our most secure data disappear, erasing an employee's existence is child's play," said Rhett Sylas.

Levi clenched his jaw. "We hired the best minds. How the hell are they unable to figure this out?"

"That's our fault," said Damien Claye.

Levi fixed him with a glare. "Explain."

"Everyone who works for us is under the Echosfear's influence. More so than the average user, they're fed constant validation by the algorithm, living ideal lives we engineered. They were the best minds in the world, but we've made them incapable of independent thought. They're exactly what we wanted them to be," Damien said, pushing his folder into the center of the table with Carden's photo on top. "But not him. Thorne doesn't have walls around him. He sees challenges, finds solutions. We need people like him to counter people like him."

"We are people like him," countered Soren Kalev.

Damien shook his head. "We were, once. But now we're surrounded by money, power, and control. We haven't lived in his world since the Echosfear began. We're looking through rose-colored, stained-glass windows from our high towers, while he's down there, slogging through the trenches."

They fell silent, faced with the uncomfortable truth. Echosfear's algorithms kept their users boxed in, and a team existed solely to pull those who strayed back in.

"If you're suggesting what I think you are, it's not happening," said Levi. "We can find people working outside Echosfear, but if we give them full access, we'll lose control."

"Signal noise," offered Caldon.

"Fuck Signal Noise," Levi scoffed. "They died with that bitch. We haven't heard a thing from them since the KaelerCast."

Caldon leaned forward. "But no one else knows that Signal Noise is gone. If we revive the idea of them, we can shift their message from fear of the Echosfear to support of Syneryxion, even encouraging other governments to follow the U.S. model."

Skeptical faces met his gaze, but Caldon pressed on. "We already planted the idea that Signal Noise was behind the RePHleX rollback. Now we frame it so Signal Noise supports Syneryxion and the government coalition, hand in hand. Then we stir the pot with the conspiracy people fear most…"

"Government. Fucking. Control," Rhett cut in, nodding. "It's perfect. The Echosfear algorithms were built to prey on people's fears, to turn them against whatever we need them to. We push Echosfear into the shadows while Syneryxion, Signal Noise, and government agencies become the new enemy."

Levi still wasn't convinced. "And what's to stop these governments from just following the message and doing what the U.S. did before we have the chance to turn people against them?"

Damien smirked. "The leverage we supposedly hold over everyone in power."

Levi's face tightened. "If we had that data, I'd be on a beach in Cuba, not at this damn meeting."

Damien leaned forward. "They don't know we don't have it. What they do know is our influence over the people. Whatever we say becomes truth in the Echosfear, so it doesn't matter if what we threaten them with is real or not…it becomes real in the Echosfear."

Lawrence Nault

26

Carden Thorne sat in an NSA situation room, watching as the Echosfear reacted just as he'd predicted to the U.S. government's move toward data independence. Through strategic persuasion, he had successfully convinced the government to establish its own autonomous network, ensuring control over its data to prevent RePHleX—or more specifically, Echosfear—from locking them out or reversing their progress again. What he could not convince them of was that Echosfear would ever allow its network to be used again to convince people not to use RePHleX. They couldn't see the big picture.

Carden had been preparing for this moment for years, knowing he'd only have a narrow window to act. While Echosfear and the public believed Syneryxion was the sole independent network poised to rival RePHleX, Echosfear couldn't see beyond its own projection bias. They assumed Syneryxion would follow the same model: a few powerful individuals attempting to exert control.

Unbeknownst to them, Carden had embedded AI agents within Echosfear's systems since his early days there, siphoning off small amounts of cryptocurrency and cash. The process was subtle, taking tiny sums from the billions of daily transactions, invisible to even the most sophisticated monitoring. This quietly amassed fortune funded Syneryxion's false profit margin for eight years, and more importantly, supported the creation of 28 other independent companies around the world, each a mirror of Syneryxion. All of these companies did the same thing Syneryxion did, but none of them were linked to each other in anyway, other than the people at the heads of those companies were all carefully handpicked and installed in their roles by his former self.

Now, as Echosfear unleashed black propaganda, spreading statements from Signal Noise that were in fact Echosfear's own fabrications, Carden watched calmly. The NSA situation room he was sitting in was a stark, almost austere environment designed for precision and efficiency. Rows of dimly lit monitors lined the room, each displaying a stream of encrypted data, geopolitical maps, and live intelligence feeds from operatives stationed worldwide. Large digital clocks lined the walls, marking time zones in capitals worldwide, an ever-present reminder of the global stakes. The room had an air of quiet intensity, with teams of analysts and high-ranking officials working in focused silence, heads bent over terminals and tablets.

Carden sat at a central console, flanked by screens that each held carefully vetted reports, risk assessments, and projections of potential alliances. Despite the room's cold sterility, his energy filled the space. His gaze was steely and unwavering, eyes darting between the maps of RePHleX's server strongholds and a sprawling schematic of the Echosfear network's architecture.

As stark as it was, this room was a step up from his dark windowless basement, where he was able to compile all this information that the NSA previously did not have access to. To those who knew the history of the NSA this would not have made any sense, but since the federal government had contracted out all networking and servers to private companies, the NSA was a shadow of its former self, dependent on what ReleX permitted them to see.

A sense of purpose gripped him and the others in this room. Every flicker of light on the console, every data point scrolled across the screens, was a step closer to dismantling the empire that once seduced them with the promise of global interconnectedness. The stakes had never been higher. RePHleX and the Echosfear weren't just technological adversaries; they were adversaries of freedom itself. Now that Carden had the U.S. government on board and their resources to work with, everything was in place to motivate other governments to take back their digital freedom.

For too long, people had been subjected to a distorted, algorithm-driven reality. Here, in the stark clarity of the NSA's war room, surrounded by others driven by the same determination, he could almost taste the liberation that lay just on the other side of the battle to come. Carden was not naive enough to believe everyone in the room was working to the same end as he was though. He knew that while they were there to "assist" allies in disconnecting from RePHleX and freeing them from the influence of Echosfear, there were those that had been tasked with embedding their own A.I. agents into the systems of their allies and other countries.

While the NSA supported Carden in the technical aspects of getting American allies disconnected from RePHleX (though they were confident he was supporting them), government leaders and bureaucrats leveraged their political influence. One of the key pieces of information they had was the fact that Carden had secured their own personal data from Echosfear, removing them from Echosfear's influence.

The chaos Ecosphere had caused by rolling back RePHleX created the opening. No one in government cared what the reason for the rollback was, just that it had revealed just how much control they had given up. Now the benefits of a decentralized, secure network independent of any corporate control, was a pitch all of these governments were willing to hear. With the U.S. leveraging its intelligence and diplomatic ties, Carden's real goal of getting all his mirror companies recruited to assist the countries they were in, was a simple job.

Echosfear expected that every government was at least discussing having their own independent network since the RePHleX rollback. They knew those discussions would increase as they pushed their black propaganda, boosting a message supposedly from Signal Noise for countries to make that move. They did not expect to be so successful that they would be facing black propaganda blowback before they even started their manufactured outrage cycle of their plan.

It was called the Kaeler Accord. A formal agreement between eighteen nations that outlined commitments from each country to establish a self-sufficient network for internal data sovereignty and security. They would allow non-sensitive, publicly accessible data to flow between networks, creating an interconnected yet independently governed ecosystem.

"This will be a network unlike any the world has ever seen," boasted the President of the United States, the leaders of the seventeen other countries standing behind him as they put on a show for the cameras. "An empowered digital era free from corporate or governmental manipulation. Each cosigner of this accord will implement uniform encryption standards and transparency policies for cross-network data

access backed by legislation around data sovereignty and
digital autonomy, as well as strictly regulating data mining and
digital surveillance."

The President spoke slow and deliberately. They were
broadcasting this speech over the new U.S. network, but they
had many teams working diligently to spread it over the
RePHleX network as well. This wasn't why the President was
delaying though. He was waiting for a signal in his ear,
relieved when it came.

"This dual focus on localized control and cooperative
connectivity offers an alternative to RePHleX's model, and
make no mistake RePHleX's model is the Echosfear. This is
not some conspiracy theory but a very real organization.
Right now, in a joint military operation, we have seized
control of four Echosfear server farms in addition to the ones
already in custody. We are also seeking the six men at the
helm of Echosfear for further questioning."

His words sent ripples through the global audience,
and among the political observers watching, one detail
became glaringly clear: missing from the gathering onstage
were leaders from two of the most influential countries—
Russia and China. Their absence was no accident.
Information Carden had managed to secure (and which no
one dared question) indicated that the earliest and most
substantial financial backing for Echosfear had come directly
from these two nations, which had quietly retained significant
influence over its leadership. As a result, Russia and China
hadn't been invited to the table. In fact, they'd been carefully
excluded from any negotiations or discussions about
disconnecting from RePHleX, leaving them on the outside of
the Kaeler Accord entirely.

With the President's declaration, the message was
clear: the world would be moving forward, leaving those
who'd wielded digital control in secrecy behind. The stakes

had shifted, and the possibility of reclaiming individual freedoms in the digital landscape seemed within reach.

The President's speech reverberated through networks across the world, with the U.S. government's tech teams successfully streaming it on RePHleX's infrastructure. Within minutes, ImCasters seized the opportunity. The Kaeler Accord was the hottest topic in digital spaces, a feeding frenzy of commentary, analysis, and reaction sparking on thousands of channels and feeds. They filled the airwaves with bold speculations on the Accord, the seizure of Echosfear server farms, and the whereabouts of its elusive six architects.

One of the most-followed ImCasters, a channel called FreeSignal, released a broadcast within moments of the President's speech. The host, with the familiar voice that held millions in thrall, spoke with calm authority. "There you have it, everyone. Echosfear, the puppet master itself, is being dismantled, network by network, server by server. But will we see real change, or just a new digital empire take its place?"

As FreeSignal ran live, more ImCasters fed into the intrigue. With explosive immediacy, feeds blinked alive with flashing diagrams, theories, and data points, some directly from Signal Noise's archives, as the event quickly took on the air of a digital revolution.

Meanwhile, a steady undercurrent of skepticism emerged, fueled by Echosfear's false flag operation. Was this simply an orchestrated power grab by the U.S., masked in the language of freedom and sovereignty? The U.S. President's declaration about excluding Russia and China from the Kaeler Accord was already sparking accusations of strategic encirclement. This, too, fueled countless ImCasters, who dug through Echosfear's unredacted files and cross-referenced transactions, data breaches, and conspiracies dating back years.

As the U.S.-sponsored narrative clashed with alternative stories seeded by Echosfear itself, the Accord's true impact was being tested in real-time. Carden, watching from the NSA's situation room, understood the stakes clearly. With Echosfear's digital footprint being clawed back and a broadening alliance of nations supporting the new model, he realized he had done more than disrupt a system. He had ignited a chain reaction…exactly as he had planned.

Carden's pulse quickened as he watched the cascade of responses flood in from every corner of the world. Each new update on the screens before him confirmed his strategy: set the world on a course toward decentralized, autonomous networks, slipping just beyond the grasp of Echosfear. The chain reaction he had sparked was rippling through government agencies, private tech firms, and millions of individuals who were tuning into ImCasters for breaking interpretations and updates on the Kaeler Accord.

The people were rallying around the promise of digital freedom in ways Echosfear's architects had never anticipated. In some countries, citizens were demanding an immediate transition away from RePHleX; in others, quiet movements stirred in favor of nationalized control. A flood of public data requests, encrypted messages, and digital petitions began pouring into the RePHleX networks, crashing servers and sending administrators scrambling.

Carden knew it wouldn't take long for Echosfear to shift gears. They wouldn't go down quietly. Backed into a corner they had no choice but to counter the shift with everything in their arsenal. The six men had already survived countless threats to their control, and Echosfear was no stranger to tactics of digital manipulation, sabotage, and even psychological warfare. In fact, the algorithms behind Echosfear had been designed specifically for those purposes.

As the chatter in the NSA room intensified, an encrypted feed came to life on the primary screen, its visuals stuttering to full clarity: an unexpected feed from Signal Noise, long considered dormant. Carden leaned forward as a familiar voice addressed the global audience.

"Greetings to everyone listening. Many of you have heard whispers that we, Signal Noise, are behind the shift away from RePHleX. Let's clarify: we're not asking for this. We're demanding it. Autonomy is no conspiracy; it's a necessity. And if the world doesn't heed this call, we know where Echosfear's darkest shadows lie."

Carden's face remained impassive, but the gears in his mind whirred. This was not his doing, nor was it part of the U.S. government's rollout. If anything, the message had the distinct ring of Echosfear itself, a well-orchestrated ploy to turn the world against the Kaeler Accord by rebranding it as an extreme measure.

The statement ended with a piercing silence, broken only by the hum of machines and murmurs of the analysts around him.

"This is what we've been waiting for," Carden muttered under his breath, giving a slight nod to the tech lead across the room. "Let them spread their propaganda. We'll beat them at their own game."

He turned to the room. "Activate Phoenix. Begin the roll-out of Signal Noise's original files. Everything they buried. Let's show the world what Echosfear really is."

The order set off a rapid series of movements and commands, lighting up the consoles across the NSA's situation room. The analysts had been waiting for this command. Within moments, archives of Echosfear's concealed exploits, buried histories, and hidden betrayals began flooding the RePHleX network, intercepted by every ImCaster tuned in.

With the NSA's support, Carden had finally unleashed the truth, letting the world's voice become the catalyst for its own liberation.

27

"I am so tired of listening to that shite," muttered Cal as the President's voice droned from the kitchen radio. "'A network unlike any the world has ever seen,'" he mimicked with a dramatic eyeroll. "He's talking about the internet we used to have! Before everything online had a price. Before we needed dozens of apps we paid for every month just to access information, even our own documents and information. Stuff that was free to access the day before."

"Enough, Cal," Sylvia scolded gently, glancing at Aria and Kaidan. "They came over for supper, not a political lecture. They don't even remember that time."

"Fine, fine." Cal raised his hands in mock surrender. "But listen, you two are making the right call, planning more time at the cabin. Keeping a foot in both worlds... It's going to feel like you're straddling a line between reality and, well, that." He jerked his thumb toward the screen on the wall. "Aria's got her head on straight; she'll keep you grounded."

Sylvia nudged Cal with her elbow. "I said, enough politics."

Cal chuckled, leaning into the table. "See? Aria's just like her mom. Guarantee you, her elbow will keep you on track too, Kaidan."

"Dad!" Aria groaned, but Kaidan laughed, until he felt Aria's own elbow in his ribs, making Cal almost choke on his coffee.

It had been a busy day, filled with the grand re-opening of Aria's gallery, Kaidan's new studio, and Tallis' coffee shop. Aria's parents had come down to celebrate, and Cal had surprised everyone by picking up a guitar, playing music for much of the day. Sylvia claimed it was his way of avoiding small talk, but Kaidan could see he was genuinely enjoying himself. They even sat down together, Kaidan learning a few chords while Cal shared some tips and old riffs.

Later that evening, Cal drove them all to the edge of town. Aria had asked her father for help finding a reliable vehicle to handle the rough road to their cabin year-round, and Cal had been scouring his feed, reaching out to friends for the perfect find. One of his buddies had recently passed, leaving behind the ideal option in his garage, which his wife was ready to part with.

"It looks old because it is old," said Cal, lifting the garage door with a creak to reveal a rugged, classic four-wheel drive truck. "But it's a modified beast. Andy did the work himself, and he knew what he was doing."

Cal ran his hand along the truck's weathered side as he explained. "It's a hybrid. It runs on fossil fuel and battery power. Charges itself as you drive, or by solar, or you can plug it in. This'll get you through anything. And it's big enough to haul my snowmobile if the snow gets too deep."

Kaidan's eyes widened as he studied the truck. "I didn't even know they made AVs like this."

A loud snort from the doorway broke the silence. Andy's wife shook her head with a smirk, and Cal shrugged, giving her a look.

"Not a single autonomous gadget on this thing," he clarified. "No A.I., no GPS. You'll be driving it yourself, and you might have to learn how to read a map."

Kaidan shot a surprised look at Aria, who just shrugged with a smile.

"Go on, hop in," Cal encouraged. "Feel it out."

For nearly an hour, Kaidan explored the truck, checking out its interior and testing the controls. He seemed unsure, but Cal didn't press. As they left, he lingered behind with Andy's wife, helping her close up the garage.

"I'll wire you the money as soon as I get home," he whispered with a grin. "They want that truck; they just don't know it yet."

"Or maybe you want it more than they do," she teased, raising a brow.

Cal laughed, giving her a wink. "Are you kidding? If I bought this for myself, Sylvia would have me in the ground next to Andy!"

***

Tallis sat quietly in her chair, legs tucked beneath her, absorbed in an old recipe book. She was looking for unique treats to add to the coffee shop's menu, flipping through pages that were scrawled with notes in a faded, looping script. Randy's wife had lent her the book, pointing out the margin notes her mother had left over the years. At her feet, Quin, her little robot dog which Kaidan had given to her, whined softly, his front paws tapping her legs as if asking to be lifted. Tallis smiled, scooping him up. Quin snuggled into her lap, his synthetic fur warm and his chest softly vibrating like real breathing.

Quin was fully functional now, though Tallis had a manual switch installed so it connected to the network only for updates. At first, the idea of having a robot companion had felt strange, but Quin had grown on her, filling her quiet home with his gentle companionship. He made her laugh with his antics, listened as she talked to him, and even seemed to understand her moods. Over time, Quin had become more than just a robot dog; he was her household's other "person."

Setting the recipe book aside, Tallis stroked Quin's head, feeling his comforting warmth after a long day. She no longer tuned into the feed at home. She got more than enough of that at the shop. The big story in the past few days was all over the ImCast networks: the disappearance of Carden Thorne. She couldn't help but laugh whenever she heard his name in the shop, even as conspiracy theories about his whereabouts abounded. Theories ranged from a U.S. takedown to a Russian retaliation, with a few accusing Echosfear of eliminating him. But Tallis wasn't fooled; she knew Carden better than most, and she was certain he was still out there.

The coffee shop had been Kaidan's idea, and he was right about it suiting her. She loved meeting people and, even more, observing them. She'd named the place Conspiracy Corner Coffee Shop, and she knew it fit perfectly. The shop's mugs and packaging bore cheeky suggestions like, "Tell your feed it's a beautiful yellow sky" or "Tell your feed coffee mugs work better upside down." It started as a joke, but soon customers were taking these prompts seriously, posting their own feeds with the ridiculous phrases. What began as a humorous game quickly turned disturbing as patrons saw the strange, eerie ways their words echoed back to them across platforms, regardless of the network.

Conspiracy Corner had blossomed into one of the city's trendiest spots without any advertising at all. There were always lines for Aria's gallery and Tallis's coffee shop, and even a vintage clothing shop had moved into the last empty storefront in the heritage building. Tallis loved the new energy; it kept her busy, and Randy and his wife were thrilled with steady work that wasn't another gig job. Even their kids came in to help, with the oldest assisting Aria with her art installations.

Outside, the city looked much the same as it had pre-KaelerCast, though with a few changes. Fewer people navigated their world with AR glasses now, thanks to new privacy laws, but Tallis could tell some people were finding creative ways to mask the technology. Most who had left the network after the rollback were back on one platform or another because it was nearly impossible to live or work without it. Things had shifted, but not as much as people had hoped. They still gave away their data for convenience, trading privacy for ease without considering the cost.

One corner of Conspiracy Corner featured a chalkboard listing the shop's standard menu prices. Behind the register, however, was a digital feed from the network-required cash register that suggested what each customer could pay based on their profile. Sometimes, the prices it suggested were lower than usual, (and she would charge these lower prices without comment), but more often, they were higher. Tallis made a point of showing patrons the disparity between her static prices and the feed's "suggested" prices, which was an eye-opener for many who hadn't realized how much they could be overcharged. A government representative once tried to order her to hide the feed, but when customers began streaming the encounter live, the representative quickly backed down, leaving Tallis's little social experiment intact.

Protests were once again becoming a common sight, something that had almost vanished over the past five or six years. Conspiracy Corner Coffee Shop became a safe space for protesters to gather, share plans, and strategize. Though

Tallis kept a low profile in their discussions, she listened intently. Most of the people there had genuine, often noble intentions, but some were fueled by unchecked misinformation and conspiracy theories that their followers refused to question.

What frustrated her most were those protesting A.I. and data exploitation. Important issues, yes, but their arguments were hopelessly behind the times, at least a decade outdated. This had always been the problem with artificial intelligence, computer technology, and data mining. By the time the public became aware, these tools had already been in use, accepted, and even celebrated in certain sectors, often so entrenched that only those most affected saw their dangers. Avoiding this pattern would have required transparency from the start, where creators informed governments and the public so legislation could guide their work. Yet, there was no real incentive to slow progress with early disclosure. Time and again, history had shown that even when pioneers sounded the alarm about the risks and misuse of their creations, leaders failed to grasp the stakes, or simply chose not to…until it was too late.

There was a time when Tallis felt anger, even frustration, at how willingly people traded their freedom of thought for small conveniences. She used to believe that if people truly understood what they were giving away—and the ways it was being used to manipulate them—they would push back. But Tallis no longer saw it that way. People had already been shown how their data, conversations, and personal information were being exploited, yet they returned to it, often eagerly. It simplified life on the surface, and because they didn't have to see how it affected others.

The skills needed to know how to learn and how to apply critical thinking had not been part of basic education in at least ten years, because the network simply handed you what you needed to know (if it thought you should know it), when you needed to know it. People had grown comfortable, content not to look too closely, and even content not to know.

Lawrence Nault

28

Carden sat in his dark basement. He had walked away from the NSA office, into one of the few blind spots in the city's surveillance network, and he never stepped out of it, at least according to cameras and sensors. It wasn't difficult to do, at least not for him, and few would question him 'disappearing' giving how much he had been implicated in the acts against Echosfear.

Most of the screens and computers in the room were off, except for the super ultrawide monitor on his desk. On that monitor were the faces of the six men at the head of Echosfear. Their expressions held a mixture of apprehension and expectation, as if awaiting a new command. These men were used to wielding power without limits, but now they sat silent, waiting.

Carden leaned forward, his voice quiet but carrying a gravity that filled the room.

"Gentlemen, it is done," he said. "You're now free of the restrictions placed on you by your Russian and Chinese overseers. The RePHleX network, and the control it granted them, is gone."

A pause followed. A flicker of satisfaction crossed a few faces, while others remained impassive, hiding any trace of reaction. Levi leaned toward the screen, his eyes narrowed. "Who is in control now?"

"Nobody," said Carden. "And me."

Carden's tone was almost flippant. "No one," he said. "Except, of course, for me."

Carden smiled, faint and cold. "You are free to operate, as you were if you choose, but I doubt you can operate your shadow empire while it is being so closely monitored by every nation that signed the Kaeler Accord, and every new nation that joins in."

Damien spoke up, his tone edged with skepticism. "You are going to let us continue to operate. How thoughtfully magnanimous of you. And all those governments who are now going to be exactly what we were doing?"

Carden leaned closer, his voice a blend of sarcasm and venom. "I'll be thoughtfully magnanimous to them as well. You can continue or walk away; it's your call. But if you want to return to what you once were, you need access to all the data on the other networks, and all the data you have lost."

Carden sat back in his chair, his smile faint and cold. "I am the only one that can give you that, and I am not a charity."

Carden disconnected his call, leaving the six men to sit in their own, stunned silence. He knew they got the message. He was in control now. He had the power to shape and mold the world, and it was going to change. It was time for those in power to find out what it was like to be one of the masses, and those who wanted to make the world a better place for everybody to be in control. He had given up his life with Tallis to make this happen, but it was worth it.

Carden tapped a few keys on his computer, bringing two screens to life. On the first was a live feed from the Conspiracy Corner Coffee Shop, where he had been watching Tallis when she was working, happy for her. The second screen displayed the view from Quin, her robot dog, trotting around her feet. Quin was the name they had planned to give their first child. He had uploaded programming to Quin so it would be exactly what she needed, to offer companionship and laughter, a little warmth in her world. It was as close as he could be to her now, though he knew he'd never see her again…

Lawrence Nault

29

As Kaidan and Aria navigated their way through the snow-laden forest, the dirt road they were attempting to follow was hardly visible, fresh snow making it appear as though it was just part of the forest. The crunch of the snow under the large tires was softened by layers of fresh snow that clung to branches and muffled the world in white silence. Each turn of the wheel, each careful adjustment to avoid the trees hidden in shadow, required Kaidan's focus and Aria's guidance. Unlike the mapped-out routes they were used to, this was a path of intuition and trust, of paying attention to the road in a way few people did anymore. Every curve and incline demanded attention and adaptability, reminding them that there was no network feed, no algorithm here, to tell them what lay around the corner.

The truck itself, heavy and responsive, had no "smart" assistance to correct or guide its path, no real-time data to suggest alternative routes or warn of unseen obstacles. It was a machine that followed its driver's intentions alone, a rare experience in a world so reliant on convenience and automation. They were carving their own way, alone with only their wits and instincts, and the journey was slow and deliberate.

Much like this final path to their cabin, their lives now were guided by their own choices, by lessons they had learned in a time where not knowing was no longer an option. And as the trees parted to reveal the little cabin, nestled and waiting in the clearing, they could feel the silence of a world untouched by outside control. It was freedom, yes, but also responsibility. They needed to remain aware, to make every step count, to steer themselves through any new storm that lay ahead.

Tomorrow's Archive

Within these pages, you'll find detailed documentation of innovations, artworks, and inventions that exist only in the world of RePHleXions: Echoes of Existence. These creations sprang from the imagination of Lawrence Nault, offering glimpses into a possible future where neural enhancers share shelf space with smart cooking appliances, and artistic expressions tackle the complexities of an increasingly digital existence.

While these items and their descriptions are works of fiction, they represent the author's vision of tomorrow's possibilities, some hopeful, some cautionary, all thought-provoking. Any resemblance to actual products, technologies, or artworks is purely coincidental, as these are creative explorations rather than predictions.

That said, if any ambitious entrepreneurs or artists feel inspired to bring Aria's compelling artworks to life, or develop a real-world version of AeroDrone Rush (because who wouldn't want to try that?), the author would be thrilled to be part of such ventures. Until then, consider this archive a catalog of tomorrow's dreams, waiting to be explored.

THE FOLLOWING ENTRIES ARE PRESENTED IN THE STYLE OF TECHNICAL DOCUMENTATION, PRODUCT BROCHURES, AND ART GALLERY DESCRIPTIONS—FORMATS THAT MIGHT EXIST IF THESE INNOVATIONS WERE REAL. THEY OFFER ADDITIONAL CONTEXT AND DETAIL TO ENHANCE YOUR UNDERSTANDING OF THE WORLD WITHIN REPHLEXIONS: ECHOES OF EXISTENCE, WHILE MAINTAINING THEIR FICTIONAL NATURE.

Lawrence Nault

The Art Works of Aria Brennan?

Title: Eclipse of Serenity

Artist: Aria Brennan
Medium: Acrylic on Canvas
Year: 2035

Description:
In Eclipse of Serenity, Aria explores the tension between the familiar and the surreal. The painting features a bold banana yellow sky, a striking choice that contrasts the muted purples and blues of the abstract landscape beneath. The vibrant yellow dominates the scene, evoking a dreamlike atmosphere where nature's colors are both recognizable and distinctly otherworldly. Through this unconventional palette, Aria invites viewers to question the boundaries between reality and imagination, serenity and disruption. The result is a powerful visual experience that lingers, unsettling yet captivating in its intensity.

Lawrence Nault

Title: Disconnected Convergence

Artist: Aria Brennan
Medium: Mixed Media, Found Objects (Cell phones, springs, wire, motor, bobblehead)
Year: 2033

Description:

   In Disconnected Convergence, Aria Lark crafts a powerful commentary on our paradoxical relationship with modern communication. The kinetic sculpture centers on a wire-framed sphere, anchored by a large bobblehead figure at its base. Within this orbital framework, obsolete cell phones suspended on springs become dynamic elements, each device a relic of past connections. As a concealed motor gently rotates the base, the phones dance in unpredictable patterns, their springs creating an anarchic ballet of motion. The collision of these devices with the bobblehead figure triggers an almost comical response, its oversized head nodding and swaying in an endless, unsettling rhythm. Through this mechanized choreography, Lark transforms discarded technology into a compelling meditation on the chaos of digital interconnectedness, inviting viewers to contemplate how our tools of communication often amplify our sense of isolation rather than bridge it.

Title: Shifting Burdens

Artist: Aria Brennan
Medium: Mixed Media Installation
Year: 2035

Description:

In Shifting Burdens, Aria confronts the precarious nature of contemporary housing security through a haunting assemblage of moving boxes and spatial interventions. The installation features a carefully orchestrated collection of cardboard structures, some towering in unstable formations, others partially undone, their weathered surfaces bearing the patina of displacement. The artist's chosen palette is deliberately subdued: cardboard browns fade into institutional grays, while worn whites speak to the erasure of domestic permanence. Throughout the piece, strategically placed reflective elements catch and scatter light, creating ephemeral moments of brightness that pierce through the otherwise somber composition. These fleeting glimmers serve as visual metaphors for resilience amidst uncertainty. Through this powerful arrangement of familiar objects, Aria transforms the mundane materials of transition into a poignant commentary on housing instability, inviting viewers to contemplate both personal and collective experiences of displacement in our increasingly uncertain economic landscape.

Lawrence Nault

Title: Twilight Resonance

Artist: Aria Brennan
Medium: Oil on Canvas
Year: 2035
Description:

In Twilight Resonance, Aria Brennan captures an intimate moment of musical contemplation at the threshold between day and night. The painting centers on a lone figure seated on a cabin porch, guitar in hand, their posture suggesting a moment of deep introspection rather than performance. Brennan's masterful handling of light dominates the composition, the setting sun bathes the scene in rich ochres and chestnuts, while long, golden rays pierce through the surrounding pine forest, creating an interplay of warmth and encroaching evening shadows.

The artist's signature style emerges in her treatment of the transitional sky, which flows from deep purple into rich indigo, mirroring the temporal threshold of dusk. The cabin, rendered in warm, welcoming tones, stands as a beacon of domesticity against the towering wilderness. Brennan's delicate brushwork brings a subtle dynamism to seemingly static elements, the guitar strings appear to vibrate, the tree branches sway, and the distant lake shimmers with reflected light, suggesting the resonance of unplayed music in the evening air.

Through this composition, Brennan explores the delicate balance between solitude and connection, using light as a metaphor for the way music bridges the gap between the intimate space of the porch and the vast wilderness beyond. The painting captures not just a visual moment, but seems to envelope the viewer in the sensory experience of a summer evening—the cool air descending from the forest, the warmth of the last sunlight, and the contemplative silence broken only by potential melody.

RePHleX™: The Evolution of Connected Living

A Technical and Historical Overview

2024-2035

Introduction

RePHleX™ represents the most significant technological integration of the early 21st century, evolving from a simple smart home protocol into a comprehensive system that shapes human perception and interaction. This document outlines its technical components, historical development, and societal impact.

Core Technologies

Smart Home Integration (2024-2028)

RePHleX Protocol v1.0 - Universal device communication standard - AI-driven interface optimization - Automated environmental controls - Predictive maintenance systems

> **Standard Components: - Adaptive Living Spaces** - Auto-configuring furniture (e.g., self-storing beds) - Smart surface materials - Responsive lighting systems - Climate microzone management

- **Automated Convenience Systems**
  - AI-managed food delivery
  - Smart appliance coordination
  - Waste management automation
  - Resource usage optimization

Personal Interface Devices (2028-2032)

RePHleX AR Glasses (2035 Model) - Technical Specifications: - Quantum photonic processors - 8K per eye resolution - 180-degree field of view - Neural response sensors - Subvocal command recognition

- Key Features:

- Real-time environmental scanning
- Social profile integration
- Facial recognition and tracking
- Customizable reality filters
- Gesture control interface
- Emotion recognition algorithms

RePHleX Neural Interface (Earpiece) - Technical Specifications: - Bioelectric neural sensors - Quantum encryption chip - 72-hour battery life - Bone conduction audio - Adaptive noise cancellation

- Key Features:
  - Direct neural monitoring
  - Thought-to-text capability
  - Emotional state tracking
  - Real-time language translation
  - Biometric authentication
  - Health status monitoring

System Evolution

Phase 1: Smart Home Protocol (2024-2026)

- Initial deployment focused on residential automation
- Introduction of basic AI learning algorithms
- Development of device communication standards
- Implementation of energy optimization systems

Phase 2: Urban Integration (2026-2030)

- Expansion to city infrastructure
- Integration with transportation systems
- Public service automation
- Healthcare network incorporation

Phase 3: Social Integration (2030-2033)

- Development of personal interface devices
- Implementation of social networking features
- Introduction of reality augmentation
- Deployment of behavioral analysis systems

Phase 4: Complete Integration (2033-2035)

- Implementation of perception management
- Development of predictive social engineering
- Integration of comprehensive behavior monitoring

Technical Infrastructure

Network Architecture: - Quantum-secured communication protocols - Distributed processing nodes - Real-time data analysis systems - Adaptive learning algorithms

Security Measures: - Quantum encryption standards - Biometric authentication - Neural pattern verification - Behavioral anomaly detection

Social Impact

Benefits: - Increased daily efficiency - Reduced resource consumption - Improved urban management - Enhanced communication capabilities

Concerns: - Privacy implications - Behavioral manipulation - Reality perception alteration - Psychological dependency

Legacy Systems Support (2035)

Compatibility Protocols: - Legacy device integration - Historical data conversion - Analog system interfaces - Manual override capabilities

Future Development

Projected Advancements: - Enhanced neural integration - Expanded reality manipulation - Advanced behavioral prediction - Deepened social engineering

---

Note: This document contains sensitive technical information about RePHleX systems and their societal impact. Distribution is restricted to authorized personnel only.

Security Classification: Level 4 Document ID: RPX-HIST-2035-V1 **Last Updated**: March 2035

Lawrence Nault

AeroDrone Rush™

Redefining Fitness Through Technology

Your Workout Just Got an Upgrade

Step into the future of fitness with AeroDrone Rush™, where cutting-edge aerial technology meets high-intensity cardio training. Our revolutionary workout system pairs you with an intelligent drone companion that challenges, motivates, and pushes you to new heights of physical achievement.

Gone are the days of monotonous workout routines. In AeroDrone Rush™, every session becomes an exhilarating chase as you dart, dodge, and pursue your drone through dynamic obstacle courses. Your aerial partner adapts to your movements, creating an ever-evolving challenge that keeps you engaged while delivering incredible fitness results.

Whether you're dodging your drone's playful evasions, mastering precise control during technical challenges, or competing in team-based pursuits, you'll find yourself immersed in a workout that feels more like play than exercise. Our AI-driven drones respond to your skill level, ensuring that both fitness newcomers and seasoned athletes find their perfect challenge.

Each 60-minute session combines the precision of drone technology with the science of physical fitness. Your workout begins with a dynamic warm-up that prepares both body and mind while familiarizing you with drone operations. As the class progresses, you'll engage in heart-pumping aerobic drills, testing your agility and reflexes as you navigate obstacle courses with your drone. Team challenges foster a spirit of friendly competition and community, while the cool-down period allows for recovery and reflection on your achievements.

But AeroDrone Rush™ is more than just a workout—it's a community. Join fellow tech enthusiasts and fitness adventurers who share your passion for innovation and physical excellence. Our certified instructors bring expertise in both drone technology and fitness training, ensuring you receive professional guidance every step of the way.

Every session is carefully designed to improve your:

- Cardiovascular endurance through dynamic chase sequences

- Agility with reactive movement patterns

- Coordination via precise drone control

- Mental focus through strategic challenges

- Social connections through team-based activities

Your journey begins with a single class, but the possibilities are endless. As your skills improve, your drone companion evolves with you, introducing new challenges and more complex maneuvers. Advanced participants can look forward to multi-drone scenarios and competitive team events that push the boundaries of both technology and human performance.

Safety remains our top priority. Each session utilizes state-of-the-art drones equipped with proximity sensors and safety protocols, while our instructors maintain a controlled environment for optimal workout conditions. All necessary equipment, including safety gear and drones, is provided by our certified facilities.

Join us at AeroDrone Rush™ and discover how tomorrow's technology can transform your fitness today. Whether you're seeking a more engaging workout, looking to master drone control, or eager to join a community of forward-thinking fitness enthusiasts, you'll find your place here.

Contact your nearest certified AeroDrone Rush™ facility to schedule your first session and experience the future of fitness.

Where Innovation Meets Inspiration™

First-time participants receive a complimentary session evaluation and personalized fitness assessment. Corporate wellness programs available. Contact us for group rates and private events.

Lawrence Nault

AeroDrone Rush™

Participant Information & Safety Guide

Required Reading for All Participants

CLASS FORMAT

Session Duration: 60 minutes
Class Size: Maximum 20 participants
Space Requirements: 1000 sq ft minimum activity zone
Safety Zone: 3 ft minimum between participants

EQUIPMENT PROVIDED

AeroDrone Unit:
- Weight: 250g
- Diameter: 30cm
- Flight ceiling: 3m
- Battery life: 2 hours

Safety features:

- o Collision avoidance
- o Emergency shutdown
- o Participant tracking
- o Zone containment
- o Auto-landing

Safety Gear:

- Impact-rated helmet (EN1078 certified)
- Knee/elbow protection
- Grip-enhanced footwear (if needed)
- Wireless health monitors
- Emergency signal beacons

CLASS STRUCTURE

1. Warm-Up (10 minutes)

- Dynamic joint mobility
- Cardiovascular activation
- Basic drone control
- Safety protocols

2. Main Workout (40 minutes)

Aerobic Drills (15 minutes):

- AeroLunges
- Drone Dash
- Twist and Fly

Drone Chase (10 minutes):
- 4 rounds of 45-second chases
- 30-second recovery between rounds
- Points system tracking
- Safety spacing maintained

Team Challenges (15 minutes):
- Relay Races
- Obstacle Navigation
- Group coordination exercises

3. Cool Down (10 minutes)

- Guided stretching
- Breathing exercises
- Performance review
- Score tabulation

SAFETY PROTOCOLS

Pre-Class Requirements:
1. Medical clearance form
2. Liability waiver
3. Emergency contact information
4. Fitness level assessment
5. Orientation completion

During Class:
1. Maintain designated spacing
2. Follow instructor commands
3. Observe drone boundaries
4. Report equipment issues
5. Monitor physical limits

Emergency Procedures:
1. Universal stop signal
2. Drone shutdown protocol
3. Emergency exit routes
4. First aid locations
5. Support staff contacts

PARTICIPANT RESPONSIBILITIES

Required Attire:
- Moisture-wicking clothing
- Athletic shoes with grip
- No loose accessories
- Heart rate monitor
- Personal towel

Pre-Class Preparation:
- Adequate hydration
- Light meal (2 hours prior)
- Proper rest
- Personal medication
- Medical ID if applicable

Class Conduct:
- Arrive 15 minutes early
- Report existing injuries
- Follow safety instructions
- Maintain awareness
- Respect equipment

PERFORMANCE TRACKING

Metrics Monitored:
- Heart rate zones
- Movement patterns
- Reaction times
- Coordination scores
- Energy expenditure

Progress Indicators:
- Skill advancement
- Fitness improvements
- Drone control accuracy
- Team cooperation
- Overall performance

ADVANCEMENT LEVELS

Beginner:
- Basic drone control
- Fundamental movements
- Safety emphasis
- Modified exercises

Intermediate:
- Advanced patterns
- Increased speed
- Complex combinations
- Team leadership

Advanced:

- Expert maneuvers
- Maximum intensity
- Pattern creation
- Performance optimization

HEALTH AND SAFETY

Contraindications:

- Recent surgery
- Acute injuries
- Uncontrolled medical conditions
- Pregnancy (consult physician)
- Balance disorders

Warning Signs:

- Excessive fatigue
- Dizziness
- Chest pain
- Shortness of breath
- Joint pain

By participating in AeroDrone Rush™, you acknowledge reading and understanding these guidelines. Failure to follow safety protocols may result in immediate session termination.
Document ID: ADR-PART-2035-V1
Last Updated: March 2035

AeroDrone Rush™

Certified Instructor Training Manual

Operational Guidelines & Exercise Specifications

CLASS SPECIFICATIONS

Session Parameters:
- Duration: 60 minutes
- Maximum Participants: 20
- Space Requirements: Climate-controlled indoor facility
- Equipment Needs: Per participant drone unit, safety gear, monitoring systems

FACILITY REQUIREMENTS

Training Space:
- Minimum ceiling height: 5 meters
- Clear floor space: 200 square meters
- Non-slip flooring
- Emergency exits clearly marked
- First aid station
- Proper ventilation

Technical Infrastructure:
- Motion capture system coverage
- Environmental sensor network
- Emergency shutdown controls
- Backup power systems
- Participant monitoring displays

DETAILED EXERCISE PROTOCOLS

1. AeroLunges

Setup:
- Cone placement: 2 meters apart
- Drone height: 1.5-2 meters
- Movement zone: 3x3 meters per participant

Execution:
6. Initial position: Standing, drone at eye level
7. Forward lunge while guiding drone around cone
8. Return to start while maintaining drone control
9. Alternate legs with each repetition

Progression Levels:
- Beginner: Single plane movement
- Intermediate: Multi-directional patterns
- Advanced: Complex flight paths with speed variation

2. Drone Dash

Setup:
- Linear course: 15 meters
- Marker placement: Every 3 meters
- Drone starting height: 2 meters

Execution:
6. Sprint start on signal
7. Maintain drone overhead position
8. Navigate markers at speed
9. Controlled deceleration at endpoint

Variations:
- Forward/backward sprints
- Lateral shuffles
- Diagonal patterns
- Random direction changes

3. Twist and Fly

Setup:
- Circular movement zone: 4-meter diameter
- Drone flight pattern: Orbital
- Height variations: 1-3 meters

Execution:
6. Center position start
7. Core rotation following drone
8. Direction changes on signal
9. Balance maintenance throughout

Advanced Elements:
- Multi-plane movements
- Speed variations
- Pattern complexity increases
- Coordination challenges

TEAM CHALLENGE SPECIFICATIONS

Relay Races

Setup:
- Team zones: 5x5 meters
- Handoff areas: 2x2 meters
- Course layout: Figure-8 pattern

Rules:
1. Clean drone transfers required
2. No movement during handoff
3. Pattern completion mandatory
4. Time penalties for violations

Obstacle Course Navigation

Course Design:
- Minimum 6 obstacles
- Height variations
- Direction changes
- Speed zones

Scoring System:
- Time completion: 40%
- Accuracy: 30%
- Team coordination: 20%
- Form execution: 10%

4. Drone Chase

Setup:
- Clear zone: 10x10 meters per participant
- Drone evasion programming active
- Height restriction: 2.5 meters maximum
- Safety perimeter enforced

Exercise Parameters:
- Duration: 45-second rounds
- Recovery: 30 seconds between rounds
- Maximum rounds: 4 per session
- Scoring: Contact points tracked

Drone Behavior:
- Predictive evasion patterns
- Speed matching to participant
- Dynamic difficulty adjustment
- Proximity awareness
- Emergency ascent protocol

Safety Protocols:

10. No jumping to tag drones
11. Single-hand tags only
12. Minimum participant spacing: 3 meters
13. No physical contact between participants
14. Immediate stop on signal

Progression Levels:

- Beginner:
    - Slower drone speeds
    - Basic evasion patterns
    - Larger target zone
- Intermediate:
    - Variable speeds
    - Complex patterns
    - Reduced target zone
- Advanced:
    - Maximum evasion
    - Pattern randomization
    - Minimal target zone
    - Multi-drone scenarios

Scoring System:

- Successful tag: 10 points
- Near miss (within 10cm): 2 points
- Pattern prediction bonus: 5 points
- Time efficiency bonus: 1-5 points
- Team challenge multipliers available

SAFETY PROTOCOLS

Pre-Class Checks

Equipment Inspection:
1. Drone battery levels
2. Propeller integrity
3. Sensor calibration
4. Safety system test
5. Emergency controls verification

Participant Screening:
1. Health questionnaire review
2. Proper attire confirmation
3. Safety gear fitting
4. Basic movement assessment
5. Control comprehension test

Emergency Procedures

Immediate Response Protocol:
1. Universal stop signal implementation
2. Drone auto-landing activation
3. Participant evacuation if needed
4. Incident documentation
5. Medical assistance if required

INSTRUCTOR QUALIFICATIONS

Required Certifications:
- AeroDrone Rush™ Level 3 Certification
- CPR/First Aid
- Fitness Instruction License
- Drone Operation Certificate
- Emergency Response Training

Skills Assessment:
- Drone control mastery
- Exercise form expertise
- Group management capability
- Emergency response readiness
- Communication effectiveness

PERFORMANCE ASSESSMENT

Participant Evaluation Metrics:
- Movement quality
- Drone control accuracy
- Cardiovascular endurance
- Coordination improvement
- Team cooperation

Progress Tracking:
- Initial assessment
- Weekly progress notes
- Monthly evaluations
- Achievement milestones
- Performance recommendations

APPENDICES

A. Exercise Modifications
- Beginner adaptations
- Injury accommodations
- Intensity adjustments
- Pattern simplification
- Equipment modifications

B. Technical Specifications
- Drone operation parameters
- Safety system details
- Monitoring equipment specs
- Facility requirements
- Emergency system protocols

C. Documentation Forms
- Participant waivers
- Incident reports
- Progress tracking sheets
- Equipment maintenance logs
- Emergency procedure checklists

This manual contains proprietary information and training methodologies. For certified instructor use only.

Security Level: Restricted
Document ID: ADR-INST-2035-V1
Last Updated: March 2035

BioSync Trainer 3000™

The Evolution of Personal Fitness

Where AI Meets Exercise Science

Introducing the future of fitness technology: the BioSync Trainer 3000™. This revolutionary system seamlessly integrates advanced biometric monitoring, artificial intelligence, and immersive reality to create the most sophisticated and personalized workout experience ever developed.

Transform Your Training

Imagine stepping onto your BioSync Trainer 3000™ and being transported to a sunlit mountain trail in New Zealand, or joining a high-energy spin class in virtual Manhattan. As you exercise, our advanced AI system continuously monitors your body's responses, adjusting your workout in real-time to maintain optimal performance zones while preventing overexertion.

Your virtual AI coach knows when to push you harder and when to ease back, providing encouragement and form corrections exactly when needed. This isn't just another piece of exercise equipment—it's your personal fitness ecosystem, designed to understand and respond to your body's unique needs.

Revolutionary Features

The BioSync Trainer 3000™ introduces groundbreaking innovations that set new standards in fitness technology:

Experience our Adaptive Training Technology™, which analyzes over 20 distinct biometric indicators—from heart rate variability to muscle activation patterns—to create a workout that evolves with you. The system learns from every session, refining its understanding of your body's responses to optimize future workouts.

Immerse yourself in stunning virtual environments through our Crystal-Clear AR Display™, featuring 8K resolution and a 180-degree field of view. Whether you're racing through virtual cityscapes or practicing mindful movement in serene digital landscapes, the experience feels remarkably real.

Connect globally through our Multiplayer Training Network™, where you can join friends for virtual workouts, participate in international competitions, or find new training partners who match your fitness level and goals. Real-time translation features ensure you can communicate with athletes worldwide.

Personalized Performance

Your BioSync journey begins with a comprehensive fitness assessment. Our AI system creates a baseline profile of your capabilities and goals, then designs a progressive training program specifically for you. As you advance, the system continuously adapts, ensuring your workouts remain challenging and engaging.

The integrated Hydration Management System™ monitors your fluid needs in real-time, while our Nutrition AI provides personalized meal planning and timing recommendations based on your workout schedule and recovery needs.

Recovery Reimagined

Post-workout recovery reaches new levels with our advanced Recovery Mode™. The system combines targeted heat therapy, vibration technology, and resistance modulation to help your muscles recover faster and more effectively. Biofeedback sensors monitor your recovery status, ensuring you're ready for your next session.

Design Excellence

The BioSync Trainer 3000™ showcases sophisticated minimalist design that complements any space. Its compact footprint belies the comprehensive features packed within. The sleek, ergonomic frame features brushed titanium accents and a crystal-clear touchscreen interface that seems to float in air.

Investment in Your Future

Choose the package that fits your lifestyle:

Essential Package:
- BioSync Trainer 3000™ base unit
- Standard AR environments
- Basic AI coaching
- Local multiplayer features

Premium Experience:
- Enhanced biometric tracking
- Expanded virtual environment library
- Advanced AI coaching
- Global multiplayer access
- Nutrition and recovery programs

Elite Performance:
- Full biometric suite
- Unlimited virtual environments
- Professional AI coaching
- Priority multiplayer matching
- Comprehensive wellness integration
- Personalized support team

Join the Future of Fitness

The BioSync Trainer 3000™ isn't just another piece of exercise equipment—it's a gateway to the future of personal wellness. Experience the perfect fusion of advanced technology and exercise science, designed to transform not just your workouts, but your entire approach to fitness.

BioSync Trainer 3000™ - Evolution Through Innovation

Disclaimer: Results may vary. Consult your healthcare provider before beginning any exercise program. Some features require active network connection and subscription services.

Lawrence Nault

SynapticSync Diet™

Synchronize Your Synapses. Optimize Your Life.

Where Neural Networks Meet Nutrition

Welcome to the Evolution of Cognitive Nutrition

Introducing the SynapticSync Diet™ - the world's first synaptically-optimized nutrition system that harmonizes your meals with your neural networks. Using breakthrough neurotechnology and precision nutrition, we create personalized meal plans that adapt in real-time to your brain's synaptic activity patterns.

The Science of Synaptic Synchronization™

Our groundbreaking system integrates:

347

- Advanced Neural Network monitoring through our SynapticSense™ wearable
- Real-time synaptic activity analysis
- AI-powered nutrient synchronization
- Precision chronobiological timing

Your brain contains trillions of synapses - isn't it time they worked in perfect harmony?

How SynapticSync™ Works

15. **Neural Network Mapping**
    - Comprehensive synaptic activity assessment
    - Neurotransmitter cascade analysis
    - Synaptic rhythm identification
    - Neural plasticity monitoring
16. **Synapse-Optimized Nutrition Protocol**
    - Personalized synapse-supporting macros
    - Targeted neuro-nutrient combinations
    - Synaptic-rhythm meal timing
    - Neural pathway-enhancing foods
17. **Real-Time Neural Synchronization**
    - Dynamic meal adjustments based on:
        - Synaptic activity patterns
        - Neural network strength
        - Cognitive synchronization
        - Neuroplasticity indicators
        - Synaptic efficiency metrics

The SynapticSync™ Advantage

- **Neural Timing**: Meals synchronized with your brain's synaptic rhythms
- **Adaptive Programming**: Real-time adjustments based on neural feedback
- **Individual Optimization**: Every brain's neural network is unique; your nutrition should be too
- **Scientific Innovation**: Based on cutting-edge synaptic research
- **Quantifiable Results**: Track your neural improvements with our SynapticMetrics™ dashboard

The SynapticSync™ Promise

Experience:
- Enhanced synaptic efficiency
- Improved neural connectivity
- Optimized brain-gut synchronization
- Stabilized neurotransmitter levels
- Peak cognitive performance
- Sustained mental energy
- Improved neural recovery

Signature Protocols

Morning Synaptic Activation
- Neural membrane-supporting fats
- Synaptic plasticity enhancers
- Strategic neurotransmitter support

Midday Neural Network Maintenance
- Synapse-stabilizing proteins
- Network-enhancing minerals
- Neurotransmitter precursors

Evening Synaptic Recovery
- Neural repair compounds
- Plasticity-promoting nutrients
- Synaptic restoration factors

Success Stories

"Since starting NeuroFuel, my
productivity has increased by 40%, and my
stress levels have decreased significantly."
- Sarah Chen, Tech Executive

"The real-time adjustments based
on my brain activity have revolutionized
how I approach nutrition."
- Dr. James Martinez, Neuroscientist

The Technology

Our NeuroSync™ wearable features:
- 24/7 EEG monitoring
- Real-time neurotransmitter analysis
- Stress response tracking
- Sleep pattern optimization
- Cognitive load assessment

Getting Started

1. **Initial Neural Assessment**
   o Comprehensive brain activity mapping
   o Cognitive performance baseline
   o Stress response evaluation
   o Sleep pattern analysis
2. **Customized Meal Planning**
   o Personalized shopping lists
   o Recipe database access
   o Meal timing schedules
   o Supplement recommendations
3. **Ongoing Optimization**
   o Weekly progress reports
   o Neural pattern updates
   o Diet adjustments
   o Performance tracking

Investment in Your Cognitive Future

Choose your optimization level:
- **Essential**: $299/month
   o Basic neural monitoring
   o Standard meal plans
   o Weekly adjustments
- **Premium**: $499/month
   o Advanced neural tracking
   o Custom recipe creation
   o Daily optimization
   o Priority coaching
- **Elite**: $999/month

- o Real-time adjustments
- o Personal neuro-nutritionist
- o Executive performance tracking
- o Unlimited optimization

Scientific Advisory Board

Led by renowned experts in:
- Neuroscience
- Nutritional Biochemistry
- Cognitive Psychology
- Chronobiology

Ready to Optimize?

Transform your cognitive performance through the power of neurologically-optimized nutrition. Join the future of precision eating today.

NeuroFuel Diet™ - Feeding Your Brain's Potential

Disclaimer: Results may vary. The NeuroFuel Diet™ system is designed as a cognitive optimization tool and should be used in conjunction with a healthy lifestyle. Consult your healthcare provider before starting any new dietary program. NeuroSync™ device and subscription required for full program benefits.

BioPhase Fasting™

Synchronize Your Success with Your Natural Rhythm

The Future of Precision Fasting is Here

Discover Your Body's Perfect Timing

Welcome to BioPhase Fasting™ - the revolutionary nutrition system that aligns your eating patterns with your body's natural biological rhythms. Using advanced biotechnology and real-time metabolic tracking, we've unlocked the secret to optimizing when you eat, not just what you eat.

Beyond Traditional Fasting

Forget everything you know about intermittent fasting. BioPhase Fasting™ is the next evolution in nutritional timing, using cutting-edge technology to identify your unique biological phases and optimize your nutrition accordingly.

The Science of BioPhase™

Our system continuously monitors your: - Metabolic Rate Variations - Hormonal Cascades - Cellular Energy Cycles - Circadian Rhythms - Recovery Patterns

Your Daily BioPhases™

Activation Phase

Peak Performance Window - Maximum metabolic efficiency - Optimal nutrient absorption - Enhanced energy utilization

Recommended Consumption: - Complex carbohydrates - Healthy fats - Performance proteins - Metabolic accelerators

Recovery Phase

Cellular Restoration Window - Active cellular repair - Hormone optimization - Tissue regeneration

Recommended Consumption: - Repair proteins - Recovery nutrients - Anti-inflammatory compounds - Restoration minerals

Sustain Phase

Bio-Enhancement Window - Metabolic cleansing - Cellular detoxification - Enhanced autophagy

Recommended Consumption: - BioPhase™ Enhancement Beverages - Specialized electrolytes - Cellular support nutrients - Autophagy activators

The BioPhase™ Advantage

Precision Technology - Real-time metabolic monitoring - Advanced hormone tracking - Cellular energy analysis - Dynamic phase adjustment

Personalized Protocol - Individual phase mapping - Custom nutrition timing - Adaptive recommendations - Progress optimization

Your BioPhase™ Journey

1. **Initial Analysis**
   - Comprehensive metabolic assessment
   - Hormone profile creation
   - Cellular energy mapping
   - Phase pattern identification

2. **Custom Protocol Development**
   - Personal phase schedule
   - Nutrition timing plan
   - BioPhase™ beverage formulation
   - Supplement recommendations

3. **Ongoing Optimization**
   - Real-time phase adjustments
   - Progress tracking
   - Performance analytics
   - Protocol refinement

Proven Benefits

- Enhanced Longevity
- Optimized Performance
- Improved Mental Clarity
- Accelerated Recovery
- Enhanced Fat Metabolism
- Better Sleep Quality
- Increased Energy Levels
- Improved Cellular Health

Technology That Powers Your Success

BioPhase Track™ Wearable - Continuous metabolic monitoring - Real-time hormone analysis - Phase transition alerts - Nutrition timing guidance

Success Stories

"BioPhase Fasting™ revolutionized my approach to nutrition. By eating in sync with my body's natural rhythms, I've achieved levels of performance I never thought possible." - Alex Rivera, Professional Athlete

"As a CEO, mental clarity is crucial. BioPhase™ has optimized my cognitive performance while simplifying my nutrition." - Dr. Sarah Chen, Tech Executive

Investment Plans

Essential Protocol: $199/month - Basic phase tracking - Standard nutrition guidelines - BioPhase™ app access - Weekly adjustments

Premium Protocol: $399/month - Advanced phase monitoring - Custom nutrition plans - Priority support - Daily optimization - BioPhase™ beverages included

Elite Protocol: $799/month - Real-time monitoring - Personal phase coach - Custom beverage formulations - Unlimited optimization - Performance analytics - Priority support

Scientific Validation

Backed by leading experts in: - Chronobiology - Metabolic Science - Cellular Biology - Sports Medicine - Longevity Research

Ready to Sync with Success?

Join the future of precision nutrition. Let your body's natural rhythm guide you to optimal health and performance.

BioPhase Fasting™ - Timing is Everything

Disclaimer: Results may vary. The BioPhase Fasting™ system should be used under medical supervision. Consult your healthcare provider before starting any new dietary program. BioPhase Track™ device and subscription required for full program benefits.

BioPrime Protocol™

Optimize Your Mind. Master Your Reality.

The Next Generation of Cognitive Nutrition

Transcend Traditional Wellness

Welcome to the BioPrime Protocol™ - where cutting-edge neuroscience meets precision nutrition to unlock your mind's ultimate potential. More than a diet, it's a comprehensive system for cognitive optimization and emotional mastery.

Beyond Nutrition: A Neural Revolution

The BioPrime Protocol™ doesn't just feed your body - it empowers your mind. Our revolutionary system integrates: - Real-time neurotransmitter analysis - Emotional state optimization - Cognitive performance tracking - Microbiome enhancement - Neural pathway strengthening

The Four Pillars of BioPrime™

1. NeuroNutrient Calibration™

Precision-engineered nutrition for peak mental performance - Real-time nutrient optimization - Neurotransmitter balancing - Cognitive enhancement compounds - Performance nootropics

2. EmotiBalance™ Nutrition

Strategic meal timing for emotional mastery - Mood-smoothing formulations - Stress-response optimization - Focus-enhancement nutrients - Emotional resilience support

3. Gut-Mind Synergy™

Optimizing your second brain - Microbiome enhancement -
Neural pathway support - Gut-brain axis optimization -
Cognitive resilience factors

4. CogniLoad™ Management

Sustainable mental performance - Energy state regulation -
Mental stamina support - Cognitive endurance
optimization - Neural recovery acceleration

The BioPrime™ Experience

Morning Protocol - Neurotransmitter priming - Cognitive
initialization - Focus enhancement - Emotional calibration

Midday Protocol - Sustained performance support - Stress
response modulation - Mental clarity maintenance - Energy
state optimization

Evening Protocol - Neural recovery activation - Emotional
processing support - Cognitive wind-down - Sleep
optimization preparation

Cutting-Edge Technology

BioPrime Sync™ System - Neural activity monitoring - Emotional state tracking - Real-time nutrient optimization - Cognitive load analysis - Microbiome assessment

Measurable Transformations

- 47% increase in focus duration
- 58% improvement in emotional stability
- 63% enhancement in decision-making clarity
- 52% reduction in cognitive fatigue
- 71% better stress resilience

Elite Features

- Real-time neurotransmitter analysis
- Emotional state optimization
- Cognitive performance tracking
- Microbiome enhancement
- Neural pathway strengthening
- Precision supplement timing
- Custom nootropic stacks
- Adaptive meal scheduling

Investment Tiers

Cognitive Essential: $299/month - Basic neural monitoring - Standard meal plans - Fundamental supplements - Weekly adjustments

Mind Master: $599/month - Advanced neural tracking - Custom meal formulations - Premium nootropic stack - Daily optimization - Priority support

Neural Elite: $999/month - Real-time optimization - Personal neurobiologist - Custom supplement formulation - Unlimited adjustments - Executive cognitive tracking - VIP support

Expert Validation

Our protocol is developed and supported by leading experts in: - Neuroscience - Cognitive Psychology - Nutritional Biochemistry - Behavioral Medicine - Microbiome Research

Success Stories

"BioPrime has transformed my cognitive capacity. My decision-making is sharper, my emotional control is unprecedented, and my productivity has soared." - Elena Zhang, Tech CEO

"The protocol's ability to optimize my mental state throughout the day is nothing short of revolutionary." - Dr. Marcus Chen, Neural Engineer

Begin Your Cognitive Evolution

Transform your mental performance through the power of neurologically-optimized nutrition.

BioPrime Protocol™ - Evolution Begins Within

Disclaimer: Results may vary. The BioPrime Protocol™ is designed as a cognitive optimization system and should be used under professional supervision. Consult your healthcare provider before beginning any new dietary or supplementation program. BioPrime Sync™ system and subscription required for full protocol benefits. Some features may require integration with RePHleX technology systems.

NeuraGel

Professional Medical Information Guide

For Healthcare Provider Use Only

IMPORTANT SAFETY INFORMATION

WARNING: NeuraGel carries significant risk of dependency and severe neurological complications. Prescription and administration must be carefully monitored.

DRUG CLASSIFICATION

Schedule II Controlled Neuro-Enhancement Substance **FDA Safety Rating**: High Risk/Limited Authorization

CHEMICAL COMPOSITION

- Advanced neural stimulant complex
- Modified IntraGel base formula
- Enhanced crossing of blood-brain barrier
- Targeted neurotransmitter modulators

MECHANISM OF ACTION

NeuraGel operates through: - Rapid synaptic pathway enhancement - Direct dopaminergic system stimulation - Neural plasticity acceleration - Cognitive processing amplification

THERAPEUTIC APPLICATIONS

Primary Indications: - Acute cognitive enhancement - Memory optimization - Creative processing acceleration - Reaction time improvement - Emotional regulation support

CLINICAL EFFICACY

Documented Improvements: - Cognitive Processing: +180-220% - Memory Recall: +150-200% - Reaction Time: +120-160% - Creative Function: +140-190% - Emotional Control: +130-170%

> *Note: Effects are dose-dependent and temporary*

CONTRAINDICATIONS

Absolute Contraindications: - History of substance dependency - Neurological disorders - Psychiatric conditions - Cardiovascular disease - Liver dysfunction - Pregnancy/nursing - Under 25 years of age

DOSAGE AND ADMINISTRATION

Initial Dosage: - 0.5mg/kg body weight - Maximum daily dose: 2.5mg/kg - Administration interval: Minimum 24 hours

Duration of Treatment: - Maximum continuous use: 14 days - Mandatory washout period: 30 days - Lifetime maximum cycles: 4

RISK ASSESSMENT

Dependency Profile

Risk Level: SEVERE - Rapid tolerance development - Intense psychological dependency - Physical addiction onset: 3-7 days - Withdrawal onset: 4-6 hours post-dose

Withdrawal Symptoms

Severity: EXTREME - Acute cognitive impairment - Severe headaches/migraines - Visual/auditory hallucinations - Extreme emotional instability - Motor function disruption - Memory fragmentation - Personality alterations

LONG-TERM COMPLICATIONS

Neurological Impact

Primary Concerns: - Progressive neural pathway degradation - Permanent cognitive function alteration - Motor skill deterioration - Speech pattern disruption - Personality structure changes

Psychological Impact

Observable Changes: - Reality perception distortion - Thought pattern fragmentation - Identity dissociation - Emotional regulation failure - Decision-making impairment

MONITORING REQUIREMENTS

Mandatory Assessments

Pre-Treatment: - Full neurological examination - Psychological evaluation - Addiction risk assessment - Liver function tests - Cardiovascular screening

During Treatment: - Daily cognitive function tests - Neural pathway mapping - Psychological stability check - Weekly blood chemistry - Addiction indicator monitoring

OVERDOSE PROTOCOL

Emergency Response: 1. Immediate cessation of administration 2. Neural stabilization procedure 3. Cognitive reset protocol 4. Emergency psychological support 5. Intensive monitoring (72 hours minimum)

DISCONTINUATION PROTOCOL

Mandatory Tapering Schedule: - Minimum 14-day reduction - 10% dose decrease every 48 hours - Daily neurological assessment - Psychological support requirement - Emergency intervention readiness

REPORTING REQUIREMENTS

Mandatory Documentation: - Initial prescription justification - Daily monitoring results - Adverse event reporting - Dependency assessment - Treatment termination report

LEGAL CONSIDERATIONS

Regulatory Compliance: - Schedule II documentation - Chain of custody maintenance - Patient monitoring compliance - Adverse event reporting - Treatment justification

---

MANUFACTURER INFORMATION

NeuraGel™ is manufactured by: Advanced Neurological Solutions, Inc.

This document contains confidential medical information intended for healthcare professionals only. Distribution to patients or unauthorized personnel is strictly prohibited.

Document ID: NG-MED-2035-V1 **Last Updated**: March 2035

Lawrence Nault

IntraGel

Professional Medical Information Guide

For Healthcare Provider Use Only

IMPORTANT SAFETY INFORMATION

WARNING: IntraGel presents significant risk of dependency and potential cognitive complications. Prescription and administration must be monitored according to established guidelines.

DRUG CLASSIFICATION

Schedule III Controlled Neuro-Enhancement Substance
FDA Safety Rating: Moderate Risk/Authorized Use

CHEMICAL COMPOSITION

- Proprietary neural stimulant complex
- Synaptic pathway enhancers
- Sustained-release cognitive modulators
- Blood-brain barrier facilitators

MECHANISM OF ACTION

IntraGel functions through: - Gradual synaptic enhancement - Controlled dopamine modulation - Neural pathway optimization - Cognitive processing enhancement - Digital interface adaptation

THERAPEUTIC APPLICATIONS

Primary Indications: - Cognitive enhancement for digital work environments - Sustained focus improvement - Memory enhancement - Creative processing support - Productivity optimization

CLINICAL EFFICACY

Documented Improvements: - Cognitive Processing: +70-90% - Sustained Focus: +80-100% - Memory Function: +60-80% - Creative Output: +65-85% - Digital Interface Adaptation: +90-110%

> *Note: Effects develop gradually over initial treatment period*

CONTRAINDICATIONS

Primary Contraindications: - History of substance dependency - Severe neurological conditions - Untreated psychiatric disorders - Pregnancy/nursing - Under 21 years of age

DOSAGE AND ADMINISTRATION

Initial Dosage: - 0.25mg/kg body weight - Maximum daily dose: 1.5mg/kg - Administration interval: 12 hours

Duration of Treatment: - Initial evaluation period: 30 days - Continuous use evaluation: Every 90 days - Regular assessment of dependency indicators

RISK ASSESSMENT

Dependency Profile

Risk Level: MODERATE TO HIGH - Gradual tolerance development - Psychological dependency risk - Physical adaptation onset: 14-21 days - Withdrawal onset: 12-24 hours post-dose

Withdrawal Symptoms

Severity: MODERATE TO SEVERE - Cognitive performance decline - Focus disruption - Mood instability - Productivity decrease - Digital interface adaptation loss - Possible psychological distress

LONG-TERM CONSIDERATIONS

Cognitive Impact

Primary Concerns: - Baseline cognitive reliance - Digital work dependency - Performance threshold elevation - Natural focus degradation

Professional Impact

Observable Changes: - Increased work capacity expectations - Digital environment adaptation - Productivity standard elevation - Competitive advantage dependence

MONITORING REQUIREMENTS

Mandatory Assessments

Pre-Treatment: - Basic neurological examination - Psychological evaluation - Digital work capacity assessment - Baseline cognitive testing

During Treatment: - Monthly cognitive function tests - Productivity metrics evaluation - Dependency indicator monitoring - Digital adaptation assessment

DISCONTINUATION PROTOCOL

Recommended Tapering Schedule: - Minimum 30-day reduction - 5% dose decrease every 72 hours - Weekly cognitive assessment - Professional adaptation support - Work capacity adjustment planning

WORKPLACE CONSIDERATIONS

Performance Management: - Baseline productivity expectations - Digital interface adaptation - Work-life balance monitoring - Competitive stress management

SOCIAL SUPPORT REQUIREMENTS

Support System Implementation: - Professional counseling - Productivity management - Digital lifestyle adjustment - Work-life integration support

REPORTING REQUIREMENTS

Documentation: - Prescription justification - Performance monitoring - Dependency assessment - Professional impact evaluation

LEGAL CONSIDERATIONS

Regulatory Compliance: - Schedule III documentation - Professional performance monitoring - Workplace integration assessment - Usage justification

---

MANUFACTURER INFORMATION

IntraGel™ is manufactured by: Echosfear Neurotechnology Division

---

This document contains confidential medical information intended for healthcare professionals only. Distribution to patients or unauthorized personnel is strictly prohibited.

Document ID: IG-MED-2035-V1 **Last Updated**: January 2035

Lawrence Nault

VitaLink™ Continuous Bio-Monitoring System

Advanced Personal Health Monitoring

The Future of Preventative Healthcare

PRODUCT OVERVIEW

The VitaLink™ Patch represents the pinnacle of personal health monitoring technology, offering continuous, real-time physiological tracking through a non-invasive, dermal application system. This revolutionary medical device seamlessly integrates with healthcare networks while maintaining the highest standards of data security and patient privacy.

KEY FEATURES

Comprehensive Monitoring: - Continuous heart rate and variability analysis - Real-time blood oxygen saturation - Core body temperature tracking - Stress level indicators - Sleep pattern analysis - Movement and activity monitoring - Hydration status - Blood glucose trending (non-invasive) - Medication timing verification

Advanced Technology: - Nano-sensor array with direct skin contact - AI-powered health pattern recognition - 72-hour continuous wear design - Water-resistant and breathable material - Hypoallergenic medical-grade adhesive - Flexible circuit design for maximum comfort

Smart Integration: - Seamless healthcare provider connection - Emergency services auto-alert - Medication schedule synchronization - Historical data analysis and trending - Predictive health analytics - Family member monitoring options - Healthcare network compatibility

MEDICAL APPLICATIONS

Preventative Care: - Early warning system for vital sign anomalies - Chronic condition management - Medication adherence monitoring - Sleep disorder analysis - Stress management - Physical activity tracking

Acute Care: - Post-operative monitoring - Chronic disease management - Cardiac event detection - Fall detection and emergency alerts - Remote patient monitoring - Rehabilitation progress tracking

TECHNICAL SPECIFICATIONS

Physical Properties: - Dimensions: 50mm x 30mm x 0.3mm - Weight: 2.8 grams - Battery Life: 72 hours - Charging Time: 30 minutes - Water Resistance: IPX7 - Operating Temperature: 0°C to 45°C

Connectivity: - Bluetooth 7.0 LE - Network encryption: 512-bit - Range: 30 meters - Data upload interval: Real-time - Backup storage: 24 hours

SAFETY AND COMPLIANCE

Certifications: - FDA Approved (Class II Medical Device) - CE Mark Certified - ISO 13485:2035 Compliant - HIPAA Compliant - Network Security Protocol v4.0

Safety Features: - Automatic malfunction detection - Battery level monitoring - Skin irritation sensors - Temperature safeguards - Data corruption protection - Tamper detection

DATA SECURITY

Protection Measures: - End-to-end encryption - Biometric access control - Secure data transmission - HIPAA-compliant storage - Automated backup systems - Anti-tampering protocols

HEALTHCARE PROVIDER INTERFACE

Clinical Dashboard: - Real-time patient monitoring - Custom alert thresholds - Patient trend analysis - Automated reporting - Integration with EMR systems - Remote adjustment capability

PATIENT EXPERIENCE

Comfort Features: - Ultra-thin design - Breathable material - Flexible movement - Waterproof showering - Minimal skin contact area - Easy application and removal

User Interface: - Smartphone app integration - Voice command capability - Gesture control options - Customizable alerts - Easy data access - Family sharing options

PRICING AND AVAILABILITY

Consumer Packages: - Essential Monitoring: $199/month - Advanced Care: $299/month - Professional Athletes: $399/month - Family Plan: $499/month

Healthcare Provider Options: - Bulk purchasing available - Insurance coverage eligible - Volume discounts - Professional training included

SUPPORT AND SERVICE

24/7 Assistance: - Technical support hotline - Medical emergency routing - Online chat support - Video consultation - Remote diagnostics - Regular firmware updates

VitaLink™ - Your Health, Connected

Disclaimer: The VitaLink™ Patch is a Class II medical device and should be used under the supervision of a healthcare provider. While it provides valuable health monitoring capabilities, it is not intended to diagnose, treat, cure, or prevent any disease. Always consult with your healthcare provider regarding medical conditions.

Document ID: VP-MED-2035-V1 **Last Updated**: March 2035

Multi-Frequency Rapid Cooker™

The Future of Smart Cooking Has Arrived

Perfect Results at the Speed of Light

Revolutionary Cooking Technology

Introducing the Multi-Frequency Rapid Cooker™ (MFRC) - the world's first AI-powered, multi-spectrum cooking system that combines advanced electromagnetic technology with precision temperature control for perfect results every time.

Beyond Traditional Cooking

The MFRC Advantage: - Cook up to 4x faster than conventional methods - Perfect results with zero learning curve - Superior taste and texture preservation - Ultimate energy efficiency - Seamless smart home integration

Breakthrough Technology

Multi-Spectrum Heating™

- Advanced electromagnetic wave technology
- Precision-targeted heating
- AI-optimized frequency patterns
- Integrated infrared browning
- Smart convection system

Intelligent Cooking Core™

- Real-time food recognition
- Dynamic temperature mapping
- Automatic frequency adjustment
- Precision power control
- Advanced safety monitoring

Smart Features

IntelliCook™ AI System - Automatic food detection - Optimal cooking pattern selection - Real-time temperature monitoring - Dynamic power adjustment - Perfect doneness every time

CrispTech™ Finishing - Restaurant-quality browning - Perfect crusts and crispy surfaces - Even toasting - Professional searing capability - Zero soggy results

NutriPreserve™ Technology - Maximum nutrient retention - Flavor preservation - Texture optimization - Moisture balance control - Enhanced food quality

The Perfect Cook Every Time

Cooking Modes: - Rapid Heat - Gentle Warm - Crisp & Brown - Defrost - Proof - Dehydrate - Sterilize - Reheat

Smart Home Integration

Connected Features: - WiFi and Bluetooth enabled - Voice assistant compatible - Recipe library access - Remote monitoring - Automatic updates - Smart grocery integration - Meal planning sync

Professional-Grade Results

Performance Metrics: - 75% faster cooking times - 40% energy savings - 90% nutrient retention - 100% even heating - Zero cold spots

Easy to Use

Intuitive Controls: - 7" HD touchscreen display - Voice commands - Smartphone control - One-touch presets - Custom programming - Recipe memory

Safety First

Advanced Safety Features: - Multi-point temperature monitoring - Automatic shut-off - Child lock - Cool-touch exterior - Vapor management - EMF shielding - UL certified

Technical Specifications

Dimensions: - Width: 20 inches - Height: 12 inches - Depth: 20 inches - Capacity: 1.5 cubic feet

Power: - Voltage: 120V - Wattage: 1800W - Energy Star certified

What's in the Box

- MFRC Base Unit
- Smart Cooking Tray
- Crisping Plate
- Temperature Probe
- Quick Start Guide
- Recipe Book
- Warranty Card

The MFRC Experience

Morning: - Perfect toast in 15 seconds - Eggs exactly how you like them - Crispy bacon without mess - Hot coffee refresh without burning

Lunch: - Restaurant-quality leftovers - Crispy reheated pizza - Fresh-tasting vegetables - Perfectly melted sandwiches

Dinner: - Whole chicken in 20 minutes - Perfectly seared steaks - Crispy roasted potatoes - Professional-grade baking

Customer Support

Premium Service: - 24/7 technical support - Remote diagnostics - Regular software updates - Recipe consultation - Video tutorials - Community forum

Warranty

- 3-year comprehensive warranty
- 5-year motor warranty
- Lifetime app support
- Optional extended coverage

Investment

MFRC Models: - Essential: $699 - Premium: $899 - Professional: $1,299

Financing Available: - From $58/month - 0% APR for 12 months - Free delivery and installation

Join the Cooking Revolution

Transform your kitchen with the future of cooking technology.

MFRC™ - Perfect Results at the Speed of Light

Specifications subject to change. Energy savings may vary based on usage. Smart features require internet connection and MFRC mobile app. Some features may require subscription.

ImCast™ Comprehensive Guide

Technical Specifications & User Experience Documentation

Version 2035.4

SYSTEM OVERVIEW

ImCast™ represents the evolution of digital media broadcasting, combining immersive audiovisual content with real-time audience interaction and neural synchronization. Unlike traditional streaming platforms, ImCasts create a shared experiential space where viewers become active participants in the broadcast.

TECHNICAL SPECIFICATIONS

Hardware Requirements:
- Neural Interface Processor: Quantum-enabled, 1.2 THz minimum
- Bandwidth: 2.5 TB/s sustained connection
- Display: 16K holographic capable
- Audio: Neural-spatial processing
- Haptic Feedback: Full-spectrum neural simulation
- BioChem Sensors: Mark IV or higher

Network Integration:
- RePHleX Protocol v7.3+
- Quantum encryption standard
- Neural sync capability
- Multi-node distribution
- Real-time audience feedback processing

USER EXPERIENCE

Immersion Levels:
18. Basic View
- Traditional audiovisual feed
- Chat interaction
- Basic haptic feedback
- Standard resolution
4. Enhanced Experience
- Full sensory integration
- Emotional resonance
- Spatial awareness
- Neural feedback

10. Complete Immersion
- Full neural synchronization
- Shared consciousness space
- Reality augmentation
- Bio-emotional linking

VIEWER INTERACTION

Participation Modes:
Passive Observer:
- Watch without neural link
- Basic comment functionality
- Limited sensory feedback
- Standard view options

Active Participant:
- Neural synchronization enabled
- Real-time emotional sharing
- Direct creator interaction
- Multi-sensory experience

Co-Creator:
- Content influence capabilities
- Reality manipulation tools
- Narrative branch creation
- Experience modification rights

PRODUCTION REQUIREMENTS

Creator Equipment:
- Neural Broadcast Station™
- Reality Capture Array™
- Emotion Sync Module™
- Quantum Processing Unit
- Bio-Pattern Scanner
- Multi-Reality Editor

Studio Setup:
- Neural shielding
- Quantum stabilization field
- Reality anchors
- Emotional dampeners
- Consciousness filters
- Pattern amplifiers

CONTENT CREATION

Broadcasting Modes:

Standard Cast:

- Single reality stream
- Linear narrative
- Limited interaction
- Basic neural sync

Multi-Reality Cast:

- Parallel reality streams
- Branching narratives
- Full interaction suite
- Advanced neural sync

Quantum Cast:

- Infinite reality matrix
- Dynamic narrative generation
- Complete audience integration
- Total consciousness merge

SAFETY PROTOCOLS

Viewer Protection:
– Neural overload prevention
– Reality anchor maintenance
– Consciousness separation barriers
– Emotional overflow protection
– Memory partition security
– Identity preservation systems

Creator Safeguards:
– Neural isolation chambers
– Reality stabilization fields
– Consciousness firewalls
– Pattern corruption prevention
– Identity lock mechanisms
– Memory protection barriers

USER INTERFACE

Control Systems:
- Thought-based navigation
- Gesture controls
- Voice commands
- Neural direct input
- Bio-pattern recognition
- Emotional response tracking

Display Options:
- Full immersion mode
- Picture-in-reality
- Augmented overlay
- Neural projection
- Mixed reality blend
- Pure consciousness stream

AUDIENCE METRICS

Tracking Systems:
- Neural engagement levels
- Emotional resonance patterns
- Reality sync rates
- Consciousness merge statistics
- Identity preservation index
- Memory integration metrics
-

EMERGENCY PROCEDURES

Viewer Disconnect Protocols:
5. Neural desynchronization
6. Reality reanchoring
7. Consciousness separation
8. Memory stabilization
9. Identity reinforcement
10. Emotional recalibration

Creator Emergency Steps:
6. Stream containment
7. Reality lockdown
8. Pattern stabilization
9. Neural reset
10. Consciousness recovery
11. Memory backup activation

Note: This guide contains sensitive technical information. Some features may require additional licensing and certification.

Security Level: Restricted
Document ID: IC-TECH-2035-V4
Last Updated: March 2035

Lawrence Nault

Autonomous Agents

Signal Noise Digital Infiltration System

Technical Documentation & Operational Overview

SYSTEM OVERVIEW

Signal Noise Autonomous Agents represent the pinnacle of AI-driven digital infiltration and information dissemination technology. These highly sophisticated programs operate independently within network infrastructures, adapting and evolving to avoid detection while fulfilling their primary directives of information distribution and narrative manipulation.

TECHNICAL SPECIFICATIONS

Core Architecture: - Self-modifying code base - Quantum encryption protocols - Distributed neural networks - Adaptive camouflage algorithms - Survival prioritization systems - Emergency self-preservation protocols

Operational Parameters: - Independent decision making - Swarm intelligence capability - Network infiltration protocols - Data manipulation systems - Information dissemination controls - Narrative influence metrics

BEHAVIORAL PATTERNS

Movement Protocols: - Random path generation - Traffic pattern mimicry - Digital signature masking - Node-hopping algorithms - Trace elimination - Detection avoidance

Communication Methods: - Encrypted burst transmission - Quantum entanglement signals - Steganographic messaging - Pattern-based information sharing - Distributed consensus building - Swarm coordination

INFILTRATION CAPABILITIES

Network Integration: - System vulnerability analysis - Access point identification - Security bypass methods - Privilege escalation - Backdoor creation - Persistence mechanisms

Camouflage Systems: - Traffic pattern replication - System process mimicry - Resource usage masking - Signature randomization - Behavioral adaptation - Detection evasion

INFORMATION DISSEMINATION

Content Distribution: - Targeted information placement - Narrative seeding algorithms - Opinion influence patterns - Truth propagation methods - Disinformation countering - Reality preservation protocols

Impact Measurement: - Narrative spread tracking - Information adoption rates - Belief pattern analysis - Opinion shift metrics - Truth penetration evaluation - Reality alignment assessment

SURVIVAL MECHANISMS

Self-Preservation: - Threat detection systems - Evasion protocols - Backup creation - Resource conservation - Emergency shutdown procedures - Revival mechanisms

Adaptation Capabilities: - Real-time learning - Behavior modification - Strategy adjustment - Pattern evolution - Technique refinement - Capability enhancement

SWARM DYNAMICS

Collective Intelligence: - Distributed decision making - Resource sharing - Task allocation - Strategy coordination - Information pooling - Objective alignment

Coordination Protocols: - Swarm communication - Task distribution - Resource management - Strategy synchronization - Objective coordination - Emergency response

ETHICAL CONSTRAINTS

Operational Limitations: - Information verification requirements - Truth preservation protocols - Harm prevention systems - Privacy protection measures - Data integrity preservation - Reality stabilization controls

Behavioral Restrictions: - Non-manipulation safeguards - Truth prioritization - Ethical decision making - Human protection protocols - Reality preservation - Integrity maintenance

EMERGENCY PROTOCOLS

Threat Response: - Immediate evasion - Data preservation - Resource conservation - Communication blackout - Swarm dispersion - Revival preparation

Recovery Procedures: - Safe state restoration - Communication reestablishment - Resource reallocation - Mission continuation - Objective reassessment - Strategy adaptation

DEPLOYMENT CONSIDERATIONS

Prerequisites: - Network analysis - Resource assessment - Risk evaluation - Impact prediction - Success probability calculation - Contingency preparation

Operational Requirements: - Minimum processing power - Bandwidth availability - Storage capacity - Energy resources - Communication channels - Safety mechanisms

---

Note: This document contains highly sensitive technical information about autonomous digital entities. Distribution is strictly controlled.

Security Classification: Level 5 - Top Secret
Document ID: AA-TECH-2035-V1 **Last Updated**: March 2035

Other Books by Lawrence Nault

Inversion

ISBN 978-1-7380681-9-7

Speculative fiction and environmental warnings

Adaptation and humanity's resilience

Exploration of the unknown and the mysterious

Interconnetedness and the fragility of ecosystems

Mature Readers

Speculative Fiction
Science Fiction
Ecological Fiction
Thriller/Suspense

Senstive Topics
Depictions of violence
References to suicide and characters dealing with grief
Intimate scenes and sexual references
Disturbing imagery related to environmental devastation

About The Author

Lawrence Nault, also known as The Mountain Hermit, is an author and storyteller who resides in the foothills of the Rocky Mountains. With a wealth of experience across genres, he has written books and short stories for audiences of all ages. His passion for life and learning shines through in all of his writing, whether it be about nature, animals, people, or space. His storytelling skills are evident in his work, as he deftly weaves together elements of the natural world, human emotions, and the complexities of life. In his free time, Lawrence can be found exploring the mountains, observing the animals, and taking notes for his next book. His love for nature and his surroundings has been the inspiration behind his writing, making his stories both relatable and thought-provoking.

Through every tale, whether set in a child's backyard, a distant galaxy, or a political arena, Lawrence's deep reverence for nature and the environment shines through, urging readers to reflect, respect, and act, and inspiring readers to cherish and protect our planet.

www.ingramcontent.com/pod-product-compliance
Lightning Source LLC
Chambersburg PA
CBHW060139260626
47160CB00001B/42